Daemon laughed. "Welcome to actually caring what people think of you."

Sora made a face. "Well, let's not take it *that* far. I'm doing this for you and me, and for Hana. Not for the Council."

He nodded. "I'm okay with that. But you know, even if your goal was to be the best taiga in Society history, for no reason other than for fun, I'd be there by your side the whole time."

There was an intensity in his eyes, but it was different from the focus of being in the sparring ring or concentrating on a difficult spell. Sora couldn't quite put a finger on what it meant. Daemon hadn't looked at her in that way before. It was so intense that it made her self-conscious.

She looked away and clapped him on the back to break through her own awkwardness. "Then let's do it. Let's be the best taigas in Society history. Let's go be legendary."

Also by Evelyn Skye
The Crown's Game
The Crown's Fate
Cloak of Night

CIRCLE of SHADOWS

EVELYN SKYE

BALZER + BRAY

An Imprint of HarperCollinsPublishers

Balzer + Bray is an imprint of HarperCollins Publishers.

Circle of Shadows

Copyright © 2019 by Evelyn Skye

All rights reserved. Printed in the United States of America.

No part of this book may be used or reproduced in any manner whatsoever without written permission except in the case of brief quotations embodied in critical articles and reviews. For information address HarperCollins Children's Books, a division of HarperCollins Publishers, 195 Broadway, New York, NY 10007.

www.epicreads.com

Library of Congress Control Number: 2018954183

ISBN 978-0-06-264373-5

Typography by Jenna Stempel

19 20 21 22 23   PC/LSCH   10 9 8 7 6 5 4 3 2 1

First paperback edition, 2019

To Tom—
the best gemina I could ever dream of

CHAPTER ONE

There are two possibilities after this stunt—we'll be the empress's favorite taigas or we'll get expelled and taken away in chains," Daemon said. His broad shoulders hunched as he bent down to talk to Sora. She was tall, but he was much taller—six foot two, officially, but six foot five when he styled his hair like this, stuck up in thick wild tufts of black.

"They won't kick us out of the apprentice program." Sora grinned. "I'm an expert at skirting the boundary between what's technically allowed and what's not, remember?"

Daemon made a face but still laughed. The slash of scars on his cheek danced, souvenirs from a fight with a wolf cub when he was two. "Trust me, no one knows better than I do how good you are at almost-but-not-quite breaking the rules." He was Sora's best friend, as well as her partner—her gemina—and that meant they were inseparable, through triumph and trouble.

With Sora, there were ample amounts of both.

1

They stood with their fellow students in the courtyard of Rose Palace, a majestic castle hewn entirely of dusty-pink crystal that filtered moonlight through its walls and shone like a prismatic beacon at the highest point of the island. Tonight, the Level 12 taiga apprentices had the honor of touring Rose Palace and performing an exhibition match before Empress Aki. Sora bounced on her toes in excitement.

She looked around the vast courtyard. Her hair, cut short along her jawline and dyed dark—as most taigas did—so she could better hide in the shadows, wisped across her face as she spun to take everything in. The palace walls were flawless and clear, soaring four stories up toward the open sky. There, the pink crystal had been cut like gems, their many facets sparkling and casting winking moonlight onto Sora's formal uniform—flowing trousers and robes made of black silk, embroidered with the moon goddess Luna's triplicate whorls in silver thread.

Beside Sora, Daemon gaped in disbelief. Rose Palace was even more stunning than they could have imagined. "I don't know," he whispered. "Are we sure we want to do this tonight?"

She wrinkled her nose at him. They had spent the entire summer plotting a surprise to be revealed during the exhibition match, and tonight was supposed to be the culmination of their hard work. "You, of all people, are getting cold feet?"

Daemon shrugged. "Maybe there are some places too sacrosanct for us to mess around with."

"Those are exactly the sorts of places that need us," Sora said. The Rose Palace invitation was an annual ritual, both to recognize young taigas in their final year before graduation and to instill in them a sense of pride at being a part of

Kichona's proud and fierce history. "Everything is beautiful here, but too serious. Besides, the empress has seen too many exhibition matches that follow the same formula. I think she'll appreciate a little change. You know my motto. Work hard—"

"Mischief harder." Daemon shook his head but smiled. "The taiga warriors are going to be really mad."

Sora glanced over at the teachers who had accompanied them to Rose Palace. Their ordinarily stern faces were even sterner than usual. And they definitely had their eyes on Sora. She and her friends had a reputation for causing trouble—at the end of every term, her report cards inevitably said she was "talented but had difficulty following rules."

They can't really blame me, though, Sora thought. *If the warriors would stop being so rigid, I wouldn't have to break their rules.* Just because things had been done a certain way for centuries didn't mean it should continue being done that way forever.

Besides, Sora liked to think that the trouble she caused was the fun sort of trouble.

She grinned at Daemon. "The warriors are going to be more than mad. And I'm looking forward to it."

Suddenly, the chatter among the apprentices extinguished, and a hush fell like a down blanket across the courtyard. Four members of the Imperial Guard—the elite warriors assigned to the empress—had marched in. Imperial Guards also appeared above, around the entire upper perimeter of the courtyard, eyes focused and weapons at the ready should they be needed.

A moment later, a young woman swept elegantly into the courtyard. Despite being just five feet tall, she could command the attention of the whole kingdom even if she were completely still. All eyes were on her now as she moved, the ten different shades of blue on her chiffon gown undulating like waves, her skirt swirling around her feet as if she were being carried in by the sea. The light from the crystal prisms above played with the gold in her hair. Empress Aki didn't need a crown; members of the Ora family were born with the gleaming color of royalty already upon their heads.

Sora and the other apprentices fell to their knees and bowed, completely prostrate to the ground. "Your Majesty," they said in unison.

"I welcome you to Rose Palace," the empress said. "And I wish you a happy Autumn Festival."

The apprentices bowed again, then rose to their feet as the empress settled into the only chair in the courtyard. The chair was surprisingly simple, made of unadorned wood. It didn't even have a cushion. The only thing that marked it as the empress's seat was the Ora imperial crest etched into the crystal wall behind it, a crowned tiger standing proudly beneath the sun and the moon, surrounded by the words "Dignity. Benevolence. Loyalty."

Then again, perhaps the simplicity wasn't so surprising. The palace may have been grand, but that was the doing of past rulers. Empress Aki was known for spending only what was necessary on herself, preferring instead to use Kichona's coffers for the good of its people. In her ten years of rule, she'd ordered all the old schools in the countryside rebuilt, and new books for every child across the island. She invested in farms and agricultural research, and thus improved harvests, making sure no citizen went hungry. The kingdom had also grown wealthier than ever, thanks to her edicts that made trading with the countries on the mainland easier, stoking appetite abroad for Kichona's colorful silks and delicate jewelry.

And then there was the constant stream of smaller details, like her frequent surprise visits to villages that had never had a member of the imperial family set foot on their soil before, or the fact that she paid for the Autumn Festival feasts throughout the kingdom. Empress Aki wasn't known as "the Benevolent One" for nothing. Sora—and pretty much everyone in the kingdom—loved her.

"Your Majesty," one of the taiga warriors said. "I am pleased to introduce you to this year's Level Twelves. It is an honor for us to be here, and they have a gift for you as a token of their gratitude." He nodded to Sora to step forward with the present, but his eyes narrowed, warning Sora not to do anything to embarrass the warriors.

She wouldn't. Yet.

Sora reached into a hidden pocket in her sleeve. Usually, she stashed a knife there—there were many such places for weapons in the taiga uniforms—but tonight she retrieved a small velvet pouch. She wasn't the teachers' favorite pupil, but that had the opposite effect on her classmates, and Sora had been elected first chair, which meant she had the traditional honor of representing Level 12 before the empress tonight.

"Your Majesty," Sora said, bowing again, "if I may, I would like to present to you a gift from our class."

Empress Aki smiled kindly, and although she was only twenty-five—a mere seven years older than Sora—she had the gravitas of someone twice her age. "What is your name?" the empress asked.

"I am called Spirit." It was the name the Society had given her at age seven, when she'd graduated from the nursery and become a taiga apprentice. No one called her Sora anymore except Daemon—also known as Wolf—who'd insisted on continuing to use their birth names so they'd have something special between them.

"Come forward, Spirit," Empress Aki said.

With the permission of the Imperial Guards who stood on each side of the empress, Sora approached and placed the pouch into the empress's delicate hands.

Empress Aki opened the drawstrings and let out a gasp of delight. A string of tiger pearls—black-and-orange-striped jewels that could be found only in the deep, underwater coves off Kichona's southwestern shore—tumbled into her palm. Daemon had rallied everyone in Level 12 to contribute more to the gift than any class before them had managed to raise. Sora could feel his joy, warm as a campfire, beaming through their gemina bond. She smiled.

"It's beautiful, thank you," Empress Aki said, fastening the pearls around her neck, right next to an abalone shell locket. "Of course, there is also something else I am looking forward to before we tour the palace. I believe you've prepared an exhibition match?"

Sora's nerves twinged. Fighting and magic were things she had no reason to be anxious about, but this would also be when she and her friends would reveal their surprise. It's what Sora had been waiting for.

"Yes, Your Majesty," she said, finding a smile. "It would be our pleasure to perform for you."

She strode back to where Daemon waited. "Are you ready?" she asked.

"Never been readier." Daemon rested a reassuring hand on her shoulder. "And so are you."

The apprentices who were not participating in the exhibition moved to the back of the courtyard. Sora, Daemon, and the other Level 12s who remained stripped off their formal robes, revealing the taigas' usual black tunics and trousers, charmed with an armadillo spell to create a thin layer of flexible armor, as soft as cotton but as strong as steel. They slid helmets made of similar armored fabric over their heads, covering everything but their eyes. And each apprentice was armed with plenty of knives, as well as their weapon of choice, which for Sora was throwing stars and darts, strapped into a leather band across her chest.

The apprentice serving as narrator began to speak, his deep voice carrying across the courtyard. "Many centuries ago, the kingdom of Kichona was born. Sola, goddess of the sun, blessed our island with wise leaders, from our first emperor, Dei the Silvertongued, to Empress Aki Ora today."

The empress dipped her head in appreciation.

The narrator continued. "Luna, goddess of the moon and Sola's sister, was tasked with protecting the imperial family and the kingdom. To do so, she blessed Emperor Dei's fledgling army with the ability to summon the powers of Kichona's animals in order to enhance the warriors' own skill.

"By casting a cheetah spell, taigas could outrun ordinary men."

A pair of apprentices sprinted across the courtyard in a blur.

"With a grasshopper spell," the narrator said, "taigas

could jump two stories in the air or leap across flooded rivers."

A group of six apprentices vaulted across the courtyard, executing quadruple somersaults in midair before landing on the parapet above.

"And with a panther spell, taigas could sneak silently through the night. With Sola-blessed rulers on the throne and Luna-touched warriors protecting its shores, no invaders could match them, and Kichona thrived."

There was an ominous pause before the narrator continued.

"Sometimes, however, the most dangerous threats come from within."

The Imperial Guards on the wall above the courtyard drew a black tarp over the open roof, casting the space into darkness. There was only a narrow hole in the center of the tarp that allowed in a small amount of moonlight. Of course, the taigas didn't need this to see; they could cast owl spells to enhance their night vision. But Empress Aki could not use magic and would need a hint of light to watch the rest of the show.

Beside Sora, her roommate pulled out a stiletto blade. She was known as Fairy because she'd always been petite, and her face was soft, with rose-kissed cheeks like a cherub. But many apprentices had figured out the hard way during sparring practice that Fairy didn't battle like a dainty pixie. Made purely of muscle and pluck, she fought fast and dirty, and she made fun of the vanquished afterward.

Sora and Fairy were playing the heroes in the exhibition, and the two girls stepped into the center of the courtyard, Sora near the back and Fairy closer to where the empress sat.

A large glass shield had been erected in front of Empress Aki to protect her. The apprentices were using practice weapons made of wood, but even those could hurt someone if they accidentally flew astray.

"Such danger came calling upon Kichona on an evening just a decade ago," the narrator said. "It is always calm before a storm, and in that silence, Prince Gin and his soldiers sprang."

Sora's stomach clenched. She'd been only eight years old during the Blood Rift, but its mention still had a visceral effect on her.

Then-emperor Kenzo Ora had died unexpectedly of an aneurysm. Afterward, his children could not agree on how to rule the kingdom. Princess Aki wanted to continue their family's legacy of peaceful prosperity, the foundation of Kichona's happiness. However, her twin brother, Gin, belonged to the Cult of the Evermore, which believed that Zomuri, god of glory, would grant them paradise on earth if enough blood was shed in his name. Prince Gin wanted to utilize the taigas' magic to build Kichona's military might, to wage war and conquer neighboring lands.

Because the princess was nine minutes older than her brother, she was first in line for the throne. But nine is an unlucky number, according to Kichonan superstition. Prince Gin would not back down, not when the future of the kingdom was at stake. Taiga warriors took sides, and a brief but vicious civil war was fought. Prince Gin's taigas battled cruelly in their attempted coup, decapitating soldiers and leaving their heads on spikes, gutting them alive, and forcing them to watch the murder of their friends.

But perhaps the most barbaric part of the Blood Rift—and

what Sora remembered most vividly—was Prince Gin's warriors setting the Citadel on fire. The inferno burned down many buildings, including the nursery, where Sora's little sister and others perished.

The terror of that night shivered through Sora now.

Daemon reached through their gemina bond to soothe her, projecting the sensation of a placid lake. As the "leader" of the enemy, he was off to the side of the courtyard, but he could still sense Sora's unease through their connection. It was as if he were saying, *Remember, this is pretend. It's only an exhibition.*

Sora swallowed hard. Right. This wasn't real.

Besides, Sora thought, *if Empress Aki has no problem with the Level 12s commemorating the Blood Rift victory every year, then I should be able to deal with it.* After all, the empress had had to battle against her own brother. That could not be an easy memory to bear.

Sora curled the fourth fingers on both hands so that they touched her thumbs and formed circles. "Sight like an owl," she chanted softly three times.

The rims of Sora's eyes tingled, and her vision sharpened just as Daemon and the other apprentices—"Prince Gin's warriors"—began to creep out of the darkness in front of her. On the other side of the courtyard, they did the same to Fairy.

Sora crouched into a defensive stance, throwing stars already poised at her fingertips.

Prince Gin's soldiers attacked, shouting, "For the future emperor!"

Sora unleashed a flurry of stars at the enemy. Two of them ducked, and one fell, feigning death.

Another wave of them came at her. She hurled more stars and darts, and then some more.

Sora spun away from an oncoming soldier, then threw a star behind her back at her attacker. It met the base of his skull. He stumbled, then fell as if dead.

She reached for another star. Her fingers ran over the band across her chest, but all she touched was leather. "Crow's eye!" she swore, as if surprised. "I'm out."

She unsheathed her daggers, one in each hand.

Prince Gin's soldiers fanned out in front of her, Daemon included. He leered as he turned his sword in his palm. "There are many dangers lurking in the night," he said. His voice oozed. "A pretty girl like you ought to stay tucked in bed if she wants to remain safe."

"I would say the same of you," Sora quipped, "except you aren't the least bit pretty."

He laughed, falling out of character for just a second. Then he yelled, "Get her!"

The soldiers hurtled toward Sora, swords raised. She wouldn't have time to use magic—it required the sacrifice of setting weapons aside in order to form mudras with her hands—but she could still take out two or three of the soldiers. Four, perhaps. Sora smiled as she flexed her fingers around her blades.

The knife in her right hand slashed the throat of the first soldier. The knife in her left plunged into the side of the second. She had the right one ready to fly as a third soldier came streaking through the air. It hit him in the chest before he landed on the ground. *Thump.*

Fairy fought her way to Sora's side.

"What took you so long?" Sora yelled over the clashing

of blade against blade.

"Oh, I'm sorry," Fairy said, sneaking in a sardonic curtsy as she avoided an incoming throwing star. "I was hosting a tea party for our visitors on the other side of the battlefield and we got rather carried away. Was I supposed to be here sooner?"

Sora smiled. In the next breath, she sliced a soldier's throat.

The narrator began to speak. "The Blood Rift was a tragedy. Many lives were lost."

Bodies littered the ground. Sora and Fairy pivoted in the center of the courtyard, backs to each other, weapons at the ready for any other enemy that dared approach.

"But after a long night," the narrator said, "Princess Aki's taigas prevailed. The prince was fatally wounded, and his warriors took his body as they fled the kingdom, never to be heard from again."

Daemon and the apprentices who played the remnants of Prince Gin's army dropped their weapons and ran to the back of the courtyard, as if boarding ships that would take them away from Kichona's shores.

Sora and Fairy remained in fighting stance for a few moments longer. Then the black tarp above them was retracted, and the moon shone brightly once more, as if the goddess Luna herself were smiling down upon them.

All the apprentices who had participated in the exhibition match stepped back into the middle of the courtyard. This was supposed to be the end, the part where they bowed.

Instead, they looked to Sora.

She looked at Daemon.

He nodded, and that reassurance was all she needed.

Sora hurled a throwing star at the hair trigger she'd set up on the parapets. The Imperial Guards knew it was coming, because Fairy had convinced them it would be a good idea; she could be very persuasive when she turned on her charm.

As soon as the star hit the trigger, the roofline over the courtyard lit up with a hundred sparklers.

"Yes!" Sora pumped her fist.

Their teachers, however, shouted in alarm and immediately began to cast spells to prepare themselves for a fight. The ones closest to Empress Aki ran to protect her from what they thought was an attack. Others began trying to shepherd the apprentices to safety.

But the Imperial Guards around the empress simply stepped in closer to her, holding their hands up to stop the teachers from leaping to her aid. The teachers stopped in confusion, until one of them turned and growled, "Spirit—"

He was cut off by the sky exploding in fireworks. Small yellow flowers, stunning purple starbursts, and red rockets careening across the glowing moon.

And finally, the pièce de résistance—an enormous tiger, composed entirely of crackling blue fireworks, topped with a sparkling gold crown. It was something Fairy and her gemina, Broomstick, had invented, a perfect combination of her expertise with chemicals and his passion for explosives.

Sora smiled so hard, her cheeks were about to break. Daemon, Fairy, and Broomstick piled around Sora, jumping and cheering.

Their teachers stood around the edge of the courtyard, seething at the ruins of what was supposed to be a solemn exhibition.

Empress Aki, however, seemed pleased. "Bravo," she said, clapping with abandon. "How different from past performances. It's very exciting that you are the next generation of taiga warriors. Kichona is truly blessed."

Sora almost burst from the pride swelling in her chest. She grinned, and the apprentices all bowed.

CHAPTER TWO

The Imperial City was made up of three parts, with most of it carved into a mountain. At the top, Rose Palace perched on a cap of steep white quartzite, with sheer faces impossible to climb. A deep moat had been chiseled around the summit, another layer of protection for the rulers of the kingdom.

Below the moat, the face of the mountain shifted dramatically from white quartzite to dark granite, with only a winding, two-mile road etched into the rock, connecting Rose Palace to the world below. Sora and the Level 12s marched down that path now, heading back to the Citadel, the Society of Taigas' headquarters on the lower third of the mountain.

Unlike the empress's castle, the Citadel was a fortress where all the buildings were as dark as looming twilight. Black was the color of stealth and, hence, of the taigas, Kichona's soldiers. The Citadel was the base of their operations, as well as where students like Sora trained. Its black outer walls were intimidating by design, severe and smooth, towering ten stories high. Inside the compound, everything was black too. Glorious, dark buildings covered in shiny, tiled rooftops as strong as armor. A black outdoor amphitheater sliced into the mountain. Even the temple to Luna was black from its pagoda roof to its wooden floors.

And then, the last part of the Imperial City was the Field of Illusions around the base of the mountain. But this was no ordinary field of grass; rather, it was a sea of black-and-white sand that shifted constantly in optical illusions, confusing and dizzying, such that the only people who could pass were taigas trained to filter out the hypnotic patterns, or those escorted by the warriors.

But tonight, Sora wouldn't have to deal with that. They were approaching the Citadel from Rose Palace, so they'd be able to enter through the rear gates. Which was a good thing, because Sora was busy reveling over the fireworks she and her friends had pulled off, and she might not have been able to concentrate well enough on getting through the illusions. She probably would have found herself face-first in the sand.

Her reverie, however, was interrupted by Fairy, who broke ranks from farther back in the formation and jogged up to Sora and Daemon.

"What are your plans before everyone goes home for Autumn Festival?" Fairy asked.

"You mean, other than packing?" Sora said as she continued marching.

Fairy skipped alongside her. "That will take you all of five minutes."

Daemon inched closer to join the conversation. "We

were going to get in one last spar if we had the time."

"Oooh, you have a wrestling date?" Fairy raised her eyebrows suggestively.

Sora laughed. Her roommate collected boys like some girls collected seashells. "You know, the male apprentices are more than just things to kiss."

"I actually prefer to think of them as fresh meat to devour. Although Wolfie here can be pretty ferocious. Maybe he'll devour *me*, which would be nice for a change. . . ."

Daemon shook his head, smiling.

"Fairy," Sora said, laughing, "you keep fishing, but it's not going to happen."

Her roommate smacked her hand sarcastically to her heart and stepped backward, nearly jostling the next apprentice in line. "Spirit! You've mortally wounded me with your cruelty!"

"I think she's broken," Sora said to Daemon. "She keeps yammering at full speed. It's like—"

"She put a cheetah spell on her mouth instead of her feet," Daemon finished.

"Hey." Fairy scrunched up her face. "I can hear you, you know."

Daemon gave her a crooked smile. "We're just teasing."

She batted her eyelashes. "I like when you tease me, Wolf."

Daemon laughed, and it blossomed through his and Sora's gemina connection like a field of golden poppies.

Sora smiled. He'd let Fairy flirt with him, but she knew he wasn't tempted. They'd all been friends for too long. And Sora was glad for that. Not that she wanted Daemon for herself. Society Code didn't allow geminas to be together,

17

because it could get in the way of their ability to serve the kingdom.

"Anyway," Sora said to Fairy, "what did you run up here for?"

She shrugged. "Oh, nothing important. I just heard that the Council is going to give the Level Twelves their scouting missions today."

"What?" Sora stopped.

The apprentice behind her bumped into her. "Hey!"

"Sorry," she said and resumed marching. She turned her attention back to Fairy.

A scouting mission. The true marker of the final apprentice year. The Council—the Society of Taigas' governing body—would be watching the Level 12s constantly this year, observing and ultimately deciding where to assign each gemina pair for their first post after graduating to full taiga-warrior status. The scouting missions were tests to show how each apprentice did in the field. The first mission would set the tone.

And yet Sora wasn't sure whether to believe Fairy. Her roommate was a monstrous gossip, and only 20 percent of what she said was true. The other 80 percent . . . who knew what she was thinking?

"How do you know the Council is handing out missions tonight?" Sora asked. "They usually wait until after Autumn Festival."

"My gemina works in their office, remember?"

Right. Broomstick—who'd been given the name because he'd been scrawny as a child—assisted the Council with administrative work, which, not so coincidentally, was the source of the 20 percent of Fairy's gossip that was actually true.

"The Council decided to give us our assignments now," Fairy said, "so we can go straight from the holiday break if we wanted to, rather than having to come all the way back here." She shrugged. "Makes sense to me."

"Wow," Daemon said. "Our first mission."

Sora nodded, unable to form words. She and Daemon had been looking forward to the first mission for different reasons—Daemon, for a chance to prove himself; Sora, for a glimpse into the future, when she wouldn't be constricted by school rules—but they were propelled forward by the same pure anticipation.

Pleased with herself for breaking the news, Fairy grinned and spun away to return to her place in the formation. As they approached the tall iron gates at the rear entrance to the Society of Taigas' headquarters, the glistening black walls of the fortress greeted them solemnly, surrounded by soaring, thick-trunked cypress trees older than the kingdom itself. The moon seemed to beam more brightly at the home of its chosen warriors.

Sora and Daemon straightened.

A chorus of voices shouted as the taiga warriors who guarded the gates surrounded the apprentices. They dropped from the roofs of the watch towers, from the trees, from the beams behind the massive gate. They were nowhere and everywhere, all at once.

The taigas always were.

Sora and the others fell immediately to their knees and splayed their empty hands on the dirt in front of them to show that their weapons remained stowed away. They touched their foreheads, too, to the ground.

"Cloak of night," one of the guards at the gate said.

"Heart of light," the apprentices recited in unison, finishing the Society's motto.

"Welcome back, Level Twelves," the gate guard said as Sora and her classmates rose to their feet. "The Council would like to see each gemina pair, in the order of your formation." He met eyes with Sora and Daemon. "That means you're going first."

Anxious yet eager, Sora reached through her gemina bond for Daemon. He was nervous too—their connection vibrated like a guitar string that had just been plucked—but her presence met his, and they stilled each other. A little.

The iron gates of the fortress swept open on silent hinges.

"Shall we?" she asked.

He looked over at her and smiled. "We shall."

Like all the buildings at the Citadel, Warrior Meeting Hall was styled in the taigas' colors—black roof tiles, black wooden frames, black rice paper windows, with just a touch of gold in places like door handles and the stitching at the edges of the black reed mats on the floors. Black paper lanterns hung on the walls, their light muted yet not at all weak. Rather, there was a refined confidence to their understatedness.

The Council Room in Warrior Meeting Hall was the black heart of the Society. Glass Lady, the stout, unsmiling commander of the taigas, presided at the head of a table made of an impossibly large black stone dredged from the bottom of Kira Lake, fully formed, polished, and flawless.

The lantern behind Glass Lady cast her long and sharp silhouette over the table, black on top of more black.

Two councilmembers—Scythe and Bullfrog, both in their fifties and therefore a good decade younger than Glass Lady—sat to her right. Strategist and Renegade, who were in their sixties, sat to her left.

"Commander." Sora and Daemon bowed together as they stepped into the room. "Honorable Councilmembers." They bowed again, to the left and the right. Then they stood before the Council table, their arms straight at their sides, palms forward and fingers open in a symbol of respect.

"Welcome, Spirit," Glass Lady said. "And, of course, Wolf."

Sora felt Daemon flinch through their gemina bond. Glass Lady had addressed Sora first, and Daemon as an afterthought. It happened fairly often, and he noticed every time.

Frankly, it was unfair. Yes, it was true that Daemon wasn't the best at magic, which meant he couldn't always enhance his stealth or his speed or his jumping as well as other apprentices could. But he compensated by fighting harder in the sparring arena than anyone else. He could win any physical fight blindfolded and with an arm tied behind his back.

But to Daemon, that was still a consolation prize. Sora knew this; she could sense it through their connection every time someone addressed her first and him second.

He had reassured her during the exhibition match. Now it was Sora's turn to make him feel better. She sent a sense of togetherness through their bond, the solemnity of their commitment gleaming like polished steel, as if saying, *Ignore her. We live and fight and die together.*

She felt Daemon's confidence steady.

"We are pleased to have a mission for you," Glass Lady said, although she looked anything but. She stared at Sora and Daemon, her eyes as cold and sharp as the jewels in her hair, which glinted like shards of ice. Glass Lady was a classic taiga, all fight and no heart. Her favorite saying: If curiosity killed the cat, it was sentimentality that killed the taigas.

"After the Autumn Festival holiday, you will travel to Tanoshi and sweep the area," she said. "Make sure everything is orderly there."

"Tanoshi?" Daemon's face fell. "It's just an ordinary village."

Not all warriors could be Imperial Guards. Some protected the kingdom's important cities, while others were assigned to ordinary patrols, acting as local police forces to keep the peace for regular citizens. Being assigned to Tanoshi for their first mission indicated that Sora and Daemon were on the path to the latter. Sora didn't care; as long as she was with her friends, she was happy. But it mattered to Daemon.

Glass Lady narrowed her eyes at him. Sora bit her lip.

"If the two of you applied yourselves more, perhaps you would have gotten a more challenging mission," Glass Lady said. "Spirit, you have the highest grades in magic even though I am quite certain you rarely practice. If you tried as hard in your training as you do at purposely breaking our rules, you could be in the Imperial Navy after graduation. But you know all this. Your teachers have told you every year, and you obviously do not care."

Sora forced herself not to shrug. The Imperial Navy was the most prestigious post possible after graduation from apprenticeship; it was the start of the path to becoming an Imperial Guard. But why would she want that? She'd spend all her days on a boat, scrubbing decks under the unforgiving sun, living in the confines of a ship. If dealing with the rules of the Citadel was bad, being stuck at sea with nowhere to escape the captain's eye sounded like a nightmare.

"Tanoshi is a perfect mission for us, Commander," Sora said.

Glass Lady let out a long exhale, as if it took all of her patience. "You're lucky we didn't refuse to give you a mission at all, after that stunt at Rose Palace tonight. We will mete out an appropriate punishment, but that will have to wait, as we have other missions to assign. For now, you are dismissed."

"Thank you, Commander," Sora said, relieved. She placed both fists over her heart, the taigas' symbol of loyalty. Daemon did the same. "Cloak of night. Heart of light," they recited.

The councilmembers saluted with double fists over hearts and repeated the Society motto as well.

"Happy Autumn Festival, and have a good mission," Scythe—the least stern of the warriors—said.

As Sora and Daemon burst out of the Council Room doors, Fairy and Broomstick left their places in line and ran up to them.

"What'd you get?" Fairy asked, her eyes as bright as if they'd been sprinkled with pixie dust.

"Tanoshi," Sora said.

"Can't wait until it's our turn to get our assignment," Fairy said. "You'll have a great time in Tanoshi. The boys there are cute."

Sora laughed, then turned to Daemon. "Can you believe it? Our first real mission!"

He frowned. "What if there's nothing in Tanoshi?"

Broomstick made a face. He may have been skinny as a child, but he'd more than made up for it over the years. He was one of the biggest Level 12s now, and he looked menacing with his shaved head and eyebrows half-singed from his experiments blowing things up. But the effect was countered by his constant smile and the fuzzy blond hair all over his arms. He was the kingdom's most lethal teddy bear. "Why would it be bad if there's nothing in Tanoshi?" he asked. "Are you afraid that the kingdom is perfectly safe?"

"No," Daemon said. "I'm afraid that there's nothing there, and we'll come back with nothing to report, and our first mission will look like an enormous zero."

"Don't worry," Sora said. "No matter what, we'll make it an adventure. Anyway, we live and fight and die together, right?" she said.

Daemon grinned. "We do." He clapped his arm around her and laughed. "But perhaps we should try not to die quite yet."

CHAPTER THREE

The next afternoon, Daemon and Sora made their way to Tanoshi. It was on the way to Sora's parents' home on Samara Mountain, where they would spend the Autumn Festival. They figured they might as well get their mission out of the way first, so they could relax during the rest of the break.

Before the discovery of tiger pearls made Kichona prosperous, the island kingdom had been unremarkable, subsisting mostly on fishing and agriculture. Many of the villages, like Tanoshi, still reflected this history, made up of small, well-kept wooden buildings with curved ceramic tiles on the roofs. Every few blocks, there was another impromptu shrine for this minor god or another. And thousands of acres of vineyards and apple orchards around Tanoshi perfumed the air with sweetness, especially now during grape harvest season.

They left their horses—and their taiga uniforms—at a coaching inn. In order to blend in to assess the state of the town, they wore ordinary layman's clothes, which was always a bit jarring. While taigas wore stark black, civilians in Kichona embraced color, and lots of it—the more vivacious, the better. Sora wore a silk blouse modeled after a violet—lighter purple at the collar and sleeves, deep plum closer to her stomach, and a vivid starburst of yellow in the center—and her trousers were green, like the stem of the flower. Daemon had on a turquoise tunic embroidered at the hem with a pink-and-orange coral reef. He drew the line, though, at garish pants, opting instead for a pair of narrow gray trousers. There was only so much he could stomach to blend in.

Nevertheless, it was good enough, for the townspeople walked past them without a second glance. Everywhere Daemon and Sora went, people were smiling, pausing to chat with each other under strings of orange Autumn Festival lanterns or in front of crates of muscat grapes. They bought each other cold bottles of freshly pressed pear juice—traditional in this region of Kichona in the fall—and drank them together on the sidewalk.

"This place is so peaceful," Daemon said, but it was more of a complaint than a compliment.

"Isn't that a good thing?" Sora asked. "This kind of life is what the Ora emperors and empresses have always wanted for Kichona."

Daemon shrugged. She was right, of course. There were pirates roaming the ocean surrounding the kingdom, but the Imperial Navy worked diligently to keep them away from shore so the regular citizens of Kichona didn't suffer. The Imperial Army kept posts throughout the island to ensure that traders from the mainland were really traders and not anything more nefarious. And there were also local police forces of taigas to keep the peace.

Even so, Daemon was jittery. "I just want something to do today, something to show for our work. If we'd been sent to a bigger ocean-side town, we could have investigated the harbors for suspicious ships. Maybe we would have found some pirates or smugglers or, I don't know, a spy from another kingdom. But here in farm country . . . what are we even looking for?"

"Don't worry," Sora said. "As long as we're thorough, we'll get good marks."

He knew it was hard for her to understand his need to prove himself. Sora was naturally good at magic. She had the luxury of not caring, because everyone knew that if she ever became ambitious, she'd blow them all out of the water. Daemon, however, constantly questioned whether Luna had made a mistake in marking him as a taiga.

But then Sora smiled at him, and he was momentarily dazed. She was tall and lean, all grace and muscle, and when the sun hit her just right—like it was doing now—he could see her curves silhouetted through the thin silk of her blouse. She had a spattering of freckles across her cheekbones, and her nose ended in a button that was an adorable contrast to her fierceness. He fought the urge to run his fingers through her hair, which fell like a painter's brush along the edge of her jaw.

He touched his own hair. His blue roots were due to be colored soon. Technically, he didn't have to dye it; it was dark enough in its natural state to comply with Society Code. But a genetic quirk gave him blue hair, and the strangeness meant he'd been teased mercilessly during their early years at the Society. As soon as he turned seven and became a taiga apprentice, he'd dyed his hair black and had kept it that way ever since. Daemon winced at the memory.

But Sora was still smiling, and his embarrassment faded away. Her mere presence made everything better.

"Should we check the north side of town first and make our way south?" she asked. They knew Tanoshi fairly well. Other than Shima, Tanoshi was where apprentices liked to go when they had weekend leave from the Citadel.

"You want to do the south side last because you're hoping to end up at a restaurant there, huh?" Daemon smirked. "Always letting your stomach lead."

"You know me so well."

His heart skipped happily.

They started down the first street. This section of Tanoshi was all business, made up mostly of stern wooden buildings bereft of decoration, lined up on a straight grid of streets numbered one through five from north to south, and named by trade from east to west. There was Accounting Street, Bookbinder Way, Architect Road, and many others. It was quiet here, and Daemon and Sora finished sweeping through the streets quickly.

Next was the residential district. The buildings here had considerably more character than the ones in the business grid. Although the homes themselves were simple in architecture—compact wood structures with brown tile roofs—each door was painted brightly to express the family's personality. One was rainbow striped. Another featured a fisherman catching an enormous fish, bigger than the sun. Another depicted the life cycle of a phoenix, from egg to bird to flames and ashes, in a never-ending circle.

In front of all this, a small group of children played in the middle of the dirt road, chasing after a ball and swatting at it with sticks.

"I wonder what it would be like to live in a place like this?" Daemon said.

"You'd go stir-crazy," Sora said. "It's lovely, but there wouldn't be enough to occupy you."

"Good point." He never seemed to have enough outlets for his energy. It was part of the reason he was so good at combat; he spent extra hours in the sparring yard to attempt to wear himself out each day. It worked. Sort of.

Farther down the road, a woman poked her head out of a doorway decorated with a pink elephant. "Keni, time for homework!" she yelled at one of the boys playing in the road. "Your father will be home soon for dinner."

Daemon quickly turned away and hurried onto the next block. If he stayed any longer, he'd start thinking again about life in a village like Tanoshi, with parents who cared about him. And then he'd wonder about knowing who his parents were at all.

As the mother's voice receded behind Daemon, he slowed his steps. Sora caught up but didn't say anything. She would know through their gemina bond how he was feeling. For years, he'd smothered his questions about who he was and where he'd come from.

But frankly, he was tired of it.

"It's our last year before we graduate," Daemon said. "After this, we won't have as much time on our own because we won't have school holidays. So I was thinking . . ."

Sora stopped in the middle of the road. "Yeah?"

He shook his head. "Never mind. It's stupid."

"Nothing you think is stupid, Daemon. What is it?"

He scrubbed his hand through his hair. That irritatingly black-but-actually-blue hair. "I was thinking that maybe I'd try this year to figure out who my parents are. Or were. I want to know where I came from, who I am."

Sora smiled. "I think that's a great idea."

He brightened. "Really?"

"Yes, really."

"Okay then." The cloud over him dissipated, and knowing that Sora supported him allowed him to put the idea aside for now. It took only another minute for him to refocus on their mission. "Let's wrap up the residential area and go downtown."

"Sounds like a plan," Sora said.

His steps lightened as they entered the noisier part of Tanoshi, full of shops and restaurants. There were artisan pottery stores, dry-goods shops carrying everything from rice to fishing rods, and stores for every other service the townspeople might need.

Daemon and Sora swept through the streets a little more slowly, since there was more to observe. But all was also in order here.

"Sorry we didn't find any illegal warehouses full of opium," Sora said.

"Guess we couldn't be that lucky on our first mission."

"Or maybe we can. A different kind of lucky." She smiled broadly as she stopped in front of an enormous red lantern. It was the entrance to an iz, a tavern that specialized in skewers of all variety of meat, from chicken thighs to chicken livers to more acquired tastes, like gecko marinated in squid ink. Panels of blue cloth hung in the doorway, and raucous conversation wafted out of the iz along with the charcoal smoke of its tireless grills.

Sora's stomach growled loud enough to be heard even over the street noise.

"Hungry?" Daemon asked.

"What else is new?"

They pushed through the cloth panels into the iz and found a seat at a table in the corner. A boy a few years younger than them appeared and asked for their order. He also appraised Daemon's shirt and, after a second, nodded, a silent compliment.

Daemon really hadn't needed garish pants to blend in.

Sora perused the menu. "We'll have two orders each of bacon-wrapped shrimp, mushroom beef, and the ginger-honey chicken skewers, please."

"And a carafe of cold sake and some tea," Daemon said.

The serving boy had been gone hardly a minute when he returned with their drinks. Daemon poured. "Cheers to us finishing our first mission."

She clinked her cup with his.

Soon, their meal arrived. The skewers were perfectly charred, each with a different sauce drizzled over the meat. Sora picked one and put it to her lips. Daemon watched, mesmerized by her mouth. Heat flushed through him.

Damn it! He jerked up his mental ramparts to block their bond, hoping Sora hadn't felt his reaction through their connection. It'd been harder and harder recently to see her simply as his gemina. Everything he'd taken for granted about her in the past had started to captivate him—her sharp intelligence, her ferocious chokehold, even the way her pinkie stuck out a little when she held a skewer in her hand.

He flinched, though, at what those feelings meant. It would be disastrous if a romantic gemina relationship failed, because you'd still be bound to that taiga for life—sharing emotions, working with each other, together despite the desperate or angry desire to be apart. That's why the Society forbade it.

Daemon poured himself another cup of sake and swallowed it in a single gulp to wash away the heat of his feelings for Sora.

At the bar behind her, shouts broke out. A glass shattered. Six men began to advance on each other, fists clenched.

Thank the gods, Daemon thought. *A distraction.*

He and Sora both stood.

"May I?" Daemon asked.

She flourished her arm in front of her. "Please, be my guest."

He grinned, hopped over his chair, and pushed his way into the fight. He bounced on his toes. This was part of what had been missing today. Adrenaline. The feeling that he could *do* something.

"Gentlemen," Daemon said, "would you kindly take it outside? You're ruining the atmosphere in here."

Two of the men who'd been in each other's faces spun around and sneered at him. "If you knew what was good for you, you'd stay out of this, boy," the bearded one said.

"Actually," Daemon said, "if *you* knew what was good for you, you'd leave like I asked."

"Smart mouth," the other man said, "but not such a smart brain." He wound up and took a swing.

Daemon dodged easily, grabbed the man's arm, and

hurled him through the air. The man sailed toward the exit, landing with an ungraceful flail as he hit the ground under the blue curtains at the door of the iz.

"Now, you can leave quietly," Daemon said to the five others, "or I can throw you out like that fellow."

The men's faces turned bright red, and despite fighting each other only a minute ago, they now united against Daemon. They all pulled out knives.

"Right," Daemon said. He could pull out a weapon too—gods knew he had enough little daggers, darts, and throwing stars hidden on his body—but he didn't want to hurt them much. They were just drunkards getting a bit out of hand. Instead, Daemon cracked his knuckles and smirked while they approached. The rest of the iz had gone silent in tense anticipation.

The first man charged at him with a knife raised above his head. *Amateur*, Daemon thought as he sidestepped while simultaneously smashing the side of his hand like an ax into the man's forearm.

The man immediately dropped the knife and fell to the ground cradling his arm. It wasn't broken, but it would feel that way to him for a little while.

The next man advanced on Daemon with quick, continuous slashes.

Daemon stepped backward, straight into a bunch of huddled diners, too frightened to be caught up in the fight but too paralyzed to flee. Daemon had to adjust his path, arcing away from the table and back toward the bar.

Of course, that's where the other three men were waiting. Their knives were out and pointed at Daemon as he backed toward them, like bayonets ready to impale him.

Daemon continued to edge closer and closer.

"He really is an idiot, isn't he?" one of the men said.

At that moment, Daemon slid himself backward, taking out the man directly behind him. Daemon swept his leg right and then left, knocking out the feet of the other two. They landed with profanity-laden crashes at the base of the bar.

Daemon spun to meet the lone man standing, who was advancing faster now. The slashing of his knife grew quicker but also sloppier, driven by rage and likely several ounces of fear.

So predictable, Daemon thought.

He lunged forward and slammed a fist to the man's throat while simultaneously grabbing and twisting the knife arm. He locked the arm, kneed the man in the ribs, and stripped him of his knife.

Only now did Daemon unsheathe a short sword from the scabbard strapped to his calf, hidden beneath his trouser leg. He brandished it at the five men on the ground.

"I'll give you one last chance to get out of here with your limbs and innards intact," Daemon said.

They glared at him, pride severely wounded. But all five of them—excluding the one already thrown to the exit—hustled out of the tavern without any further threat.

The iz erupted into hoots and applause.

Daemon nodded his head in a small gesture of acknowledgment and went back to his table, where Sora waited.

She was smiling. "You really are art in motion when you fight."

He flushed from the tips of his ears down to his neck.

Luckily, he was saved by the bartender, who set another carafe of sake on the table. "You two are taiga apprentices, aren't you?"

"Yes," Daemon said, beaming proudly. "You could tell?"

The bartender chuckled. "Normal people don't fight like that, and they aren't as honorable. Thank you for keeping the peace."

"It was my pleasure," Daemon said, his cheeks beginning to hurt from smiling so hard. "And thank *you* for the sake."

CHAPTER FOUR

Finished with their mission and officially on Autumn Festival break, Sora and Daemon rode all the next day to Samara Mountain, and then up dusty switchbacks, passing only a handful of people with their mules, and even fewer houses. The mountain sliced into the cerulean sky like jagged shards of slate, its crooked pines tucked into crevices and clinging to the steep rock. It was always with mixed emotion that Sora returned here. She loved her parents, but she'd spent her whole life with the Society of Taigas, and after eighteen years, the Citadel felt more like home than this place where she'd been born.

Across Kichona, the other taiga apprentices were also home to celebrate the Autumn Festival. They would light lanterns with their families and hang them over their doorways. There would be feasts to pay homage to the major gods—steamed whole fish to honor Nauti, god of the sea; bowls overflowing with noodles for Silva, goddess of wealth;

platters of sautéed morning glory stalks for Sola, goddess of the sun; and a variety of stewed vegetables on beds of rice for Emmer, god of the harvest.

Daemon had come home with her because he didn't have family to return to. Unlike the other apprentices, he hadn't been brought to the Citadel by adoring parents and dedicated to service to the kingdom. Rather, until age five, Daemon had lived in Takish Gorge, a remote, uninhabited part of Kichona, with a family of wolves, eating, hunting, and playing in the forest with his lupine brothers and sisters. The trapper who found Daemon would have left him in the canyon—ferocious as he was, with his snapping teeth and his nails grown out long and sharpened like claws—if not for Luna's silver triplicate whorls on the small of his back, a mark that glittered even when the sun was gone.

Daemon was well aware that this sounded like a fairy-tale trope. But he wore the badge with amused pride, at least outwardly. Only Sora knew that he hated not knowing who his parents were, why they'd left him, and how he'd come to be raised by wolves.

Nevertheless—or perhaps *because* of this—Sora and Daemon spent the second half of their Autumn Festival break in Takish Gorge every year, visiting the only place he knew as his. And if he wanted to find his parents this year, Sora would help him.

As the sun began to set, they reached a solitary wooden home perched on a ridge, as if the house had grown like a bonsai out of the stone. It overlooked the turquoise waters of the sea, which surrounded the kingdom, a natural barrier from the rest of the world. The colors of dusk settled into the sky like the inside of an abalone shell, a muted iridescence no less stunning than a daylight rainbow despite its subtlety.

A small woman in a long red-and-blue-striped skirt and a blouse as yellow as the sun swept the stone path in front of the house. Her pale blond hair—the same almost-platinum shade as Sora's beneath the black taiga dye—was tied back neatly in a bun, and she wore no jewelry except a single golden pearl at her throat. As she worked, she hummed a lilting melody, like wind chimes on All Spirits' Eve. The aroma of braised fish and bamboo shoots, cooking on the outdoor stove, mingled with the mountain air.

Because taigas tread lightly, it wasn't until Sora and Daemon stood with their mud-spattered boots halfway down the path that her mother noticed them. Her mother looked up, up, up at the tall girl and the even taller boy in front of her. She took in the Society uniforms that Sora and Daemon wore now—black tunics, loose trousers, and the thin, cloth-covered armor—as well as the throwing stars strapped on the leather band across their chests, the knives on their belts, and the sword and bo staff on their backs. There were more weapons, tucked into the secret pockets of sleeves and other folds of fabric, of course, but Sora's mother didn't see those.

"Your Honors," she said, bowing.

Sora blushed and took her mother's hands, pulling her upright. "Please, Mama, how many times have I asked you to just call me Sora?"

Her father, a wiry man with a kind, downward tilt at the corners of his eyes, came out of the house and stood behind his wife. "It is the greatest privilege a Kichonan can ever hope for, to have a child blessed by Luna to serve the empress. Let us have the small pleasure of reminding ourselves of that and addressing you by your title." Papa bowed to both her and Daemon.

Sora rolled her eyes but smiled. "You two are always so stubborn."

"I know someone else who's very stubborn," Daemon said, looking at Sora.

"Where do you think she gets it from?" Mama said with a wink.

"Come," Papa said. "Your mother has cooked up quite a feast. We'll stuff our bellies, and then when we're as round as rice balls, we'll roll ourselves down to the base of the mountain to join in the village festivities."

Sora laughed.

They dined outside beneath the full moon, on the small balcony behind the house, overlooking the sea. A salty breeze whispered through the pine needles, and waves hit the cliff below in a soothing, rhythmic rasp. Papa sat across the table from Sora and Daemon, smiling the entire meal despite his long mustache continually blowing into his food. Mama kept a steady supply of hot, spiced tea in their cups. And Sora had helping after helping of miso-glazed butterfish, fried shrimp, buckwheat noodles, and bamboo shoots braised in sticky soy sauce.

"Doesn't the Society feed you?" Papa joked.

Sora responded by popping another fried shrimp in her mouth.

When she'd finally had her fill, Mama brought out an Autumn Festival cake, an extravagant, ten-layered confection made with an entire block of butter, eggs, lemony yuzu, and almond flour, and dusted with confectioners' sugar. It resembled the full moon, in honor of Luna. Sora cut slices for her parents, despite their protests that she and Daemon serve themselves first.

Sora took a bite of the cake, and she sighed as it melted in her mouth. It tasted like happiness, and she warmed as if she'd drunk an entire carafe of Kichonan rice wine.

She managed to eat three more slices.

Papa shook his head in awe.

"She has two stomachs," Daemon said. "One for regular food and one for dessert."

"You're just jealous," Sora said.

Papa cleared away the plates when they were finished. Mama folded her hands on the table. But her smile at having her daughter home began to fade.

The wine-like warmth inside Sora turned to vinegar. She'd known this was coming. It always did. And yet whenever Sora came home, she tried to pretend she wouldn't have to face it.

"Would you like to visit your sister's shrine before we go down to the village?" Mama asked.

Sora nodded weakly. Not because she was disrespectful of Hana's memory and didn't want to go. But because every time she thought of her little sister, the mountain air suddenly felt too thin.

Daemon squeezed her shoulder. "Do you want me to come with you?"

She sighed. "No, I need to do this myself."

"Then I'll wait for you here."

Papa came back out on the balcony, with a small slice of Autumn Festival cake on a plate. "Take this with you."

The incense in the shrine would bring the spirit of the cake to the heavens, for Hana to enjoy.

Sora tried to stay composed. But despite all her taiga training, she couldn't placate the quiver in her hands as she took the plate from her father.

Sora sat beneath the canopy of trees, in front of a small wooden shrine composed of red beams. There was a short dais, which held a vase of white chrysanthemums and a tiny brass cauldron full of uncooked rice, with sticks of white incense protruding from it. Sora had placed the slice of Autumn Festival cake next to the flowers. In front of the dais, a curved sword lay displayed on a white lacquered stand.

White was the color of mourning in Kichona.

She had been here for almost an hour, and the incense sticks had long ago burned out. But she just kept staring at the sword. It was supposed to honor who Hana had been— there were always ceremonial swords at the shrines of deceased taigas—but to Sora, it was also a symbol of everything that *could* have been. And everything that wasn't. The tiny fingers that had never had a chance to grow big enough, strong enough, to hold a sword. The quick little legs that never got to experience a grasshopper or cheetah spell. The big, brown eyes that wanted nothing more than to be a taiga warrior, fighting side by side with her sister, but instead never saw beyond her sixth year.

Mama's footsteps sounded on the gravel path leading down from the house to the shrine. Sora nodded but didn't say anything when she sat down on the ground beside her. Mama carried a worn, leather-bound book with her, embossed on its cover with the Teira family crest of the sun rising out of a vase of flowers. Their family had always been renowned for their ceramics; Sora's father was a tenth-generation pottery master.

"I know it makes you sad to be here," Mama said. "But while we should always mourn your sister, we should also honor her memory by using our lives to do what she could not." She opened her book to a page marked with a ribbon, its blue satin faded with years of age. "I wrote something a long time ago that I've never shared with you. Will you let me read it to you?"

Sora smiled a little, as much as one could when sitting before Hana's shrine. Mama was a famous storyteller. While Papa told his tales on clay, shaping emotions and beauty into ceramic, Mama created in words. Her books were renowned throughout Kichona.

"I would love to hear it," Sora said.

The branches above them rustled and then quieted, as if they too were settling in to hear Mama's story.

She cleared her throat, and then she began.

A long time ago, a girl was born among the clouds and mist of Samara Mountain. She came writhing and screaming into the world, as if she were not ready to leave whatever dream she'd inhabited inside her mother's womb, as if she were unwilling to enter this reality. The midwife had to swaddle her tightly to calm her hysterics, but even warm blankets could not quiet her wailing as it echoed off the cliffs and over the sea.

The baby cried the length of the day, and continued into the dusk. Her father rubbed his red-rimmed eyes and left their tiny house so he could have a moment of peace. Her mother curled into a ball on the reed mats upon the floor.

In the deepest hours of the night, when the trees creaked in the darkness and the sea sparkled under the moonlight, a masked figure slipped silently into the house. She made not a sound but walked with sword drawn, the blade of it black as pride yet bright as honor.

It was Luna, goddess of the moon and divine protector of the Kingdom of Kichona. She picked up the baby and cradled the girl against her moonlit chest. The crying ceased.

Then Luna raised her sword and brought it across the baby's back in one quick, shallow slash. A wound opened, then quickly healed, replaced in its stead by a swirl of silver triplicate whorls, like a birthmark upon the girl's skin.

The baby did not shed a single tear. Instead, she smiled, for she was marked by Luna.

The girl had been blessed as a taiga.

When Mama finished reading, she closed the book in her lap and rested her hands on the cover, her fingers circling the family crest. The trees around them remained still, no breeze in the branches, the whole mountain hushed in appreciation of the moment.

"It's beautiful," Sora said. "Is it about Hana?"

Mama shook her head. "It's about you."

A lump formed in Sora's throat.

"It is the greatest privilege in the land to serve Kichona as a taiga," Mama said. "You have done well in school, and your father and I are very proud of you."

"Thank you."

"Your sister would have been proud as well."

Sora closed her eyes, already welling up. Maybe by

shutting them, she could keep the sadness inside, stop it from spilling out into the rest of her life. As if that hadn't already happened.

"I think you should have this," Mama said softly, taking off her necklace. It was a simple chain with a golden pearl on it, more affordable than rare tiger pearls.

"But that's your memorial for Hana." Sora blinked the tears from her eyes. "I couldn't take that from you. You've worn it since the Blood Rift."

"And it helped me through my mourning. But now it has a new purpose." Mama fastened the necklace around Sora's throat.

"Your Honor, there's something else I want to say . . ." Mama reached out and touched her knee. Sora stilled, holding her breath.

"Despite your high marks in class," Mama said, "I know these years haven't been easy on you. You carry the burden of your sister's memory with you. But it's time to stop."

Sora frowned; she was unaccustomed to the reprimand in her usually deferential mother's tone.

"Before I read you the story, I said that we should remember Hana by using our lives to do what she could not. Do you understand what I meant by that?"

Sora bowed her head and kept it down, even more respectful than if she were before the Council. "You're saying I shouldn't take being a taiga for granted."

"Yes," her mother said. "But not only that—honor your sister by becoming the best you could ever be."

She looked up now. "The best taiga."

"Yes, that. Try harder in school. Push yourself when you become a warrior. But more important, be the best *person* you can be." Mama squeezed her knee, losing the harsh edge in her voice. "Think of Empress Aki. She has done great things for our kingdom, but she doesn't brag and doesn't require loud adulation. Maintaining peace and quietly improving our lives is harder than it seems, and it is not glamorous. But there is a nobility in the way that she leads."

Sora's cheeks flushed. She was suddenly a bit ashamed of how she'd courted the limelight by shooting off fireworks at Rose Palace, not to mention the umpteen other stunts she'd pulled off in the past.

"Your Honor," Mama said, "it is your duty to do more than most. To *be* more than most."

The moon seemed to shine brighter. It filled Sora, as comprehension set in. *Hana never had a chance to reach her potential. But I do.*

Her teachers had been telling her for years that she was wasting her talent, that she could be so much more if she simply tried. But Sora hadn't wanted to.

Until now. Thinking of what Hana could have been— that little girl who was so proud to be a taiga someday, so proud of having a big sister who was already an apprentice— let Sora see her purpose in this world in a different light.

I've been so selfish, Sora thought. She moved her hand and clasped Mama's fingers in hers.

"I carry Hana's memory with me," Sora said, touching the golden pearl with her free hand. "I understand what you're saying—I live this life for the both of us."

Mama nodded, eyes glassy with tears. She held Sora's hand more tightly. Sora stopped fighting her own sadness, and she let the tears spill over onto her cheeks. Hana had been a part of Sora's life for six years, but just because she was dead didn't mean Sora couldn't keep her close to her heart now. Hana would be Sora's inspiration; her death would not be in vain.

After a little longer at the shrine, Sora and her mother climbed together up the mountainside and back home.

Sora immediately went to Daemon. He'd been outside her father's workshop, admiring the latest ceramic vases and platters. She had put up her mental ramparts while she was away so that he couldn't feel her sadness. But Daemon's forehead creased as soon as he saw the dried trails of tears on her face, and he set down the bowl in his hand and rushed to her. "Are you all right?"

She paused, but then nodded. She told him what had happened at the shrine, and through their bond, she shared the small swell of ambition inside her. Sora was talented enough to be part of the Imperial Guard, eventually. It would take years to become one—only the most accomplished warriors, with at least a decade of experience, could qualify for the honor—but the path started early. Hopefully, it wasn't too late to change the trajectory of their careers.

"Mama's right—I owe it to Hana to be more than just a decent taiga. From now on, I don't want to be just some mischievous kid. I want to see what I'm capable of."

Daemon laughed. "Welcome to actually caring what people think of you."

Sora made a face. "Well, let's not take it *that* far. I'm doing this for you and me, and for Hana. Not for the Council."

He nodded. "I'm okay with that. But you know, even if your goal was to be the best taiga in Society history, for no reason other than for fun, I'd be there by your side the whole time."

There was an intensity in his eyes, but it was different from the focus of being in the sparring ring or concentrating on a difficult spell. Sora couldn't quite put a finger on what it meant. Daemon hadn't looked at her in that way before. It was so intense that it made her self-conscious.

She looked away and clapped him on the back to break through her own awkwardness. "Then let's do it. Let's be the best taigas in Society history. Let's go be legendary."

CHAPTER FIVE

While the taiga apprentices had gone home for the Autumn Festival, the Council convened for their annual retreat on Isle of the Moon. Kichona was an archipelago, with the main island shaped like a leaping tiger, and Isle of the Moon was a crescent to the north, arcing over the tiger's head. Glass Lady strolled through the manicured gardens here, past deep-green topiaries shaped like tigers and feather-tipped maples with leaves so bright red, they looked like candied apples. The evening air was crisp with autumn, and she allowed herself a rare moment of relaxation as she strolled across a bridge over one of the many ponds, brimming with koi of every shade imaginable, as if they'd escaped from a painter's palette. Behind her, the famed Constellation Temple stood stoic yet richly ornamented, six stories high and composed of orange beams, capped off with a gleaming silver-tiled pagoda roof. Its white walls shone bright under the sun, and windows opened atop balconies carved with stars.

After her walk, Glass Lady went to the dining room, part of a high-ceilinged building with a glass roof that provided an unobstructed view of the sky. The other councilmembers had arrived a few minutes earlier and were already tucking into their dinners, their raucous laughter and conversation mingling with the rasp of chopsticks against ceramic bowls. Glass Lady nodded at their pleasure. It was, after all, the main point of assembling here.

The other point was to remind them of the history and identity of Kichona.

She strode up to the table. "My fellow warriors, I hope you enjoyed your first day here yesterday. It is certainly an extravagance to be able to gather on Isle of the Moon to enjoy the luxuries offered here. This would not have been possible without the generosity of our heavenly empress, who never hesitates to pay for this annual rejuvenation of our Council." Glass Lady raised a teacup in the air. "To Empress Aki, the Benevolent One."

The councilmembers lifted their teacups. "To Empress Aki, the Benevolent One!"

Glass Lady sipped her tea, then set it on the table. She had just opened her mouth to begin her speech when a sudden roar tore through the room. It filled the air like the exhale of a dragon who had been prodded, unhappily, awake.

In a hairbreadth of a second, every councilmember brandished swords and retrieved sickles and chains, darts, and other weapons from the pockets of their uniforms and the holsters on their backs.

Glass Lady looked up at the top of the dining room. Through the glass, a wave appeared, larger than any typhoon she had ever seen.

She dove beneath a table for cover. The wave crashed through the ceiling. Glass rained down like razor-edged hail.

"What's happening?" Bullfrog, the nearest councilmember, shouted from beneath a chair he'd used as a shield.

"I don't—" Another wave crested and smashed through the ceiling before she could finish.

But there wasn't anything to say anyway. The sky had been clear this morning with no sign of storm. Had there been an earthquake somewhere that triggered a tsunami?

Whatever it was, the Council could not remain here. Glass Lady sprang to her feet, even as her entire body trembled. The next wave was already growing and looming overhead. "Evacuate to higher ground!"

The warriors sprinted for the doors.

Outside, the wind howled, toppling topiaries and ripping branches off the trees. The councilmembers began weaving their way through the flooded garden toward the highest point on the isle, Constellation Temple.

Another typhoon wave roared and crashed down on them. It knocked Glass Lady off her feet, sending her careening into a broken lamppost. Thick splinters from the wood beam pierced into her torso. Salt water swallowed her whole, and she struggled to surface while blood blossomed from her wound.

No. Despite being in her mid-sixties, she was still strong. She kicked frantically and pushed with her arms. Her lungs burned. She found the ground beneath her and shoved up, breaking the surface of the churning water and gasping for air. She'd deal with the injury to her side later.

The waves kept coming.

Finally, the taigas made it to Constellation Temple. Battered and soaked, the councilmembers tumbled into the temple and climbed the stairs quickly, straight to the observation pavilion at the top.

"Commander," Strategist said, his gray beard looking like a drowned squirrel. "You've been wounded."

Glass Lady glanced at shards of wood still protruding from her side. She waved him away. "Later. There are more important things right now."

She turned to the ocean in the direction from which the waves came, expecting a wide swath of water that swelled and grew like a wall.

Instead, the waves came from a single point in the sea.

"It's not a storm," Glass Lady whispered.

"What do you mean?" Scythe asked.

Glass Lady squinted at the ocean. Was that a black spot on the water? "Someone find me a spyglass," she said.

Strategist ran down the stairs into the temple. A minute later, he returned and placed a telescope in her hand.

She focused on the point from which the waves seemed to emanate.

"Daggers!" she cursed. "There's a ship out there."

"They'll never survive the typhoon," Bullfrog said. "Should we attempt to rescue them?"

Another wave rose to monstrous heights and sped toward the island. It slammed into where the dining hall had been.

Gods help us. That was no Imperial Navy ship out there, nor was it a merchant or even pirates. It was nothing Glass Lady knew how to handle.

She turned to the councilmembers and shook her head. "There's no way we could save that ship. Besides, they don't need rescuing. They're causing the waves."

"What? How?" Strategist asked.

She tried the spyglass again, but visibility was poor. "I don't know. But the waves are originating from that ship. We have to get out of here. Whoever and whatever that is out there, this is an attack, and we have no way to fight it. We'll cast sailfish spells on ourselves and swim from Haven Cove."

It was the most direct path from Isle of the Moon to the shores of Kichona, even though the waters would be rough.

"Rough" was an understatement.

Glass Lady kept an eye on the mysterious ship as the taigas evacuated. But she couldn't see much through the typhoon. The wind was so violent, it was hurling water high into the sky. And the massive waves kept growing and coming for the island.

"Commander?" Strategist said. "We need to go."

She hesitated for a moment, paralyzed by not knowing what it was they faced.

"Commander. Now."

She blinked. Nodded. They sprinted for the cove.

When they arrived, Bullfrog turned to her. "What are we going to do about this? How do we fight a threat we don't even understand?"

"Just focus on swimming right now." She gave him a stern look, even though he was also a councilmember. As if acting unafraid would actually make it true.

Bullfrog either didn't pick up on Glass Lady's fear or he was too well trained to question her. He put both fists over his heart. "Yes, Commander."

The Council cast their sailfish spells to help them hold their breath longer underwater and swim faster. Glass Lady forced herself not to look back at the ship. And they dove into the vicious, frigid sea.

CHAPTER SIX

Kichona's empress was up late, perusing a report on the projected wheat and rice harvests, when a messenger rushed into her study.

"Your Majesty," he said, huffing to catch his breath, "the commander of the taigas is here to see you."

"What? Why?" Aki rose from her desk, alarmed. Glass Lady was a meticulous planner. She had come to Rose Palace unannounced on only one occasion before.

"All I know is it's an emergency," the messenger said.

"Have her brought to the throne room. I'll be there soon."

He nodded and ran off to carry out her orders.

Aki hurried out of her study. As she stepped into the corridor, Imperial Guards surrounded her and strode with her.

They reached the throne room, and Aki settled into the velvet cushions that had once belonged to her father. The moonlight sparkled brightly here, focused through the crystalline prism of the ceiling like a celestial beam upon the empress's head. Sometimes, the effect was a reassurance, reminding Aki her reign was blessed by Sola, the sun goddess. Other times, she felt unworthy of the spotlight, as if she were an imposter. It was her father who was supposed to be sitting on this throne.

Aki shifted uncomfortably. But she didn't have time for self-doubt, for the commander of the taigas entered the room.

Glass Lady was completely disheveled. Her hair—usually pinned with great precision—stuck to her face, stiff from the salt of the sea. Mud streaked her uniform. Her boots squelched as she moved. Aki gasped.

Despite her appearance, the commander was as poised as ever. She dropped gracefully to her knees and laid herself prostrate on the marble floor. "Your Majesty, I apologize for interrupting your night."

Aki rose shakily from her throne. "What happened?"

"A typhoon hit Isle of the Moon this evening, and the Council had to evacuate," Glass Lady said as she stood up.

It was then that Aki saw the sticky dark red that covered the left side of the commander's uniform. It had been camouflaged by the wetness of the fabric. "You've been injured!"

The commander waved at her to sit down. "I'm fine; I'll have a doctor look at it when I return to the Citadel. It's much more important that I finish my report to you first."

Aki had the distinct sensation that she was swimming in deceptively calm waters but about to be carried out to sea by a riptide. She didn't want to sit down. But the commander gave her a firm look, like a tutor scolding her student. Aki obediently sat.

"Um, please continue," she said, trying to regain her authority as empress.

"It's not typhoon season," Glass Lady said. "What struck us today was not a storm. It was a calculated attack, using magic we've never seen before."

"I . . . I don't understand," Aki said.

"There was a ship in the distance, launching the wind and waves at the isle. We don't know how. But whoever or whatever that was, I'm certain this will not be their only attempt at Kichona. They must have known the Council would be there. It's possible they wanted to wipe us out because we run the Society of Taigas."

The whole room seemed to pitch. Aki gripped the armrest of her chair. The last time Kichona had pitted magic against magic—the Blood Rift—was still raw in her memory. Aki had barely won that time, and she'd known it was coming because it was her brother she'd faced. But now? She couldn't prevail if she didn't know her enemy or what they were capable of.

"Which of the nearby kingdoms is attacking?" she asked. "And why?" Other than its tiger pearls, there was nothing special about Kichona, and it hadn't bothered anyone in decades. The kingdom traded pleasantly with countries on the mainland but otherwise minded its own business—wasn't that enough to have everyone else in the world leave Kichona alone? Aki's breath hitched as if the riptide were swirling around her, testing its grip. "What do we do?"

"All squadrons will be immediately dispatched back to their posts around the kingdom," Glass Lady said. "We don't know who the enemy are or what they want, but when they attack again, they will most likely hit close to where we saw their ship. For that reason, we will send additional taiga warriors to reinforce the squadrons already based in the cities in the north."

"And what of their magic?" Aki asked.

"Our best scholars will research day and night until we figure out what sort of magic can control the elements, and how we can defeat it," Glass Lady said. "They will sleep in the library if they have to."

The fact that the commander seemed confident was like a life preserver thrown to Aki. *This is the Society's job*, she reminded herself. *I am empress, but I don't have to solve all the problems alone.* She exhaled, even though she still drummed her fingers on the cushion of her chair.

"I think we should keep the knowledge of this attack within the Society," Aki said, "until we have a better understanding of what or who it is out there. I don't want the citizens to panic."

Glass Lady dipped her head. "I agree that is wise."

"What do you need me to do in the meantime?" Aki asked. "Anything the Society needs, it's yours."

Glass Lady closed her eyes and exhaled deeply before she opened them again and spoke. "You only need to stay safe, Your Majesty. And pray."

CHAPTER SEVEN

If the Imperial City was the eye of the tiger of Kichona, Takish Gorge was part of the tiger's tail. For the last part of their Autumn Festival break, Sora and Daemon left Samara Mountain and rode south, through sparsely populated farmland and rice paddies to land not populated at all.

Now they raced through towering cypress trees atop the edge of a canyon, their horses pushing through dense green ground cover and soft soil. It was also a good thirty degrees cooler here, as if winter were creeping in early on the Kichonan autumn's reign.

Daemon gasped as he looked up at the delicate, feathery pink clouds above.

Sora glanced up and smiled. It was as if the gods had cast an ethereal lace in the sky. "Welcome home," she said.

He simply sighed. She heard the actual sigh as well as felt the echo of it in their gemina bond, the wisp of contentment like a shadow trailing behind the original.

Daemon closed his eyes and took a long, deep breath. Sora

followed suit. The air here smelled evergreen, as though it had been kissing the dew on the trees for millennia. Breathing it in was Daemon and Sora's ritual each autumn when they returned, a marker to the start of another school year together. And this breath felt more significant, because it was their final year before graduating.

They sat still on their horses for a few minutes, simply breathing.

When Daemon cleared his throat, Sora opened her eyes. He smiled at her, recharged, and it seemed almost as if the air around him buzzed with his renewed energy.

"Let's climb some trees," he said.

She laughed. "You know, sometimes I think you belong in the sky, not on the ground with the rest of us."

Every night at the Citadel, Daemon climbed out his window and onto the boys' dormitory rooftop to lie under the stars. He said there was something about the sky's vastness—its possibility and infinity—that comforted him. There were too many limits imposed down on the earth.

Sora dismounted and tied her horse to a tree. "Shall we climb?"

"Yes, please. I'm itching for height."

They hiked into the woodland. After a few minutes, he picked a tree, cast a squirrel spell, and quickly scaled the trunk, into the branches. Sora followed, and the crisp smell of the evergreens greeted her again. She watched as Daemon inhaled deeply before he pushed off and jumped into the next tree. He bounded from bough to bough, working his way farther down the canyon but higher into the treetops. Sora leaped from tree to tree in a path parallel to his.

Eventually, she landed on the tallest cypress in the area

and climbed up until she was on the highest, thickest branch that would support her weight. She wrapped her legs firmly around the trunk and stood up, opening her arms and tossing her head back toward the sky. The wind blew her back and forth, as if she were a mere dandelion swaying in the breeze. Contentment washed through her.

"You see?" Daemon shouted from where he had also found himself a cypress towering into the sky. "This is why I love being up high."

A raptor soared above her and let out a shrill whistle. Sora whistled back.

The bird jerked in flight and steered away from her, as if offended by Sora's birdcall.

Daemon laughed.

"Oh, shut up," Sora said.

She looked over in his direction. A waterfall came into view, crashing hundreds of feet to the whitewater pools below. And then, beyond that, the trees cleared, and she could see straight down into the bottom of the gorge.

What in Luna's name——?

She leaped through the trees until she was beside Daemon. "I think there's an Autumn Festival celebration going on down there."

He squinted. "Really?"

Sora formed her hands into tapered oval shapes and chanted, "Eyes like a hawk. Eyes like a hawk."

The skin around her eyes tightened, and her long-distance vision sharpened. She homed in on the canyon floor.

"Whoa," Sora said. "There's an entire encampment of red tents, with long yellow-and-green banners whipping in the wind. Thirty or forty people are dancing around a fire."

Daemon tried to cast a hawkeye spell too, but a few seconds later, he muttered a string of half-intelligible curses under his breath. "Stupid mrphrk bumbling grffff magic never works . . ."

"I think we should sneak in and join the party," Sora said.

"I don't know. . . . It's weird that there's a celebration in Takish Gorge. No one ever comes out here. This is wolf and bear territory."

He was right about that. Takish Gorge was far from civilization; Paro Village was the closest town, and because it was already one of the remotest parts of Kichona, its residents wanted to go into the heart of the kingdom when they traveled, not farther away. The canyon was also known for its unfettered wildness, home to a dense population of wolves, bears, cougars, and poisonous, camouflaged snakes. Takish Gorge was not the kind of place most people wanted to go, especially for a celebration known for its carefree, gluttonous, and drunken excess.

"Besides," Daemon said, "I thought we just decided to get serious. Would the heroes in your mother's stories crash a party?"

Sora paused to think about it. But then she grinned. Being mischievous and being renowned weren't mutually exclusive. "The most legendary figures did all sorts of outlandish things. It's part of what makes their tales worth retelling. So yes, if there's a once-in-a-lifetime event in the middle of nowhere, I think it would be part of Kichonan lore. And we should definitely go."

As they got close, though, Sora frowned. A wall of wood surrounded the camp, looming eight feet high above them. She'd seen it from far away, but Sora had been so focused on the party inside, she hadn't registered that the beams were actually spiky protrusions, more like fortifications to protect from enemies.

"That's . . . strange," Daemon said.

Sora nodded. But then she shrugged. "Like you said, Takish Gorge is full of wolves and bears and other predators. It would really ruin a party if any of those got inside." She walked right up to the logs and began to study them, figuring out the best way to get inside.

Daemon hung back a moment. "This isn't an ordinary Autumn Festival celebration. Maybe we should rethink going in."

"Nope. We already agreed that we should *definitely* go in if it's not an ordinary Autumn Festival celebration."

He chewed on his lip, then sighed. "All right. But let's cast moth spells on ourselves before we go in." It would mute their whispers to an ultrasonic level inaudible to the human ear, but which they could use to communicate while in the camp.

Sora laughed. "You *really* want there to be a hidden conspiracy so we can report something interesting to the Council, don't you?"

Daemon looked so mortified, though, that Sora shut up. She shouldn't have said that. They quickly formed finger-fluttering mudras and chanted the moth spell. Sora's voice box tingled as the enchantment took hold. Daemon needed a few tries before his spell worked.

They slinked up to the edge of the camp and hoisted themselves over the wall of logs. Sora landed on the ground as quietly as a ghost—her near-soundless movement, after all, was why she'd been given the taiga name Spirit.

Daemon lowered himself from a nearby section of the perimeter wall, tugging on a wire that trailed him. He'd secured one end to a tree outside the wall and planned to tie off this end inside the camp. It would be easier to leave via tightrope on their way out than scrambling over these slippery logs again.

Lanterns on posts cast a dim red glow over everything. Sora and Daemon crept through the spaces between the tents, sticking, as always, to the shadows. After a few minutes, she found a tree they could climb to get a better view.

She glanced over her shoulder to confirm they were still alone before she wriggled her fingers in a mudra and whispered: "I am a spider, I am a spider, I am a spider." Immediately, her fingertips felt fuzzy, as if there were hundreds of thousands of tiny hairs to help her climb and grip.

Then she jumped to the tree. Her hands and feet made quiet contact with the bark, and the spider spell adhered her to the trunk. She scuttled up the tree, limber and arachnid quick. Daemon followed, although he didn't need a spell. He'd been climbing trees since he could crawl.

There was a sound below them, a rock skittering over the ground. Sora and Daemon froze.

A few seconds later, a pair of guards in light armor walked by. They didn't look up.

She exhaled but spun to face Daemon. "Why would an Autumn Festival celebration require armed guards?" she asked, audible only to him at this moth level.

"I don't know," he said. "Probably the same reason they would have log fortifications. I told you something was off about this party."

The easy, feline grace that had accompanied Sora now tensed. On alert, she was more panther than cat.

She pushed her way through the branches and climbed to the roof of the nearest tent. They hopped their way across the camp until they were just outside the circle of dancers and the bonfire.

A reedy melody weaseled itself through the air. It came from a long woodwind with a curved bell.

"What is that?" Daemon asked.

Sora had never seen nor heard that instrument before. "I don't know," she said. But the number of "I don't knows" was beginning to heap up to an uncomfortable pile.

As the music intensified, the crowd of dancers stilled. It was then that Sora noticed their clothing.

"Daggers," she swore. "Daemon—is it me, or are their tunics and trousers eerily similar to the taiga uniforms?"

He took a few seconds to study them. "Their belts are green; ours are black. Otherwise, they do look similar. But then again, how creative can you make a tunic and trousers? It's not as if the Society owns the color black."

"Maybe . . ."

At that moment, the flaps of a nearby tent parted, and a man in a hooded cloak stepped out. He folded his arms behind his back and walked casually to the dancers.

The fire flared. Then its flames changed from orange to green.

Sora gasped. *How is this happening?* Flames were yellow,

orange, sometimes blue . . . but not green. Not like this.

The fire stretched taller. The tips of the flames rounded, and narrow eye slits formed in each one.

Fiery mouths yawned open and forked green tongues flicked at the sky. They looked like serpent heads.

Sora's heart pounded like a taiko drum.

"What in all hells is happening?" Daemon whispered.

"I don't know," she said again.

"I think we should go before we get caught," Daemon said. "We have enough to report to the Council."

Sora glanced down at the bonfire and the cloaked man. They were not the fun sort of trouble.

The man let the hood fall away, and even from this distance, Sora could see how the light and shadows of the flames taunted the scalelike ridges of his face.

"Impossible," Sora whispered.

But she knew who he was. All of Kichona did. This young man had been burned in a kitchen accident when he was a child, leaving half his skin covered in reptilian scars. Because of this, some called him the Dragon Prince.

Officially, however, he was known as Prince Gin.

Sora's mouth fell open. Daemon's shock reverberated through their gemina bond at the same time.

"He's supposed to be dead," Daemon whispered.

But here he was now, right in front of Sora. Her stomach lurched, not only because this traitorous, violent prince had returned, but also because he was the reason her sister was dead.

Ten years ago, as the Blood Rift was brewing, Sora and the other taiga apprentices had paid little attention. The politics surrounding Rose Palace had seemed too removed from them. On the same day the prince's and princess's factions prepared to fight, Sora had been preoccupied with much more interesting things.

"Is it Friday?" six-year-old Hana had asked earlier that afternoon. It was her last year as a tenderfoot—the rank of children marked by Luna but too young to be apprentices—so she lived and slept in the nursery. But on Fridays, she had a standing date to sleep over in Sora's dormitory with the older girls, and she looked forward to it every week.

Sora had been eight then. "Yes, stinkbug, it's Friday," she'd said with a sigh. She loved her sister, but Friday evenings were when Daemon and her other apprentice friends began the weekend, and there was always mischievous fun to be had, like casting puffer fish spells on each other and then attempting to wrestle in the pool with ballooned bodies and useless limbs.

"You'll come pick me up after dinner for our sleepover?" Hana asked.

Sora looked over her shoulder wistfully, toward the apprentice dormitories. She sighed again as she turned back to her sister. "I'll be here at seven o'clock, as always."

Except when seven o'clock neared and Sora was ready to go over to the nursery, Daemon and their friends burst into Sora and Fairy's room.

"Are you coming for Cookies and Cards tonight, Spirit?" one of the apprentices asked.

"She can't," Daemon said. "Friday is her night with her sister."

"Come, just once," Fairy said. "We have empress cakes."

Sora stopped and spun around. "You have what?" Her mouth watered. Empress cakes were rich little confections made of a thin, delicate pastry crust and filled with almond paste, quince, and goldenberries. Sora's favorite.

"We're leaving now," Fairy said. "One of the Level Nines is going to take us up in the dirigible."

Empress cakes *and* a ride in the taigas' airship? The dirigible was usually reserved for upper-level apprentices and warriors. This was too good to be real. Sora looked at Daemon.

He nodded, almost apologetically, as if to say, *Surprise. Fairy's telling the truth.*

Sora glanced in the direction of the nursery, but it was all the way on the other side of the Citadel.

Hana will be all right, she told herself. *A little disappointed, but she'll be all right.*

Sora left with Daemon, Fairy, and the others.

But Hana was not all right. While Sora was eating empress cake in the dirigible, Prince Gin's warriors launched their attack. The skirmish with Princess Aki's soldiers lasted only two hours, but in that short amount of time, friends brutally killed friends. The prince's warriors slaughtered innocent palace servants and decapitated taigas, leaving their heads on spears. They took the headless bodies and set them aflame on a pyre.

Then they set the Citadel on fire. The southern part of the headquarters burned to the ground. And the nursery—with Hana and many other tenderfoots inside—perished in the flames.

Eventually, Prince Gin was wounded gravely in the

battle. Princess Aki's taigas took advantage of that, and they forced the rebellious soldiers to retreat. They fled to the sea, casting the prince's body into the waters in an ancient Kichonan funeral rite, and then never returned. The entire kingdom heaved a sigh of relief.

Except Sora. She'd never forgiven herself for that night. If she'd been with her sister, Hana might still be alive.

And now the Dragon Prince had returned, on the tenth anniversary of that horrific battle. Sora could practically feel the weight in the air, like humidity composed of blood.

Her knees buckled beneath her. Daemon caught her.

The men and women in the eerie, taiga-like uniforms bowed in unison to Prince Gin.

"We need to go," Daemon said. "Now."

Sora touched the pearl on her necklace and clung to the memory of Hana to help her summon strength. She climbed down from her perch. Moments later, Daemon appeared beside her, and they slinked between the tents. Behind them, the wordless music and dancing had started again.

Daemon scaled the cypress where their escape wire was tied. He slid off his belt, slung it across the wire, and zipped down it like a clothesline.

Sora climbed onto the wire, choosing to run it like a tightrope. She put one foot in front of the other, again and again, methodically making her way across.

Almost there. Almost there.

Across and over the log wall.

Before the line ended, Sora dropped fifteen feet to the ground. She took one more look at the camp behind them, the bonfire lighting up the night as though the hells had opened a rift from the canyon floor.

"We definitely have something to report to the Council now," Sora said, trying to make a joke because she couldn't fully process what they'd just seen.

But what she did know was that if Prince Gin was back, things were about to change for Kichona, in a really bad way.

CHAPTER EIGHT

Sora and Daemon raced back to the Citadel as fast as their horses could gallop. When they arrived three days later, they immediately ran toward Warrior Meeting Hall.

Sora heaved open the heavy black doors and burst into a dark corridor.

Broomstick, Fairy's gemina, rounded the corner from the direction of the Council Room, where he helped with administrative tasks.

"Thank the gods you're back," he said. "Fairy and I were worried about you."

Sora looked at him quizzically. "You already know what happened?"

Broomstick stared at her for a second, as if she were dense. "Um, yes . . . everyone knows about the attack on Isle of the Moon."

Daemon gaped. "What? The Council was attacked?"

"Yes, although by whom or *what*, we don't know," Broomstick said. Then he paused. "Wait a minute. I thought you said you knew what happened."

"Not that part," Sora said, "but we saw something else, and I have a suspicion it's related. Tell us about Isle of the Moon."

Broomstick filled them in on the strange typhoon attack. He didn't know much—the Council was keeping information close to their chests while they tried to understand what they were up against—but being part of the Society's administrative office staff, he'd gleaned enough to know this was formidable magic the Society would be up against.

"Stars," Daemon cursed, as he leaned against the corridor wall for support. "I've never heard anything like it. Magic to control something outside of our own bodies?"

"We've seen magic like this, remember?" Sora said. "The fire at Takish Gorge." She turned to Broomstick. "We saw Prince Gin. He's back."

Broomstick blinked at her. "What?"

A door opened and closed in the distance. A few moments later, Glass Lady turned in to the hallway. She walked quickly past the apprentices without even nodding to acknowledge them.

"Wait, Commander," Sora said.

Glass Lady stopped and peered over her shoulder at her. "What is it?"

Sora's insides nearly froze just from the commander's stare. But she managed to speak. "Wolf and I have returned from our mission, and we saw something we think you'll want to hear about—"

"I have much bigger things to worry about right now than Level Twelve missions," Glass Lady said. "Submit the report in writing." She began to walk away again.

"With all due respect, Commander, you'll want to listen to this." Daemon grabbed Glass Lady's arm to stop her.

Sora and Broomstick both gasped.

Glass Lady stiffened. She turned and glared at where Daemon's hand touched her. She let out a slow, chilly exhale. "You are not disrespecting a warrior—a councilmember— like I think you're doing, are you?"

Daemon dropped his grip instantly. "N-no, Your Honor. I'm sorry. It's just . . . please. We only need a few minutes of your time."

"*One* minute," Glass Lady said, crossing her arms.

Sora nodded. "One minute."

"Then talk."

"We saw Prince Gin," Sora blurted.

Glass Lady raised a brow skeptically, as if she were listening to a tenderfoot's story. "You did, did you? And how, pray tell, did that happen?"

Sora bristled. She'd never cared in the past about being taken seriously, but after the talk with Mama, Sora didn't want to be merely a troublemaker anymore. Maybe Daemon was right—maybe it did matter now what other people thought of Sora, at least in some respects.

"Your Honor," she said, standing tall with her arms by her sides as if she were giving a formal report in front of the entire Council. If she acted respectably, perhaps it would also command respect. "While on our annual trip to Takish Gorge three days ago, Wolf and I stumbled across a camp of nearly fifty people. They had a wall of logs around them like a fortification, and they danced around an enchanted bonfire. The flames changed colors and flared like green serpents. Then a cloaked man joined them, and when his hood fell away from his face, it was scarred. Like the Dragon Prince's."

Glass Lady's expression remained emotionless. "They were dancing? Last I checked, that was not a violation of Kichonan law."

Daemon pushed his way forward again. "Your Honor, the magic in the fire wasn't taiga magic. Doesn't that worry you given what happened at Isle of the Moon? And we saw Prince Gin!"

Glass Lady shook her head and sighed impatiently. "Spirit, Wolf, I appreciate your enthusiasm. Apprentices are often overly excited about their first missions. But think about it—you saw this during the Autumn Festival holidays. You yourselves just finished a reenactment of the Blood Rift. Other Kichonans across the kingdom also carry out similar playacting to celebrate Empress Aki's victory. I'm sure what you saw was a masked actor. As for the color of this supposedly magical fire, that can likely be explained by the addition of a chemical—copper sulfate or alum—to the flames. Spirit's roommate would know."

Sora reddened. Fairy was obsessed with potions and poisons and all kinds of other concoctions. How could Sora not have thought of something as simple as the dancers throwing a chemical powder into the bonfire? Perhaps she *had* gotten too swept up by her new desire to be more than just another apprentice.

But then the image of Hana's and the other tenderfoots' charred skeletons after the Blood Rift flashed in Sora's memory. She pulled her shoulders back and said, "No, Your Honor. I know what we saw. It wasn't just stagecraft that made that fire."

Glass Lady crossed her arms. "The typhoon attack was five days ago, and you saw this bonfire just two days later. If it were the same people, they wouldn't have been able to travel the entire length of Kichona in that short period of time. However . . . we are investigating all possible leads to explain the attack on Isle of the Moon, so I suppose I can have a dragonfly messenger sent to the taiga outpost in Paro Village and have them send someone to investigate."

The dread in Sora's stomach settled, just a little. Glass Lady had listened to her. The warriors would handle this. "Thank you, Commander."

Glass Lady walked away without saying anything else.

Broomstick spoke up once she disappeared down another corridor. "I'm glad she's going to have someone look into that camp. But for everyone's sake, I hope you're wrong about the Dragon Prince being alive. It would ruin Kichona if he tried to resurrect his quest for the Evermore."

The brief relief Sora had felt disappeared. The Evermore. That's what had nagged her when she saw Prince Gin in Takish Gorge. It's why he'd come back. She'd just been in too much shock that he was still alive to think it all through.

The Evermore was a story in Mama's most famous books, the Kichonan Tales, a collection of the kingdom's legends, written before Sora was born. It was common knowledge that, as a child, Prince Gin had spent hours poring over the volume known as *The Book of Sorrow*—stories about lakes that consumed people with nightmares, of days when the sky rained not water but blood, of an era when men prayed not for wisdom and compassion but for riches and power and glory.

Prince Gin's favorite story had been "The Evermore."

Every tenderfoot, including Sora, studied it as a cautionary fable against greed. But sometimes, avaricious souls like the Dragon Prince read the story as truth rather than myth.

As a prophecy, rather than a warning.

It was Prince Gin's quest for the Evermore that had caused the Blood Rift. The burning of the Citadel. The murder of Hana and the tenderfoots.

The dread in Sora's stomach returned. The Dragon Prince had returned to finish what he started.

CHAPTER NINE

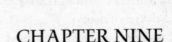

I don't know why you like that story," Aki had said when they were ten years old. They were lying on the carpet of Gin's bedroom and reading together, albeit from different volumes of the Kichonan Tales. She had volume one open, *The Book of Tranquility.* Her brother had volume three, as usual, *The Book of Sorrow.* "It's bloody, and it gives me nightmares."

Gin had shrugged. "That's because you're reading it wrong. There's a paradise at the end of it, and immortality. That's a happy ending."

"There's a cult devoted to that story. That's how you know it's crazy. And Father would be upset if he knew how obsessed you were. You should stop reading it."

"But it's not just a story!" Gin slammed the book closed, and Aki jumped. His scarred face had gone red. "Why is it that some stories of the gods are accepted as true—like Sola blessing our family and Luna gifting the taigas with magic— while others, like the Evermore, are said to be myth?"

Aki rolled over on the carpet and put her hand on her brother's cheek. He hated his skin, but she always told him it made his outside as unique as his inside, and whenever she touched him, it helped calm him down.

But this time, it didn't. He ripped her hand away. "The only reason the Evermore is called a myth is because we don't already have it," Gin said, seething. He turned away from his sister and clutched the book to his chest. "People don't have enough faith to believe in something they can't see."

The Evermore
As retold by Mina Teira

In Celestae, the gods' floating island in the heavens, fruit is so sweet, its mere scent drips syrup from the stars. Beauty is so pure, it bestows joy from miles away. And youth is eternal, such that muscles never grow weak, nor minds, feeble with age. This is the paradise of the gods, a playground of power and immortality and bliss in the sky.

But when Kichona was a young kingdom, its emperor Mareo decided he wanted a version of Celestae on earth. He appealed to Sola, who ignored his summons. He called to Luna, but she did not reply. The gods, it seemed, were too far away to notice or care.

There was one deity, however, who had chosen to live on earth. Zomuri, god of glory, lived in sulfurous caverns in the center of Kichona. And so Mareo embarked on the long and treacherous journey there.

When he finally found the god's home, he was on the cusp of death. Still, Emperor Mareo laid out many offerings for the god. There was gold. There was silk. And mounds of tiger pearls. Zomuri hoarded riches.

On the eighth day, Zomuri appeared. He was a giant wearing an elegant silk robe decorated with embroidered flames. He stroked his long beard with a ten-fingered hand, then picked up the gold and the silk and the spears in turn.

Emperor Mareo looked up through muddied strands of hair. "Great Zomuri, I—"

The god waved at him. The gesture choked off the emperor's voice.

"I know what you want," Zomuri said, scoffing. His breath smelled powerfully of spoiled eggs. "Did you think that gold and silk would be enough to buy you paradise?"

Emperor Mareo shook his head furiously. Through sheer force of will, his voice broke through the god's magic. "This was merely an offering. But I am willing to pay whatever it takes."

Zomuri eyed him now with an inkling of curiosity. It was nearly impossible to break through a god's spell. And yet Mareo had managed to speak.

"If it were possible to grant you paradise on earth," Zomuri said slowly, "what would you do to achieve it?"

Mareo swiped the grimy hair from his face and looked eagerly at the giant. "I have my entire life to give. I have my entire soul to dedicate to you."

The god considered this. It would be quite a coup to have an emperor worship him rather than Sola. But then Zomuri shook his head. "Your life and your soul are not enough."

Emperor Mareo hesitated. But he pulled back his shoulders and said, "I promise all the lives it shall take. All the people I conquer shall worship you. All I kill shall die in your name."

Zomuri smiled. "Do what I bid of you, and you shall have your paradise on earth. You shall have the Evermore."

The curse was made.

Emperor Mareo's legs buckled beneath him from exhaustion, and he hit the ground. He wept, but out of gratitude rather than pain. "Thank you, my lord. Thank you."

Zomuri picked him up by the scruff of his neck and stood him back on his wobbling legs. "Do not thank me yet. There is much work to be done. You will broaden Kichona's borders as far as the eye can see. You will convert the people of the lands you conquer to our faith and make them worship me. And you will pay your tithe to me in blood."

The emperor quivered under the burden with which he'd been bestowed. But he had asked for it. And he wanted the Evermore.

"The first tithe you owe comes due to me as soon as you return home. You shall find Kichonans aged one to one hundred, a male and female each, and sacrifice their lives to me in the Ceremony of Two Hundred Hearts. Only then will I grant you the right to seek the Evermore."

Emperor Mareo's jaw hung open. "You want me to kill two hundred of my own people? Babies? Old women?"

Zomuri huffed, and a cloud of sulfurous air billowed from his nose. "The Evermore is the greatest prize of them all. Blood must be shed to make Kichona into the empire I want. Therefore, the first step is a ritual to prove to me that no life is too precious for you to spare, whether young or old, Kichonan or not."

The emperor stood in the cavern, knees quaking. It was unspeakable, what Zomuri asked.

But it was also a small price to pay to bring paradise to the rest of the kingdom.

With this mission bestowed upon him, Emperor Mareo returned to his palace. He called for volunteers throughout the kingdom, *a male and a female for each age between one and one hundred, promising them glory. And then, away from curious eyes, he slaughtered them, offering their hearts to Zomuri.*

After that, Mareo's armies massacred tens of thousands overseas, and he pursued his goal to the end of his days.

But when he died, Kichona's borders barely skimmed the edges of the mainland. The mantle of the curse would have to be picked up by another disciple, who would, like his predecessor, offer the blood of many, many others.

Thus, it continued. There were periods of peace, when no one was foolish enough to desire what Zomuri had offered, not at so high a cost. But the avarice of men always rears its head again, and in time, another would try for what those who had come before him had failed to achieve.

But there was never enough blood to quench Zomuri's thirst for glory in his name. Never enough for the god to grant heaven on earth. Therefore, it was not man who achieved immortality but, rather, the curse, which trailed their greed like an unshakable, eternal shadow.

The Evermore was never worth its price.

CHAPTER TEN

A crowd had formed in the center of the camp in Takish Gorge. The Dragon Prince walked to the edge of it. He cleared his throat.

The warriors turned. As soon as they saw it was him, they bowed and said, "Your Highness," and stepped aside.

A path quickly appeared. Two taiga warriors from Paro Village had been captured that morning, and they were being kept in cages made of the skulls and femurs of foxes and wolverines and other forest animals, held together and unbreakable by magic. It was a specialty of another one of Gin's soldiers.

The Dragon Prince strode to the cages and peered inside. "New recruits?" he asked.

The prisoner on the left gawked at him.

Was it because she was surprised to see him? Or was it the hideous scars on his face? Gin fought the urge to draw the hood of his cloak over his head. A true leader showed no fear. He had to project the aura of impenetrability.

Meanwhile, the taiga prisoner in the other cage spat at him. "I'd rather die than join a traitor like you."

"Oh, really?" one of Gin's warriors in the crowd asked. It was Skeleton, the one who'd built these cells. "Let's see how true that is."

Without his even forming a mudra or uttering a chant, the bones of the cage began to arc inward. As they did so, the bars splintered, turning into hundreds of bone stakes and spears. They closed in on the taiga rapidly.

"Stop!" her gemina cried.

Gin let it go on for another second, then held up his hand. The killer instinct in his warriors' veins was a good thing. However, the taigas were not enemies. They might resist Gin at first, but they were part of the kingdom he meant to rule, to raise to great heights.

Once his warriors were abroad, though, Gin would unleash them and all their magic on their true adversaries.

On his command, the bones of the cage ceased their crushing movement inward.

The taiga in the cage quivered visibly, but contempt still glinted in her eyes.

"Skeleton," Gin said, "I'd appreciate if you didn't kill our prisoners before I've had a chance to decide what to do with them."

"Yes, of course, Your Highness," Skeleton said, bowing. "I let my excitement run away from me. Please accept my apologies."

Gin turned to the prisoners. "I understand why you hate me. History is written by victors. I lost the Blood Rift; therefore, I'm the enemy. But the truth is, I care for Kichona as much as my sister does. We simply have different views on what's best for the kingdom."

The promise of the Evermore swelled in Gin's heart. It was soft, like the petals of a golden rose trying to bloom, and yet it ached, for it was a dream so big, it couldn't fully unfurl in the space of one human being. He wanted to share his hope with the kingdom, to make the fantasy a reality for all of Kichona.

It would, of course, mean sacrifices had to be made along the way. Lots of blood would be shed, but it would be outweighed by the happiness, the paradise, that would come. That was Zomuri's point. Only a truly courageous leader would have the fortitude to do what needed to be done to achieve the Evermore for his people.

Gin had the ability to do it.

Actually, more than that. When he was born, Luna had passed over Aki but had chosen to bless Gin as a taiga. Then, after the Blood Rift, he'd been on the brink of death yet somehow survived. His warriors had fled with him overseas and nursed him back to health in the rugged mountains of Shinowana, where he recovered and discovered new magic. All these improbabilities couldn't have been an accident. The gods wanted him to know he was special.

Therefore, Gin had the *responsibility* to pursue the Evermore, to bring the best future possible to his people. It burned like a torch in the center of his chest.

He looked at the two prisoners again. Gin focused on the air around him. His magic appeared, like the dust of a million emeralds ground into glitter, floating in the breeze.

Take control of their minds, he willed the sparkling green particles.

They streamed toward the taigas, flurrying around

their heads in a maelstrom. The taigas couldn't see them, and they stared ahead, oblivious. The magic funneled in through their ears and into their heads.

The effect was startlingly sudden. One moment, the taigas were scowling, and the next, they smiled. For them, Gin's control of their minds would feel like the soothing sound from inside a conch shell. They were still themselves—mostly—but they could relax, no longer burdened by the stress of whether their own decisions would be right or wrong. Gin would take care of everything. His presence in their heads gave them the security and purpose they'd always hoped for.

"We are proud to serve you, Your Highness," the prisoners said, their declarations coordinated through their gemina bond.

Gin nodded, swallowing the tinny aftertaste of what he'd done. He hadn't needed to enchant any of his original Blood Rift warriors to follow his commands; they had believes in his cause from the start. But his plan to capture the Council at Isle of the Moon—and, in effect, control the rest of the Society—had failed, so now it came to this. If the Society wouldn't join him willingly, he'd make them his soldiers by force. With magic.

It's necessary, he reminded himself. *This is for my people. My kingdom.*

Gin interrogated the two taigas before him, and they told him everything he needed to know: someone had seen him here in Takish Gorge, the Council had sent them to investigate, and they were to send back a dragonfly messenger immediately with a report.

"If the Council is waiting to hear from you, I suppose I

can't compel you to stay here." He thought for a moment. "You'll return to Paro Village and report that you found nothing here except the trash from an Autumn Festival celebration. You won't say a word about me or this army."

"Yes, Your Highness."

He ordered them freed, and they hurried away to return to Paro Village.

"Congratulations, Your Highness," Virtuoso said. She was one of his most talented warriors and potentially his deadliest weapon. "This is so exciting. Your plans are falling into place—"

Gin held up a hand. Virtuoso was also one of the younger of his soldiers, and her unbridled enthusiasm was too much at the moment. "I have a headache. Order the camp packed up. I'm going to my tent to rest."

It was a lie, the part about the headache. It was Gin's conscience that hurt.

But he couldn't let it stop him. Not for too long.

He'd been put on earth for a purpose—make the taigas and Kichona the greatest they could be. Bring glory to Zomuri. And give his people eternal joy and immortality.

Gin clenched his fists. "This life was given back to me when I should have died. And so I swear on it: I *will* achieve and claim the Evermore."

CHAPTER ELEVEN

Fairy perched on the short wooden bench in the towel room of the boys' bathhouse, tilting her head so her hair cascaded down like a sheet of mahogany silk. The light from the narrow window above hit her at just the right angle to emphasize the heart shape of her face. Across from her sat Racer, a Level 10 who had enough stubble along his jaw to almost pass for a Level 12. Fairy was fully clothed, but she knew well how the fabric of her tunic draped over her curves, and she also understood how, sometimes, more was a lot better than less.

"Has anyone ever told you that you look like you could be the empress's sister when the sun illuminates you that way?" Racer said, trying to lean casually against the shelf of towels. His desire to cross the two feet of distance between them and smash himself against Fairy was obvious, but he didn't. He knew the rules—he could look but he couldn't touch, not until she gave him permission to. Racer was working very hard to stay on his side of the tiny linen room.

"No one's ever said I look like the empress," Fairy said coyly, even though loads of boys had given her that compliment before. "You're terribly sweet to say so." She leaned forward so that the collar of her tunic gaped slightly. A shadow concealed her cleavage, but the fact that the fabric was open was enough to make Racer's Adam's apple bob visibly. A thrill fluttered through Fairy's chest.

"I really want to kiss you," Racer said. He held on to the edge of the towel shelf, as if that were the only thing keeping him from closing the last twenty-four inches between them.

"I'm wearing cherry-flavored lipstick today," she said.

"Oh gods," he groaned. "Please."

"What have the other boys told you about me?"

He shook his head. "No one has said a word."

Fairy smiled her cherry-lipped smile. "That's right. Because if anyone kisses and tells, I'll rip out his manhood and serve it to him on a platter. Right?"

Racer's Adam's apple bobbed again, but for a different reason. "Right," he whispered.

"Good. I'm glad we understand each other." She stepped forward until she was only an inch away. Her head came up to his chest. She looked up at him through her lashes and reached up to cup his face, drawing his mouth down toward her. He held his breath as her lips approached his.

Someone rapped on the door.

Racer jumped and smacked his back against the towel shelf. Fairy, on the other hand, whirled around in a huff. Every apprentice knew that a closed towel room door meant it was occupied.

She opened the door a crack, ready to tear into whoever was on the other side.

It was Broomstick. "A dragonfly just came in from Paro Village. Your ramparts were up so I figured you were here. I wouldn't normally bother you, but I thought you'd want to know."

"Stars, yes." Fairy stepped outside the towel room and shut the door behind her. "What did the message say? Was it really Prince Gin?"

Technically, Broomstick wasn't supposed to have access to the dragonflies. The Council's communications with the Society command posts across the kingdom were strictly confidential. But Broomstick was the kind of person who everyone couldn't help but like. He had an easy smile and stopped by every office in Warrior Meeting Hall each morning to say hello to all the staff. He remembered their birthdays, where their families were from, and what their hobbies were. Everyone in the building relaxed around Broomstick and chatted freely with him, because conversation with him was an effortless joy.

It also meant they told him all sorts of things he wasn't supposed to know.

"The message said there was only garbage from a messy Autumn Festival celebration, and the 'fortifications' were simply part of a reenactment of the Blood Rift, mimicking the Citadel walls."

Fairy frowned. "Have you told Spirit and Wolf yet?"

Broomstick shook his head. "We should go do that."

"Wait." She opened the towel room door and popped her head in.

"Racer, something came up. I'm sorry, but we're going to have to do this another time," she said.

His face fell. "Oh. When do you think—?"

"I don't know. But I'll come find you, okay?" She didn't know when, if ever—it really depended on her mood—but she wanted to let him down easily. Besides, he was cute.

He smiled eagerly.

"All right then . . . see you later." She shut the door, leaving Racer inside, and rejoined Broomstick.

"You know Spirit is not going to be happy about this, right?" she said as they exited the bathhouse and turned across campus toward the girls' dormitory.

"I know. But I'm guessing it'll spur some new scheme of hers."

When they were nine years old, one of the other Level 2s bullied Broomstick about his then-puny size. Sharktooth drew pictures of Broomstick, pummeled him when the teachers weren't looking, and stole his lunch nearly every day. So Sora "borrowed" a laxative from Fairy's lab and baked a batch of cookies. Broomstick happened to bring them for lunch the next day. Sharktooth helped himself to them . . .

And never stole Broomstick's lunch or uttered another mocking word about him ever again.

Fairy nodded now as they walked. "I feel a little guilty that the message didn't turn out the way Spirit wanted it to, but I'm curious to see what she has up her sleeve next."

CHAPTER TWELVE

Sora sat with Daemon on the lawn between the girls' and boys' dormitories. He'd gotten them pumpkin ice cream wrapped in pancake cones from the mess hall, in an attempt to get her to eat something while they waited for the taigas' report from Paro Village, but Sora just sat there, staring into the distance as the ice cream melted and dripped all over her hands.

As soon as she saw Fairy and Broomstick approaching, though, she jumped to her feet, her cone abandoned on the grass. The ice cream rolled in a sloppy globe into a patch of dirt.

Daemon sighed and rose too.

"Did the dragonfly come in?" she asked.

Broomstick nodded. "The conclusion was that what you saw was an Autumn Festival celebration. Prince Gin was just part of a reenactment."

"What? No! Those were real scars we saw, not makeup.

There were fortifications around the camp. And what about the fire?"

"You know, you can turn fire green with several different chemicals . . ." Fairy said.

Sora glared at her.

Fairy put both hands up as if in surrender. "Whoa. Hold on. I hadn't finished. No need to scowl me to death."

Sora still glowered, but she turned down the heat a bit.

Her roommate wisely did not challenge her but instead continued patiently. "You can turn fire green with chemicals, but you can't change the flames into serpent heads."

"So you believe us?" Daemon asked.

"If you think something's off, then something's off," Fairy said.

"I do feel that way," Sora said. "It's like a cannonball in my stomach. Aren't we taught to marry evidence with instinct? But the Council writes us off after one pair of taigas gives a once-over to a pile of trash."

"It's because we're mere apprentices," Fairy said. "The warriors expect us to act like adults until it's inconvenient for them. Then we're just children to them again."

"I suppose it's also my fault they don't take us seriously," Sora said. "I've spent years goofing around and doing anything I could to make life difficult for them. Why would they think any differently of me now?" She sank down onto the lawn.

Daemon, Fairy, and Broomstick joined her, and Fairy rested her head on Sora's shoulder, her hair like a silky blanket for Sora's cheek. They sat like that for a few minutes in silence, which Sora knew was difficult for her roommate, who usually couldn't keep her mouth shut. Sora appreciated it and let her own head rest on Fairy's.

It didn't mean her mind stopped whirring, though.

I understand why the Council closed the matter, Sora thought. They'd sent a team to look into it, and when the answer came back a definitive negative, Glass Lady and the others had moved on to other leads. This was a crucial time; the Council and all the taiga warriors were stressed and researching every possible explanation for the magic at Isle of the Moon. There were scholars in all the libraries across the kingdom, poring over old texts, day and night. The outposts throughout Kichona were on high alert and on orders to send dragonfly messengers about anything and everything suspicious. And the councilmembers themselves were hardly sleeping as they sorted through all the incoming reports.

But Sora didn't accept that what she and Daemon had seen was unimportant. It just meant that the Society was short on resources right now and couldn't spend more time on chasing a lead that seemed, on its face, easy to explain away.

I have time, though, Sora thought. Classes were going to be canceled this week, because the Society needed every taiga warrior—teachers included—to help with their research and to be ready to defend the Imperial City should the Isle of the Moon threat appear here. That meant apprentices like Sora were without a task, and without much supervision.

Daemon sat up and arched a brow. An idea was percolating in Sora's brain. He could feel the pinging of anticipation through their gemina bond.

"What's the plan?" he asked.

Fairy and Broomstick turned to Sora too.

She took another moment to think through her idea, just to make sure she really believed in it.

She did.

"We need to go back to Takish Gorge," Sora said. "Or near it. We have to find those people again. The Council won't investigate this any further now, but just because they're busy pursuing other leads doesn't mean we should let this go ignored. Maybe we really are wrong. But what if we're not and it really is the Dragon Prince? If we do nothing, we will have failed as taigas. Our job is to protect Kichona. Prince Gin would destroy it."

Fairy sprang to her feet. "When do we leave?"

Sora frowned. "About that . . . The warriors might not notice if two of us are gone, but four are too conspicuous. I think it should be just me and Daemon."

"But I want to go!"

"She's right," Broomstick said to Fairy. "The Warrior Meeting Hall staff would definitely notice if I'm not at work. Besides, if you and I stay, we can help cover for them." He turned to Sora and Daemon.

Fairy slumped. "I feel left out."

"Don't," Sora said. "If we do find Prince Gin, we're not just going to take notes and then leave him. I want a way to stop him. Whatever the Dragon Prince is here for, it can't be good, and I need you."

Fairy scrunched her nose, confused. "How can I help with that?"

"You could pack up some poisons for me."

"You want to kill a member of the imperial family?" Fairy's eyes went wide in shock. Broomstick gawked at Sora. Even Daemon, despite his gemina bond that had clued him in on her feelings leading up to this, was numb with shock.

"No," Sora said. "I want to kill a traitor to the kingdom, who would upend the entire planet in his selfish quest for the Evermore if he could do it."

What she didn't say out loud, but which was equally true—

I want to kill the man who murdered my sister.

CHAPTER THIRTEEN

Sora and Fairy climbed up to the third floor of the girls' dormitory. The building's black rice paper windows were thrown open, so even indoors it smelled like sunshine. It was a jarringly cheerful sensation, given that Kichona's destruction loomed on the horizon.

They turned down the hall, passing several doors until they reached theirs. Sora slid it open and stepped inside, nearly tripping on the nunchucks she had left haphazardly in the middle of the floor before going on the Autumn Festival break.

"Yipes!" Sora said as she caught herself on a bedpost.

Fairy merely shook her head. There was an unofficial but obvious line down the center of their room. Sora's side was littered with dirty uniforms and unread books and the occasional nunchucks. Fairy's side was spotless and tidy, especially her botanicals lab—a small desk and set of shelves lined with jars full of dried leaves and vials of flower nectar, as well as flasks of experiments, some successful and some not.

"I'll, uh, tidy up your side of the room while you're gone," Fairy said.

"You shouldn't have to," Sora said. "I'll do it when Wolf and I return. But I know you'll worry while we're gone, so if you need something to occupy your mind, maybe you can work on Wolf's birthday surprise?" His birthday was only a couple weeks away, and after the success of their firework tiger at Rose Palace, Sora had an idea that she thought he'd love.

Fairy smiled a little. "That's a good plan."

But already, Sora was thinking of the journey ahead. And the last lines of the Evermore fable also lingered, a haunting reminder of what was at stake.

It was not man who achieved immortality but, rather, the curse, which trailed their greed like an unshakable, eternal shadow.

The Evermore was never worth its price.

But the opposite was also true. It was worth any price to stop Prince Gin and everyone else who pursued the unattainable legend of the Evermore.

Sora threw open her closet and grabbed a bag. She'd need some clothes, a canteen for drinking water, which she could fill in ponds and streams, and a cloak for concealing herself and keeping warm in the night.

And of course, weapons. She unhooked two leather bands from the wall. One had her usual throwing stars, and the other had spikes, poison darts, and exploding eggshells filled with blinding powder. She strapped several more knives onto her body and into the hidden pockets in the sleeves and every fold of her tunic.

When she turned around, Fairy handed her a small leather pouch. Her favorite, which she always kept strapped to her belt.

Sora's mouth fell open. "Fairy . . . you don't have to give me your satchel. I can just take a few of your concoctions—"

"I want you to take it," she said. "Then I feel like . . . I don't know. This is stupid. But I'll feel like a part of me is there with you, helping."

Sora hugged the satchel to her chest. Inside were half a dozen squat glass vials of poison, each with its own slot. These were Fairy's babies wrapped in blankets, all in a row. She didn't like going too long without cradling them. It was a big deal to hand them over to someone else. "Thank you."

Sora jostled the finicky latch and opened the leather flap. She admired the different poisons, which Fairy lovingly milled and distilled herself.

"What is this syrupy amber one again?" she asked about the leftmost one.

"Demon sugar. One drop on a cake or in a cup of tea will send the victim into paralysis and a slow, strangled death."

"Right," Sora said. "The blue powder, I remember, is ground gaki berry mixed with salt from the Emerald Sea."

"Yes. A little sprinkle of that on a dish, and the victim will get so hungry, he'll go crazy and eventually devour his own limbs to satisfy his appetite." Fairy went on to explain the other four powders and serums in the pouch.

When she finished, she whirled abruptly and hurried to a set of drawers, the one that seemed like a bottomless pit of anything one could possibly need. It was, of course, meticulously organized inside into little trays. Sora had seen Fairy retrieve everything from hair clips to seaweed strips to a romantic novel from the drawers' depths. Now Fairy came back with a small red envelope.

"Hold out your hand," she said. She took what looked like two pink coins out of the envelope and placed them in Sora's palm. They were heavy too, like coins. Lines crisscrossed the disks.

"What is it?"

"Pressed rira powder. In small doses—like an eighth of this disk—it will put someone to sleep. In large doses . . ."

Sora's heartbeat stumbled. But perhaps that was the point. Fairy was giving her and Daemon a way out, in case they got in over their heads, and in case the dancers' camp really did turn out to be Prince Gin and a small army.

"I hope we don't have to use them," Sora said softly as she slipped the rira disks into the leather pouch.

Fairy looked away. "I hope not too."

CHAPTER FOURTEEN

Getting out of the Citadel hadn't been a problem for Daemon and Sora. The Council and the other taiga warriors were too busy preparing for another attack from their mysterious assailants to pay attention to the apprentices. He and Sora simply had to show the guards at the gate their leave passes, which Broomstick had gotten for them.

A day after leaving the Citadel, Daemon and Sora arrived at the base of Samara Mountain, where Sora's parents lived. The trails that led up its steep face were as dark as the taigas' cloaks, obscured entirely by the night and the fog. The Kichona Sea tinged the air with salt, and its waves smashed themselves into the saw-toothed cliffs.

Sora bit her lip as she looked upward. Her fear seeped through their gemina bond and into Daemon's pores.

"I know I've been obsessed with the idea that we saw Prince Gin," she said. "And I know that maybe we were wrong. But that doesn't mean there's no threat. I'm scared about the attack at Isle of the Moon. What if it happens again? And what if next time it's not an island with just five taigas on it, but a place like this with ordinary people too? People like my parents. They could be hurt."

Daemon nodded. Being this close to her family made the threat more real. He brought his horse next to Sora's and squeezed her shoulder. Even though what he really wanted to do was wrap her up in his arms and tell her everything would be all right. But he couldn't do that, for multiple reasons.

"We should probably stop for the night," Sora said, trying to shake off her worry.

"Yes, but let's ride a bit longer. I recall a creek not far from here." It wasn't that Daemon wanted to travel more tonight; they'd been riding hard enough to make good time. It was that he thought it would be better to draw Sora away from Samara Mountain. Unlike Glass Lady, Daemon believed that emotion could be beneficial to a taiga, providing motivation when it was needed. But in this case, the mountain was such a looming reminder of what was personally at stake for Sora, it was probably the right choice to move on.

Brows knit tightly, she looked up the switchbacks once more before she nodded and nudged her horse to continue.

They rode until they heard the lullaby of the water. There was a clearing set back from the road, sheltered by a cluster of ancient camphor trees, their moss-covered trunks as wide as Daemon's horse was long, their fissured branches plunging deep into the fog. A patch of muddy grass would have to do as both grazing for the horses and bedding for him and Sora. The air smelled of damp and camphor mint.

They brought their horses to the water and tied the

reins to the trees. Daemon caught a few small carp from the creek, which they cooked over the fire Sora started. Soon after dinner, a chill sliced like a scythe into the night.

Sora shivered as she unrolled her sleeping mat.

"Cold?" Daemon asked. "You can have my blanket."

She smiled but waved him off. "I'll be all right. Thank you, though."

Daemon looked at her a few seconds longer than he needed to. When he caught himself, he coughed and glanced away.

Sora lay down on her mat and pulled her wool blanket over herself. "Do you think we're doing the right thing?"

"Yes," he said without hesitation. "I do. Do you think the camp will still be there when we arrive?"

But Sora had already fallen asleep.

Daemon lay on his own sleeping mat and listened to the featherlight in-and-out of her breath. After a while, her teeth began to chatter.

He removed his own blanket and spread it over her. He'd make do with his riding cloak.

But he couldn't sleep. His mind raced with thoughts about Isle of the Moon, about the Evermore story that he'd hated as a kid, about the scars on that man's face in Takish Gorge. Maybe his scaly skin had been stage makeup, as the Paro Village taiga report suggested. That would be good. Daemon and Sora could return to the Citadel knowing that there was no Prince Gin, that he was (still) dead, and they'd leave the Isle of the Moon attack to the Council and actual warriors to deal with.

Then again, if the hooded man really had been the Dragon Prince, Daemon and Sora could return to the Citadel as heroes for having uncovered it. Maybe they could even sneak into his camp and assassinate him. Daemon imagined riding triumphantly through the iron gates at the Citadel, the evil Dragon Prince's body thrown over the back of his horse.

He let his mind wander to other versions of victory.

But eventually, he got up. His inexplicable need to see the stars nagged at him, tugging at him from up high. *I need to clear my head.*

Daemon found a tall pine nearby. He climbed quickly, and when he broke through the fog at the top, he cried out like a man in the desert who'd finally stumbled on an oasis of water. His cloak was cold and damp from the mist, and pine needles poked into his hair, but none of it mattered. There was sky, sky, sky, not the suffocating blanket of fog. There were stars and there was the moon, glowing fiercely into the night.

Why did he crave this so badly? Was it simply because he'd been raised in the wild? Or was there something else in his past that made him need the freedom he found at the tops of the trees? Maybe he'd spent his infancy in a mole tunnel or something.

But then Daemon closed his eyes, and he imagined not only the comforting, dark infinity of the sky around him but also the smell of leather and steel mixed with black currant and sandalwood. The curiously alluring scent of Sora's weapons and her soap. Daemon breathed in deeply and let his mind wander, just a little, to Sora's smile, the taut lines of muscle on her body, and to a recent sparring session when she'd pinned him to the dirt floor of the arena and straddled him, pressed her knife against his throat, and leaned forward to whisper, "It looks like I win."

Daemon had grinned, though, because he'd felt he was the winner of that match. Not because of the fight itself, but because she'd been so close to him, her lips nearly grazing his ear, the razor edge of her hair skimming his cheek as she declared victory . . .

He exhaled.

Everything was going to be fine. It had to be.

CHAPTER FIFTEEN

Paro Village was a town swallowed by the forest. Trees draped in long sheets of flowering vines curtained the buildings, so thick that a traveler could easily pass the city by, if not for the fact that the gravel roads ended abruptly here, going no farther south. The shops and homes themselves were made of stone and covered in thick blankets of moss, as if they'd risen from the forest floor as part of the natural landscape. And a waterfall in the nearby cliffs kept the air thick with chill.

Gin stood in the village square—really, a grassy field in the middle of the town—as the citizens assembled. Even the people here seemed a part of the woods, preferring rough-spun clothing the color of bark, their hair untamed in the breeze that whistled through the trees. Shopkeepers stood in the doorways of their stores. Families brought the elderly and the young. Whether it was because they were curious or scared or both, everyone turned out to see the Dragon Prince.

On the edges of the crowd, the Paro Village taiga warriors stood at attention. Hypnotizing them had been Gin's first order of business here. Since he'd failed to take control of the Council at Isle of the Moon, this was plan B—stealthily enchant as many taigas as possible to create an army, then march on the Imperial City and take the rest of the Society. Without the taigas guarding his sister, Gin could seize the throne.

But that wasn't all he needed. In order to begin his quest for the Evermore, Gin would have to perform the Ceremony of Two Hundred Hearts. He needed to persuade ordinary Kichonans to give their lives to Zomuri.

A ripple of nausea rolled through Gin's stomach, the warning of seasickness before a storm.

Am I really going to do this?

He looked over at his original taiga warriors, who had stood by him since the Blood Rift. He remembered how close to death he'd been, and how dedicated they'd been to bringing him back to health. And then they'd spent years training in the Shinowana mountains, fumbling with this new magic, bruising themselves while sparring, and finally, mastering it.

This was what all that time and effort was for. To bring Kichona and its people a glorious, immortal paradise.

Gin turned his attention back to the assembling crowd in the square. *Taking away their free will is a necessary sacrifice. The Ceremony of Two Hundred Hearts is part of the process. It's for the ultimate good of the kingdom.*

"I've spent a decade dreaming of coming home," Gin said. "You're my kin. I missed you deeply." He smiled.

A little girl in the front row shrieked. "His face is so

ugly!" She buried herself in the folds of her mother's skirt.

The woman flushed and took several steps backward, all while wrapping the fabric of her skirt around her daughter, as if doing so could make her disappear. "I-I'm sorry, Your Highness. She's only three. She doesn't know what she's saying."

Gin clenched his fists. But he didn't respond. The girl—and everyone else—would love him soon enough.

Now, in fact.

Emerald-green particles whooshed through the air, falling like snow on the people's heads. A moment later, they smiled drowsily.

Gin glared at them. "As I was saying, I've been looking forward to coming home. You missed me too, didn't you?"

"Yes," the crowd answered in chorus. Their eyes twinkled with the kind of blissful peace only Gin's enchantment could give them.

Perhaps free will was overrated.

"I'm here to bring eternal paradise to Kichona," Gin said. "But I need your help. Are you willing?"

"Whatever you require, Your Highness," the villagers said.

"Good. My sister has been empress for a while, but I intend to take the crown from her, so that I may lead you to glory and everything our kingdom deserves. There will be a coronation, and I would like to invite citizens from throughout Kichona. Is anyone interested?"

"Me!"

"Over here!"

"Your Highness, pick me, pick me!"

The crowd erupted in clamoring chaos.

Gin motioned for Virtuoso, one of the most reliable of his original warriors, to come over. "You know what to do, right?"

She nodded. "Two hundred slots that need to be filled. Ages one to one hundred, a male and female each."

"We don't need to find all of them here. We'll make plenty more stops before the Imperial City as we amass our army. But go ahead and choose some here."

Virtuoso nodded and began shouting at the people for order. The other taigas jumped in to herd them into lines to submit their names.

Gin turned his back on the square. He strode away, pushing through the curtains of flowering vines to the outskirts of town, where his warriors' horses waited. Even from here, he could still hear the people shouting over each other as they argued for the honor of going to his coronation. For the privilege of sacrificing their lives for Zomuri.

Another little shudder of nausea rippled through Gin.

But this time, the guilt was smaller, and it passed quickly. Because after a lifetime of dreaming and ten years of planning in exile, everything was starting to come together. Gin had the makings of a magical army that no one would be able to defeat. He'd begun collecting Hearts.

And the fantasy of the Evermore was within reach.

CHAPTER SIXTEEN

Fairy and Broomstick pushed their way through the streets of Shima. Obnoxious, sweaty hawkers stood on the narrow sidewalks, each shouting louder than the previous one that their gambling hall had the most honest dealers, the greatest odds of winning, and the cheapest tobacco and beer. In every alley, crowds of people huddled in circles, exchanging bets and watching roosters screech and fight in a mess of blood and feathers. And pretty girls with too much makeup hung on the arms of men strolling through the tawdry city.

Usually, taigas liked to dress in street clothes when they were on leave. Kichonans respected taigas immensely, because the gods interacted with humans in only two situations—when they blessed babies as taigas, and when they were summoned by an emperor and empress. Thus, people bowed at the taigas' feet and called them "Your Honor" wherever they went, and it wasn't unusual for small children to run up and ask taigas—even apprentices—for their autograph. It was hard to blend in and enjoy a brief leave from school or duties when wearing a black uniform.

But there were other occasions when a Society uniform was needed. Going into Shima was one of those times. Fairy had worn a red dress here on her first leave as a Level 9 and had received enough leers to last a lifetime. She swore never to do that again.

Fairy and Broomstick finally arrived at their destination, a tiny herbal medicine shop that was sandwiched between a gentleman's club and a pawnshop. The owner, Mrs. Mura, was from a long lineage of respected herbal masters, and she sold dried plants that had been used in ancient remedies for centuries. Unfortunately, the demand for traditional medicine was dying, so she found she had to cater to a less savory clientele to keep her shop open; she sold relaxing grasses and hallucinogenic mushrooms in the main part of her store. But Fairy was here for the rare seeds and crushed leaves that she needed for her botanicals. Like Sora had said, she needed something to distract her while her friends were off hunting a Dragon Prince.

Mrs. Mura's seemingly permanent frown melted away as soon as she saw who had walked in her door. She pushed up the heavy spectacles on her nose and straightened her blouse, which was decorated with a pattern of brightly colored flowers and herbs, spiraling out as if seen through a kaleidoscope.

"Your Honors, welcome back. I cannot tell you how happy I am to see your faces. What can I do for you today?" Not only did she respect Fairy and Broomstick as taigas, but it was also a relief to be able to serve someone who actually appreciated her plants. It wore Mrs. Mura down to sell areca nuts to the patrons of the gentleman's club next door.

"It's great to see you again," Broomstick said before wandering off to look at the amusing collection of pipes in the display window. There was one shaped like a laughing banana, another like a pig's snout, and more. Broomstick didn't smoke—taigas weren't allowed to, and besides, he didn't see the allure of tarring up his lungs and coughing all the time—but the pipes were something to look at while his gemina did her shopping.

Fairy handed a piece of paper to Mrs. Mura. "I made a list of what I need for my experiments. Do you have any of these?"

Mrs. Mura put on her glasses. "Two ounces of swallow's saliva, one ounce each of dried wood-ear mushroom, cherry blossom petals, and mangrove bark, half an ounce of bitter almond extract . . ." She read the rest of the list in silence. When she finished, she took her glasses off and said, "I think I have most of these. I'll be right back."

"That's a lot of ingredients," Broomstick said. "You're going to spend your entire apprentice allowance on them."

Fairy shrugged. "I gave my satchel to Spirit, so I want to make new batches of some of my standbys. Plus, I need some of them for Wolf's birthday project. . . ."

"Oh yeah!" He grinned. Then he picked up a pipe shaped like a hairy, bare foot. The mouthpiece was the big toe. "Who in their right mind would want to put this in their mouth?"

She laughed. It caught her by surprise, because she'd been so anxious since Spirit and Wolf had left. But it was a welcome surprise, even if it was only temporary.

Mrs. Mura came back with a tray of tiny glass jars and vials.

Fairy flitted back to the counter.

"Your Honor, I have everything on your list except the wood-ear mushroom."

"It's okay. I can forage in the woods for that. Everything else is harder to come by."

Mrs. Mura rang her up, and as Broomstick predicted, it cost Fairy her whole allowance. It was a good thing Mrs. Mura was out of the wood ear.

"Someday when you have more time," Mrs. Mura said, "I would love to hear what you're cooking up with all these ingredients."

Fairy smiled and clasped Mrs. Mura's wrinkled hands. "I will definitely tell you all about it once I get better at brewing these potions."

"I'm looking forward to it," Mrs. Mura said. "Thank you again for coming by, Your Honors. I hope to see you soon."

Fairy waved, and then she and Broomstick were out the door, hurrying back to the Citadel. There was lots of work to be done on Wolf's surprise, and they had only a couple weeks left.

Not to mention that their best friends were on a potentially dangerous mission, and Fairy and Broomstick had to do *something* to keep their minds off worrying.

So they would go back to her lab and play with chemicals. And explosives. Because that's what fairies and broomsticks did best.

CHAPTER SEVENTEEN

Takish Gorge was as pristine as Sora and Daemon had left it.

Or, perhaps, a bit *more* pristine.

As they rode to the top of the canyon walls and peered down, they saw exactly what they'd expected to see the first time—a roaring waterfall, towering cypress trees, and a rocky floor through which various sharp-toothed creatures and their prey darted. What Sora and Daemon did not see was the camp, other than the log walls.

"Stars," Sora swore, even though they knew the Paro Village taigas had reported nothing here but the remnants of a celebration.

"It's been less than a week since we were here," Daemon said. "Maybe we can still pick up their trail."

Sora sighed. "Maybe. I suppose we should go down to the campsite to look for clues."

They descended into the gorge. There weren't paths

here, so they had to make their own, pushing through spaces between boulders and steering their horses around trees downed by lightning.

Hours later, they reached the canyon floor. They were dusty and sweaty, and their legs ached from holding tight against their saddles during the climb down. Sora dismounted first, just outside the strange log walls. Most remained in place, but a twenty-foot length of it had been eased open like massive doors.

Sora ran her fingers between two of the logs until she reached the corner, where it hinged out from the rest of the fortifications. "There's nothing holding them together. No mud or other daubing between the wood, and no notches to lock the logs into place. It's as if they're just . . . balanced on top of one another."

"Magic?" Daemon asked.

She shook her head. "I don't know."

Daemon kneeled into the dirt. "Add something else to our list of this camp's strangeness—there aren't hoofprints or wheel ruts here. It looks like they opened the log wall in order to leave and then rolled out in something giant."

Sora bent to examine the dried mud. The ground had, indeed, been flattened by something wider than a cart or carriage. "Or maybe they marched and rode out of here like normal but had something follow them to erase their footprints?"

"Why would that matter? We could still follow the path crushed by . . ." Daemon's voice trailed off as he looked in the direction of the path. It disappeared just a stone's throw away from the logs, as if no one had been here at all. "So much for that theory." He chewed on his lip, puzzled.

"Let's go through the camp to see if there are any other clues," Sora said.

They walked slowly through the site. Where there had been crimson tents last time, now there was emptiness, not even a stray stake left unpacked. Despite the Paro Village taigas' report, there was no trash left behind, besides some horse dung in the area that had been their stables. And other than a handful of tree trunks that had been sliced a bit too cleanly, as if a sword had glided through them rather than a saw, there was no indication that magic of any sort—green fire or otherwise—had been here.

Sora and Daemon stood in the middle of the campsite, completely flummoxed.

A howl sounded at the edge of the forest, too close to the campsite. Sora froze.

Another howl responded. Then another and another.

The wolves were surrounding the camp.

"I don't like the sound of that," Sora whispered, drawing her sword and placing her back at his so they could fight attacks from both sides.

But Daemon hadn't drawn his bo or any of his other weapons. Instead, he tilted his head up to the sky and belted out his own howl.

Sora whirled around, eyes wide. Her terror shivered through their gemina bond.

Daemon put a hand on her arm to calm her. "The wolves were issuing a warning to us."

"I figured that out," she said, "which is why I have my sword out. Why aren't you armed? Why are you howling and letting the wolves know precisely where we are?" She shook her arm free from his grip and began to pace in an arc again, ready for an attack.

"Because they aren't after us," Daemon said. "They're trying to warn us against the ones who were here before."

She lowered her sword. Daemon often downplayed his ability to communicate with wolves—he called his language skills "rudimentary eating and fighting words," since that's pretty much all he remembered from his wolf cub days—but Sora thought he sold himself short. Other taiga apprentices might have been better at magic, but how many of them could be left in the wild for years—or even weeks—and survive alongside predators like the wolves, bears, and cougars of Takish Gorge? Not many.

Sora watched as he tilted his head up and let out another cry, his eyes closed and lashes fluttering as he poured himself into his past self, lost for a minute from this world. He usually kept his wildness stashed away, but in moments like these, Sora saw his true essence, and she swelled with pride. She also, irrationally, felt safer, knowing that her gemina had this ferociousness in him. She silently thanked Luna for bonding her with Daemon.

The wolves streamed in now from the surrounding parts of the canyon, into the center of camp. They were all colors—gray and black and snowy white—and their leader was a mottled brown, grizzled and scarred from winning his place at the top of the pack. The muscles beneath his fur heaved, fierce and taut, and he bared his fangs as he growled, teeth shiny and sharp in the sunlight.

Daemon crouched on all fours and bowed his head in submission. Sora mimicked him.

The alpha wolf barked.

Daemon lifted his head, growled, and barked in return. Despite living as a civilized human for thirteen years, he still seemed surprisingly at home in the company of wolves.

"What are you saying?" Sora asked.

"Shh," Daemon said, as the wolf answered. They exchanged a few more rounds of barking and guttural growling. The effect echoed through Sora's gemina bond, and she felt the rumble deep in her core.

Daemon finally turned to her. "I don't understand everything he's telling me, but from what I can gather, the people in the camp could do a lot more than turn a bonfire green. The wolf said the log fortifications were built in less than a day. Trees were ripped from the forest throughout the canyon and then flew through the air here."

"Flew through the air?" Sora said.

"Yeah. He also said something about giant balls rolling out of the camp . . . they were made of ice and fire and . . . something about insects?"

Sora frowned. She didn't want to doubt Daemon, but by his own admission, his wolfish *was* a little shaky, and what he was translating made no logical sense.

But he had enough doubt about his abilities as a taiga. Sora wasn't going to undermine him now.

"Do the wolves know when the group left the camp, and did they see where they went?" she asked.

Daemon faced the brown wolf again and barked his questions.

The wolf consulted two others near him, then replied.

"I see." Daemon was so fully in wolf mode, he pointed his nose—rather than his finger—northeast to indicate to Sora where they had gone.

"Huh. I wonder where they're going?" Sora envisioned a map of Kichona in her head. They were in the tiger's tail, and there wasn't much else there. "Paro Village, maybe?" It was a short distance inland.

"Possibly," Daemon said, his voice still rough from the transition between wolfish and humanspeak.

He said something else to the wolves.

The alpha barked.

Daemon went quiet, but their gemina bond blanched white.

"What is it?" Sora asked. "What did he say?"

Daemon stayed still for a minute, then looked up, swiping at his eyes. "He expressed condolences for my pack. The last of my wolf family passed on in the winter."

"Gods, I'm so sorry."

He waved it away. "Wolves in the wild don't live that long usually. They had full lives."

The alpha wolf growled again.

Daemon composed himself and nodded.

"The pack will accompany us to the top of the canyon," he said. "They want us to exact revenge against those who came in and cut down their trees and disrespected the gorge."

Sora bowed her head to the wolf to convey her thanks and accept his charge. Daemon reinforced it with a string of barks.

"I guess we'll head in the direction of Paro Village and see where it takes us," Sora said. Her heartbeat was already sprinting ahead.

"And if we don't find them?" Daemon asked.

"We report what the wolves told you."

"That'll go over even better than trying to convince Glass Lady of what we saw." He twisted his mouth downward. "It always sounds ridiculous when I say I can talk to wolves."

Sora crossed her arms. "Well, they'll have to deal with it, because you know what else sounds ridiculous? A magical cult cutting down flying trees and rolling around in balls made of ice and fire. But if that's what Kichona is about to face, then the taigas had better listen."

"And if they don't?"

"Then I suppose we'll have to take matters into our own hands."

CHAPTER EIGHTEEN

Sora and Daemon emerged from the unfettered wildness of Takish Gorge only to be greeted by the different sort of wildness of Paro Village. They rode into town, their horses pushing through curtains of flowering vines every few feet. It was difficult to see where they were going.

"This is the strangest-looking town I've ever been in," Sora said. "It's like they cleared the land a long time ago to build the village, but then the forest came back with a vengeance, and the people didn't bother to fight back."

"Maybe we should leave the horses," Daemon said. "It might be easier on foot."

They secured their horses to a nearby post and crossed over a mossy bridge to the main street where most of the shops were concentrated. Even here in the center of town, the forest was so thick that they had to elbow their way through the greenery. Sora almost shoved her arm into someone's face accidentally as she was pushing through some vines.

"I'm sorry!" she said.

The woman laughed pleasantly. She was short and red-nosed from the cold. "It's all right. It's a part of life here. Are you a tourist?"

"Not really. We're looking for the taiga outpost."

"Oh, of course, silly me." She nodded at Sora's and Daemon's uniforms. "But I'm afraid there are no taigas here, Your Honor."

Daemon frowned. "What do you mean, no taigas? There's a Society post here. We received a message from them a few days ago."

"They went with Prince Gin, to make him emperor! He is so very kind." She smiled blissfully.

The color drained from Sora's face. The Dragon Prince had been here.

But the Paro Village taigas wouldn't support him, let alone leave this outpost unguarded in order to go with Prince Gin. That made no sense. Those who'd fought for him during the Blood Rift were either dead or gone. The taigas who remained in Kichona were on Empress Aki's side.

Daemon cleared his throat. "You realize that Prince Gin's sister is still the empress, right?"

The woman shrugged and looked entirely unconcerned. "Prince Gin has picked many here in this village as his Hearts! Including me."

Sora choked on a breath. "His Hearts?"

The woman beamed and nodded. "Yes! We are to go to the Imperial City soon as special guests for his coronation."

Sora grabbed Daemon's arm. "You know what that's a reference to, don't you?" she whispered.

"The legend of the Evermore?"

"Yes. And the Ceremony of Two Hundred Hearts." Sora

120

fought the dizzying sensation of the ground giving way beneath her feet. Prince Gin was tapping people to become his blood sacrifices to Zomuri, so that he would be granted the right to pursue the Evermore. Two hundred men, women, and children, who would cut out their own hearts and offer them to the god, all in the name of glory.

Sora grabbed onto a nearby vine to steady herself.

The woman blinked at them, as if she'd forgotten what Sora and Daemon had been asking her about. "Hey-o, did you say you were tourists? You really should visit the Paro Bakery. They have the most divine persimmon twists, especially if you can get them straight out of the fryer. I think I might go see the baker right now. Would you like to join me?"

"Um, no thank you," Sora said.

The woman smiled vacantly and drifted off like dandelion seed in the wind, murmuring to herself about persimmon twists.

"Should we try to figure out who all the 'Hearts' are here and tie them up or something?" Daemon asked.

Sora shook her head. "We don't have time. We need to get to the Society outpost to see if the taigas really are gone, and to send a message to the Citadel."

A man with an ax pushed through the vines on the other side of the street and began crossing the road toward them. But as soon as he saw Sora's and Daemon's uniforms, he veered back to the other side of the street and disappeared behind the flower curtain through which he'd come.

The hairs on Sora's arm stood up. "I don't like the feeling of this," she said.

"We'll find the Society outpost ourselves," Daemon said. "Paro Village is small. A black building can't be hard to find among all this green."

They made their way through town, practically swimming as they pushed aside armfuls of vine. They almost collided with several more people, but again, as soon as their uniforms came into view, the people quickly changed direction.

Sora and Daemon reached the end of the main street and nudged their way through a particularly dense curtain of vines. There was nothing but steep mountain ahead of them.

"I guess the Society building isn't as easy to find as I thought," Daemon said, kicking at the rocks at his feet.

But Sora reached over and touched his arm. "Look up."

Above them, platforms spanned the arms of half a dozen trees. A series of black buildings with black thatched roofs traversed them.

"It's a tenderfoot's dream post," Daemon said, staring in wonder at what was essentially a giant treehouse. A very well-constructed one. The Society outpost here was as unique as the rest of Paro Village.

At that moment, a little face popped up in one of the open windows. "Oh no, it's the enemy!" he cried out. "Sound the alarm!"

A handful of other children peeked out from various windows. They were just boys and girls playing. Real tenderfoots all lived and trained at the Citadel. But where were the taiga warriors who were supposed to be here? They wouldn't have let their post be overrun like this.

"Attack!" one of the children yelled.

Acorns hailed down at Sora and Daemon. "Stop!" Sora shouted. "We're taigas!"

"It's the enemy! Empress Aki's taigas are here!" the first boy cried. "Show no mercy!"

The enemy?

More acorns.

"Stand down!" Daemon yelled. "We must speak to the taiga warriors and send a message to the Citadel."

"The dragonflies are all dead!" a girl from the highest platform shouted. She whirled to the other children. "Keep fighting, everybody!"

A storm of rocks pummeled down from the treehouse this time. They were a lot harder than acorns.

"This is ridiculous," Sora said, as she ran for cover. Daemon was right behind her. They plowed through the curtain of greenery that had initially blocked their view of the outpost.

When they were shielded from the acorns and rocks, Daemon said, "What in all hells is going on here?"

Sora's skin crawled as if there were ants beneath the surface. Where had the Paro Village taigas gone in the short span of days between when they sent the dragonfly to the Citadel and now? And why were the people here so fiercely dedicated to Prince Gin?

Unfortunately, there didn't seem to be a way to get any of that information from here.

"Come on," Sora said, heading back toward their horses.

"Where are we going?" Daemon asked, falling into step beside her.

"Kaede City." It was south, on the tiger's leg of Kichona. They'd be able to send off a message to the Citadel. Sand Mine was technically the closer Society outpost, but it was difficult to get to. So Sora chose Kaede City. "Hopefully Prince Gin hasn't been there already too."

CHAPTER NINETEEN

"What do you think Fairy and Broomstick are up to right now?" Sora asked as they rode along a dirt road. They were halfway to Kaede City and a long way from the Citadel. She was really beginning to miss their friends.

"Fairy has probably accidentally gassed the girls' dormitory a couple times with experiments gone awry, and Broomstick might have blown another hole in the wall of his room."

Sora smiled, but then grew serious again. "Do you think they're worried about us?"

Daemon went serious too. "Yeah. I'm sure they're worried sick and trying to keep themselves occupied so they don't have to think about it. But we'll—"

"Shh." Sora stuck out her arm to stop him and his horse. There were voices in the distance, and hooves. Lots of them. "Quick, into the woods," she said.

They yanked their horses into the trees just in time. A caravan of a hundred or so people appeared on the dirt road coming from somewhere inland.

While Daemon hid the horses farther in the forest, Sora crept back out close to the road, staying hidden in the low shrubbery. She lay on her belly as she pulled out a spyglass.

"Is that them?" Daemon asked, when he crawled up beside her.

Sora trained her glass on the banners above the wagons. They were the yellow-and-green flags they'd spied last time at the Takish Gorge camp. Red canvas peeked out from the carts, possibly tents.

"Yes," Sora said. "It's them."

She moved her spyglass to the people then, part of her hoping to see mere dancers, prancing around as if celebrating by a fire. But instead, she saw actual fire. A sphere of it, nearly eight feet tall, rolling at the head of the caravan.

Her mouth hung open. "Gods . . ."

"What is it?"

Sora let her arm drop and held the spyglass limply to Daemon.

He took it and focused on what she'd been looking at.

"Daggers," he swore in disbelief. "Are those flames?"

"Unless our eyes are both deceiving us." It turned out Daemon *hadn't* misheard the wolves about enormous spheres of fire.

"There's . . . a person inside."

"What?" Sora grabbed the spyglass and peered through it.

Inside the orb, a silhouette marched. Occasionally, the flames parted, and Sora saw the actual woman inside. She was propelling the entire sphere forward.

Holy heavens. What was this magic? It was nothing

like what the taigas could do. Every muscle in Sora's body tensed. "The fire doesn't even hurt her; it just obeys her. I'm afraid to look at what else is over there."

"Me too."

And yet a hard determination crystallized between them. It was a fragile bravery, like thin ice in a pond full of dread. But it was courage nonetheless.

Sora took a deep breath. Then she raised the spyglass to her eye again and scanned the rest of the column of people in the caravan.

Crow's eye.

A snowball ten feet in diameter rolled after the fire orb, freezing the scorched ground as soon as it touched the dirt and leaving a trail of frost behind.

A small tornado followed the snowball, sucking up the frost. Like with the sphere of flames, there was a person visible inside. He collected the frost and occasionally hurled the snowflakes back out like icy throwing stars.

Never in any of Sora's studies or even in the myths and legends her mother wrote had Sora heard of magic like this.

Her spyglass focused on a boy gliding on a platform of something wriggling. Sora gagged.

"What is it?" Daemon asked.

She coughed and pointed the spyglass in the direction of the caravan. "Insects," she said hoarsely. "There's a boy being carried by a moving platform made of insects. Just like the wolves said."

Daemon's eyes widened, and his skin shaded green, as if his body was warring between the shock of disbelief and the desire to throw up.

And at the very end of the procession, two massive,

muscled horses carried the last of the mysterious group. Both wore dark green cloaks with hoods that hid their faces from view, but there was a sternness to them that hammered another crack into Sora's courage.

"Maybe we should go back to the Citadel," Daemon said. "This isn't just harmless magic. It's too big for you and me."

Sora shivered, but she shook her head. "We already lost them once when we reported back to the Citadel. We can't lose them again. There's too much at stake. After what we saw at Paro Village, there's definitely something bad going on."

"Then what do you propose we do?"

She lowered the spyglass. "Stick to our plan. Follow them, learn what we can, and then I'm going to kill Prince Gin."

Sora and Daemon waited for the caravan to pass, then followed as if they were ghosts, disappearing into trees and melting into the shadows. As the sun reached its afternoon peak, they arrived at a fork in the road. One path went farther inland into farm country, the other, out toward the coast. The fire orb at the front of the procession chose the road toward the sea.

"They're heading to Kaede City," Daemon said. "How convenient for us."

Sora nodded. Maybe they could sneak past the caravan once they got closer to the city and report to the taiga outpost.

An hour and a half later, the smell of the ocean blew in from the coast, tingeing the air with brine. Kaede City was a short distance away, a small harbor town with roots in fishing and seafaring.

The caravan stopped in the sparse forest just outside the city. Sora and Daemon ducked behind a cluster of mossy boulders.

One of the cloaked figures rode up from the back of the line.

He removed his hood. The reptilian scars were undeniable.

The man who had burned down the Citadel. Who killed Sora's sister. Who wouldn't stop at battlefields soaked in blood in his quest to achieve the Evermore.

A furious cocktail of fear, hatred, and a hunger for vengeance swirled inside Sora. It was so potent, Daemon actually gasped as the feeling shot through their bond.

Prince Gin faced the soldiers who had gathered around him.

"My formidable ryuu," he said, his voice low and gravelly. "I'm so proud of where we have been, how hard you've worked to come this far, and where we're all headed together."

Sora gripped Daemon's shoulder. "What are ryuu?" she whispered.

"I think that's what they call themselves," he said.

The sound of the word sat like a lump of lead in Sora's gut.

The other cloaked figure rode up beside Prince Gin. "May I say a few words?"

It was a girl's voice. A little raspy, but definitely a girl.

"Before we enter our next target," the cloaked ryuu said, "let me remind you that we are embarking on a course of action that will not only bring glory upon each and every one of you but also usher Kichona into a new age. Too long have the abilities granted to us by the gods lay dormant.

Taigas shouldn't just be police; we can be so much more than that. And with our new power, we'll unleash our potential. We will make Prince Gin emperor, and we will build a new kingdom worthy of the people of Kichona and the gods."

"Huzzah!" the soldiers shouted, as they stamped their feet.

Fear shivered through Sora's veins.

But then, as she remembered what the prince had done to Hana, what he'd done to the Society, anger blazed through her like flames on an oil-soaked wick. Her grip on Daemon's shoulder tightened like a vise. "The Dragon Prince as emperor?" Sora whispered. "He staged a coup, murdered taigas, and tried to kill his sister. He'll be emperor over my dead body."

"Well, like I said before, I'd rather we didn't die quite yet," Daemon said.

"Good, because I don't plan on him becoming emperor, ever," Sora said, grabbing Daemon's hand and pulling him into the woods. "Come on. We're going to beat them into Kaede City to warn the taigas and transmit the information to the Council and Empress Aki. They need to know that, without a doubt, the Dragon Prince is back."

CHAPTER TWENTY

The market was in full swing as Sora and Daemon entered Kaede City, looking for the taigas' command post. The open-stall market covered several square blocks in the center of town, and it was a cacophony of activity as housekeepers, kitchen maids, and page boys hurried around, running errands.

A butcher unloaded fresh cuts of beef to display at his stall. A hawker shouted about the hot noodle soup he had for the afternoon special. And a fishmonger huffed by with crates laden with mackerel and ice, shoving past a page who was in his way.

Daemon walked up to a stall selling silk scarves and hair combs carved from abalone shells to ask for directions to the taigas' post. The girl who worked there wore a heavy quilted coat that looked as if it had been made from every color of fabric ever invented. She had an equal rainbow of ribbons tied through the braids in her hair.

"Good afternoon," she said in a south Kichonan accent,

one that lilted softly like the ripples of a lake. "Are you looking for a gift for your girlfriend?" She tilted her chin at Sora.

"I'm not his girlfriend," Sora said brusquely.

Her quick response was like a little stab in Daemon's chest. But he smiled through it.

"I'm sorry," the girl said, casting her eyes downward in a manner that was demure yet slightly flirtatious at the same time. "I just assumed."

He cleared his throat. "Right. Well, um, I was actually wondering if you could direct us toward the Society of Taigas' command center here?"

The girl's mouth twisted a little in confusion. Then Daemon remembered he was in civilian clothes, that hideous turquoise-and-coral shirt again. After the Paro Village incident, he and Sora had decided to switch to "normal" clothes so it wouldn't be obvious that they were taigas. But that made it so this girl didn't understand why he'd need to find the Society post.

He laughed as if embarrassed. "I'm just coming through Kaede City, and I heard there was a taiga outpost here. I've always wanted to see a real live taiga in person."

She smiled then. "Boys. My little brother is obsessed with the taigas too. But I didn't expect it of you. You're so . . . strapping. And handsome." She twirled one of her ribboned braids around her finger.

Daemon could feel Sora's amusement through their gemina bond, the hop and skip of a smirk.

"Er, thank you," he said, tracing the tines of a comb decorated with tiny seashells that looked like lemon drops so he wouldn't have to watch the girl ogling him. "Do you know where the Society's post is?"

She nodded eagerly. "By the harbor. There's a tall wooden building, all black. You can't miss it."

"Thank you," Daemon said.

"Anytime," the girl said. "What are you doing tonight? I finish work at four o'clock. . . ."

"I, um, will have left town by then. But have a nice day!" Daemon hurried away.

Sora caught up with him and shook her head, that smirk he'd felt plastered on her face. "You don't even have to do anything, and girls fall at your feet, don't they?"

Daemon threw up his mental ramparts for a moment, so Sora couldn't sense what he was feeling. "Not all the girls," he said.

There was an awkward silence. At least, Daemon thought it was awkward. Maybe Sora wouldn't notice.

Then suddenly, the sky exploded.

Sora dove for cover. Daemon threw himself over her. Screams engulfed the marketplace.

Green mist burst from the explosion. It billowed everywhere, filling the air and blotting out the sun.

Daemon could hardly hear over the pounding of his heartbeat.

"A bomb?" Sora asked, as she clambered back into fighting stance.

He leaped to his feet too. "Possibly—"

The mist started to move. Not innocently like a bank of fog, but with determination. The clouds of green streamed together, hissing loudly and drowning out all other sound.

"This is really not good." Daemon drew his bo from the holster on his back. But despite standing ready to fight, he gawked at the sky, unsure of what to do next.

The fog formed into a massive serpent. Its body stretched several miles long, with scales glistening like green drops of dew.

A girl nearby shrieked. All the color drained from her face, and she fainted, knocking down her entire display of hats.

The snake circled above Kaede City, red eyes narrowed and glowing. It opened its jaws to reveal a mouth full of razor-sharp teeth, icicles reflecting the cowering sun.

"Luna help us," Daemon said. If ever there was a time he wished he was better at magic, this was it.

Sora looked over at him, sensing his doubt through their gemina bond. She punched her fists to her chest.

It reminded him that he wasn't alone. Daemon saluted back, then spun his bo in his hands. Whatever was coming, they would handle it together.

The mist serpent snapped its teeth, and he jumped as the sound ricocheted through the air like a thunderclap. The force of it sent tremors through the city. Flowerpots careened off window ledges. Pedestrians fell to their hands and knees in the street.

The marketplace erupted in confusion and noise.

"What was that?" a woman behind Daemon shrieked.

"The gods are punishing us!" someone else yelled. "I told the mayor he needed to be more generous with his gifts to the sea!"

Rumbling came from down the road that led into the marketplace. The sound grew louder and louder, until it rattled the stalls, shaking wares off tables and drowning out all the shouting.

A large black orb shot toward the far edge of the

marketplace. A collective, high-pitched, insect whine filled the air.

Holy heavens. Daemon nearly dropped his bo. The bug boy had seemed so much less threatening on the road, when he was far away.

"Run!" Panicked shoppers and vendors screamed and fled, shoving each other, abandoning baskets, and tripping over fallen wares. Hundreds of thousands of cockroaches rushed at them, like a black-brown tsunami of antennae and legs. Then a second surge of them came, this time carrying a boy on the crest of the wave.

"Nines," Sora cursed.

"I guess we won't have time to warn the taigas," Daemon said, tightening his grip on his bo. "It looks like the ryuu are already here."

The cockroaches scurried over Daemon's feet and up his trousers. He tried to bat them away. They crawled in spirals around his entire body and skittered across his shoulders and up his neck, and he gagged as their aggressive little antennae waved in his face. Around him, people screamed and moved in frenzied jerks as they tried to shake off the roaches. Tables crashed, and stalls collapsed into one another.

Daemon swiped at them with his bo, sending cockroaches flying into the air.

"Try to get everyone out of the market safely!" Sora shouted to Daemon. "I'll focus on the bug boy."

Daemon nodded. He wanted to fight too, but part of being a taiga was knowing what was more important for the people they were protecting.

Sora ran off in the direction of the ryuu.

A cloud of wasps swarmed toward the screaming people, who were shoving each other and falling down in their hysteria. "Daggers," Daemon cursed. If he didn't do something soon, the stampede would kill someone.

I need to make a path for evacuation, he thought. Until there was a space clear of insects, the vendors and shoppers wouldn't know how to exit. They'd trample each other to death.

Daemon stashed away his bo and shut out the feeling of tiny legs crawling all over him. He grabbed at the silk scarves on the racks near him and flung them like nets, taking swathes of wasps with them. Then he snatched a tarp from the top of a fallen stall and threw that at the wasps too. Finally, he hurled a pot full of simmering miso soup, dousing the insects' wings so they could no longer fly.

"This way," he yelled to the terrified marketplace. He waved his arms, directing them toward the space temporarily free of wasps.

The people closest heard him and began to run. The rest followed. The girl from the comb stall paused for a second before him, her face streaked with tears. She pecked him on the cheek, then fled out of the market.

Daemon stood a little taller. But he couldn't bask in the pride of doing his job, not when Sora was fighting something as formidable and unknown as a ryuu.

He glanced over his shoulder to find her. He couldn't see her. But there was no fear in their gemina bond, just intense focus as pointed as a hunter's arrow, searching for her prey.

The stalls in the marketplace were in disarray. Tables broken down the middle. Scarves and dumplings and signs all trampled together in the mud. But the people were gone, and miraculously, no one lay dead on the ground. Daemon heaved a sigh of relief.

It was short-lived, however, because Sora was still out there. He had to find her to help against the insect ryuu.

Daemon crept as quietly as possible over broken bowls and smashed cockroach carcasses, weaving in and out of the collapsed stalls.

But there was no sign of the ryuu. Or of Sora.

His heart pounded and he quickened his pace through the market. "Sora!" he whispered loudly. He knew he shouldn't. If she were hiding from the ryuu, it could give her away. But fear for her overrode Daemon's intuition.

She burst through the eastern exit of the marketplace.

"Sora!" He leaped over the destruction around him and ran to her. "You're all right!"

"I chased him," she said, eyes darting back in the direction from which she'd come. Her words were ragged as she tried to catch her breath while talking. "I think the ryuu were tearing through the city, looking for taigas." She gulped for more air. "But bug boy didn't notice us, because we were dressed like ordinary shoppers. After he wreaked havoc here, he headed toward the harbor."

"The Society command post," Daemon said, understanding sinking in his stomach like an anchor.

"We have to help," Sora said.

Daemon began to run. Sora matched him stride for stride.

Now he would get the chance to fight.

CHAPTER TWENTY-ONE

The air at the port hung heavy with the tang of iron, snarled together with the brine of the sea. The ships creaked and pulled at their lines. Usually, there would be men all over the docks, cleaning ships, unloading whales for blubber, bringing sails down to patch their tears. But the harbor was empty now, except for the fifty-some taigas who stood on the black-tiled roof of the Society building, guarded by at least two dozen ryuu.

Sora lunged in the direction of the taigas' building, but Daemon grabbed her arm and pulled her into the shadow of the harbormaster's shanty.

"They're prisoners. We have to do something," Sora said, trying to step toward the outpost again.

He held her fast. "No. If we get caught, we're no good to the Society or to Kichona."

"So we just stand here and let the ryuu execute our own warriors?"

"I know you want to be the best taiga you can be, but do

you think running in and getting yourself killed is the way to achieve that? Because that's what will happen if we try to storm the roof, Sora." He forced her to look him in the eyes. "There are close to thirty ryuu up there, and the rest are swarming around here somewhere. You saw what happened in the marketplace. The magic of one ryuu can take out at least twenty of us, probably a lot more."

Sora didn't like it, but Daemon had a point. Taigas were trained to give their lives for the greater good, and sometimes that meant allowing others to die. Yet Sora couldn't stomach just watching the execution of the taigas on the roof.

"I won't believe there's nothing we can do," she said. "We have to at least try to help."

A grim smile caught the corner of Daemon's mouth. "Stubbornness really does run through your veins. All right, then, what's the plan?"

Sora heaved a sigh of relief that he was willing to do this with her. Of course, she'd known, mostly, that he would— Daemon would be loyal to the end.

I just hope this isn't the end, she thought.

She pointed at the alley next to the taiga command building. "We dart in there and use gecko spells to scale the wall. We'll coordinate our timing to spring onto the roof. If we surprise the ryuu, it will buy us a little time to take more of them out and allow the taiga warriors to also join the fight."

Daemon looked from where they stood against the harbormaster's shanty to the alley. They'd be exposed while they ran across the docks to the alley. A moment later, he said, "All right."

She nodded. They checked their weapons, making sure they were where they were supposed to be and easily accessible, and cast moth spells to dampen their whispers. Then they prepared to cross the pier to the alley.

Daemon watched the ryuu on the roof. Most were turned toward the taigas in the center, but a few patrolled the edges of the building. Sora waited impatiently, itching to sprint.

Suddenly, the wind began to shriek. Dust and rocks and leaves kicked up from the ground. Sora and Daemon shielded their eyes as the wind blew harder.

"All hail Prince Gin," a voice like a frigid breeze said. Goose bumps prickled on Sora's skin.

A moment later, a violent tornado tore down the length of the pier, ripping up boards and tearing out posts. A ryuu spun in the center, powering the storm.

But at the top, Prince Gin sat as calmly as if riding in a palanquin.

The tornado paused right in front of the Society building, then shot upward to the roof.

"Now!" Daemon said, lunging out toward the alley, using the noise and chaos of the dust storm for cover.

Sora didn't wait to follow. She darted out behind him, and a few seconds later, she plastered herself against the black-walled side of the alley, along the taigas' building.

"What in Luna's name was that tornado?" Daemon whispered.

"Another ryuu. Come on, we need to climb."

Sora splayed her fingers into a gecko mudra, with precisely five-eighths of an inch between each finger. She quietly chanted the spell that would allow her to stick to the wall as she climbed.

Next to her, Daemon did the same thing, although it took him several attempts at spreading his fingers, whispering the spell, shaking out his hands when he'd failed, and starting again. He got it on the fourth attempt. His embarrassment at his magical shortcomings again manifested itself like a cringe through their gemina bond, their connection actually contracting.

"We can do this," Sora whispered. "I believe in you. In us."

He sighed in frustration but nodded.

They began to scale the wall, the tips of their fingers like suction cups.

Before they reached the top, the noise and wind from the tornado disappeared as violently as it had come, its fury replaced by a sudden vacuum of movement and sound.

The taiga warriors above gasped.

"It can't be," a woman said. "You died during the Blood Rift."

Prince Gin laughed, but it was joyful, not condescending at all. "I'm alive and well, and grateful for it," he said. "My taiga brothers and sisters, how I have missed you and Kichona. Not a day has passed in ten years when I didn't think of you. I can't tell you how happy I am to be home."

"I'm not sure we are as happy as you," the same woman who'd spoken up before said. "What is the meaning of terrorizing the city and rounding us up like cattle?"

Prince Gin sighed. "I apologize that it was a bit . . . rough. But I needed to show you how things are different from a decade ago. I still believe that Kichona is destined for greatness, and that you—the taigas—are destined for greatness as well. We didn't have the means to achieve that in the past, but we do now."

Daemon glanced over at Sora. "Because of the new magic?" he whispered.

"I think so."

They began climbing upward again.

Another taiga warrior spoke up. "How have things changed since the Blood Rift? Because other than some flashy circus tricks with firework snakes and rings of fire, it seems that your warriors' tactics are the same as ever—destructive to the point of disregard for the very citizens we are meant to protect. Your Highness," he added hastily, as if remembering to whom he spoke.

Sora frowned. Despite Prince Gin being a known traitor, he nevertheless commanded respect.

There was a contemplative moment of silence, and then Prince Gin said, "I appreciate your opinion, and again, I apologize for our unruly arrival. I love every citizen of this kingdom. I've come back because of them."

"And what about us?" the first woman asked. "Will you murder us like you did our fellow warriors during the Rift?"

"Your Highness," a raspy girl's voice said. "I think it may be wise if you used your—"

The prince let out another sigh, but this one was colored with a hint of impatience. The ryuu who'd spoken up stopped talking.

The wind around the Society command building kicked up again. But though it should have been cold here, the breeze kissed Sora's cheek like a woolen blanket, warm and soft from years of loving use. She closed her eyes for a moment, basking in the sensation of being fireside with her friends, telling each other stories and filling their bellies with butter cookies and rose-apple wine. She felt a lingering trace of tension, but she couldn't remember why she'd been stressed a moment ago. All her worries melted with the warmth and trickled away.

"As I was saying," Prince Gin said, "it is for the taigas and the people of Kichona that I've returned. I know you thought me dead, but I've only been in exile. Let me tell you about the past decade."

"Yes, I want to know," the previously confrontational woman said, her tone now the complete opposite, brimming with curiosity and subservience.

I want to know too, Sora thought. A pleasant buzz saturated her every cell, like she'd drunk a cup of spiked coffee.

Then she frowned. Why had she thought that?

Something was off. But she wasn't quite sure what.

No, a feeling inside of her countered. *Nothing is wrong. Prince Gin has only the best for Kichona in mind.*

"It's true," Prince Gin said to the woman who'd spoken up earlier, "I was near death at the end of the Blood Rift. We fled across the ocean and lived in exile in the mountains of Shinowana. It took over a year to nurse me back to health. But one day, I woke up, and it was as if the gods had given me new eyes. Some people see light when they're dying. I saw light when I began living again. It turned out to be a greater form of magic, and I believe the gods showed it to me for a reason.

"Now, I've come back to Kichona to bless all of the taigas with the ability to perform this ryuu magic. To unlock each of your potentials. To make this kingdom as great as

Zomuri—and Sola and Luna, of course—deserve it to be."

"You would teach us your magic?" one of the taigas asked.

"Yes," Prince Gin said. "Do you want it? Do you want to become a ryuu and bring glory and paradise to Kichona?"

"Yes, Your Highness," the taiga shouted.

"Yes, Your Highness," Sora said.

The moth spell had kept her answer muted so the ryuu couldn't hear, but Daemon crawled sideways over to her. His eyes were wide with alarm. "What do you think you're doing?" he hissed into her ear.

"The prince is wonderful," she said. "I like what he's offering."

"Gods, no." Daemon stared at her for a second, as if not understanding the momentousness of Prince Gin's return. Then he clamped one of his sticky hands over Sora's mouth. "He's got you under some kind of spell. You have to fight it."

His panic was as sharp as a pike through their gemina bond. But Sora didn't understand why. Everything was lovely.

She released one of her hands from the wall and pried his fingers off her face. "Prince Gin suffered exile for a decade but then had the generosity to come back to Kichona to share his new gift with us. He wants what is best for the kingdom. Just like we do." She felt even happier now, explaining it to him. Her insides were all warm and mushy, like a vat of pudding just off the stove.

Daemon grabbed her and wrapped his left arm around Sora's throat.

"What are you—?"

He jabbed his right thumb into a spot at the top of her

head, a place that was soft in newborns but grew hard when the skull solidified. Hard, that is, unless you were trained in hidden pressure points.

Sora let out a strangled cry and writhed against Daemon's grasp.

He tightened his hold against her windpipe.

She gasped.

And then she went slack.

CHAPTER TWENTY-TWO

Sora was limp against Daemon. The dead weight of her body almost made him fall backward onto the ground.

He hastily smacked his right arm back toward the wall, adhering his fingers to the wood, then untangled his left arm from around Sora's neck.

Daemon looked at her, unconscious but still attached to the wall by her gecko spell. *What did Prince Gin do to you?*

It had all been so swift. One moment, Sora had been alert and focused. Then the next, the emotion emanating through their gemina bond had muddled, like a carafe of milk ruining a clear pot of tea. Prince Gin had put Sora under some kind of hypnotic spell, and the girl Daemon had known better than anyone else suddenly wasn't herself anymore. He could hardly breathe.

He had knocked Sora unconscious so he'd have time to think. He also didn't know how he'd managed to stay free of the spell. But until he could figure that out and teach it to Sora, he couldn't let her scuttle up onto the roof to offer herself to the ryuu.

Daemon pressed himself against the wall and forced his lungs to work. He couldn't pass out too.

He looked at Sora again while he breathed. Her hair swung like a fringe curtain as her head bobbed limply. But she was safe, for now.

His heart calmed enough that he could think straight, and he remembered why he was here. To collect as much information as he could about what Prince Gin was up to. And to stop him if at all possible. Daemon climbed up the wall a little and listened to what was happening above.

"I'm so happy you're all eager to begin our work together," Prince Gin was saying. "Now I'll gift you with the ability to see ryuu magic, and you'll join us."

Daemon inched closer to the roof, in danger of being spotted. What did it mean to "see" ryuu magic?

"Taiga power stems from the exact same magic as ryuu power," Prince Gin said, "but taigas don't know how to use it to its fullest potential. They don't understand that magic is tangible, visible."

Daemon's jaw hung open. Magic was visible? Did that mean that any taiga could perform ryuu-level magic, if they could see the source? Maybe not someone as clumsy with spells as Daemon, but someone like Sora . . .

Prince Gin continued talking to the captured taigas. "You see, mudras and chants are crutches the taigas need to focus their attention, in order to even find magic. But we ryuu already know where it is. It is all around us, like emerald dust. Once I give you Sight, your vision will be more attuned to the magic, and you'll be able to see the ryuu particles for yourselves. Then all you'll need is a thought, and the magic will do your bidding.

"I'll touch each of your eyes," Prince Gin said. "When you open them again, look for the green particles that float all around you. That is magic."

Oh. Daemon's hope sank. There wasn't a simple solution. A taiga couldn't simply start using ryuu magic by virtue of knowing it existed. There was still some special Sight that Prince Gin had to give them.

A solemn silence swept across the rooftop as he approached the first taiga to touch her eyes.

Then there was a loud, long gasp, like the sound a branding iron makes on sizzling skin. It tapered off to a quiet chill, like the steam that rises off the surface of snow.

The same sound repeated itself, starting hot and ending cold, over and over until the Dragon Prince had touched all fifty-four taiga warriors.

Daemon shivered and held tight to the wall.

"Now," Prince Gin said, "step to the front edge of the roof, and we'll finish your initiation."

Daemon frowned. What else could be involved in transforming a taiga to a ryuu?

He glanced over at Sora. Her body sagged away from the wall, but her hands and feet still held on. Assured that she was all right, Daemon climbed his way toward the front of the building until he was at the corner.

"I think the quickest way to help you see the emerald dust," Prince Gin said to the recruits, "is to make it a life-or-death situation."

"What do you mean, Your Highness?" one of them said.

"My ryuu will show you," the prince said. "Now."

With that, they shoved the taiga warriors off the rooftop.

No!

There was a chorus of surprised cries. The closest taiga hurtled far enough away from the building for Daemon to see.

He almost lunged to try to save her, stopping himself at the last moment.

What was the Dragon Prince doing? Did he toy with them, bringing them to his side just for fun, before he killed them?

"Look for the magic!" Prince Gin shouted.

There was a split second of flailing taiga arms and legs, the same fear Daemon was feeling.

But then stoicism graced the recruits' faces as they pulled themselves together and focused.

The taiga closest to Daemon grabbed at the air. Her hands closed around something. Like a rope, it jerked her to a stop in midair, then swung her back to safety along the front of the Society building.

Sight, Daemon realized. *She somehow must have seen the ryuu magic.*

At the same time, the other taigas snatched at the invisible ropes in the air. Once their feet touched the wall, they climbed back up to the roof.

They all cheered.

Daemon clung to his side of the building, paralyzed. He'd watched that taiga near him plunge to certain death. But then she hadn't. How? What, exactly, was this ryuu magic that seemed to manifest itself in so many different ways? Something consistent had saved all the recruits, but outside that, he had already witnessed Prince Gin conduct mass hypnosis, a boy command all manner of insects, and a serpent made of mist biting through the sky.

He had a sinking feeling that this was only the beginning. The ryuu hadn't even begun to show off what they could do.

Prince Gin clapped from the rooftop and said, "Welcome to the ryuu. Now, let's get ourselves a new ship and be on our way. We have more taigas to recruit."

They leaped off the roof fearlessly and ran to the harbor.

Daemon's stomach swan dived even more deeply as clarity hit him.

The Dragon Prince was going to rebuild his army by ransacking the Society. He could lure taigas at other outposts like he just did here. That was probably what he did at Paro Village, why there were no warriors left there.

If taking the throne from Empress Aki was the extent of it, that would be bad enough. But Prince Gin wanted the Evermore. The stakes were much, much higher.

First, innocents like the woman in Paro Village would be slaughtered in the Ceremony of Two Hundred Hearts. Then the taigas and the rest of Kichona would become mindless pawns under the Dragon Prince's hypnosis, carrying out his will. Prince Gin would declare war on all of the kingdoms on the mainland, murdering people abroad and bringing bloodshed to Kichona's shores when their enemies stormed the island in retaliation.

So many lives lost. Taigas and ordinary Kichonans, conscripted as infantry. Helpless children, both here and overseas, with an ocean of blood between them. All in pursuit of the Evermore, a promise that might not be more than fable.

Daemon shuddered.

He had to learn more about Prince Gin. Not just how to free oneself from the Dragon Prince's charm but also how ryuu magic worked in general. Whether it could be used by taigas without becoming ryuu. Whether it had any weaknesses the taigas could exploit.

Whether Kichona, as Daemon knew it, had a chance at all.

CHAPTER TWENTY-THREE

Sora woke to the world jostling. Or was it her body? She couldn't quite tell, because all the blood was in her head, and when she opened her eyes, the ground was up and the sky was down.

"Whass happenig?" she slurred.

"I'm saving you from yourself," Daemon said.

She blinked several times before she understood that he was carrying her over his shoulder, balanced like a precarious sack of taro root, while he climbed down the side of the taiga command post's wall.

Sora jolted upright.

"Holy heavens!" Daemon cried out as he slammed himself and Sora's lower half into the wall. "What are you doing? You almost hurled both of us to the ground!"

But what he was saying only partly registered. Now that Sora was awake again, she resumed basking in the sunshine-like warmth of Prince Gin's promises.

"Are we going to the Dragon Prince?" Sora asked. "Did he make us ryuu?"

"I swear on Luna's name, I'm going to knock you unconscious again if you don't shut up about the traitor," Daemon said. He secured Sora over his shoulder and began his descent again. He couldn't go as quickly as usual with her as cargo, but she was starting to get the feeling that he wouldn't want to let her climb down on her own.

"Daemon . . ." she said slowly, "do you *not* want to become a ryuu?"

"No, Sora, I do not."

She frowned. "But why wouldn't you want to join in Prince Gin's cause? He wants what's best for the kingdom. Plus, he's going to teach us incredible magic. You would love being good at magic, wouldn't you?"

She felt him flinch. Perhaps that wasn't the best thing to say to someone who was sensitive about his abilities.

"I mean, also, I want to be the best taiga ever," she said, attempting to cover up her flub. "With ryuu magic, we could be better than anything we could do with just taiga magic. I mean, you saw what the ryuu could do with fire and wind and . . ." She trailed off because she couldn't remember what else they'd done.

But I'm sure it was incredible.

Daemon reached the ground and smashed Sora against the wall. He had a hand around her throat and a knife pressed under her rib cage. "He did something to you."

"What are you—? *Who* did something to me?" Sora's pulse quickened, but at the same time, she analyzed their position for ways she could escape.

"Prince Gin. He magically brainwashed everyone to

convince them to switch allegiances. It must be the new magic he learned while he was exiled, because he certainly wasn't able to persuade taigas that easily during the Blood Rift."

Sora frowned and shook her head. The sunny awe the Dragon Prince made her feel couldn't possibly be a lie. It ran too deep, as though it was woven into the fiber of her being.

Oh . . . Maybe Prince Gin had rejected Daemon. Maybe he was angry because he was upset. Sad or embarrassed or jealous to be left behind again. . . .

"If the prince said you couldn't join him, I'll talk to him," Sora said. "I'll tell him you're great, and I'm sure—"

"I don't want to join him!" Daemon said, pushing Sora into the wall again. "Listen to me. The Dragon Prince does *not* want what's best for Kichona. He wants to raise an army of taigas—or ryuu, whatever—to go out like mindless pawns and conquer other countries to expand our kingdom. But if he does that, do you think our people will get to continue leading their peaceful lives with Autumn Festival celebrations and apple harvests and quiet, lazy mornings of fishing?

"No," he continued. "If the prince gets what he wants and starts attacking other countries, they won't sit back and let him take them. They will attack Kichona. They will storm our coastal cities. Torch the crops and the countryside. Pillage towns, rape women, kill children. Empress Aki has preserved Kichona's stability, prosperity, and peace. But Prince Gin will bleed other kingdoms to conquer them, chasing that stupid Evermore legend, and in turn other armies will come to Kichona and burn our country to the ground.

"So just . . . please," Daemon said, the anger in his voice

suddenly giving way to desperation. "Please snap out of it. I can't do this without you. I can't save the whole gods-damn kingdom on my own."

A sharp electric shock zapped through their gemina bond, and Sora jumped. It fried the pride and sense of purpose Prince Gin had inspired, and the literal jolt Daemon had sent through their connection jostled her brain awake. For a minute, all she could see was bright blue light, bursting like sparklers and engulfing everything in its brilliant determination to set her free. Even her nerves vibrated.

When the blue light faded, the remnants of the spell were gone, and horror set in. "Stars, Daemon, I'm sorry," she said. "He got into my head. If it weren't for you, I'd be . . ." She couldn't bear to finish the sentence.

Daemon narrowed his eyes. "Is this a trick? How do I know you've really come back to your senses?"

"I don't know. . . ."

But then she did. She let the shame she felt flood through their gemina bond. It was like waking up in sewer water.

"Oh, Sora. There was nothing you could have done." He released his hold on her throat, lowered his knife, and embraced her.

That sent a surge of a different kind of spark through their bond, this one gentler. Soft, like a lullaby.

She relaxed into it.

When she released him, though, she asked the obvious question. "If there was nothing I could have done to resist Prince Gin's magic, how did you escape it? And how did you break me free?"

"I-I don't know." He worried his lower lip. "All around me, you and the taigas toppled like dominoes to the Dragon

Prince's words. But I didn't feel any different. I don't know how he charmed all of you and why it didn't affect me."

"Maybe that's the superpower you've been waiting for," she said.

He let out a short laugh. "Right. I'm terrible at magic, except I can resist one random thing."

"It's a pretty good thing to be able to resist."

"I suppose so." He grew solemn. "You know what this means, right? Prince Gin can force everyone to love him."

Sora's insides clenched violently, like she'd eaten spoiled fish. "Crow's eye. The woman in Paro Village who told us she had been chosen as a Heart . . . He's not only hypnotizing an army of taigas but also ordinary people. He'll turn Kichona into a kingdom of bewitched puppets."

Daemon nodded. "They'll march overseas with him and give up their lives, just because he asked them to. And he could do it to anyone. Our friends. The people in your hometown. Your parents."

Sora had to lean against the wall to support herself. The Dragon Prince had already hurt her family once by murdering her sister. She wouldn't let him do it again, not to her family or any other.

Her fingers went to the small leather pouch on her belt. Fairy's satchel of deadly powders.

"We can't let them leave the harbor without us," Sora said. "We need to get on the Dragon Prince's ship."

CHAPTER TWENTY-FOUR

Most of the ryuu had gone either into town with Prince Gin to help him herd together the citizens and charm them or to raid the captain's quarters of the other boats in the harbor in search of wine and other spirits. The new recruits, however, gathered in the front of the caravan of wagons that carried their supplies to begin loading the ship Prince Gin had decided to help himself to.

The rest of the caravan, though, was unattended. Still, Sora's nerves jostled with every step as she and Daemon sneaked among the wagon wheels to find places to hide.

The last cart was full of tents. Too risky. The ryuu probably wouldn't load the entire cart but, rather, just the tents themselves. There was no way for a person to hide in the canvas without falling out as soon as the tents were separated from the pile.

They slinked up to the next wagon. Sora opened the doors. This one was packed with large rattan trunks. She hopped silently into the flatbed and opened the lid on one of them.

"Uniforms," she whispered to Daemon as she looked down at stacks of neatly folded black tunics.

Daemon climbed into the wagon, and together they riffled through the trunks to find tunics and trousers the right sizes. They should disguise themselves as ryuu if they were going to stow away on board. Just in case they were seen.

The ryuu uniforms were similar to taiga ones, except there was a green belt, and Luna's triplicate whorls on the cuffs were embroidered in green, rather than the Society's silver.

They turned away from each other and changed quickly into their new clothes. When they were finished, Daemon looked at the trunk again. "If we got rid of some of those uniforms, we could fit in there."

Sora looked it over. "You're right. Let's empty it out a bit and then I'll stack some clothes on top of you for cover. I'll dispose of the extra uniforms before I find a different place to hide."

"Wait." His eyes went wide. "You're going to hide somewhere else?"

"I wasn't planning to climb into the same trunk as you." As soon as Sora said it, Daemon's face went red.

"Gods," Sora said, "I didn't mean to suggest anything untoward. Obviously I don't think about you like that. We're geminas."

He nodded quickly. "Obviously. And, um, good."

"Anyway," Sora said, "I don't think it's smart to hide in the same place. But once we're on board and it's safe, let's meet in the cargo hold at the bottom of the ship."

"And if it's never safe?" Daemon asked. He couldn't look at her.

Sora knew how he felt. Not just because she could feel his anxiety through their gemina bond but because . . . well, yes. Because of their gemina bond, but in a different way. She wouldn't know what to do if Daemon weren't on the other side of it.

"What if something happens to one of us?" he asked.

She shook her head. She didn't want to think about that.

"Then the one remaining does everything he can to get off this ship alive." Sora looked him square in the eyes, because they both knew they were really talking about what would happen if Sora was caught and he wasn't. He might look like a brawny killing machine, but inside, he was all loyalty, a wolf dedicated to his pack until the very end. If she didn't make it explicit, he would stay. "You save yourself, Daemon. You get to shore and back to the Society with everything you know."

Daemon pursed his lips. Sora could feel the tension of his worry, like a rubber band pulled so taut, it could snap at any moment.

"It'll be fine," Sora said, even though she couldn't promise a thing. "Now get in the trunk." She shoved him gently.

He laughed despite the circumstances and reluctantly climbed in. "See you in the cargo hold."

Sora nodded. Then she piled stacks of ryuu uniforms over him and shut the lid. There were slits in the rattan weave of the trunk to allow Daemon to breathe.

Soon afterward, she found a cart filled with drums of fruit and crates of vegetables. Sora curled up in a barrel that was partially full of oranges. *At least it smells good in here,* she thought.

She had hardly settled herself in when voices approached.

"You're in charge of transporting the food to the ship," a ryuu said. Her voice still had the reedy quality of youth, but there was also a corrosive bossiness to it that made it clear she was in charge despite her age. It sounded like the same ryuu from before, the one in the cloak with Prince Gin. "Can you handle the responsibility?" she asked.

"Yes, Virtuoso," a recruit said.

Virtuoso. Sora made note of the name. She wouldn't make the same mistake as the report on Takish Gorge, when she didn't have enough specific information to share with the commander.

"Recite the steps I taught you," Virtuoso ordered the recruit.

"Look for the green particles of magic, coax them to form small hands, and command those hands to lift and carry the crates and drums to the ship."

"I'll watch you cast the first spell," Virtuoso said. "Transport this one." She thumped hard on the top of Sora's barrel.

Sora nearly jumped out of her skin. She tensed every muscle in her body to prevent herself from knocking the oranges inside the barrel around. It would be a dead give-away that something or someone was inside. Citrus wasn't supposed to move on its own.

It was quiet for a minute. Was the recruit concentrating on seeing the magic? Daemon had explained to Sora about Sight.

The barrel lurched upward a foot into the air. Sora braced

her hands against the inside of the drum. It continued its bumpy ascent, jerking slightly left, accelerating right, pausing, zooming up and left again . . .

And then a sudden drop. Sora barely stifled a gasp as her insides plummeted along with the barrel.

A split second later, the drum came to an abrupt halt. Sora's heart pounded so loudly, it wouldn't be a surprise if the ryuu outside could hear.

"At this rate," Virtuoso said scathingly, "it'll take us days to leave Kaede City. Either that or we'll set sail without the food, and everyone will starve at sea."

"I'm sorry," the recruit said.

Virtuoso huffed impatiently. "You're overthinking it. Taigas rely too heavily on their chants to will the magic into a spell. You're a ryuu now. Simply see the magic and use your thoughts to imagine what you want it to do."

"Let me try again," he said. There was steel in his voice that Sora recognized as the resolve taught to all taigas from a young age. She could practically hear the teachers making them chant the mantra every morning before class: *Failures are not end points. They are merely challenges to be mastered.*

Her barrel of oranges began to rise. It was a rocky ascent again, but swifter, as if the magical hands were balancing the drum on their palms this time, rather than juggling it like before.

Then Sora's barrel flew sideways. Toward the ship? About ten seconds later, the speed tapered off, and she was lowered slowly until the bottom of the drum thunked onto wood.

She remained very still and quiet, resisting the temptation even to brush away the hair tickling her face.

Something else heavy thudded down near her barrel. Followed by another and another. Sora kept count. There had been thirteen crates and three drums, besides her own, in the back of that cart.

When her tally reached sixteen, the thumping stopped. *That's it*, she thought.

Sora smiled and rested her head back against the oranges. She was on Prince Gin's ship.

CHAPTER TWENTY-FIVE

Empress Aki paced the courtyard inside Rose Palace. "I don't like this," she said to Glass Lady.

There hadn't been any new typhoon attacks, which ought to have been good news. But there also hadn't been any hint of the ominous magic or the ship that Glass Lady had seen. Aki got the feeling that an enormous trap was being set up around them, and they were too oblivious to realize it was happening.

"Are we receiving daily updates from the Society outposts around the kingdom?" Aki asked.

"Yes," Glass Lady said. "The only post we did not hear from this morning was the Paro Village taigas, but that isn't unusual. Things are slow out there, so they don't always report daily."

"What if that's where the enemy is?"

"Unlikely. There's nothing out there. There's no reason why an enemy would want Paro Village over the larger, more valuable targets in Kichona."

Aki stopped pacing and whirled to face the commander. "So we're just sitting around, waiting for them to strike again?" As soon as she asked the question, though, she realized how much she sounded like a shrill teenager, accusing a grown-up of not knowing better despite all her years of experience. "I'm sorry," Aki said. "That didn't come out the way I meant it. I do not doubt the Society's methods, but it's frustrating that we don't know anything more."

Glass Lady nodded. "Believe me, I wish we knew more as well. But until we catch sight of our enemy again, all we can do is practice extreme vigilance. Taigas around the kingdom are on high alert and have been ordered to double their patrols. The navy is on constant watch for anomalies, everything from unregistered ships coming to port to unexplainable weather patterns. And the scholars at the Citadel are diligently combing through our libraries for references to the kind of magic I saw, whether it's in historical scrolls or texts collected from other kingdoms or our own folklore. We have the very best on the job, Your Majesty, and when our enemy decides to rear its head again, we will be ready."

"Very well, Commander." Aki restrained herself from demanding that she see progress soon. The Society would get her information as soon as they had it.

But it wasn't enough for Aki to do nothing while waiting. After Glass Lady left, the empress turned to Graystone, one of her Imperial Guards. "I need to go to the temple," she said.

Graystone bowed. "I will fetch your kit, Your Majesty."

"Thank you. I'll meet you there."

Luna was the taigas' patron deity, but her sister, Sola, ruler of the sun, was the goddess of the imperial family. All emperors and empresses were blessed by Sola to rule Kichona.

Aki climbed the spiraling gold steps that led up to Rose Palace's highest turret. Unlike the other towers, Sola's temple was constructed of red and orange crystal to honor the fiery light of the sun. It stood alone in the center of the palace, and at the top of the staircase, a fountain of cool, clear water bubbled eternally, needing no rain or underground spring to replenish it.

At the threshold to the temple, Aki stepped out of her shoes, leaving the delicately embroidered slippers on the last stair. She washed her hands in the fountain, rinsing herself of the impurities of earthly life before she addressed the goddess. When she was clean enough, she walked into the small chamber of the temple itself. The Imperial Guards remained outside; gods and goddesses appeared only for the royal family.

The interior of the temple varied in color, depending on the time of day and the mood of the sun. Sometimes light streamed through the crystal and cast a pale orange everywhere. Other times, the room was a swirl of red and gold, like an autumn leaf made of sunbeams.

Today, however, the temple was dark crimson. *This is not a good sign*, Aki thought.

She knelt before the shrine and lit a stick of incense. Its smoky pomegranate scent wafted up toward the heavens but did nothing to soothe the empress's nerves.

Aki set down the blue velvet roll Graystone had fetched for her. She untied the gold ribbon and unfurled the velvet on the low table, her fingers shaking. The contents of the roll constituted "the kit" given to each emperor and empress on coronation day: a long needle forged of pure gold; a small, rose-crystal disk; and a white handkerchief, embroidered with the imperial family crest. The Ora tiger wearing a crown graced the corner of the silk.

She centered the crystal disk on the velvet roll. Then she raised the needle to her finger. "I am Aki Ora, empress of Kichona, servant to Sola. I give my blood as proof that I am who I claim, and that it is my honor to offer my life for Kichona." She pricked her skin, inhaled sharply, and held her finger above the crystal disk. A single droplet of blood fell, as dark as the crimson of the room.

Aki pressed the square of white silk to her finger. The handkerchief was never to be washed or replaced. The blood accumulated over the years was a record of many things, not only the length of an emperor's rule, but also the number of times Sola's advice had to be sought. Peaceful reigns required fewer visits to the temple. Turbulent ones left the silk entirely stained with red.

This was only the second drop of blood on Aki's handkerchief. It could be seen as a victory, evidence of her tranquil reign as the Benevolent One. But Aki frowned at it. Two bloodstains were two too many.

Her blood glistened on the crystal, shiny and round like the most valuable of rubies. Aki waited. Every beat of her heart felt like a century.

Half an hour later, the temperature in the temple warmed, as the sun beamed brighter through its walls. The blood on the disk sizzled. And then it evaporated.

Sola appeared. Even though Aki had seen her once before, she still gaped slack-jawed in awe at the goddess's radiance.

The light surrounding Sola was so bright, it nearly blinded Aki. Even so, she could make out the figure of the goddess within—tall and imposing, with orange flames curling around her head instead of hair. A long red gown, her belly round beneath it, pregnant with the possibilities of the next day. And a face that was smooth as a baby's one moment, then wrinkled and spotted as a great-grandmother's the next. The sun goddess had existed for so long, she knew no age.

Simultaneously, Aki felt as if a sliver of herself had been carved away. She gasped, even though she had expected it. Seeking answers or favor from Sola was not free. Age was real for humans, and each visit from Sola cost a year of life. The goddess had just shortened Aki's by another 365 days.

But it's for Kichona, Aki reminded herself. *It's worth it.*

"You have asked for me," Sola said, her statement blowing through the temple like a desert wind.

"Yes, my lady," Aki said, bowing deeply and grateful to be on her knees, since her legs were shaking.

She would have to be quick in explaining what she needed. The daily lives of humans could not hold the gods' interest for long, and Sola would vanish back to Celestae, island of the gods, if she grew bored.

What bravado Aki had presented when talking to Glass Lady, she shed now.

"My kingdom has been attacked, my lady, but I don't know what it is that we face. What should I do? Who is this enemy? Will Kichona be safe?"

While Sola considered this, the chamber heated up more as the sun focused its beam on the temple. The crystal acted as a magnifying glass, and Aki grew light-headed. She held on to the shrine's table to steady herself. The only other time she'd come—to consult Sola about what would become the Blood Rift—Aki had nearly passed out under the goddess's fiery gaze.

But Aki hadn't fainted, and she wouldn't today, either. *I am as strong as I was then*, she thought. *Or stronger. Even if I don't feel it.*

Sola strolled over to the dais where Aki had offered her blood and lit incense to send her request to the heavens. The goddess picked up the handkerchief.

"I do not like to be called upon to settle petty human disputes."

Aki fell to the ground and bowed again. "I'm sorry, my lady. I didn't know where else to turn."

Sola scrutinized her. The intensity of her stare was like the heat of a bonfire.

Just as Aki felt as if she would be roasted alive, the goddess relented. "You are young, and therefore unsure," Sola said. "But I see in you great love for Kichona and unwavering conviction. Stay true to your compass, and you will prevail."

Aki looked up from the floor. "Thank you, my lady. But you didn't tell me—who is this new enemy we face?"

The goddess glanced at the handkerchief in her hand. She traced a finger across the silk, ending at the embroidered Ora tiger. "You don't need me to tell you. You already know."

She released the handkerchief and let it flutter to the ground, landing in front of where Aki lay prostrate at the foot of the shrine.

Suddenly, flames shot through the center of the silk in a

violent, thin line, precisely where Sola's finger had traced. Aki jumped backward as the handkerchief flew in the air.

The fire extinguished a moment later. The incense stick snuffed itself out. The temperature in the temple dropped back to normal.

Sola was gone.

Aki collapsed back onto her hands and knees, sweat dripping from her forehead. The handkerchief lay on the floor, cleanly singed and split down the center. Half of the Ora tiger had fallen to Aki's left, and the other half, to her right.

Her heart nearly stopped.

She had learned how to hold herself up like a proper empress over the past ten years, to deal elegantly with whatever challenges presented themselves, but this . . .

Aki could make excuses about interpretations. She could come up with ways to explain away what Sola had meant.

But it wouldn't change what was right in front of her— the Ora tiger, torn in two.

Could it be?

Aki pulled on a chain around her neck, freeing an abalone shell locket from beneath her collar. Inside were two portraits, side by side, of a gold-haired little girl and her twin brother, the pictures done in profile so it looked as if they were smiling at each other.

She ran her finger over the boy's portrait. They had been inseparable once. That is, until he began training as a taiga. Because he was royalty, he was taught privately in Rose Palace, rather than with the other apprentices at the Citadel. But being a magical warrior in the making went to her brother's head, especially since Aki was not blessed with Luna's magic. Arrogance and avarice moved in between the siblings. Gin gained a taste for power. Aki lost her best friend.

She didn't want to breathe. Her brother could be alive. How many nights had she lain awake in bed, dreaming that she hadn't stood up to Gin back then, imagining a world where the Blood Rift hadn't happened and she'd let him wear the crown instead of fighting him for it. A world where she still had a brother, a twin.

"Is it really you, Gin?"

But then she remembered what happened when those fantasies intersected with reality: if Gin were on the throne, he would chase Zomuri's legend. He'd use the Society to attack and colonize other kingdoms, and this peaceful, steady life established by their father and the Ora rulers before him would cease to exist. War was not conducted in a vacuum. Bloodshed on the shores of other kingdoms meant bloodshed on Kichona's shores in return.

So if this split handkerchief meant what Aki thought it meant, then what was coming wasn't just a reunion between brother and sister. If Gin was the one who possessed the new magic, he'd have a chance to get what he always wanted— the throne, Kichona, and the Evermore.

Aki pressed the locket to her chest.

Her brother would destroy everything.

CHAPTER TWENTY-SIX

Daemon sat with his knees to his chest in a dark corner of the ship, behind several wooden boxes in the cargo hold. The air was dank and heavy down here, since there was no ventilation. It stank of stale water and damp rope and old, rotted wood; even if the sailors who'd previously manned this ship pumped the extra water out of the bilge every morning, it was still impossible to get rid of all of it, and years of seafaring seeped into the groaning planks, infusing the ship with every algae- and salt-water-soaked journey in its history.

In spite of the stench and the unsteady rocking of the ship, though, Daemon's stomach growled. He hadn't had anything to eat other than a handful of rice crackers and dried fish, before they arrived at Kaede City.

You're going to have to wait, Daemon thought to his stomach, *even if you have to eat yourself.* There was no way he was leaving this part of the ship until Sora arrived.

The passing of each minute was excruciating, as if the

wheel of time needed oiling and had slowed to a creaking, halting pace. He clenched his teeth as he waited for her.

Don't be ridiculous, he chastised himself. *There's no panic coming through the bond. Sora's fine.*

But still, Daemon ground his teeth some more.

Forty-five torturous minutes later, Sora dropped down from the ladder and snuck into the cargo hold. The tension in Daemon's neck and shoulders released as soon as he saw her, but he remained in his corner, tucked away in the shadows, watching as Sora darted around boxes and coils of rope that cluttered the floor. Her movements were fluid yet precise. She was a beautiful, deadly weapon. He never got the chance to simply admire her, and this rare opportunity might never come up again.

When she made it close to his hiding place, he finally stood. Sora smiled when she saw him.

Daemon grinned. "What took you so long?"

She punched him on the shoulder. "I had to wait until foot traffic died down in the hold I was in. It was busier up there."

"I bet it smelled better, though." The humid potpourri of mildewed rope and fetid water momentarily overpowered him again.

Sora wrinkled her nose. "Yeah, it did." She began to explore the hold, looking for a place they could hide more permanently. "Anyway, before I got on the ship, I overheard a girl called Virtuoso teaching one of the new ryuu how to use their magic."

"Learn anything useful?"

"Maybe. I couldn't see what they were doing because I was inside a barrel of oranges, but I have an idea, in vague terms, of how ryuu magic can work, at least on a beginner level." She frowned at the boxes around them. "There aren't any good places to hide that won't be exposed by a ryuu just walking through here."

Daemon pointed at a collection of trunks and an old armoire along the back wall. They'd been obscured by netting, usually used to hold cargo against the walls in the case of turbulent seas. "I wonder if any of those are empty?"

They shoved past the nets. The wood on the trunks and armoire were molded and nibbled at the corners.

He opened the first trunk slowly, trying not to make too much noise with the rusty hinges. "Damn. It's packed full of rope and broken buoys and other junk."

Sora pulled on the door of the armoire. Once. Twice. Three times. "This one's jammed."

"Leave it. I don't want us to get stuck inside a closet." Daemon moved to one of the trunks they hadn't examined yet. He opened it and found this one only half full of water-damaged books in another language. This must have been a merchant ship from a kingdom on the mainland.

"We could stack those on the floor," Sora said, behind him now.

He shivered at the feel of her breath so close to him. But when he turned around, Daemon had control of himself again. "Good thinking. You can finish telling me about ryuu magic while we move the books."

Sora caught him up on what she'd overheard. It seemed that the ryuu didn't need chants or mudras to cast spells; focused thought was enough to command the green particles of magic floating in the air.

Daemon chewed on his lip, thinking about it.

"Can all ryuu do the same things with the magic?" he asked as he set down the last of the books. "I assume commanding the particles to make little hands to lift things is basic, since that's what Virtuoso had the recruit do. But what about the ryuu we've already seen in action? Do they get to choose if they like bugs or fire or whatever?"

"I don't know. Maybe they do get to choose. Or maybe they have a natural inclination or talent for something." She looked inside the trunk. "That's going to be a tight fit for both of us."

Daemon thought of sleeping pressed up next to Sora.

It was suddenly very hot on this part of the ship.

He shoved up his mental ramparts and tried to think about ice. No, not just ice, but dunking himself in an entire bathtub full of it. No, wait, glaciers. Swimming in a frigid, glacial pool . . .

Sora looked at him with her mouth twisted. "Are you okay? You look like you just ran headlong into a forest ogre."

"Hmm? Oh, yeah, I'm fine, never better. Great. Fantastic."

Sora's stomach growled. Daemon's rumbled in return.

Saved by our bellies, he thought.

"Hey, now that we have a place to hide out, why don't I try to find us some food," he said.

Her stomach agreed loudly. She laughed. "That sounds like a smart idea. I'll come too."

"No," Daemon said, perhaps a little too quickly. But he needed to put some distance between them, just for a bit, so he could cool down. Thinking about glacial pools took him only so far. "You stay here."

"And do what?" She crossed her arms.

"Um . . . try to see those green ryuu magic particles?"

"I don't have Sight."

"But you're good at magic."

She shook her head. "As a taiga, not as a ryuu."

Daemon frowned. "Well, unless you're planning to knock on the Dragon Prince's cabin door to turn yourself in, which I doubt, we need to find another way to learn about their magic. Prince Gin might grant Sight to the recruits, but he had to have discovered the particles the first time, right? What if it's possible to use ryuu magic without Sight, but it's just harder than with it?"

"You mean, if *knowing* the magic is there is half the battle?"

"Maybe." He shrugged. "To be honest, I'm making it up as I go along."

Sora nodded. "Me too."

They stood there by the trunk for a minute, contemplating the recklessness of their plan. They could be caught at any minute and either executed or hypnotized into service. Daemon may have been able to fend off Prince Gin's charm once, but there was no guarantee he could do it a second time, and Sora was certainly susceptible to it.

But they hadn't really had a choice. Or, at least not a choice that Daemon and Sora wanted to pick. Before the ryuu left the Kaede City outpost, they had destroyed all the taigas' dragonfly messengers, just as they had at Paro Village. Even if Daemon and Sora had stayed behind, they wouldn't have been able to communicate with the Citadel. At least on the ship, they could attempt to gather more information so that the next time they landed somewhere with a Society post, they'd have more to share.

Plus, there was Sora's plan to poison the ryuu. They had originally plotted to target only Prince Gin, but now that they knew how loyal his soldiers were, it seemed wiser to take them all out. And frankly, they were more likely to succeed if they aimed for all of the ryuu instead of specific ones.

He shuddered to think about killing everyone on board. Many of them had been loyal taigas just a day ago. And all Daemon had was the taigas. He didn't have family. The Society was it.

But he also thought about the rira disks that he and Sora had stashed away. Taigas would rather die than allow themselves to be captured. If the ryuu recruits knew what had happened to them—that Prince Gin had made them prisoners within their own minds—they would prefer Daemon and Sora poisoning them over continuing as mind-controlled tools of the enemy.

Poisoning all the ryuu on board really was the best option for everyone. There was no other way that two apprentices were going to be able to stop them.

Daemon's stomach interrupted the downward spiral of his thoughts by growling again.

"You were on your way out to get us some food, right?" Sora asked.

"Um, yeah," he said, coming back to the present. "I'll go now."

"While you're at it, why don't you break into Prince Gin's cabin and find out all his plans too?" Sora asked. It was supposed to lighten their mood, but given how much was at stake, the joke came out a bit flat.

Daemon appreciated the effort, though, and tried to play along. "Is that a challenge?" he asked.

She smiled grimly. "Work hard, mischief harder. You break into the Dragon Prince's quarters, and I'll find a way to access ryuu magic without Sight."

He nodded. "Challenge accepted."

CHAPTER TWENTY-SEVEN

Sora sat cross-legged on the ground. She was hidden by the cargo nets, so if someone came into the hold, she could dive into the trunk.

How do I find this godsforsaken magic? She stared intently at the air in front of her, brows knit together and eyes narrowed. All she saw was nothing.

Prince Gin had said the particles were everywhere, and the only reason taigas didn't see it was because they didn't know the magic was tangible.

But now I know, Sora thought. "Magic . . . come out, come out, wherever you are." There was a beam of light coming in from a hairline crack in the wall. She focused on it. Maybe it would be easier to see the ryuu magic there.

And then . . .

Aha! A particle!

Sora smiled.

When she looked again at the beam of light, though, the particle was gone. And come to think of it, it had been white, like ordinary dust, not green like Prince Gin had said.

There was an awful lot of dust swirling around in that sliver of light. Sora sighed.

Concentrate, she told herself, squinting harder. *Where are you, you little green things?*

She stared and stared until her eyes crossed and actually began to ache.

She thought she saw the particles, and she jumped.

Her head smacked into the ceiling. *Crow's eye.* Sora rubbed the spot she'd bumped.

She sat down again, allowing her eyelids to flutter closed for a minute.

Think, Sora, think. There must be something.

Maybe she wasn't looking hard enough.

Or maybe she was looking too hard.

What if I tried a different sense?

People could smell sea salt in the ocean air and feel dampness before a storm. If the ryuu particles were floating everywhere, wouldn't there be other ways to find them besides seeing them?

Sora inhaled slowly and deeply. And gagged. She'd gotten used to the stench of mold and wet rope and dank air, but a giant lungful all at once was a wallop to her chest.

She took a moment to recover, then took another breath. A smaller one.

This one still stank, but she pushed that into the background and searched out more subtle smells. The lingering scent of paper from the books piled nearby. Dried algae from the broken buoys.

This was too general. Sora's nose needed something more specific to home in on. But what did magic smell like?

She got on hands and knees and started sniffing around.

Iron.

More stale water.

Dirt.

And the slight hint of rotting food . . .

"Ugh." Sora found herself directly in front of a rat's nest of random things: scraps of old cloth, soggy bills of lading, and bits and pieces of partially consumed food, some to enjoy soon, others to be saved until they ripened to the rat's liking.

She got to her feet, wrinkling her nose in disgust.

Sora couldn't quit, though. Right now, she and Daemon were the only things standing between Prince Gin and his superpowered army.

Sight and smell weren't working for finding ryuu magic. But there were still other senses.

All right, she thought. *A short break, then another try.*

CHAPTER TWENTY-EIGHT

Virtuoso stood with arms crossed on the main deck of the ship. Above her, the sails filled with wind, like puff-chested flag bearers hurtling the ryuu around Kichona to Tiger's Belly, a trading port on the island's eastern side. The air was bitter and sharp, and salt spray leaped over the railings, dampening her hooded cloak with coldness.

She was not on deck because she enjoyed the abuse of the sea, however. She was here because she had been tapped by Prince Gin to give the recruits a crash course on ryuu magic.

This was important. She was one of the youngest of the original ryuu, but she'd proved herself more adept with magic than any of the others, and she'd become the Dragon Prince's protégée. Training the new army was the biggest responsibility yet. Her stomach knotted at the possibility.

But she quickly untied it and focused on the task at hand. Virtuoso had learned at a very young age not to get her hopes up when there was any measure of uncertainty. She would earn the right to stand by Prince Gin's side. She would make sure there was no room for chance.

The new ryuu stood before her, already bruised and exhausted from loading the ship and from the hour of training she'd already unleashed upon them. A large wave rocked the ship violently, and some of the recruits almost fell over.

"Are you tired?" Virtuoso asked, hands on her hips.

"No, Your Honor," they replied despite being soaked through with sweat and the salt water that had come from the last wave.

"Good. Because I'm not even close to finished with you." Besides making herself indispensable, it was also critical to the Dragon Prince's plans that he amass the largest army possible. The more soldiers Prince Gin could count on, the better. "After you've mastered the basics, you will each begin to discover what your specialty is. If you were an excellent swimmer as a taiga, your ryuu ability may manifest itself as control of the water. If you used to tend the stables as an apprentice, perhaps your ryuu ability will be communicating with animals. But first, let's review what you've learned."

She looked at Chainbreaker, a brute of a man who was strong but not the most accurate. She pointed at a straw-stuffed dummy on the other side of the deck and then at the racks of knives next to the recruits.

"Attack the enemy, as I've taught you, but this time, you must also avoid me." Virtuoso stepped into the center of the deck, in the direct path between the knives and the dummy. He'd have to arc the knives around her to get to the target.

Chainbreaker cracked his knuckles and stepped forward. He squinted his eyes until they were the size of pinheads, concentrating on the green particles in the air. Virtuoso watched as they obeyed him, turning into small hands. He sent them to the rack, and each nebulous hand latched onto a dagger. He glanced at her and the dummy far on the other side of the deck.

"Do it," Virtuoso said.

She pretended not to be worried. It was important to put on a cold, hard exterior, especially to counteract the fact that she was half the age of many of these warriors. But the truth was, she'd never taught anyone else how to use ryuu magic before. All Prince Gin's soldiers had learned together, fumbling through it in their refugee camp in the mountains of Shinowana.

And yet, the future of the Dragon Prince's revolution rested on Virtuoso's shoulders. She *had* to make proper ryuu of these new recruits.

Chainbreaker eyed the dummy behind Virtuoso one more time. She held her breath.

Several dozen blades launched themselves across the deck, whizzing around her. The fabric of Virtuoso's hood rippled around her face, and her insides flipped at every single knife. It took effort not to grip the railing to steady herself.

The blades embedded themselves in the dummy's torso, plus one dagger directly in the middle of its forehead.

Not a single piece of Virtuoso's cloak had been nicked.

She let out a silent exhale and hurried to put on her mask of unflappability again.

"Acceptable," she said. "Of course, I learned those skills within the first ten minutes of being a ryuu." It came out a little more loudly—and cruelly—than she'd meant it to.

But Chainbreaker nodded and returned to the other

recruits. Taigas were used to harsh training.

Virtuoso nodded at a woman. "Coyote, it's your turn."

She stepped up. Her jaw was set hard, and there was fire and challenge in her eyes. Without waiting for Virtuoso's signal, she set the green particles upon the knives embedded in the dummy's body. The daggers dislodged from the straw and flung themselves past Virtuoso to the rack, where they executed flip turns as if they were synchronized boomerangs. Then they hurled themselves back past Virtuoso, whirling so fast, they whistled, and lodged into the dummy's torso in a straight line down the center. The fire of ambition flared hotter in Coyote's eyes.

Underneath her hood, Virtuoso smiled. This was a good start. Very good. Prince Gin, she hoped, would be pleased.

CHAPTER TWENTY-NINE

There were plenty of skills that Daemon was mediocre at, but stealth was not one of them. When he was a toddler in Takish Gorge, he was often tasked with catching foxes, raccoons, and other prey from the trees. The pack would identify a part of the forest for hunting, Daemon riding on the back of the mother wolf, and when they arrived, he would climb silently up into trees, aware of every twig or leaf that could brush against him and sound an alarm to his prey waiting above.

The element of surprise was always helpful. But sometimes, trickery was also required, some way to draw a weaker or more curious member of a raccoon family away from the others, before pouncing and knocking him out of the tree to the waiting pack below.

It was these skills that Daemon called upon now. He smiled at the chance to do something he was actually good at.

On the main deck, Virtuoso trained the new recruits.

Daemon had listened in but quickly moved on. It was difficult to understand what was happening without actually seeing it, but going onto the main deck itself was out of the question with so many ryuu up there.

Acquiring food was a priority, but that ought to be easy enough. Sora had come onto the ship in a barrel of oranges, and there were more barrels and crates of provisions in that cargo hold close to the galley. Daemon would pilfer some supplies on the way back to their own hold, but not yet. He didn't want his pockets laden with food while he tackled the challenge Sora had given him—acquiring information on Prince Gin's plans.

Daemon made his way to the deck on which the captain's quarters were located. *If I can get inside, I can look for maps and notes.* That was probably the most useful information he could contribute to the mission.

But how would he get Prince Gin out of his cabin?

It would be dinnertime soon. Daemon could stay hidden and wait for the prince to get hungry . . .

Except captains usually had their meals brought to them, didn't they?

Ugh. There's no way the Dragon Prince is going to eat with the rest of the crew. Daemon racked his brain for other ideas. He kept coming up with the same conclusion—he had to draw him out.

Not in person, though. Prince Gin would probably recognize that Daemon didn't belong here. Unless it was possible he could be mistaken for one of the new recruits?

Still too risky. Daemon didn't know if he'd be able to fend off the Dragon Prince's hypnosis again. Plus, if he got caught, so would Sora.

However, there was one trick from Daemon's wolf cub days that might work here. One or two wolves would do something to draw out the prey from its hiding spot. The prey would be focused on the source of the distraction, and the other wolves would pounce on it from another side.

Of course, Daemon didn't have a pack with him. He had only himself.

I can play the other roles, though.

He stepped out of the shadows to knock on the door of the captain's quarters. But he'd only raised his arm when someone climbed down the ladder from above deck and said, "Hey, what are you doing?"

Daemon whirled around, his heart in his throat. The ryuu looked at him suspiciously.

If the first strategy during a hunt goes wrong, don't panic. Adjust and find a different way to get your prey.

Right. Hunting often didn't go as planned. A nearby bird could startle and set the prey on alert that something was amiss. Or there might be more raccoons than antici-pated. Daemon could handle this.

He puffed out his chest and acted confident. "I was just about to ask the captain what he'd like for dinner."

The ryuu took several steps closer. "You're one of the new recruits? Aren't you supposed to be training with the rest of them on the main deck?"

Daemon smiled. "I was, and it was incredible. I can't believe what we can do with this new magic, and I was dis-appointed when I was ordered to head down to the galley to begin cooking dinner. Hey, do you think you could take my galley shift instead, so that I could go back to training?"

The ryuu snorted but also retreated toward the ladder.

"One of the benefits of having fresh blood is that recruits like you can take over cleaning the head and sweating in that cramped galley, so the rest of us don't have to anymore. But you won't be able to get the prince's dinner order right now. He's a deck up, examining the weapons we collected from Kaede City and brought on board."

"Oh, thank you," Daemon said. "Otherwise, I'd be standing here knocking for ages like a fool."

The ryuu snorted again, then climbed down the ladder, going below to wherever he'd been headed in the first place.

Stars, that was close. Daemon leaned against the wall and took several long breaths until his heart dislodged from his throat and slid back where it belonged in his chest.

The good news, however, was that Prince Gin wasn't in the captain's quarters. Daemon slipped inside.

Flickering, palm-sized spheres floated near the ceiling, lighting the room with their soft glow. A spartan futon took up one of the far corners of the room, its sheets crisp, as if untouched since they were laundered, and a thin blanket—folded at precise angles—lay at the foot of the bed. Daemon chewed on his lip, disappointed. He'd thought that a man claiming to be the rightful emperor would have more luxurious quarters.

There was also nothing that looked like they might be plans. No notebooks or scrolls, only a desk with a completely bare surface. Double disappointment.

Then Daemon noticed the lock on the front of the desk, and he grinned. "I bet you I know what I'll find in there."

He pulled a series of small, slender tools from one of the hidden pockets in his tunic. There were two essentials that taigas never left home without: weapons and lock picks. It didn't matter that he was wearing a ryuu uniform. Daemon had made sure to transfer his throwing stars, knives, and picks as soon as he'd tied on the green ryuu belt.

It took him only a second to assess the lock and another second to slip the necessary tools into the keyhole. He listened carefully as he shifted the curtain pick and moved each of the tumblers one by one.

There was a click and a satisfying give. Daemon didn't smile, though. Being able to break into a lock like this was expected of apprentices as early as Level 4.

He opened the drawer and . . . there was nothing in it.

Daemon ran his fingers over the bottom of the drawer, but it was perfectly smooth. He slid his hands into the back corners of the drawer, feeling for anything out of the ordinary but finding only wood and an abandoned stopper to an inkwell that had dried up and been discarded long ago.

Hmm. It was possible that it really was empty. But why would Prince Gin bother locking his desk then?

No, there had to be something inside. Daemon knelt down so the drawer was at eye level. He retrieved a small metal pellet—scatter shot, a new, discreet kind of throwing weapon that one of the taiga weapon masters was testing—and placed it on the right side of the drawer. It rolled toward the front.

But the ship was rocking from side to side.

If there was a false bottom on the drawer, its contents could be pushing up on the panel unevenly, hence the pellet rolling forward. Since there was no obvious release switch, though, maybe this one was pressure-mounted.

Daemon placed his palms flat against the bottom of the drawer and pushed down gently.

It gave a little, then lifted up with a tidy pop.

Cheers to me, he thought.

There was, indeed, a pile of papers tall enough to cause the unevenness in the false bottom of the drawer. Daemon flipped through them. They appeared to be profiles of each ryuu: height, weight, age, and most important, details about their "specialty."

Tidepool could command the sea.

Insects responded to Beetle.

Firebrand was the orb of flames.

For all that is good and holy . . . Daemon felt ill and had to hold on to the desk for a minute, but it wasn't from seasickness. Skimming ryuu profile after ryuu profile hammered home the fact that if the Dragon Prince were allowed to build his army even bigger, they would be virtually invincible.

A warrior who could grow ice.

One whose hands became powerful magnets to attract away enemy weapons.

Two who could break bones, just with their minds. Even when the bones were still inside a living person.

How did the taigas stand a chance?

Stay calm, Daemon thought. *The Society needs this information, and I'm the only one that can get it to them.* He couldn't steal them right now, though. If Prince Gin checked—which he might, because he would have profiles to add for the new recruits—it would be too obvious if they were all gone.

But Daemon would come back later to get them. Sometime, somehow.

He set the profiles back into the desk and was about to replace the false bottom when his fingers grazed a ribbon on the underside of the panel. Puzzled, he flipped it over.

There was a large map of Kichona. Colored dots marked various points around the kingdom, each connected by a green ribbon, beginning at Isle of the Moon, then Paro Village, Sand Mine, Kaede City, and onward.

Were those Prince Gin's targets?

He touched the map. Each colored dot had a corresponding number written on it.

Isle of the Moon, 5

Paro Village, 26

Sand Mine, 30

Kaede City, 54

Tiger's Belly, 200

Striped Coves, 300

Lionshead Pass, 622

Gorudo Hills, 1,100

Red Harbor, 1,810

Toredo, 2,000

They were cities and other landmarks throughout Kichona, but what did the numbers mean? Daemon studied them some more.

He gasped. There had been five councilmembers at Isle of the Moon over Autumn Festival, when the typhoon hit. Twenty-six taigas had come from Paro Village. And he and Sora had seen fifty-some taigas hypnotized at Kaede City.

These must be the number of taigas posted at each target. The number of new ryuu that Prince Gin plans to recruit.

It dawned on Daemon that if the prince had been successful at Isle of the Moon, the rest of this list might have been moot. The Dragon Prince would have captured Glass Lady and the other councilmembers and made them his puppets. They would have been able to command the Society to overthrow Empress Aki, and then Prince Gin could seize the throne.

Daemon felt a wisp of relief.

But that quickly passed, because it only meant that Prince Gin had been forced to a backup plan—all these other targets around Kichona. It looked like he was starting at smaller outposts, which he could easily overwhelm with his existing ryuu. Then, as the ryuu ranks swelled, he would begin to take on bigger targets to grow his army and collection of Hearts even faster.

Other than that, though, the ribbon traced an unpredictable path around the kingdom, such that it would not only take the Society a little while to catch on to what he was doing but also make it impossible for the taigas to know where he would strike next.

Finally, the ribbon ended at the Imperial City. The Citadel and Rose Palace would be the biggest prizes of all.

"Stars. If we don't stop him soon, he'll have so much momentum and power, we'll be as good as dead." Daemon sank into Prince Gin's chair. "We have to poison him and every ryuu on this ship. And we have to get the list of targets to the Citadel, just in case Sora and I fail." Saying the plan out loud somehow made him feel better. It gave him a bit of confidence—however unjustified—in the face of this daunting enemy.

There was a knock on the door.

Daemon jumped out of the chair. Then he hastily stuffed the false bottom of the drawer back in place, closed up the desk, and dove under the futon.

Gods dammit. His lock picks were still on the desk chair.

Whoever it was knocked again a minute later. Maybe this was the ryuu who had actually been sent to inquire of the Dragon Prince's dinner preferences.

After no response, however, the person left. Daemon exhaled.

Time for me to go too. He'd lingered too long anyway. Prince Gin might come back any second.

Daemon grabbed his lock picks and slipped out the captain's quarters door. He had just stepped back into the dark corner nearby when he saw legs descending the ladder. Daemon dove behind some boxes and buried himself beneath the coils of rope on the floor.

"Your Highness?" someone above said.

The prince stopped on the ladder. "What is it?"

"I was sent to ask what you would like for dinner."

"Do we have fresh fish?"

"Yes, Tidepool swept up a section of ocean and had the waves deposit a school of mackerel for us."

"I'll have that then," Prince Gin said. "Oh, and wine. Not just for me, but for everyone on the ship. You've all worked hard today. We deserve to celebrate."

"Thank you, Your Highness!" the ryuu hurried off to report to the galley.

Daemon waited until the prince went inside his cabin. Then he ran for the ladder and scrambled several levels down to Sora in the bottom hold.

Their grumbling stomachs would have to wait.

CHAPTER THIRTY

Fairy crawled through the narrow space beneath the floorboards of Warrior Meeting Hall. Broomstick followed, but he was bigger and had to scoot on his stomach, which made him lag behind.

"How did you even know this was here?" he whispered, even though they'd cast moth spells to keep from being overheard.

"My boys and I have use for secret nooks and spaces," Fairy said.

Broomstick groaned.

She laughed.

But she quickly grew stern again. The Council was holding another meeting and Empress Aki was going to be in attendance. The apprentices had not been given any updates about the Isle of the Moon attacks, and even worse, Fairy and Broomstick hadn't heard a thing about Spirit and Wolf. Broomstick had leveraged all his relationships in the office but learned nothing.

So Fairy had decided to take matters into her own hands and eavesdrop on the source.

The space beneath the Council Room was tighter than that below the rest of Warrior Meeting Hall, and Fairy also had to get onto her stomach. She used her arms to crawl forward, stopping every so often to blink away the dust puffing up from the dirt on the ground. Despite what she'd just told Broomstick, this was not one of the places she brought her boys; she'd tried it once and never again, because it really wasn't much fun to mess around with someone when there wasn't space to do said messing around.

Finally, she reached a pinprick of light that shone down through a minuscule hole in the floorboards.

"I barely fit here," Broomstick said. "One less inch, and I'd be stuck like a cork in a bottle."

"Good thing you passed on that second helping at dinner then," she said.

"Ha-ha." He punched her in the arm.

Above them, the Council filed in. The only reason Fairy knew that was because shadows passed over the tiny beam of light. Otherwise, there was no sound, because the councilmembers treaded so lightly, there were no footfalls.

A minute later, though, there was plenty to hear as Empress Aki arrived.

"Your Majesty." It was followed by a pause as the councilmembers presumably bowed.

They settled back into their chairs.

"You have a report of your latest findings?" Empress Aki asked.

"Yes, Your Majesty," Glass Lady said. "I know you like to see all the details, so we've compiled summaries of the reports from each outpost, as well as the research our scholars have yielded thus far." There was some shuffling of paper as she passed it across the table.

"As previously discussed, we are actively patrolling the seas and have increased the numbers of warriors on watch at every station around the kingdom. Ships and outposts send reports to the Citadel every twelve hours, rather than every twenty-four, as was the previous peacetime model. The most recent dragonflies from the navy this morning indicate nothing unusual in the seas—no unidentified ships or unusual weather. The reports from around the island are likewise—"

"Wait," Empress Aki said. Papers rustled. "There still hasn't been a dragonfly from Paro Village? And now Sand Mine and Kaede City have also failed to report."

Beneath the floorboards, Fairy's breath caught. Spirit and Wolf had gone to Takish Gorge. That wasn't too far away from Paro Village. Had something happened to them? She reached for Broomstick's hand.

He clutched his fingers against hers.

"What if—?" she began.

"I know," he said.

"But Spirit . . . she always manages to figure a way out, right?" Fairy said weakly.

"Yeah, she'll know what to do," Broomstick said. His conviction was as uncertain as Fairy's. It didn't make her feel any better.

Above them, Glass Lady cleared her throat. "Forgive me, Your Majesty, for not leading with Paro Village, Kaede City, and Sand Mine. I wanted to give you some comfort that the seas are safe for now, that no new threats, like an incoming navy, have appeared. But it is indeed concerning that there has been no communication from three different outposts in the south. A ship has been dispatched to investigate, but it will take a few days, since those regions are remote, and the ship will need to sail around the tiger's leg to access them."

"Have we no taigas who can get there more quickly by land?" Empress Aki asked.

Bullfrog spoke up, his voice croaking a bit, as always. "It is unwise to divert resources from our other command posts, Your Majesty. And since the Imperial Navy is already patrolling the ocean, it makes sense to investigate via water. Besides, we haven't received any distress calls from those three posts. If something bad has happened, surely one of them would have managed to send off a dragonfly."

Fairy wanted to believe this reasoning. But how did they know something hugely bad hadn't happened? What if a massive typhoon took out the entire southern part of Kichona, and that was why there weren't any dragonflies coming in?

Oh gods, Spirit and Wolf could have drowned. She imagined them floating facedown among the wreckage of a typhoon, their bodies lifeless.

Broomstick almost crushed Fairy's hand. He could feel her terror tremoring through their bond. "Whatever is going on in that head of yours, stop it. It's not true."

"But it could be."

"There are an infinite number of possible outcomes. You can torture yourself imagining the worst, but it's just as likely to be true as Spirit and Wolf being fine. They could be on their way back here right now. Think about that. Think about Spirit and Wolf's victory as they ride into the Citadel with news about the south, *before* the navy gets us word."

Fairy tried to smile. But she couldn't.

Above them, Empress Aki sighed loudly. "I appreciate the speed at which the Society has mobilized to address this unidentified threat. However, I can't help but think that we're approaching this in the wrong way."

"How do you mean?" Glass Lady asked. "We are doing what has worked for centuries, based on the Society's experience protecting the kingdom from everything from coordinated pirate raids to full-scale foreign incursions."

"Yes, but that's my point. The attack on Isle of the Moon is like nothing we've ever seen before. In all those centuries of experience, have the taigas ever faced an adversary who wielded magic stronger than yours? Or have you faced another enemy with magic at all?"

The Council was quiet, seemingly taken by surprise by someone questioning their expertise.

A minute later, the commander recovered herself. "Your Majesty," Glass Lady said, "we have succeeded in defending this island under all manner of conditions for ages. Despite the novelty of this situation, you do not need to worry. Our methods are proven. We will get to the bottom of this mysterious assault, and you will continue to rule this kingdom as your father and your ancestors have done before."

"I feel as if I'm being talked down to because of my age."

"Not at all!" Glass Lady rushed to say. "Your Majesty, we have the utmost respect for you. For gods' sake, you prevailed in the Blood Rift when you were only fifteen. We have no doubt in your leadership. But what we are asking is that you also have faith in ours. Protecting Kichona is what the Society does. Believe me when I say that we are doing everything we should be. It is my job, and I will die before I watch anything—magical or not—threaten our kingdom."

Empress Aki sighed again. "My patience is running thin, Commander. I feel like we're having the same conversations over and over again. Therefore, I want you to start thinking about alternate approaches to what you've done in the past. In the meantime, keep me up to date if anything changes, and let me know as soon as the navy sends word on why we've no communications from the southern outposts."

The meeting was over. The empress rose and left the room, with the councilmembers accompanying her out of the building.

Fairy stared at the underside of the floorboards. She was as frustrated with the Council's lack of progress as the empress was.

"I know they have a way of doing things," she said, "but why haven't they found anything yet? It's like they're afraid to stray from their tracks, for fear of stumbling into an unknown they can't handle." Resigned, she laid her head down, her cheek pressed flat into the dirt.

But then she thought of Spirit and Wolf, out there, brave but alone, in the midst of the unknown.

Fairy lifted her head.

Broomstick looked at her expectantly.

"If Spirit were here, she'd come up with a plan," Fairy said. "But since she's not, we'll have to do it ourselves."

"What do you have in mind?"

"Right now, nothing. But like Empress Aki said, she wants the taigas to start thinking differently. Maybe we can combine your knowledge of the inner workings of the Society with my talent for being in places I'm not supposed to be, and come up with something."

Broomstick nodded slowly as he considered it. "Work hard, mischief harder, right?"

Fairy was able to muster a small smile now. "Yeah. Let's mischief harder."

CHAPTER THIRTY-ONE

Sora was experimenting in the cargo hold again, now with a different sense. On the rooftop of the Kaede City command post, Prince Gin had described ryuu magic as emerald dust. What if, like real dust, it was something that could be touched?

Sora lifted her hand in front of her face and blew gently into the air.

Nothing happened.

She kept blowing.

Nothing.

More air.

Nothing.

More, more, more . . .

Sora was light-headed. She paused so the room would stop spinning.

Daemon hurried in. He was a little paler than usual, and his hair was mussed up. But there was also an electric sort of energy in the way he bounced around the hold, unable to stand still, kinetic and fully charged.

He stopped moving for half a moment to say, "I did it. I broke into Prince Gin's quarters." Daemon promptly resumed pacing again and told her what he'd discovered in the maps and notes upstairs.

When he was done, Sora sank down to the floor. "Prince Gin is building an unstoppable army. War is coming."

"No," Daemon said. "War's already here. It's just that the rest of Kichona doesn't realize it yet."

The nauseating image of the tenderfoot nursery on fire flashed through Sora's memory. She could still smell the smoke and see the charred remains in her head. And then afterward, once the embers had died, she'd wrenched herself away from the arms of the teachers who tried to comfort her, to restrain her, and bolted into the middle of all the ash. It had flown up around like a snow flurry from the hells.

Beneath it, there had been bones. Tiny, blackened bones, the skeletons inseparable from one to the next. The tenderfoots had died huddled together.

Sora bent over, dry heaving.

Daemon rushed to her side.

She shoved the fiery memories aside and tried to breathe. In. Out. In. Out.

Breathe.

"We can't let this ship make it to Tiger's Belly," Sora said. "We can't let him choose more Hearts or take more taigas. We have to poison everyone here, and soon."

"We really have to kill everyone?" Daemon asked.

Sora felt his unease keenly, not only because it coursed through their gemina bond like milk gone sour, but also because she wasn't convinced that killing everyone was necessary either. Or at least she didn't want to do it.

She kept focusing on her breaths as she rethought her plan. She opened Fairy's pouch and looked through the vials. Then she saw a tiny transparent packet fastened to the inside of the leather flap. Sora gasped. It was kagi powder.

"What if we use this?" she asked, showing the fine white powder to Daemon. "It's ground kagi leaves, which cause the equivalent of very vicious food poisoning. They'll retch to the point of passing out."

Daemon nodded as he processed what she was suggesting. "It'll debilitate the ryuu long enough for us to isolate and kill Prince Gin. Maybe, without a leader, the rest of the ryuu will stop their advance through Kichona."

"Exactly."

However, poisoning the meal wouldn't be easy. There were people in the galley, cooking. Sora and Daemon would have to distract them, or hope that there was a moment before dinnertime when the food was left unguarded.

They climbed up a level to where the galley was located and slinked in between crates of vegetables and drums of oranges until they were close to the kitchen. From what she could see through the galley door, there were three ryuu recruits in there, likely relegated to dinner duty because they were the lowest rungs of the ladder.

"Keep watch," Sora said to Daemon. "Remember, if one of us is captured, save yourself."

He hesitated.

"It's the only way," she said.

He shook his head. "No. We won't get caught."

Sora sighed. "And you say *I'm* the stubborn one."

He shrugged and positioned himself at the ladder in case any other ryuu decided to make an appearance.

Sora crept a little farther through the food stocks, as close as possible to the galley door without being exposed. She reached into the pouch in her sleeve and confirmed that the small square of paper, folded like an envelope, was there. The kagi powder would blend into whatever it was that was bubbling on the stove.

She also checked that her pink disk of rira was easily accessible. It was the poison that Fairy had given her in case she was captured. Daemon had one on him too.

Sora stalled. Both she and Daemon were 100 percent nerves, and their gemina bond was as taut as a tightrope.

We were blessed by Luna to do this, she reminded herself. *And we have trained our entire lives to protect Kichona*. It didn't make her any less nervous, but it was enough to push her forward with her plan.

One of the ryuu was tasting what was in the pot. Another was pulling trays of roasted mackerel out of the oven. The third put a vat of pickled radish on the small counter.

"I think this is done," the one at the pot said. "Let's ring the meal bell."

Oh no, Sora thought. If they rang the bell, the deck would be swarming with ryuu before she could get to the pot.

She had to disable the bell. But it hung right outside the galley door, which meant she risked exposure even running to it, let alone trying to tinker with it while the ryuu were a foot away.

It was a risk she had to take.

Sora glanced at Daemon on the other side of the deck to signal what she was going to do. He shook his head and raised his arms up in confusion. Her pantomiming hadn't made any sense.

Never mind that. She had only seconds to get this done. Sora darted to the bell.

She pressed herself flat against the wall of the galley and wrapped her fingers around the cold brass clapper dangling inside the bell. But how would she dampen it? She couldn't yank the thing out; it was connected by a metal ring.

I might've acted a little hastily.

She let go of the bell for a moment and retrieved a knife from her sleeve. Then she sliced off the cuff of that sleeve and began to wrap the fabric around the brass clapper.

A spike of panic, like the prick of a cold stiletto blade, pierced her gemina bond.

At the same time, someone cleared her throat behind Sora. "What, exactly, do you think you're doing?"

Sora jumped.

She recognized that acid-tinged voice. It was Virtuoso, the girl who'd been training the recruits.

"I'm, um, fixing the bell," Sora said, her back still to Virtuoso.

"How interesting. I didn't realize bells could be fixed with cotton. Or kagi powder."

Sora whirled around and saw with horror that the little paper packet of poison had fallen out of her sleeve, probably when she grabbed her knife to cut the fabric. And now the envelope was in the hands of Virtuoso, the top flap open where white powder spilled out.

She looked up from Virtuoso's hands. The ryuu's face was shrouded by the heavy hood of her cloak.

She didn't dare spare a glance past Virtuoso, to where

Daemon was, for fear of revealing him.

Run! she wished she could say. She tried her best to convey the feeling of it through their gemina bond.

Resistance pushed through the connection.

Sora pushed back. *Go, go, go!* She sent the urgency to him. He couldn't stay. He couldn't get caught too.

His sadness harpooned through their bond. But he'd made her a promise, and his intention reverberated through their connection. He would get off the ship. He would make it to shore, somehow, because he knew that otherwise, Sora's sacrifice wouldn't be worth it.

She saw out of the corner of her eye when he fled.

Please get away safely.

She focused on Virtuoso again. Sora dared to reach for her sword.

Virtuoso took a step back, as if momentarily caught off guard. But then she laughed. Green mist coalesced out of thin air. It was shaped like a snake's head, a smaller version of the one that had menaced over Kaede City.

"I'm ordering you to stop." Sora pointed her sword to strike at the snake.

But it snapped its misty jaws around the tip of the blade, then sucked it down. Sora's sword disappeared, eaten in a single gulp.

She jerked back in shock.

The mist snake coiled around Sora, locking her arms against her body. She struggled to get free, but the snake might as well have been made of iron, not fog.

"You'll never pull this off," Sora said, hands balled into fists. "The Society will fight you. You'll never get what you want."

Virtuoso sighed. "Trust me, I'm used to not getting what I want." A resigned kind of sadness tinted her tone. It was almost as if the ferocity and arrogance from before was a facade.

She stepped toward Sora. Then she pulled the hood of her cloak off her head.

She really was just a girl. One with pale blond locks, almost platinum, the same color as Sora's beneath her taiga-black dye.

And a similar sprinkle of freckles across her cheekbones.

And the same button nose.

The ship seemed to lurch all around Sora, and she grabbed onto a citrus drum for stability.

I must be seeing things.

But she wasn't.

Virtuoso wasn't just any girl.

Sora's sister was alive.

CHAPTER THIRTY-TWO

Sora gasped. "Hana."

Her world spun. The deep pit she'd felt in her heart for the past ten years, everything she thought she'd known about the Blood Rift, no longer made sense. How was her sister standing before her? Alive?

The girl nodded curtly. "You recognize me."

"Th-the hair. The freckles, like mine. And you have Mama's nose and Papa's sharp jawline." Sora's voice was barely louder than a whisper.

Hana bit her lip. "I wouldn't know. I don't remember them." Her voice was a little sad, but also bitter. The years apart had left their mark.

"We still remember you," Sora said. "Stars . . . Mama and Papa will be beside themselves when they find out you're alive."

Sora could see Hana's return home now—Mama tripping over the hem of her long skirt as she ran down the pebbled path in front of their house to greet her, her face already splotched from crying, and Papa standing back to let his girls reunite, quiet tears streaming down his face as he looked on. They would spend the first evening at home, just the four of them. Mama would cook a feast of all of Hana's favorite foods. Papa would begin sketching a new piece of pottery to commemorate her homecoming. Sora would read from Mama's newest stories as they curled together in front of the fire. And in the morning, they would walk down the mountain path together and dismantle the shrine, perhaps offering one last slice of cake to the gods to thank them for Hana's safe return. They would be an unbroken family again, no more ghosts whispering guilty things in their ears, no more sad, burnt skeletons in memories anymore.

Several ryuu recruits emerged from the galley, and Hana's tough outer shell snapped back into place. "What are you staring at?" she said. "Sound the alarm. Alert Prince Gin and the others that we have a stowaway, and search the ship to see if there are more. I suspect that, at the very least, this taiga's gemina is on board."

The steely prick of panic pierced Sora again, although this time, it was her own. But Daemon would feel it and know they were after him now.

Please, please, get off the ship.

The ryuu rushed off to carry out orders. Hana turned back to Sora.

"You say you remembered me," Hana said, the harshness of giving orders still lingering, "and yet no one tried to come after me. If you and the Society cared as much as you claim, someone would have pursued us. We were tenderfoots, for gods' sake. I waited for you that Friday night for our sleepover, and you didn't come. You just left me in the nursery for them to take us."

Sora staggered at the anger in her sister's eyes, as savage as a tempest. This was not the Hana she'd known.

"What do you mean, let them take you? Who is 'they'? I thought you *died*. The nursery burned down that night. I . . ." Sora could hardly choke out the words. "I saw all the little bodies."

Her sister scowled. "Some tenderfoots died, but Prince Gin's warriors took others."

"Why?" The question came out as a whisper.

"Because we were small and they could hoist us over their shoulders as they retreated. Why would Prince Gin leave an entire generation of talent for the Society, when he could have them for the day when he returned to Kichona?"

If not for the mist snake holding her up, Sora would have collapsed onto the ship floor.

"I'm so sorry, Hana. I didn't know." The memory of that night came rushing back, as well as all the heavyhearted nights thereafter when Sora would relive the decision to go with her friends on the dirigible instead of getting Hana for their sleepover. Sora would wake with tears soaking her pillowcase, only able to calm down after Daemon soothed her through their bond.

"But I'm here now," Sora said. "And so are you—"

"Just because I wanted you to be with me ten years ago doesn't mean I want you now," Hana said flatly. Her features were pinched, as if saying this cost her something. "Prince Gin raised me. The ryuu are my family. And stop calling me Hana. I go by 'Virtuoso' now."

If it were possible for Sora's heart to sink, it was

happening now. Straight out of her chest, through the bottom of the ship, to the ocean floor.

She slumped against the mist snake's coils, looking at her sister and trying to reconcile the strong-willed sixteen-year-old before her with the eager-to-please, clingy little girl she'd been a decade ago.

"Enough talk," Hana said. "I can't deal with this right now. And Prince Gin will want to see you. He can be very . . . charming."

But Sora already knew that. She wriggled in the snake's grasp, to no avail.

She was about to lose her mind to the Dragon Prince. Again.

CHAPTER THIRTY-THREE

Daemon dove into the sea just as the alarm was sounded on the ship. He wanted to stay on the surface, to look back at where he'd left Sora, but he couldn't. The future of the kingdom was at stake, and he'd promised Sora he would do his part, even if it meant leaving her alone.

But if anyone can take care of herself, he told himself, *it's Sora.* Daemon tried to take comfort in the fact that Prince Gin probably wouldn't kill her. He wanted to recruit more taigas, and he would bewitch Sora to join him.

Maybe I can do whatever it was that I did last time to jerk her out of his spell, Daemon thought. Even though he wasn't quite sure what it was he'd done.

Daemon kicked his legs and swam as hard as he could in the frigid water. For once, his pathetic magical ability had cooperated, and he'd successfully cast a sailfish spell on himself, which would allow him to hold his breath longer. He pushed and pulled with his arms, diving deeper, putting more space between him and the ship.

Suddenly, a shock wave rattled his gemina bond and colored it black, like ink injected into water.

Sora! Daemon gasped and swallowed seawater. He choked and his lungs burned. His legs instinctively kicked upward.

When he broke through the surface, he coughed and gulped for air.

Ryuu swarmed the ship's deck. Some were up in the rigging. One was in the crow's nest with a spyglass pointed at the ocean. All were searching for him.

At the same time, his gemina bond prickled with pins and needles, as if Sora had been emotionally stung by a jellyfish. What had just happened?

Daemon's limbs went heavy with dread.

But he couldn't stay here for long. If he didn't move, he'd either drown or be caught by the ryuu.

Either way, he'd be no good to Sora.

His mission was to get to the Society outpost at Tiger's Belly to send a dragonfly and let the Citadel know what was happening. But after that, he had another mission—he would come back to save Sora, no matter what it cost.

Daemon took one last look at Prince Gin's ship. Then he took a breath, dove deep, and swam.

CHAPTER THIRTY-FOUR

Sora knelt on the main deck. Hana stood behind her, flanked by a half dozen ryuu. There was no need for the mist snake anymore, for she was more than adequately guarded.

Prince Gin approached. The ryuu bowed.

Sora cringed. But it wasn't just his immense presence. It was every little detail—the way he walked with his arms folded behind his back, as if he had nothing to fear and therefore didn't need his hands at the ready. His smile, surprisingly warm and disarming, despite the fact that it tugged awkwardly at the scarred ridges on his face. And the adoration radiating off his warriors, which wasn't servile but, rather, seemed of mutual respect.

Before the prince reached Sora, another ryuu ran up to him. "We found no evidence of any other stowaways on board, Your Highness."

For a moment, Sora forgot the fear of being in the Dragon Prince's presence, and she heaved a sigh of relief. She'd been pretty sure Daemon was safe—she felt his adrenaline through their gemina bond, and it was a determined kind of drive, not a panicked one—but hearing the ryuu verify he'd escaped was even better confirmation.

Prince Gin nodded at the warrior to acknowledge the report. Then he strode to the center of the deck and scowled at Sora. "I hear you were attempting to poison me and my warriors. Do you know who I am?"

Sora swallowed and nodded, keenly aware again that she kneeled before the man at the helm of the Blood Rift slaughter.

"Then you understand that an assassination attempt against me is an act of treason. I could have you beheaded right here on this deck."

She took a deep breath and tried to steady herself. Pushing aside her feelings—her fear—might help. Glass Lady would tell her to focus on logic.

What Prince Gin says isn't true, she reasoned. *Trying to kill someone who is a known traitor probably isn't treason.* Sure, he was born into the Ora family, but after he tried to murder his own sister, was he still considered part of the imperial line?

But Sora kept her smart remark to herself, because she did know one thing for sure—the Dragon Prince *could* take off her head right now if he chose.

"Where's your gemina?" Prince Gin asked. "Surely you didn't board my ship alone?"

"I did," Sora lied. "I took extended leave after the Autumn Festival. My gemina is at the Citadel with the rest of the apprentices."

Behind her, Hana cleared her throat. "I don't believe

that. You and Wolf were always inseparable."

Sora winced. Was that another reference to the fact that she'd ditched Hana the night of the Blood Rift because Daemon and their other friends were going to ride on the dirigible? *I'm sorry I left you behind*, Sora thought. *But I promise I'll make this right. Somehow. I just need time to figure it out.*

"Hmm," Prince Gin said. "Lying to me, in addition to trying to poison me. The charges of treason are racking up. You know, I haven't killed anyone in a long time. I returned to Kichona with a plan to spare as many of our taigas' and citizens' lives as possible, since they will constitute my army. But one life won't matter in the long run. Besides, the legend says Zomuri requires blood."

Sora tried to muster some bravery, but all she could feel was how fragile her neck was. She was used to believing she was strong—so much muscle from years of training—but in reality, it was just flesh and bone that could be sliced through with a blade or snapped with whatever ryuu magic struck the prince's fancy.

"Your Highness, wait!" Hana stepped forward.

Sora frowned. What was she up to? She had seemed ready to cast Sora into the sea not long ago.

"This taiga is my sister," Hana said.

Sora blinked. Hana was coming to her aid?

Prince Gin arched his brow. "You didn't tell me this before."

"I'd disavowed my family. For the past ten years, Spirit didn't exist for me."

It felt as if Hana were stomping on Sora's heart, which already lay at the bottom of the ocean.

"However," Hana said, "because we share blood, she

probably has the same ryuu power that I do, just like how Skullcrusher and Skeleton both excel at controlling bones."

The Dragon Prince considered this new information. Every ryuu on the ship was silent, waiting for his verdict.

Sora was the only one looking at Hana. What was her special power that made it tempting enough for Prince Gin to commute Sora's sentence in order to have one more soldier?

A slow smile crept across his face. "Spirit, you've been trained by the Society and spent the last decade under my sister's rule. I know there are some things about my past that may have been . . . skewed. I wasn't here to offer my side of the story. But as you can see, there are many smart and accomplished warriors who support me, including your sister. I hope you'll let me share my perspective."

That warm, mushy porridge sense of calm she'd felt at the Kaede City outpost began to fill her. For a split second, she was aware that he was casting his hypnotic spell on her, but it was too fleeting a moment for her to do anything about it. Not that she'd be able to fight off his magic anyway. No one could, except Daemon.

Prince Gin told her what had happened after his warriors fled Kichona a decade ago. It was the same version he'd given the taigas in Kaede City. Sora nodded along, rapt. "I can give you access to our new magic," he said. "Would you like that?"

Yes yes yes. Giddiness welled up in Sora's eyes as the feeling of security and conviction inside of her warmed even more. There was a niggling in the back of her mind, as if Daemon would disapprove, but she couldn't figure out why. And the tickle of wrongness was soon subsumed by the rightness of what the Dragon Prince offered. "Yes, Your Highness. I'd like to be a ryuu, more than anything. I'd like to be reunited with my sister, who up until today, I had believed lost to me forever. It would be an honor to serve you."

She took a deep breath, knowing from Kaede City that the next part of becoming a ryuu required Prince Gin doing something that might hurt. Daemon had told her about the surprised cries from the taigas on that rooftop. But no matter what the Dragon Prince was going to do, it would be worth it. Everything was worth it for Prince Gin.

He smashed his fingertips to Sora's eyes. She barely managed to close them in time so that he didn't gouge her eyeballs directly. It felt as if his nails were drilling through Sora's lids, and then as if hot iron was burning right through them. But even though it hurt, she didn't care. The sound of magic whooshed around her like a small dust storm, and Sora smiled as she lost herself in the chaotic melody.

Prince Gin yanked his fingers away as suddenly as he'd started.

Sora rubbed at her eyes. When she opened them, she gasped.

Emerald particles floated everywhere, tumbling through the air and sprinkling down on her like colored sugar. She cried out in wonder. And then she stuck out her tongue. It tasted sweeter than apple sidra, than cherry ice cream, than golden empress cakes. She sighed with a deep-seated happiness as the ryuu magic twinkled all around her, the sweetest of snowflakes.

Prince Gin turned to Hana, his expression harder than

before. "You asked for her, Virtuoso. She's your responsibility. Train her and show me that I didn't make a mistake in letting your emotions get the better of you."

Hana paled. But then she squared her shoulders. "Yes, Your Highness. I won't fail you."

Sora should have been worried, both for herself and Hana. It was unknown whether she would be able to command magic the way it was implied that her sister could. And yet Sora was too entranced by the emerald dust to register rational feeling. Even though it was hardly dusk, the world was lit up like it was made of emerald galaxies. Everywhere she turned, the air sparkled. Even the Dragon Prince's mutilated face looked handsomer amid the glitter, as if he were a fairy prince come to bless the kingdom with beauty like nothing anyone had ever seen before. Sora's mouth dropped open as she continued to spin around, drinking it all in.

Prince Gin's forehead wrinkled a little. "Can you already see the magic?" he asked.

Sora nodded. "It's magnificent. It's as if the entire universe has come to earth."

"Maybe something *does* run in the Teira family blood," Prince Gin said.

He watched both Sora and Hana as if something else were occurring to him.

Prince Gin turned his focus to Sora. "One more thing, Spirit. Pull up your mental ramparts. You are a ryuu now, and you have your sister back. You won't need your gemina."

Sora frowned. Her gemina connection yawned, as if telling her it wanted to stay open.

But the reassuring warmth of Prince Gin's smile encouraged her. He wouldn't tell her to do something if it wasn't right. She nodded and followed his orders. With a slam, she blocked off her gemina bond.

I am a ryuu now, she thought, her happiness at being on the same team as her sister buoying her spirits as if she were floating on a balloon. *I don't need Daemon anymore.*

CHAPTER THIRTY-FIVE

Afterward, Hana stood at the bow of the ship, ostensibly watching the final approach to Tiger's Belly, but really, thinking about her sister's unexpected return.

She had known there was a good chance that she and Sora would cross paths as the ryuu swept through Kichona, since Prince Gin intended to hypnotize every tenderfoot, apprentice, and warrior in the Society to make them his. But she'd thought she had long ago buried all the emotions that came with thinking about her family. If there was to be a reunion with her sister, it was supposed to come later, at the Citadel, where apprentices were based. Instead, Hana had run into Sora sooner than expected—*too* soon—and she wasn't prepared.

In the distance, the lights of Tiger's Belly's harbor twinkled, reflecting in the water much like the thousands of candles that were lit around the lake at the Citadel during All Spirits' Eve. Tenderfoots were not allowed to partake in the midnight festivities because it was much too late for them to be awake. But each year, Hana had longed to stay up to watch the skit where the older apprentices dressed up in costumes like the mythological animal constellations from the sky, and the music played into the early hours of the morning, and the teachers drank too much sake and fell asleep on the benches of the amphitheater underneath the stars. So when Hana was five years old, Sora had "borrowed" the joey part of the kangaroo constellation costume, put Hana inside, and carried her around all evening, pretending she was just an inanimate stuffed toy. That's how she'd gotten to see the All Spirits' Eve celebrations.

Hana almost smiled now. But then she remembered that it was also the *only* All Spirits' Eve festival she'd ever witnessed, because after that, she'd been whisked away from Kichona during the Blood Rift, and Sora and the Society had done nothing about it.

"I hate you, Sora," Hana said in an attempt to remind herself how to feel.

But the wind swallowed her declaration and stole it away.

Prince Gin walked up to the bow of the ship. He stood silently beside her for a few minutes, looking out at their next target.

Finally, he spoke. "Family reunions aren't always pleasant. You think blood is strong enough to bind you, but the truth is, sometimes those bonds are shattered irreparably. In the end, it's better to choose your family than to remain prisoner to what you were born into. Do you understand what I'm saying?"

Hana nodded. The prince was sharing his own experience, and she realized how much that sliver of vulnerability was worth. Most of the original ryuu saw him only as their passionate leader, who would stop at nothing to bring to Kichona the glory it deserved. It was not a bad thing at all for the Dragon Prince to be regarded this way; it's why the original ryuu had fought with him during the Blood Rift, willing to give their lives for their prince and his noble cause. They didn't need to be hypnotized to follow him to the ends of the earth.

She herself had been a little harder to convince. She'd only been a child when she was taken from Kichona, and at first she was frightened and cried to go home to the Society. But the warriors had taken care of her, and when Prince Gin recovered from his Blood Rift injuries, he recognized that she had more talent for magic than anyone else. He took her under his wing, and she felt like she was home again.

Of course, he would often try to break her during training, expecting more of Hana than he did any other soldier. But he also mended her afterward with moments like this one now. Advice to make her stronger. She appreciated the tough love, that he recognized she could handle it. That it made her better.

"I'm going to take you off the duty of training our new recruits and give that responsibility to Firebrand," Prince Gin said.

She took a step back, caught off guard. "Why? I should be the one training the new ryuu."

"Because you need to focus one hundred percent of your energy on whipping Spirit into shape. Our army will reach critical mass before we know it, and then we'll march on the Imperial City. If your theory is correct that your sister harbors the same talent in her veins as you do, I want her ready. You're my secret weapon. But if I can have two such weapons when we face Aki and the Society stronghold at the Citadel, then I want you and Spirit both ready and at full power. You can do this for me, can't you?"

Hana's stomach twisted. When she was little, it had been her dream to fight by Sora's side. But her sister hadn't turned out to be who Hana had held aloft; by abandoning Hana, Sora had shown herself as helpless and ordinary. And then Hana had gone on to prove that *she* was actually the extraordinary one, that she could rise above the taigas and every single ryuu except the prince himself.

I'm supposed to be his most valued soldier. But what if Sora ended up better than her?

"Virtuoso," Prince Gin said. "Did you hear me? Treat Spirit as you would any other recruit. Or harder. I want her as ferocious as you promised me. And soon."

"Of course, Your Highness. I'll be merciless in her training."

She bowed and retreated a bit to give Prince Gin space. He liked his solitary moments at the bow, like a small meditation with the sea before reaching land.

She didn't feel calm, however. The thought of being able to punish Sora—to force her to spar until her legs were too weak to stand upon, to deny her sleep as she practiced magic, to push her until she threw up and then push her some more—should have made Hana happy. It was payback for her sister abandoning her all those years ago.

But instead, Hana's hard exterior cracked, like the desert floor after a decade of drought.

No, she thought, as she gritted her teeth. *I will not feel sorry for Sora. She left me on my own, and this is who I've become. I am immune to sentimentality.*

It was a lie, and Hana knew it. But she held on to it anyway.

CHAPTER THIRTY-SIX

On the main deck, away from the bow, the ryuu were preparing for their arrival at Tiger's Belly with a scrimmage, which seemed to Sora to be a combination between magical sparring and a rally to get their adrenaline pumping. The scrimmages were duels where two ryuu cast spells, and the others judged which was more impressive. A scrimmage ring had been set up in the middle of the deck, and ryuu surrounded it, shouting and laughing and placing bets on the next two warriors to fight. It was fascinating— a look at the kind of power she would soon have once she practiced—and Sora wanted to get closer.

She found a spot against a post to lean on. The bug boy popped up beside her, grinning as he took a bite from the dessert sandwich he held in his hands. It was made of two soft sugar cookies, filled with chocolate and sliced pear.

"This is your first scrimmage, huh?" he said. "It's exciting stuff. We haven't met yet. I'm Beetle." He stuck his hand

out for Sora to shake. His fingers were smeared with chocolate.

But Sora didn't take it, because she was too busy staring
at him. How had she not noticed before how young he was?
He was barely a teenager, his cheeks still holding on to some
baby fat, just the faintest hint of down on his upper lip.

*He must have been one of the tenderfoots who was kidnapped
with Hana*, she realized. Instinctively, she stepped back,
anticipating his wrath that the Society had not come to his
rescue.

But the boy kept smiling. There was no resentment, as
there had been with Hana.

*Maybe he was too young when he was taken to remember any-
thing about the Citadel and the Society*, Sora thought. Hana had
been six during the Blood Rift. But the boy would have been
two or three. *He had no fond memories of the taigas, and no hopes
or expectations that they would come to his aid.*

Sora shook his sticky hand. "We've met, sort of. I saw
you in the marketplace at Kaede City."

He was about to take another bite of cookie but stopped
before it reached his mouth. "You did? But I didn't come
across any taigas."

"I was disguised in layman's clothing," Sora said.

Suddenly, a memory of turquoise flashed through her
mind. And coral pink. She scrunched her nose as she turned
the colors over in her head. They were insistent, poking at
her like real, sharp coral in a shallow lagoon, as if they were
trying to tell her something. Where had they come from?
What did they mean?

She focused on the colors more intently, and they began
to take shape into something familiar—Daemon's hideous

shirt from Tanoshi and Kaede City.

Oh. Sora frowned. She hadn't thought of him in a while. How long? An hour? Two or three? But now, as she remembered him, she felt a slight pressure on her gemina bond. There was something not quite right about it, similar to the sensation of diving too deep in the sea and forgetting to clear her ears.

Where was Daemon? Why wasn't his presence in her head?

Instinctively, Sora reached out toward her gemina connection. She hit a wall.

Huh? Why was it closed? On her side?

And then she remembered. Prince Gin had asked her to close her mental ramparts.

Everything was fine. He wouldn't lead her astray.

He loves his warriors. He loves his people. He loves his kingdom.

She smiled. Just thinking of the Dragon Prince filled Sora's head with a warm cloud of contentment, like walking into a bakery and breathing in the aromas of cranberry tarts and hazelnut cookies coming out of the oven and pots of chrysanthemum tea on the counter.

What was I thinking about before that? She shook her head but couldn't remember.

Probably wasn't important.

Beetle was sitting in front of her, though, looking at her with his head cocked sideways. "You still there?"

"Huh?"

"Your eyes got all dreamy for a minute."

"I'm . . . fine. More than fine." The pastry warmth still floated through her head. Maybe the cookie sandwich Beetle was eating had something to do with it too.

"So you were about to tell me why you were in layman's

clothes in Kaede City?" he said.

"Oh, right," Sora said. "I was trying to spy on your army. But that was before I heard Prince Gin speak. Now I understand how naive I was. I'm thrilled to join the ryuu."

Beetle grinned more broadly before he took a big bite of his cookies. "Yesh," he said with his mouth full. "We're really lucky to get to use this magic and fight for the prince."

Two warriors—a man and a woman—stepped into the scrimmage ring.

"Oooh, this one's gonna be good," Beetle said. He was so intensely focused, he forgot to finish chewing.

Sora leaned forward too.

"Ready?" the ryuu serving as judge called out. "Three-two-one, scrimmage!"

The man began to circle.

The woman simply sat cross-legged in the middle of the ring.

What in Luna's name?

A moment later, a rumbling came from the cargo hold below. Oranges rolled up the ladders, in neat but hurried lines. They rushed to the scrimmage ring and piled atop themselves to form an enormous citrus gorilla. The gorilla towered over the ryuu, its broad orange chest heaving, as if it were really alive. Then it bent down and opened its hand. The woman stepped onto its palm, and it lifted her twenty feet up into the sky.

The entire spell took a span of ten seconds.

Sora gawked. Who would have thought a bunch of oranges could be so imposing? It was phenomenal. A gushy sense of pride bloomed inside of her, just by virtue of being part of the ryuu.

The crowd broke out into hollers and applause. Beetle cheered with his mouth full, flinging his arms up, cookie crumbs tossed into the air like sloppy, sweet confetti.

"Are there limits to what we can do?" Sora asked Beetle over the noise.

He shrugged. "Sort of. Everyone has their strengths and weaknesses. But I think it's like anything else. Some people are really good at math, and others stop at algebra. Same with magic."

Fascinating. Sora grinned so hard, she knew she must look a little stupid, but she couldn't help it. Everything about being a ryuu was new and intriguing. There'd been this whole other world, right beneath the taigas' noses, and they'd never known. But now Sora would get to be a part of it.

"It seems like all ryuu are geniuses with magic," she said.

"Nah," Beetle said. "Smart, maybe, but not geniuses. Except Prince Gin. And Virtuoso. That's why she got her name. While most of the ryuu took a while to learn what they could really do with the magic, she was a natural from the start."

The other warrior in the ring looked up at the gorilla. He nodded, as if acknowledging its grandeur. Then he puckered his lips and whistled. A keening, high-pitched noise sliced through the air. Sora and everyone around her smashed their hands over their ears.

Seemingly out of nowhere, hordes of bats filled the sky, blotting out the moon for a moment.

"Fruit bats," Sora said as she realized what they were.

The man raised his hand, ready to give the signal for his

bats to descend on the orange gorilla. To devour it.

"Halt!"

Someone whispered, "Virtuoso!" and the warning floated through the air like a winter ghost. Every ryuu on deck froze, afraid to move. If there was anything soft left inside of Hana, she didn't show it to the other warriors.

Hana strode to the center of the scrimmage ring and smacked the man upside the head. "Menagerie, you will not have your bats eat all our oranges. Think before you act. We need those."

He set his jaw, angry that she'd stopped him before his grand finale. But then he said, "You're right, Virtuoso," and whistled to call off his bats.

"I declare this scrimmage a draw," Hana said. The ryuu who was supposed to be judge didn't try to protest.

The gorilla crumbled, oranges cascading gently downward and bringing with them the woman on her platform. She landed quietly on deck as the last of the oranges rolled away, back down the ladders and, presumably, into their drums.

Hana paced the ring, examining every ryuu who stood around it.

"Personally," she said, "I think these duels encourage idleness and speculation." She glared at a place in the crowd where money was changing hands. The truing up of bets ceased immediately. "But His Highness sanctions them, believing them to be good practice for you. So then, let us make this a worthwhile exercise."

She pulled a knife from her sleeve, whirled, and pointed it in Sora's direction. The ryuu parted as if they were actually in the blade's path.

Sora found herself staring at the deathly tip.

"Step forward. It's time for your training to begin."

"But I don't even know how to use the magic," Sora said. She knew the ryuu particles were everywhere, like emerald dust glittering in the air, but she couldn't see them right away as she had after Prince Gin granted her Sight. There had been a rush of power during the initiation ceremony, but since then, it had leveled off, and she had to concentrate to find the ryuu particles. Even when she did, she didn't know what to do with the magic.

"Nothing better than a little public humiliation to get you started," Hana said. There wasn't a trace of humor in her words. "Now step forward."

Sora swallowed hard. But she didn't have a choice. Everyone was watching her. She was on a ship in the middle of the sea, traveling at sailfish speed. There was no way of getting out of this.

She walked through the path created when the ryuu had parted and met Hana in the scrimmage circle.

Hana vanished. Literally disappeared.

Sora gasped and whipped around.

Some of the ryuu in the crowd snickered.

So that was her little sister's specialty. No wonder Prince Gin wanted Sora trained. Siblings had the same power, and invisibility would be an incredible advantage over any enemy. If the Dragon Prince could have two ryuu like that . . .

A swipe knocked Sora's feet out from under her, and she slammed into the floor.

"Use your senses, Spirit!" Beetle shouted.

Sora lashed out to grab an ankle or a leg. Her fingertips

touched only air. Hana laughed cruelly, already half the length of the ship away.

Sora jumped back onto her feet. She felt a slight shift in the air a split second before Hana's head barreled straight into her stomach. Sora flew backward into a mast. It knocked the wind clear out of her lungs, and she crumpled onto the deck.

From the sails above, Hana said, "Get up. You're an insult to the blood we share."

So angry. But instead of hurting, the taunt stoked Sora's competitiveness. *I was using magic while you were still in diapers,* she thought. *Someone needs to put you back in your place.*

That was part of the job of being an older sister, after all.

Sora gritted her teeth and pushed aside the ache of the already-forming bruises on her back, and she rose again.

"Find me!" Hana, still invisible, yelled. "Stop flailing like a Kira Lake fish and use the Sight that Prince Gin granted you!"

Sora squinted and remembered what the green particles looked like. A moment later, she saw them whirling in the air, as if a breeze were stirring the magic. Sora followed the disturbance. The specks parted as an unseen force ran through them, then halted at the highest point of the ship—the crow's nest.

There. That's where Hana perched.

Sora stared for a few seconds. It wasn't possible, was it? Had she really found Hana?

But then it began to sink in that she was a ryuu, and that meant she could do ryuu things. Sora grinned, then leaped up the mast, several stories high. It was a movement unimaginable to a taiga, but now it was surprisingly effortless, as if the magic that floated everywhere existed simply to buoy her up and extend her trajectory. Sora reveled in the feeling of being tossed upward, like her legs were made of springs. All she'd done was think about jumping up the mast, and it had happened.

This is incredible. It was the same magic the taigas called up with their mudras and chants, but the ryuu could do so much more with it. How could it be that this power had been there all along, but the Society hadn't fully understood it?

Because the taigas are limited by their mudras and chants, Sora realized.

She found solid grips and footing on the mast. She looked for Hana but saw nobody.

There was a shout from the crow's nest above, and suddenly, Hana slammed into her.

Sora plowed into the mast, the wood scraping the entire left side of her face, blood spattering onto her tunic. She rebounded out of the crow's nest.

She got caught in a sail on the way down, slowing her rapid fall. It was the only way she didn't die when she hit the deck. Still, the impact slammed every bit of oxygen out of her body.

"Spirit! Are you okay?" Beetle ran up to the edge of the scrimmage ring. She'd nearly forgotten she had an audience. But of course she did. This was, as Hana had put it, a public humiliation.

"I'm all right." Sora wiped a smear of blood from her cheek. Hopefully it made her look fiercer than she felt, like war paint instead of defeat.

And she would not be humiliated. Not by her little sister. Sora got to her feet.

The last time she and Hana were in the same place, Hana had been so resentful. Sora didn't want to see that in her sister's eyes anymore. She wanted both Prince Gin *and* Hana to be proud of her.

Sora was supposed to have the same power as her sister. But even if Sora didn't know how to make herself invisible yet, it might still be possible for her to see how Hana did it.

"You're still thinking like a taiga." Hana's voice came from somewhere else on the deck, that now-familiar corrosive condescension returning to burn the edges of her otherwise youthful voice. Sora's ears were still ringing from the fall and she couldn't quite place the source. "Magic is like another reality," Hana continued. "Or rather, one layered on top of the world that ordinary people—and taigas—see."

Sora remained light on her feet, hands up in fighting stance, while she pondered this.

That was it! Ryuu magic was invisible to taigas. But now that Sora had Sight, she could use it if she focused. She'd seen the oranges in the gorilla, infused with the green of particles. The bats' wings had glittered with ryuu magic inside them.

If she looked harder at the emerald dust, maybe she'd find Hana, saturated by the magic in much the same way.

Sora bit back a smile, in case it was premature. But that had to be it. Hana wasn't actually invisible. She'd simply asked the magic to camouflage her from ordinary reality. With that thought, the barriers of Sora's preconceptions began to fall away.

And there was Hana, like an emerald version of herself, reclining on the edge of the ship's railing.

Sora pretended to wander aimlessly. But when she was

within range, her arm shot out and knocked Hana off the railing. Only because Sora grabbed a fistful of her tunic did her sister not fall overboard.

Hana reappeared.

"Holy heavens," Beetle said, dropping the last half of his cookie sandwich onto the floor. "No one else has been able to see Virtuoso when she was invisible."

All the other ryuu stood equally stunned that someone— a recruit, no less—had bested the undefeatable Virtuoso, who now dangled off the side of the ship.

Sora braced herself for Hana's scowl.

What she got, though, was her sister looking up at her, eyes bright and clear and wide, the exact expression of surprise and awe she used to give Sora when they were young. Sora glowed. *This* was what she'd wanted. This was what she'd missed.

But the admiration was quickly replaced with Virtuoso's signature glower. Hana scrambled back onto the railing and shoved Sora aside. She landed on deck and stormed off.

Those two seconds, though, were enough.

I am so glad to be here, Sora thought. Not only to be able to play with magic more powerful than she'd ever imagined possible. But also to be reunited with Hana, even if her little sister hadn't come around yet to accepting her.

Sora couldn't wait to spend more time with Hana. She would become the ryuu that Hana had promised Prince Gin she would be. And hopefully, she would permanently earn back that look of love and admiration that had flitted in her little sister's eyes.

CHAPTER THIRTY-SEVEN

Daemon swam all night. He swam until his muscles cramped, and then he pushed on some more, the magic of his sailfish spell allowing him to continue past ordinary human limits. His lungs burned and his lips cracked from the seawater, and still, he kept swimming. He would never make it to Tiger's Belly before the ryuu. Their magic could command the sea. Even against an ordinary ship, Daemon's arms and legs would be no match. But he could do his best and swim ashore on one of the smaller islands nearby.

At the same time, he tried to project the will to resist Prince Gin through his gemina connection. Where was that electric feeling he'd had before, the sharp spark he'd used to shock Sora out of the Dragon Prince's spell? He needed to send it to Sora again.

But he couldn't find it. Perhaps Daemon had to be under attack by Prince Gin's magic in order for his own defenses to rise. There was no blaze of resistance now, just his own thoughts reciting, *Be strong, Sora, be strong*, over and over again.

And yet, even that was useless. His urging went nowhere, like throwing a ball at a cushioned wall. It simply bounced back, muted. It was as if Sora's mental ramparts were up.

Why were her ramparts up?

Oh gods, he thought, his arms growing heavier in the water. *What if Prince Gin has already hypnotized her?*

Part of Daemon wanted to let himself drown. He couldn't bear to think of Sora stolen by the Dragon Prince. His strong, brilliant gemina reduced to one of the lemmings who followed the prince around.

But another part of Daemon knew that he had to keep going. If Sora had fallen under the charm spell, she'd need him now more than ever. And that part of him guiltily liked that he had a chance to be the hero of the story for once. Between the pair of them, Sora had always shined brighter. Daemon didn't even know who his parents were or where he'd come from, for gods' sake.

He heaved himself onto shore, his arms too tired to take care not to slice himself on the coral.

Officially, these islands were called the Sanran Atoll, but Kichonans had long ago nicknamed them the Belly Lint Atoll, since they were a sprinkle of tiny islands south of Tiger's Belly, and on a map, they looked like specks of navel dirt.

Daemon flipped onto his back and lay there, panting. Because he was no longer in the water, the sailfish spell left him, and with it, his sailfish endurance disappeared, too. Suddenly, human exhaustion caught up and slammed into him. Not two minutes from climbing out of the sea, Daemon passed out.

The sun was up when Daemon woke. His eyes flew open in a panic. Was it morning already? How much time had passed? Gods, he couldn't afford to fall asleep!

Waves lapped at his legs, and the salt water stung the myriad cuts on his skin. The pain helped him focus, and he realized that whatever time he'd lost couldn't be recovered, so worrying over it was a waste. All that mattered now was getting to Tiger's Belly as quickly as possible.

I need a boat. I can't beat Prince Gin there, but maybe I can still get to Tiger's Belly before they leave with the new batch of recruits. In time to save Sora.

Daemon rolled over and got to his feet. His legs felt like jelly, but he forced himself to jog toward the cluster of thatch-roofed huts farther up the beach.

Half a dozen fishermen sat on a small pier, some sorting through the day's catch, others mending nets. It must have been later than Daemon thought it was. *Please let the ryuu still be at Tiger's Belly.*

"Yah-ho!" he shouted when he was close enough.

The men looked up at his greeting.

Daemon stopped at the edge of the pier and gave a short bow of his head. "Hello there. I was hoping you could help me."

They blinked at Daemon, as if he were a strange apparition. He must have looked like some sort of sea creature, dripping wet with seaweed and sand clinging to his clothes.

"Look at his hair," one of the men whispered. "It looks like the midnight ocean."

The others gawked.

"Um . . ." Daemon ran his fingers through his hair. Damn blue roots. Once this was all over, he was going to dye them again. But first, he had the small order of business of defeating a magical, vengeful prince bent on hypnotizing all of Kichona. Easy.

After a few more seconds of gaping, the first man who'd noticed Daemon's hair dropped to his knees and lay out prostrate on the pier, as if bowing to the empress herself.

"What are you doing?" Daemon asked, blood rushing to his cheeks. "Get up. I'm not royalty."

"Nauti is testing us," the man said to the others.

They murmured their understanding that they were in the presence of the god of the sea, who in some myths had hair as blue and black as the deepest part of the ocean. They immediately fell to their knees and laid themselves before Daemon.

"No!" Daemon said, the ridiculousness of the scene pushing back on his own embarrassment. "I'm not a god. Especially Nauti, who I'm pretty sure wouldn't look like a drowned dog if he wanted to appear before you. Look, I'm only a taiga."

The men crawled up from their bows a little, although they remained on their knees, just in case. "A taiga?"

"Yes, I am called Wolf, and I am in dire need of your assistance. I need a boat so I can get to Tiger's Belly. Whatever it costs, the Society will reimburse you, and then some. But please, get up. I need this boat quickly."

They studied him, then discussed among themselves for what seemed like an eon. Finally, the first man stood up.

"We do not have much to offer, but whether you are

Nauti or Wolf, it is our honor to help you. We'll row you ourselves, wherever you wish to go."

Daemon nodded. *I suppose if believing I'm a god means they'll get me to Tiger's Belly, I'll let them go on believing.* He'd donate next month's apprentice allowance to Nauti's temple as an apology for not setting the record straighter here today.

"Thank you," he said. "You are truly honorable citizens of Kichona. Now please, let's go."

CHAPTER THIRTY-EIGHT

Soon thereafter, the ship swept briskly into Tiger's Belly. The ryuu disembarked, led by Hana, who refused to meet Sora's eye.

The harbormaster ran down the pier, waving papers angrily. "This ship is not registered! You cannot take up a berth!" he shouted.

Prince Gin took his time walking up to him.

"My ship serves Sola, Luna, and Zomuri," he said. "You insult our gods by refusing me in your port."

"I don't know who Zomuri is—"

Prince Gin flicked his wrist.

The harbormaster's head snapped cleanly off his neck.

Sora gasped. The man's body remained standing for a few seconds, as if, in its shock, it still expected its head to return. But a moment later, it collapsed onto the pier, splattering blood everywhere.

The new recruits joined Sora in her surprise, but Prince

Gin turned to them and said, "We aim for peace while in our own kingdom, but sometimes, expediency requires sacrifice. Blood is a price we must be willing to pay for glory. I also wanted you to see the power we have within us. This is what we will be able to do when we invade other kingdoms. We'll make Kichona one of the most feared and revered kingdoms in the world. We will be unstoppable."

Yes! Sora thought, as the fire of ambition in her belly flared, hot and ready to fight. Her mother had entreated her to do more, to be more. And now she was fulfilling her promise, serving the greatest leader Kichona had ever seen and using Luna's gifts to their greatest potential. And with her sister, no less.

Mama will be proud, Sora thought.

By now most of the ryuu had disembarked, leaving a small crew behind to guard the ship. Prince Gin divided his warriors into small groups, each in charge of attacking a sector of the city, securing it, and rounding up any taigas they found. Everyone had been assigned a unit—even the new recruits—except Sora.

"Where do I go?" she asked, but everyone was already gone, assembled with their groups farther down the dock.

"You haven't been trained yet," Hana said, as she appeared seemingly from nowhere. "You're stuck with me until you're ready. Unfortunately."

Shrug it off, Sora thought. She reminded herself of how Hana had looked at her earlier, when Sora had managed to find her when she was invisible. She also held on to the fact that Hana could have let Prince Gin execute her, but had saved her instead. That didn't mean nothing.

"I won't let you down," Sora pledged, touching her necklace. *Not this time.*

Sora stood inside the shrine to Emmer, god of the harvest. While Tiger's Belly had a port, it was only a small one; this part of Kichona was mostly rice paddies and silos, growing and supplying the kingdom with grain. Fittingly, this was a modest shrine, with plain wooden beams supporting a clean but basic pagoda roof.

It did, however, have an excellent vantage point from which to observe the network of farms inland. Hana would be able to watch the ryuu's progress while she trained Sora in their magic.

"Lie down," Hana ordered.

"Here?"

"Where else?" She tapped her foot impatiently. It was a role reversal. It used to be Sora who complained that Hana was too slow, that she was always holding up Sora's plans.

Sora lay down on the thin reed mat covering the shrine's floor. Marigold wreaths on rickety bamboo stands, offerings to Emmer from the locals, surrounded the perimeter.

"You could see me when I was invisible," Hana said. "Which means that, in theory, you might be able to disappear too."

Sora sat up. "You're going to show me how?" Eagerness for more ryuu magic bubbled inside her.

Hana put her foot on Sora's chest and shoved her back on the floor. "Don't get ahead of yourself. We'll start with the basics."

Sora sighed but nodded.

"Find the ryuu particles. Once your Sight homes in on them, they will respond to your thoughts. No stupid chants and mudras to tie up your hands. Ryuu can actually cast spells and fight at the same time."

Oh! Sora hadn't thought of that before. Taigas always had to choose between holding weapons or using their fingers to begin a spell. But now she'd be free to use both superior magic and throwing stars simultaneously. The ryuu were the future of Kichona. Sora smiled.

But if she wanted to be part of Prince Gin's revolution, she'd better practice. Sora refocused, shifting her vision to look for the magic. After a few seconds, the ryuu particles winked into view.

"I see them," she said.

"Now tell them to lift you up."

Sora made her body as stiff as a corpse.

Buoy me, she thought to the emerald dust floating around her.

They eddied for a moment, then came together like droplets of water forming a wave. They swept under Sora's left side and scooped her up, suspending her an inch above the shrine floor.

She let out an unintentional gasp. Whereas taiga magic was like warm, liquid chocolate coursing through her body, ryuu magic was a sauna—hot and intense, but in a good way. It both energized and relaxed her. There were even notes of cedar in the air. Sora smiled as she relaxed into the ryuu power.

Now take me higher, she thought at the particles.

Her body rose in the air, steadily. Then she accidentally sped up, and she smashed into the bells and banners hanging from the ceiling. She tumbled back to the ground and smacked into the reed mat. The force of her landing knocked over several of the marigold wreaths nearby.

Hana laughed. But when Sora looked at her, she smacked her hand over her mouth. All traces of amusement were wiped away in an instant, replaced by schoolteacher sternness. Or what Hana probably thought a teacher looked like when disciplining an apprentice. She'd never had a chance to be part of the taiga school.

"Make the particles lift you up again," Hana said.

Sora obeyed, but not because she was scared into obedience. It was because the would-be-teacher look on Hana's face reminded her how young her sister had been when she was kidnapped.

She used to be small enough to fit in Sora's lap. Sora hadn't been much bigger, but two years made a difference back then, and Hana would curl up against her, with a smile that could light up the Imperial City whenever Sora paid her any attention. On Friday night sleepovers, Hana would beg Sora to tell her myths from their mother's books, stories Hana was still too young to read on her own, and Sora would recite fables about rich, greedy children who tried to steal the moon from Luna, legends of past taiga warriors who fought against monsters from the sea, and myths about girls riding on the backs of horses made of comets. Every time, Hana would murmur happily and curl tighter into Sora's lap, and Sora would know the moment she fell asleep by the rhythm of her breath, the content slowing of the ins-and-outs as she drifted off to her own dreams full of brave warriors and mysterious storybook creatures.

Sora ached to have that again. Not exactly the same, because they were grown now, but she wanted her sister back. She wanted to bundle her up in her lap and keep her safe from the world, with the promise that when the monsters came, she and Hana would fight together, sister by sister, sword by sword.

And so she listened to Hana and commanded the ryuu particles to buoy her again.

Sora went up and down ten times, and by the last round, her control was much improved.

Satisfied that she'd mastered the spell, she released her command of the particles and landed back on the shrine floor as gracefully as if she were a flying carpet.

"You're awfully smug for just making yourself go up and down," Hana said. "Let's see how smug you are after this." She glanced at the reed mat beneath Sora. Its edges leaped to attention, flying up and lifting Sora into the air. It wrapped her inside. Then it squeezed itself, rolling more tightly, trapping her like a human spring roll.

Sora struggled with her arms clamped by her sides. The mat pressed in on her, almost crushing her ribs. She could manage only shallow breaths.

With her arms pinned, she couldn't use a knife to slice her way out. She tried to command ryuu particles to retrieve her knife for her, but even they couldn't do it, because her blades were stashed in various pockets and sleeves, which were also smashed tightly against her inside the mat.

"Nines," she cursed between quick breaths.

She wiggled her feet, the only parts of her that were really free, but that didn't do any good.

Think, Sora, think.

Wait. Her eyes lit up as an idea came to her. Maybe she could untie herself.

She searched for the ryuu particles again, needing only a few seconds for her vision to shift to ryuu reality. The narrow space inside her rolled mat sparkled green.

Let me out, she commanded the particles. She envisioned the magic flowing in a stream of green at the string that wove the reeds together, unraveling through the threads, and setting her free.

But instead of following her command as she'd imagined it, the particles flew around in a chaotic swirl. Then they rushed forward, into the reeds themselves, as if the magic had been absorbed. The reeds turned from brown to a bright shade of glowing green.

"Oh no. What's happening?"

The mat unrolled, then disappeared, and Sora again slammed to the floor.

"What in all hells?" Sora looked again, but it wasn't as if she could miss it. The mat had been right there, all around her. And now it was gone.

The magic had done her bidding. She'd asked it to free her from the mat. It just hadn't done it in the way she'd imagined.

She gasped and looked at Hana. There really was something about sharing the same blood.

Sora rose and began to walk toward her sister, but not two steps later, she tripped on something and fell. She swore, as she stumbled and tumbled to the shrine floor for the third time.

Yet she was an inch off the actual floor, even though she wasn't asking the ryuu particles to help her levitate. What was going on?

She ran her fingers over the air beneath her. It wasn't air.

It was a reed mat. Invisible, but there.

"Gods," Sora said, as she ran her fingers over it again.

Like how Hana hadn't truly vanished, she realized. During the scrimmage, the visible part of her sister had just been camouflaged, but her physical body still existed in the ordinary world. The same had happened with the reed mat—it was both here and not.

Hana had told her to focus on basic firsts. But Sora never had been one to follow the rules.

"I'm going to make myself invisible too," she declared.

Her sister's veil of disdain lifted, as if Hana had forgotten she wanted to dislike Sora. It was replaced by a cautious curiosity. "Try," Hana said, her mouth parting into a small O as she watched.

Sora located the emerald dust. *Make me invisible*, she willed it.

Her hand trembled, but nothing happened.

Try again. Make me invisible.

Again, nothing.

She thought about what had happened with the reed mat. The magic had swirled around and then the reeds had soaked them in.

Sora smiled. She rose to her feet. Instead of asking the ryuu particles to come to her, she would go to them.

The emerald particles flurried before her. She hurled herself into them, as if diving into a pool.

Stars! They absorbed her, or she absorbed them, and they were cool and hot at the same time, on her skin, in every blood cell, penetrating all the way to her core. She inhaled sharply. This wasn't just the sauna-like feel of the magic before. Sora lit up from within. The ability to make herself invisible was a thousand Autumn Festival sparklers inside of her, and she laughed, spinning in a circle with arms out, intoxicated by the power.

Hana made herself invisible too, but she appeared to Sora as if shimmering, like the form of her sister but composed entirely of green jewels. Sora looked down at her hand. It was delightfully the same.

"We're made of emeralds," she said.

"I can't believe you figured out how to do this so quickly." There was nothing but wonder in Hana's voice.

"I'm learning as fast as I can for you," Sora said, her belly filling with warmth, as if she'd just eaten the most delicious, hearty stew. Being a part of Prince Gin's ryuu made her feel as if nothing could go wrong. Fate had put her here, in this time and place, to be a ryuu. With Hana. "I want us to be able to do things together. I want to share your ambitions. I want to be your sister again."

Hana frowned, her defenses going back up a little. "You're doing this for Prince Gin. It's because of his vision for Kichona that we're all here."

Sora shrugged. "Yes, for Prince Gin. But also for us. We'd get to fight together, Hana. We can forge a new path for Kichona, make history and be part of building a kingdom together. I know it's hard to have me here all of a sudden, but you have to believe when I say I love you and always have, and I would have come after you a decade ago if I could. But I was eight."

Hana tensed.

That was the wrong thing for me to say, Sora realized. Because no excuse was good enough, not when you were as scared and lost and hurt as tenderfoot Hana must have been.

All she'd wanted was her sister, and Sora hadn't been there.

"For what it's worth," Sora said, "if anything happened to you now, I would fight to the ends of the earth to save you."

Hana blinked as if surprised. She opened her mouth to say something.

But then a horn sounded. The ryuu had rounded up all the taigas from the vast countryside in Tiger's Belly. It was time to assemble them in the Society outpost building so that Prince Gin could speak with them.

Giddiness burst inside Sora like a geyser in Rae Springs, and the conversation with Hana was immediately forgotten. Sora jumped up. "Come on! Let's go see the new recruits get initiated." Prince Gin's charisma was addicting, and she craved being in his presence some more.

She hurried toward the stairs that led down from the shrine's tower. "I can't wait to see His Highness honoring some of the citizens as Hearts too!"

Hana rolled her eyes. It was a typical little sister thing to do, though, and Sora shrugged it off. Also, Hana had probably seen enough of the Dragon Prince's speeches that she wasn't awed by them anymore. But that wouldn't stop Sora from enjoying this. Or dragging her sister along.

"Please, Hana? I don't want to miss any of it."

Her sister rolled her eyes again—it was a wonder they were still inside her head—but then she said, "All right, all right."

Sora grinned, and they ran down the stairs together.

CHAPTER THIRTY-NINE

The ryuu were gone by the time Daemon and the fishermen rowed into Tiger's Belly. Daemon had known this would likely be the case. And yet the emptiness on the pier—the quiet berths and complete lack of sailors and merchants and the other men who usually populated the harbor—nearly brought Daemon to his knees. Prince Gin had come and gone through another outpost, stealing its taigas for his army, hypnotizing all the citizens, and likely selecting more Hearts for sacrifice. He was one step closer to the Ceremony, and Daemon was one step farther from stopping him.

And then there was the deafening silence in Daemon's head. Nothing was coming through his gemina bond, and what he tried to send to Sora just bounced back. Was she safe? Had Prince Gin brainwashed her? Would Daemon ever get her back?

He hadn't realized how much she completed him, until she was gone.

But Daemon couldn't feel sorry for himself. Because if Sora was alive, she needed him. They were in this situation because she'd decided she wanted to do all that she could for Kichona, to be the best that she could be.

He had to follow suit.

"Thank you for your assistance," Daemon said to the fishermen. "I'll see to it that the Society knows of your good deeds."

"It was our honor to help," the eldest man said. They all bowed, then pushed off to return to their atoll.

Daemon hurried down the silent pier to the harbormaster's office and pushed his way through the door.

"Agh!" a man shrieked from beneath the desk. "Please don't kill me."

Daemon jumped. He already had blades in his hands before he realized that the man had screamed in defense, not attack. He put away his knives. "Why do you think I want to kill you?"

The man wouldn't come out from his hiding place. Daemon walked around the desk instead. "I promise you, sir, I don't want to hurt you."

A bespectacled fellow was sitting in a puddle of his own piss, and from the smell of it, it was likely he'd soiled himself in another way too. As soon as he saw Daemon, he started sobbing. "Please! I'm just the assistant to the harbormaster! I had nothing against your ship docking on the pier! Please don't decapitate me."

Apparently, the ryuu had cut off the harbormaster's head. Daemon shuddered.

He looked down at himself and realized he was wearing a ryuu uniform. Not that a taiga uniform would have calmed the assistant down any. The man saw black clothing and weapons on Daemon's back, and that's all he needed to know to cry for his life.

"I know you've been frightened," Daemon said as he kneeled by the man, "but I swear I'm not with the people who attacked Tiger's Belly. I'm here to help, but I need to know where the Society's command post is."

The assistant peered up, his puffy eyes magnified through his glasses. He didn't say anything.

"Can you tell me where the Society of Taigas' command post is located?" Daemon asked again, making his voice as soft and patient as possible. It was quite an accomplishment, given that his blood rushed through him, urging him to run too. But he needed to know where to go.

The man nodded, his head seeming to bobble all over the place. "Th-the taiga post is on the outskirts of town, where the grain silos are."

"Is the fastest way to cut through the city itself, or is there a better path?"

The harbormaster's assistant just stared at Daemon. He pulled his knees up to his chest and started rocking back and forth in his puddle.

That was all Daemon would get out of him. He wished he had a spare pair of trousers to leave the fellow, but all he had were the wet clothes he wore and the weapons stashed within them. "The Citadel will send more help soon," Daemon said. He didn't know if it was true, but the man needed hope, so that's what Daemon gave.

He left the office and sprinted into Tiger's Belly. Like Paro Village, the citizens wandered around with blissful, if slightly blank, looks on their faces. The stone streets were littered with the detritus of the ryuu's hasty and violent search for taigas—overturned carts, shopwindows blasted into shards, a trampled stuffed toy lying muddy in the gutter—but the townspeople didn't seem to care.

And because the residents of Tiger's Belly avoided him, Daemon made quick progress to the grain silos. They bordered the edge of town and the farmland, rising like a forest of cylindrical towers from the ground. Amazingly, the silos were largely untouched by the ryuu. Perhaps because they didn't think taigas would be hiding inside.

The Society's local command post, however, was a different matter. It was a manor made of black stone, large enough to house the majority of the taigas who were stationed in this region, although there were probably some smaller safe houses farther out in the country for warriors when they were on rotation there. The manor had probably been impressive a few hours ago, but now its black rice paper windows were blown out from the force of ryuu-controlled wind, and the wooden roof had been torn off unceremoniously, like a toupee ripped rudely off a gentleman's head. Daemon winced at the humiliation of the once grand building.

But this was not why he was here. Even though all the taiga warriors were gone, their dragonfly messengers were hopefully still alive. If they were, Daemon could send a missive to the Citadel to let them know what had happened and where the Dragon Prince planned to hit next.

Daemon stepped through the space where the front door had been, careful to tiptoe around the debris. He was 99 percent sure the ryuu were gone, but he'd be quiet, just in case.

He slipped through the entryway. Upstairs and in the

back of the manor, there would be living quarters, but here on the ground floor, Daemon passed by meeting rooms where the sliding doors had been torn off their tracks, meditation spaces with the reed mats wrenched from the floors, and a dining room where the tables had splintered when they were hurled against the walls.

Finally, he found the communications office. There ought to have been terrariums full of dragonflies here, trained to deliver taiga messages throughout the kingdom. This was how the command posts throughout Kichona communicated with the Citadel every morning, and vice versa.

Unfortunately, the ryuu were not stupid. As with the previous posts, all the terrarium tanks before Daemon lay in pieces on the floor, the glass slivers interspersed with charred dragonfly bodies.

"Daggers," he swore. Had it really been necessary to incinerate helpless insects? He growled under his breath. Growing up with wolves meant he was particularly sensitive to the treatment of animals, dragonflies included. Daemon kicked at the lone desk in the room, throwing quiet caution out the window. There was nothing here but destruction anyway.

He let out a long, frustrated exhale. He was trying his best, yet it still wasn't enough.

Daemon couldn't stay in the communications office. Not with the dragonfly corpses all over the floor. He stormed out into the hall.

But now what? How would he get in touch with the Citadel? It would take too long to find a horse and ride it all the way back to the capital. By then Prince Gin would have taken at least another target or two, and the size of his army would near the critical mass needed to overwhelm the Society.

If only a single dragonfly had survived.

"I'm an idiot!" Daemon tore through the manor and into the kitchen. Broomstick had told him a while ago that there were always backup dragonflies kept in a separate location at every post, in case disease or heat stroke or something else happened to the squadron in the communications office. It was not common knowledge—only those who worked on receiving and dispatching messages knew—but a small contingent of dragonflies were kept in a frozen, suspended state inside a special icebox in the kitchen.

Daemon threw himself into the walk-in icebox. His teeth chattered within seconds, but he methodically searched each shelf and drawer. There were hunks of frozen beef still in crates. Tubs of peach ice cream, probably made from fresh fruit and milk from Tiger's Belly farms. And giant, frost-dusted blocks of ice. But no dragonflies.

The hair on his arms now frozen stiff, Daemon stumbled out of the icebox. He paused for a moment to allow himself to warm a little.

Then he tackled the shelves of pots and pans, tossing each one aside with a clang when he found nothing there. Next, the cabinets full of plates and bowls, which he only sort of tried not to break in his hurry. Then he dug headlong into the pantry of dry goods, leaving clouds of flour and slashed bags of rice in his wake.

Maybe I'm wrong. Maybe there isn't a backup set of messengers.

Daemon leaned against a workstation in the center of

the kitchen, the weight of the day pressing against the countertop.

It gave way behind him. He jumped up, away from the workstation.

Part of the countertop had unlatched and slid open to reveal a secret compartment inside.

Ice. And a small crystal box.

Daemon whooped and pumped his fist. Then he lifted the box carefully out of its frozen chamber and took off the lid.

Wisps of cold floated out. They evaporated and revealed six dragonflies lying on beds of blue satin edged in gold, small soldiers honoring Kichona's colors even in slumber.

As the warmth of the room thawed the dragonflies, their tiny legs began to wiggle. Their wings fluttered, rasping against the satin.

Daemon smiled at them as he carried the crystal box back to the communications office. He hated to go in there again, but he needed the miniature scrolls and needle-tipped pens that the taiga dispatchers used to compose messages small enough for the dragonflies to carry.

When he arrived, he set the box down on the desk and quickly found the supplies he needed in the top drawer. He secured the miniature scroll onto a board with fasteners designed to hold its corners down. At the edge of the desk, a magnifying glass on a long brass arm stood waiting to be called to action; Daemon extended it so it was positioned directly above the scroll. Then he began to write with the dispatcher's pen. It was no easy task. Dispatchers needed not only impeccable penmanship but also a steady, detailed hand, for each letter was no bigger than half a millimeter.

Daemon painstakingly recorded what he'd discovered of the Dragon Prince's plans. It took multiple sheets of paper, and he hoped the Council could read what he wrote, but he did the best he could. If he were still a Level 2 or 3 apprentice, this scroll would be the highest mark he ever received in handwriting class. But alas, there were no such rewards for composing messages about impending doom.

He rolled up the scroll and secured it to one of the dragonfly's legs using tweezers and thread. Then Daemon tried to set it free. It should know what to do, how to fly to the Citadel.

The dragonfly stood around the desk awkwardly, one-sixth of its legs bound to a scroll.

"Hmph," Daemon muttered.

He tried nudging the dragonfly.

It remained where it was.

He tried talking to it, as if it could understand what he wanted.

Nothing.

Then, as Daemon was about to give up, the dragonfly seemed to wake up from its daze. Perhaps it had still been groggy from the icebox. It bolted into the air, circled the communications office twice, and zipped out a hole in the window.

Daemon exhaled and collapsed back in his chair.

He let himself rest for all of two minutes.

And then he launched himself into the other part of his self-appointed mission—he had to get through to Sora.

Hey-o, he called out through their bond. She wouldn't be

able to hear his words, of course, just feel his presence and his emotion, but sometimes he spoke to her to help convey his feelings.

But as before, his greeting seemed to ricochet off something and smack back into him. He actually ducked, as if the rejected "hey-o" could hurt him.

Undeterred, he tried again. *Sora?*

Her name boomeranged back.

The silence in their bond ached. Daemon's and Sora's minds had been interwoven, their partnership omnipresent, for eleven years. When they were children, they used to do everything together—eat together, spar together, study spells together. For things they couldn't do together, like sleep, they'd stay connected to each other until the last moment, sending soothing thoughts through their bond until they were drowsy enough to fall asleep.

He took the pain of not having Sora and drilled that into their connection, shoving it like a battering ram. It would not be a nice emotion for Sora to receive, but that was the point. Maybe he needed something intense—like his terror when Sora was hypnotized by Prince Gin at Kaede City—in order to smash his will through their connection.

There was resistance, stubborn and solid like the Citadel's fortress walls.

He drilled his anguish into their gemina bond over and over again. The battering ram kept smashing against Sora's ramparts. Daemon broke out into a sweat. At one point, he felt a slight give, like he'd made a dent in the blockade, but then there was no more progress after that.

Daemon fell back against the chair again, utterly drained.

The dragonflies flitted in front of him, as if concerned.

He waved at them, shaking his head. "Thank you, but this is on me alone."

Maybe he couldn't get to Sora without better understanding what it was that he'd done in the first place. Or what had triggered it.

Daemon hesitated to think there was something special about him. Other than the odd origin of being raised by wolves, he had spent his life being decidedly *not* special. Sora could pick up new spells on the first try. Fairy had a golden touch with botanicals. Broomstick more than played with fire. But Daemon didn't excel at anything besides physically fighting people to the ground, and honestly, even an ordinary Kichonan could be good at that if he trained hard enough.

There had to be an explanation for his strange ability to resist Prince Gin's hypnosis. *I'm stuck here until I get a dragonfly response from the Citadel,* he thought. *I should spend some time doing research.* He'd seen a small library down one of the halls. Burying himself in stacks of books wouldn't be as active as trying to reach Sora, but he wasn't doing any good on that front and needed a break. Besides, good reconnaissance was as much about what one saw as what one understood about those observations.

Daemon pushed back from his chair. Who knows? Maybe this was a blessing in disguise. Maybe he'd learn something about his strange magic that would give him a clue about where he'd come from.

CHAPTER FORTY

Aki paused outside the Council Room. The commander had summoned her, and she had come swiftly from Rose Palace. But now that she was here, she stopped. *Why am I running to them like I'm one of their warriors?* she thought. *I'm the empress. It should be I who summons the Council, not the other way around.*

Besides, what had the Society accomplished since the attack on Isle of the Moon? Aki had let them do things their way, but the old system had proven too slow.

She had great respect for the taigas, but now it was time for Aki to take charge.

She pushed her way into the room before the guard could properly announce her.

The councilmembers jumped at her entrance and hastily laid themselves prostrate at her feet.

Aki strode over to the commander's high-backed chair. "I'm sitting here today," she announced to Glass Lady, leaving no room for debate.

The commander, only halfway up from her bow and still on her knees, looked stunned for a moment. But proper etiquette meant she had to defer to the empress, so Glass Lady dipped her head in concession and pulled up an extra seat. Now she and the other councilmembers sat opposite Aki across the black stone table, the shift in power evident.

"This came in today, Your Majesty," Glass Lady said, passing a stack of miniature papers, curled at the edges, to the empress. "You were right. Prince Gin is involved. And now we know his plans."

Aki took the magnifying glass offered to her by Scythe, one of the councilmembers. She took her time reading the details of her brother's attacks on Paro Village, Sand Mine, Kaede City, and Tiger's Belly, as well as his subsequent targets.

"This message didn't come from your naval ship," she said when she'd read the pages twice.

Glass Lady's usual arrogance faltered. "No, Your Majesty. It's from an apprentice."

"An apprentice? I thought you said you didn't have any taigas who could reach the far outposts before the navy could?"

"Er, we didn't send Wolf," Glass Lady said, looking down at the table. "He and his gemina, Spirit, slipped out of the Citadel on their own initiative."

Spirit? The name sounded familiar. Aki glanced up from her magnifying glass. "Was Spirit the one who set off the fireworks at Rose Palace?"

One of the other councilmembers, Bullfrog, made a croaking noise. "Unfortunately, yes. She and her friends have a penchant for breaking rules. Or at least for finding the loopholes in them."

"And you say the Council didn't sanction Spirit and Wolf leaving the Citadel?"

"No, Your Majesty."

Aki pondered this for a moment. The Council had been spinning their wheels, unable to figure out the mysterious assault at Isle of the Moon or protect against Gin's stealth attacks. They were relying on a specific way of doing things, which may have worked in the past, but clearly wasn't getting them anywhere right now. In the meantime, Spirit and Wolf had tossed traditional methods aside and uncovered Gin's plot on their own.

Interesting. Perhaps this was what Kichona needed. An unorthodox approach to an unorthodox enemy.

"We must stop my brother before he grows his army further," Aki said. "Can you send a dragonfly to the Striped Coves before he arrives?"

"I cannot guarantee it, but we'll try."

Aki nodded. "Good. Tell the Striped Coves taigas to evacuate the citizens. And then the taigas themselves should hide."

Strategist smacked both hands on the table. "You want the taigas to hide like cowards?"

Glass Lady glared at him. She turned to the empress with an apologetic dip of her head. "What my colleague means, Your Majesty, is that, with all due respect, we don't think it's advisable to leave the Striped Coves completely unprotected."

"I don't mean for them to abandon their duties. The

Striped Coves are a valuable part of Kichona, and we won't leave it open to pirates. But they can't stay at the Society post there. The taigas would be captured by Gin, and we'd be handing him an army, which is precisely what he wants." Aki sat back in the commander's chair and crossed her arms. "I want half of them to stay in the Striped Coves, and the other half to regroup here to protect the capital, which I guarantee is where Gin will end up. I appreciate your perspective, but *with all due respect*, I defeated my brother once. I can defeat him again. We will do this my way."

The councilmembers held their tongues. She knew they didn't approve. They probably thought her inexperience was leading her to act rashly. *But the old guard's way isn't working*, Aki thought. *Gin certainly isn't following the old rule book.*

"Actually," she said, "have this message posted at the harbor for my brother: I would like to meet with him in neutral territory where there is nothing to tempt him—let's say, Dassu Desert—to discuss a cease-fire and peace treaty."

"He'll use his magic to hypnotize you," Glass Lady said.

Oh. Aki hadn't considered that. Now the Council really would think she was just plowing headlong into folly.

There was some scuffling beneath the floor of the black stone table. The councilmembers leaped to their feet, weapons trained on the source, while the Imperial Guard grabbed Aki and began shoving her toward the door to safety. Her heartbeat skittered.

"Don't hurt us!" a boy shouted, his voice muffled but loud, as if he were pressed right up against the floorboards. "It's Broomstick. And Fairy."

"What are you doing down there?" Scythe asked.

Glass Lady rolled her eyes. "Eavesdropping, I'd wager."

Bullfrog grumbled. "Like I said. Penchant for breaking rules."

The councilmembers muttered a spell that allowed them to heave the boards off the floor. Two apprentices climbed out, covered in dirt and coughing.

"Aren't you two already in enough trouble for Spirit's last stunt?" Glass Lady asked.

Broomstick screwed up his face. "Yes, Your Honor."

"And you thought it would be wise to tempt fate by crawling under the floorboards of the Council Room to eavesdrop on the most confidential of conversations?"

Fairy shrugged sheepishly. "It seemed like a good idea at the time?"

Glass Lady sighed. "Your Majesty, meet Broomstick and Fairy. They're two of your fireworks hooligans."

CHAPTER FORTY-ONE

Fairy and Broomstick laid themselves prostrate on the ground.

When they rose, Fairy said, "We're sorry for the, uh, intrusion."

"I suppose it's all right," Empress Aki said, as she returned to her seat. Her Imperial Guard remained close by. It almost made Fairy laugh out loud. *As if I'm a threat the Imperial Guard needs to protect her from.*

"We wanted to speak to you because we have an idea," Broomstick said.

Bullfrog grumbled. "Normal people with ideas to present come in through doors, not floorboards."

Fairy's tongue tripped over itself.

But then Empress Aki said, "Normal isn't working. You say you were part of the league of rogues who rigged the fireworks in my palace? Well then, I want to hear what you have to say. After all, we are dealing with my brother here. Some trickery is almost certainly afoot."

League of Rogues! Despite the gravity of the matter at hand, a grin spread across Fairy's face. Beside her, Broomstick did a better job of hiding his, although she could feel through their gemina bond his pleasure at being recognized by the empress as worth listening to.

"We heard you suggest a meeting with Prince Gin in Dassu Desert," Broomstick said, "but as Glass Lady mentioned, if you get close to him, he can hypnotize you and make you his puppet."

"That's right," Empress Aki said.

"But what's the purpose of the meeting?" Broomstick asked. "Do you really expect him to agree to a cease-fire? I'm guessing not. I think this is just a stall tactic to allow the taigas from around Kichona to centralize here, so we can fight Prince Gin with a bigger army, right?"

The empress smiled. "You have quite a head for political strategy for someone so young. I'm impressed." ·

Broomstick flushed. "Thank you, Your Majesty."

She nodded. "You're correct. Gin has no incentive to actually agree to peace, even a temporary one, when momentum is on his side. But I do think asking him to meet with me will buy us time. If only because he'll be tempted to stray from his current plans to try to hypnotize me. Or kill me."

Fairy trembled a little, knowing what was next in her plan. But being stuck here at the Citadel, unable to do anything while Spirit and Wolf were out there, was like being caught in a pixie trap. Fairy had been rattling the cage bars for days, wanting to get free, but those who had captured her had forgotten her because she was too small. She didn't want to be insignificant anymore.

She took a deep breath and said, "Which is where our

idea comes in. You may have noticed a resemblance between us. Not that I would ever claim to be as radiantly beautiful or intelligent or poised as you, Your Majesty," Fairy added hastily.

Empress Aki smiled gently. "There's no need for flattery. But yes, I do see a resemblance. If your hair were gold, you could pass for a younger version of me to someone who didn't know me well."

"Exactly. Let me go to this meeting in your place. Your brother hasn't seen you in ten years; it could work. And with enough Imperial Guards, maybe we have a chance of capturing your brother or . . ." Fairy stopped. She couldn't suggest killing the prince. Even though he was a traitor, talking about assassinating a member of the royal family was treason.

"It's all right," Empress Aki said. "This is war, and in war, there is always the possibility that someone will die. However, I cannot allow you to sacrifice yourself to save me."

Fairy walked all the way up to the edge of the Council table. "But Your Majesty, that is the purpose of the taigas. We serve you and the kingdom, whatever and however you need. You *must* stay alive and with your wits about you if Kichona is to survive Prince Gin's attacks. As one of your soldiers, it would be my honor to do this for you and our kingdom."

"Fairy . . ." Broomstick said.

"I won't change my mind." They had argued ferociously beneath the floorboards about this, muted by their moth spell. But she had prevailed then, and she would again now. Two of their best friends were out there, in danger. She wouldn't sit here at the Citadel any longer, doing nothing.

Broomstick slid his hand down her arm to her hand and squeezed it. "Then of course I'm going with you. And I won't change my mind either."

She squeezed his hand back.

Glass Lady opened her mouth to object. But Empress Aki held up her hand to silence her.

The empress looked at Fairy and Broomstick with grief already in her eyes. "This could be a suicide mission."

A quiver fluttered through Fairy's chest. But then she held Empress Aki's gaze for a moment, before laying herself prostrate again on the ground. "Like I said, Your Majesty. We serve you and Kichona. Whatever and however you need."

CHAPTER FORTY-TWO

As soon as Broomstick had a moment alone, he snuck into the dispatcher's office in Warrior Meeting Hall.

I can't believe we're doing this.

But of course he could. This was what they'd trained their whole lives for. Fairy had already been worried and itching to do something. And now the future of the kingdom was at stake. On top of that, their friends were out there. They knew from Wolf's dragonfly that Spirit had been captured.

Still, Broomstick's hands shook as he prepared the tiny scroll and composed a new message to Wolf. Hopefully he was still at Tiger's Belly and would receive it.

> *Wolf,*
> *Fairy and I are headed to Copper Bluff in Dassu Desert with Empress Aki for negotiations with Prince Gin.*
> *Please meet us there.*
> *—Broomstick*

He couldn't write the truth, that Fairy would be bait, masquerading as the empress. He couldn't risk the message being intercepted. But he needed Wolf there. It wasn't just for support. It was because, if there was going to be any way out of this, they'd need as many of their heads together as possible.

And they'd always said that if they were going to die, they wanted to die fighting together. All four of them.

Maybe it was better that Sora wouldn't be there. Maybe she would be spared.

Broomstick rolled up the miniature scroll and secured it to a dragonfly.

"Gods-speed," he said, as it dashed out the window to the Society outpost at Tiger's Belly. "Gods-speed to both you and Wolf."

CHAPTER FORTY-THREE

The pearlescent orange-and-black buildings along the Striped Coves' coastline glimmered in the midday sun. As the center of Kichona's tiger pearl industry, the ocean-side city was always bustling, full of diving outfits harvesting the gems, jewelers creating world-famous baubles, and wealthy trading companies taking the goods abroad and bringing back chests full of gold.

But rather than catch the city unawares, the ryuu found something was already waiting for them when their ship pulled into the harbor at the Striped Coves. An enormous wooden sign with a letter tacked to it. It was clearly marked in large script: "Prince Gin."

Hana leaned so far out over the railings to get a better look, she nearly fell over the edge.

"Virtuoso," Prince Gin said, as he strode to the gangplank. "Come with me."

As usual, he took his time. He was the one with the upper hand; he didn't need to rush. Hana matched her steps with his, practicing the gravity of power.

When they reached the sign, the prince charmed the letter to untack and open itself. It remained suspended in the air as they read it.

Dearest Brother,

What a surprise to find you have returned to Kichona.

I understand you have been poaching my taigas, to which I, of course, object. I have ordered the Society to take precautions and evacuate outposts you may be tempted to take possession of.

I also request that you cease and desist your activities, and that we meet for peace talks and negotiation. I am sure we can come to an acceptable compromise.

Please meet me at Copper Bluff in the Dassu Desert in three days' time. Bring only yourself and one warrior.

Your sister,

Aki

Prince Gin took a long, slow breath. When he'd finally exhaled, he said, "It seems my dear sister has figured out what we've been up to."

"It appears so, Your Highness," Hana said. "But it's not unexpected. You knew she'd catch on to your plans sooner or later."

"Yes, but I'd hoped to capture one or two more cities before we were discovered."

Prince Gin glanced at a small cage hanging from the bottom of the wooden sign. There was a dragonfly inside, presumably so he could respond to the Society. "They're still using these messengers," he said. "How quaint."

He quickly scrawled a note to Empress Aki, accepting her request for a meeting, and simply enchanted the scroll to fly itself to the Citadel, without the dragonfly.

"You're going to go?" Hana asked, mouth hanging open in disbelief.

"It's a trap. I'm sure of it," he said. "And yet, this would be a good opportunity to get Aki off the throne, away from all the witnesses in the Imperial City. Then I could take the crown without being seen as killing my own sister."

"You could have one of the ryuu do it, Your Highness. You'd avoid the risk of being ambushed yourself while still achieving your goals."

The prince's expression was uncharacteristically conflicted, his eyes shadowed and mouth turned down at the corners. Was it just that he was unsure of what to do next? Or was there something more that made him hesitate?

But then he nodded. "That's an excellent idea. Make it happen, Virtuoso."

Hana's breath caught. Crow's eye, she hadn't meant to volunteer herself. She didn't know if she could do it. Hana wanted Prince Gin on the throne, but his sister was still the ruler of the kingdom. Assassinating an empress with one's own hands was a very different thing than talking about someone else doing it. As much as she hated to admit it, Hana still respected the symbol of the throne, even if the person sitting on it was the wrong one.

But the relief in Prince Gin's expression—the way the creases around his eyes and the frown lines at his mouth smoothed at her suggestion—extinguished her doubts. Hana would get this done for him. Somehow.

Prince Gin looked again at his sister's message hovering

in the air. "Take Spirit with you. Two invisible ryuu are better than one. And it will be a good test of her abilities."

Great. Not only do I have to do the impossible, I have to do it with my sister.

But even as she told herself that, she knew she was starting to feel differently about Sora. And Hana reluctantly admitted that it was unreasonable to have expected her sister to come after her a decade ago. As Sora pointed out, they were children then. A bunch of eight-year-olds couldn't have commandeered a naval ship and sailed after the kidnapped tenderfoots. There was nothing they could have done differently during the Blood Rift.

Hana could try to forgive her. Or at least work with her, for Prince Gin's sake. There were many who were sacrificing more than their pride to move Kichona closer to the Evermore.

"Of course, Your Highness," she said. "Spirit and I will go to Dassu Desert, kill your sister, and bring her body back to you."

CHAPTER FORTY-FOUR

A diver emerged from the sea, climbing onto the rocky shores with a heavy net full of oysters. Sora stood on the cliff above the Striped Coves, watching one of Kichona's oldest trades. Pearl hunting was a family legacy, the expertise passed down from generation to generation. It took years of training to learn how to dive to depths of a hundred feet on a single breath alone, how to navigate the dark underwater caverns, how to identify the oysters with the most beautiful tiger pearls. She wondered how many centuries this diver's family had been hunting for the orange-and-black-striped jewels, and how they'd discovered them in the first place.

The man sat on the slick rock for a minute, letting the sun warm him as he filled his lungs with precious oxygen. His nearly naked body shimmered, coated in coconut oil to keep him warm beneath the surface. But if he knew Sora was there, he didn't care. Tourists often came to gawk at the process. One girl on the cliff wouldn't bother him.

Soon, he upended his net and dumped the oysters onto the rock. In one deft motion, he inserted a small knife into the shell, slid it around the edge, and popped the oyster open. He pressed on the soft mollusk inside, and a second later, a large pearl slipped out into his fingers.

"It's perfect," Sora whispered. With her hawkeye spell, she could see the famed orange and black stripes on it, gleaming even though the jewel was unpolished. The pearl was round too, not oval or lopsided, but an exact sphere. And it was nearly an inch in diameter.

The diver nodded to himself, as if approving, set the pearl on top of a small silk pouch to dry, and moved on to the other oysters in his net.

Daemon had spearheaded the Level 12 fund-raiser to buy Empress Aki a string of tiger pearls during Autumn Festival.

Sora startled at the thought. She'd almost forgotten her gemina existed, which was a horribly disloyal thing, since they'd been best friends for ages. Mortified, Sora latched onto the memory.

But as soon as she tried to hold it, it wriggled away, like an eel. She lunged for it again, but it began to fade, the memory swimming into the murky depths of her mind.

This had happened before, hadn't it? She'd remembered Daemon, but the thought had disappeared quickly, subsumed by something else.

She also felt strangely guilty for thinking about him. Or was it that cutting him off was wrong?

The diver shouted in alarm. Sora rushed to the edge of the cliff, her cloudy musings forgotten at the sound of someone needing help.

Three ryuu had suddenly appeared, riding on a wave. They were all women, and they surrounded him like sirens circling a stray sailor.

"Hello, handsome," one of the ryuu said. "Did you find some good pearls?"

The diver tried to take a step back, but he bumped into another of the women.

"Hey," she said, "Tidepool asked you a question. It's rude not to answer."

"W-what are you? Where did you come from?"

Tidepool smiled maliciously. "We're your darkest fantasies come true. And your nightmares."

The two other ryuu laughed and closed in on him. They put their hands on his chest and his back, holding him prisoner as they began to kiss his oiled skin.

"Stop!" Sora shouted from the cliff. "What do you think you're doing?"

"Leave them be," Prince Gin said, approaching behind Sora.

She fell to her knees and bowed. "Your Highness."

He gestured for her to rise. "The ryuu have been working hard. They deserve a little reward."

Sora frowned. She wanted to believe him, to agree with his words that warmed her like sweet wine, but something felt wrong. "They're forcing themselves on him."

Prince Gin shrugged. "And they'll kill him afterward. Those three have earned themselves the nickname 'the Black Widows.'"

"No . . ." Sora shook her head. Again, that sensation that she wasn't seeing the whole picture nagged at her. It was like that eel of Daemon's memory, lurking in the muddy water just out of reach.

"The diver is one of our people," Sora said. "I don't understand. Aren't we fighting so we can make all of Kichona happier?"

The ridges on Prince Gin's face tightened as he pursed his lips together. Was he thinking? Was he considering what Sora had said?

A few moments later, he grunted and walked to the edge of the cliff. "Black Widows," he said, "stop what you're doing." He didn't have to yell. Somehow, his voice just carried on the wind down to them.

Tidepool pouted. "Why? You've always allowed us playthings."

"That was in Shinowana. But this is our home country, and that diver is one of us. Save your appetites for the war abroad. Then you'll have free rein to do what you want. It won't be much longer that you have to wait."

The women grumbled but backed off the diver. They rode off on a wave Tidepool commanded.

"As for you," Prince Gin said to the diver, who stood shivering but immobile from his encounter with the Black Widows, "they didn't hurt you. Everything is all right. Yes?"

The man looked up in wonder. A smile broke across his face, and his body stopped trembling. "Your Highness. You've come home."

"I have."

The man nodded. "Then yes, everything is all right."

Prince Gin waved his hand, and the diver quickly

gathered his oysters and pearls and dove back into the sea, swimming in the direction of home.

"Is that better?" the prince said, turning to Sora.

She saw him as if through a haze of heat. At the same time, a swell of ambition and purpose washed through her, and she couldn't recall why she'd protested a minute ago. How silly to question the Dragon Prince. He knew what he was doing. He had Kichona's best interests at heart.

She looked down at the sleeve of her uniform, where the green triplicate whorls of the ryuu reflected the sunlight off the surface of the water. She smiled and traced the embroidery. So beautiful. Like pride and power woven straight into the threads.

"Yes, everything is better," Sora answered the prince.

"Good. Because I have a mission for you and Virtuoso."

"A mission? For Hana and me?" Happiness bubbled up inside Sora, like a cauldron of sweet tapioca soup, overflowing. The Dragon Prince wanted her to do something for him. And with her sister. What an embarrassment of riches!

"That's the kind of enthusiasm I like. You'll have to pack quickly. I need you to leave within the hour."

Sora didn't care. She would have left yesterday if she could.

"What's our mission?" she asked.

Prince Gin looked at the ground and kicked a rock over the cliff's edge. "You're going to assassinate the empress."

Sora nodded. "It's time the empress's rule was put to an end."

"This is the most important task right now," he said. "Are you ready for it?"

She could hardly wait to run back to the ship, grab her

things, and go. She had to put her palms on her legs to force herself to stand in place for just another minute, to have some dignity in front of the Dragon Prince.

"Yes, Your Highness," Sora said. "I'm more than ready."

CHAPTER FORTY-FIVE

Sora tore through the treetops, chasing after Hana, who sprang from branch to branch as if she'd been born a panther. "You call that fast? I call it pitiful," Hana yelled, only half teasing as she darted into a hole between cypress branches and emerged several tiers below.

Sora concentrated even harder. It wasn't that her legs were too slow. It was that she wasn't completely accustomed yet to the way ryuu saw the world, everything brighter and sharper, as if she'd been myopic before and had only now discovered this marvelous invention called spectacles.

Of course, there were no spectacles, not real ones. And yet the world was new. Besides the omnipresent emerald specks of magic in the air, there were smaller things that surprised Sora. Being able to see a faint green path through the seemingly chaotic mess of forest, for instance. Hana was beating her right now because she not only saw the path between trunks and jagged branches clearly; she also trusted it. Sora had the vision but had not yet acquired the trust to fling herself headlong toward wherever the magic directed her.

She caught up to Hana only when they reached Ao Hills, their stop for the evening. It was another two days to Copper Bluff. Perhaps less, considering ryuu speed.

Sora dropped to the dry grass on the ground. Hana was already roasting a fox she'd somehow caught and skinned in the time it took for Sora to arrive. The blond pelt had been cast aside.

How do I talk to her? Sora wondered. Hana had spoken little since they'd left the Striped Coves. Besides confirming that they were going to kill the empress, Hana hadn't given any more details. Not how they were going to do this or where they were going. Sora wasn't even sure if it was progress in their reconciliation that Hana had agreed to the mission, or if it was just following Prince Gin's orders.

Maybe I'm thinking about this the wrong way. I'm focusing on me. I should think about her.

Maybe the best way to start a conversation would be to appeal to what Hana was most proud of—her ryuuness.

"I'm hesitant to hurl myself through the trees, even though the path is obvious," Sora said. "I only hope I can be as good with the magic someday as you are. How do you do it?"

Hana didn't say anything for a few minutes. Sora let her turn the spit in silence, with only the crackling flames to interrupt.

"You're slow because you're afraid of crashing into a trunk or not being able to fit through a crooked opening between trees," Hana finally said. She didn't look away from the flames as she spoke. "But the magic won't steer you wrong. If you let yourself go and have faith in it, it'll work."

The fox meat suddenly caught on fire. "Crow's eyes!" Hana cursed.

For a moment, Sora found a tiny spark of joy that her little sister still favored the swearwords that Sora had always liked, the ones she used to tell Hana she was too young to use. Sora grabbed a dead branch and used its leaves to slap at the flames on the meat.

The fire snuffed out, leaving a charred carcass on the spit.

Hana's fierce exterior broke, and she looked young all of a sudden, not the hard Virtuoso she usually liked to be.

Oh, stinkbug, Sora thought. She wanted to gather her sister in her arms. But it was too soon for that.

"We can scrape off the burnt part," Sora said. "I'm sure the meat underneath is still edible."

"I'm not hungry," Hana said. She pouted at the other supplies they'd brought. A jumble of poles and canvas leaped to attention and assembled itself, magically, of course, into a tent in less time than it had taken for Sora to put the fox fire out.

Sora smiled. There was pride in watching your little sister surpass your abilities. Even if it stung a little.

She left Hana alone to let out her frustration. If this was anything like the tantrums she used to throw when she was a tenderfoot, Hana would run out of steam in a few minutes. Sora turned back to the smoldering remains of the fire, the embers still popping in the remnants of the wood.

As she sat there watching the smoke curling into the sky, though, a dull headache took root. It wasn't sharp, but more like a constant thrum or a quiet drumbeat at the back of her skull. The rhythm was so well established, it was as if it had been there for a long while. There was also something strangely familiar about it.

What was it?

The mild throb continued, slow and steady. For some reason, it reminded Sora of being asleep, on the cusp of waking.

Thump. Thump. Thump. Like muffled knocking on a door. *Thump. Thump. Thump.*

Oh. Sora sat up and pressed her hand to the back of her head. She could practically feel the beat in her fingers.

Her gemina bond.

The drumming felt like Daemon pushing gently against her mental ramparts on weekend mornings when she slept in, trying to wake her so they could go to the sparring ring. Is that what this was now? Daemon trying to get her attention.

She hadn't thought about him much recently, just occasional bursts now and then that quickly faded away because she'd been moving nonstop since becoming a ryuu. But now the balance in her mind felt off. Sora's feelings weren't supposed to be alone; Daemon's were their companion, rounding Sora out to make her whole.

She missed the sensation of his laugh, that feeling like a field of wildflowers had all bloomed at once. She craved the smirk of his jokes. She even wanted the way his emotions leaned on her when he felt insecure.

Sora moved to lower her mental ramparts.

Immediately, though, the warm tide of her promise to

Prince Gin rushed in, washing away her yearning for Daemon like a wave erases marks in the sand. *You've outgrown him*, it seemed to remind her.

Yes, she thought, as the heat of ryuu conviction flowed through her, renewed. Sora's commitment to the Dragon Prince was the only gemina she needed now. The thrumming in Sora's head faded until it was nearly inaudible. Merely distant background noise.

Sora settled back into her spot in front of the campfire. She remembered her sister, and looked over at where Hana stood by the tents, arms crossed, still huffing.

Hana had been too talented for her own good, in some respects. Among the ryuu, she was always the best, and she was unofficially Prince Gin's second in command, even though she was only sixteen. Because of all her early success, she didn't deal well with failure. Being less than perfect seemed to bother her, even if it was something as inconsequential as burning dinner.

"Hey," Sora said gently, "come back and eat. It's not bad at all once the char is scraped off. I promise." She held out a chunk of meat skewered on a twig.

Her sister crossed her arms and huffed. But a minute later, she came back to the fire and accepted the offering. She took a bite.

"See?" Sora said.

Hana grumbled. "It's all right."

They devoured the entire fox—learning new magic made Sora even hungrier than usual—and licked their fingers when they were done. With bellies full, Hana relaxed a little, leaning back against a log.

"Is it a secret, where we're going?" Sora asked, careful

not to sound accusatory. "I only ask because you're doing everything on your own right now, but I could contribute if you told me how."

Hana nudged a twig into the fire. The flames crackled.

"I can't let the prince down," she said, rubbing her face with her hands. "But I . . . gods, this is stupid."

Sora scooted closer to her. "Nothing's stupid. Tell me, and we'll fix it."

"I drn rahr ri I cah rii rit," she mumbled straight into her hands.

"Didn't get that," Sora said.

Hana ripped her hands away and glared at her. "I don't know if I can do it, okay?" she shouted. "I hate Empress Aki. But that doesn't mean I can kill her. She's the gods-damn empress. I mean . . . as ryuu, we're trained to protect the Dragon Prince. Yet that somehow gets twisted in my head, and I get stuck on the idea that I should protect—not hurt—the current ruler. Oh gods, it makes no sense. Please don't tell anyone. I swear, I'm one hundred percent loyal to Prince Gin."

Sora dared to wrap her arm around Hana. And to her surprise, Hana tucked her head into the crook of Sora's neck, just like she used to do when they were little.

Her sister's doubt about carrying out this mission made sense too. The Society was built on a rigid hierarchy, and even though Hana had been there for only a short time, her mind had always operated well under that kind of order. She'd looked up to Sora not only because she was her older sister but also because Sora outranked her. It was the same reason Hana went stomping around and barking at the ryuu now. She outranked them, and she felt compelled to remind everyone of it.

The problem, however, was when Hana was asked to disrespect someone higher up in the chain. Like the empress.

"What kind of ryuu am I, if I can't even help Prince Gin with the most crucial first part of his plan?" Hana asked. But then she sighed and said, "You wouldn't understand. You're under the prince's spell."

"Huh?" What was Hana talking about?

"Never mind."

"But I don't understand."

"It's, um, not important," Hana said. "What *is* important is that Prince Gin needs us to take Empress Aki out of the picture, so that he can claim the throne. He *ordered* us to do this."

The warm tide coursed through Sora's body again. It was like a kiss of heat that began in her heart, then spread down her spine, through her limbs, to the very tips of her fingers and toes. She smiled and nodded. "I can kill her."

Hana sat back up. "What?"

"I understand what you're going through. It's possible to believe in a cause but still have trouble doing what you're supposed to do. That was my life story in the Society, remember?"

"You did have a hard time following their rules."

"Yeah," Sora said. "So I understand how you feel. You want Prince Gin to be emperor, but that doesn't mean it's easy to carry out what he's asked you to do. I have no qualms, though." The warmth had become a self-assured blaze inside her now. "If you can take out the Imperial Guards at Copper Bluff, I'll take care of assassinating the empress. I'll do it so you don't have to."

Hana looked like she might cry, but it was a happy sheen of tears over her eyes. "You'd really do that? Even after I was nasty to you?"

"I'm your sister. Anything within my power, I'd do for you."

Hana laughed dismissively, but she nestled her head back into the crook of Sora's neck.

Sora brought her in more tightly and buried her nose in Hana's hair. She smelled of dirt and sweat, but Sora didn't mind. She had thought her little sister was gone forever. But here she was, alive and in her arms.

I will never lose you again.

CHAPTER FORTY-SIX

Daemon wiped the sweat from where it dripped off his soaked headband. He'd gotten Broomstick's dragon-fly, and he was on his way to meet them.

The desert was brutally unforgiving. Daemon wore a straw hat, but he'd also tied a cloth around his hairline to keep the inevitable additional sweat out of his eyes. And yet it trickled through anyway, first a few droplets, and now a steady stream. It was nothing short of blistering here.

Disappointingly, he hadn't found anything in the Tiger's Belly library to explain his immunity to Prince Gin's charm. The closest thing was an ancient legend about a taiga who had allowed himself to be possessed by a demon named Dassu. Dassu combined taiga magic with devilfire and tried to bring the hells to earth by magically torching Kichona. He managed to burn down a large part of the center of the island before the gods found out (they did not pay much attention to the daily lives of humans, as a general matter). Luna was livid that the magic she'd granted to the taigas had been distorted. So she smothered him, suffocating both the warrior and Dassu inside.

Daemon had shuddered when he finished reading the story. *I really hope I'm not the spawn of the devil*, he'd thought. He didn't want Luna to smother him for being able to do more than what a taiga was usually able to do. Maybe there *was* an argument for not being special.

He shuddered again now as he rode through Dassu Desert, named after the old legend that had otherwise been forgotten.

After two days of travel, Daemon finally arrived at a reddish brown plateau that shimmered under the sun, the only rise in the flat topography of the desert. He cried out at the sight of it and sagged forward in his saddle, nearly falling off his horse out of both exhaustion and relief. Empress Aki had chosen an oasis in which to conduct her negotiations with Prince Gin. As soon as Daemon got above the scorching sand, the temperature dropped twenty degrees. Acacia trees provided ample shade, and a sprawling watering hole sparkled like a pale sapphire in the midst of it.

"Halt!" an Imperial Guard shouted at Daemon's approach. "Identify yourself!"

I guess I don't get to fall off my horse quite yet, Daemon thought.

He held both hands in the air to show he had no weapons. "I am Wolf, Level Twelve apprentice, here to join your forces."

"Dismount. Slowly."

Daemon followed the directions, keeping his hands in clear view.

The Imperial Guard studied him carefully.

"Wolfie! What are you doing here?" Fairy sprinted past the Imperial Guard and hurled herself at Daemon.

"Oomph," he said, as he caught her against his chest. She was tiny, but she definitely made an impact.

"I take it you know this apprentice," the Imperial Guard said.

"Yes. I verify that this is Wolf." Fairy gave the taiga one of her dazzling smiles.

The warrior ran his hand through his hair almost sheepishly. Her smile tended to have that effect on whomever she trained it, sending the recipient into a temporary daze. Daemon couldn't help a small laugh.

The Imperial Guard gave Daemon a final once-over, then left them alone.

Fairy buried her face back into his chest and clutched him harder. "Am I glad to see you."

"Same," Daemon said. He closed his eyes. Even here in the middle of the desert, Fairy's hair managed to smell like plums and sweet cream. He didn't know how she did it, but he was glad for the familiar comfort. Also, he was happy to let her hold him for a minute, because he really was about to fall over.

"Wolf," a boy said. "Pleased you could join us."

Daemon opened his eyes. Broomstick stood before him, a crooked, if somewhat solemn, grin on his face.

Fairy released Daemon.

"Did you ask him to come?" she asked Broomstick.

"We need him."

Daemon and Broomstick slapped each other on the back. "I'm rather pleased to join you too," Daemon said. "Although what would really make me happy right now is some cold water. And a spot in the shade to lie down for a bit."

"Maybe I could lie down with you," Fairy said, winking.

Daemon laughed. "I've missed you."

She faked a pout, but quickly dropped it and laughed too. "I had to try."

"I do love your persistence."

"It might be my last chance." There was an unexpected seriousness in her voice.

Daemon frowned. "What do you mean?"

Broomstick slapped him on the back again. "Don't listen to her. We'll catch up in a little while. But let's get you some water first."

Daemon watched Fairy for a few seconds more before he shook his bleary head. "Right, water. Also, I need to report to the empress about everything I saw firsthand about her brother. I could only fit a fraction of it on my message."

Fairy kicked at the sand. "About that . . ."

"No," Broomstick said. "Let him rest for a bit. Wolf is about to keel over." He tried to steer Daemon toward the oasis.

Daemon anchored himself to the ground and crossed his arms. "What are you keeping from me?" There was something about Fairy that seemed different, but he couldn't put his finger on it. Dehydration and the heat made thinking difficult.

She walked up to him, put both hands on his shoulder, and pulled him down so she could whisper in his ear. For a moment, he was taken again by the sweet smell of her hair.

But then she said quietly, "Empress Aki didn't come. If she did, she might die or be subjected to Prince Gin's magic."

"So then . . ."

Oh gods. Fairy had always been the prettiest of the Level 12s and this wasn't the first time her resemblance to the empress had been noticed. Fairy smelled so good now because she wasn't here as a warrior.

And her hair was dyed gold.

Daemon's stomach sank into the blistering sand. Stars, how had he not noticed her hair? Was he really that exhausted?

"You're here as a decoy for the empress, aren't you?" he asked weakly.

"I'm not supposed to be out here," she said. "I'm supposed to stay in the tent. But it's boring in there, just books and makeup. There aren't even any boys to play with. You'd think that, as empress, I could at least get my own harem of strapping young men. Especially if I'm about to die."

Daemon gaped. "How can you joke about that?"

Fairy shrugged, but it wasn't as casual as she hoped it would look. "Besides trying to convince myself that dying for Kichona really is an honor, joking about it is all I can do. Help me by not moping over it, all right?"

He swallowed the lump in his throat and nodded. He saw her in a different light now, and it wasn't just the desert sun. She held herself taller, those birdlike shoulders more eagle than sparrow. Her lips had a determined set to them too, which was somehow more entrancing than the normal pink pout that all the other boys wanted. And that flash of vulnerability in her eyes made her more real. In the past, Fairy had been almost all show. Now she was courageous but also afraid, and that made her not merely pretty, but beautiful.

Daemon had known Fairy was strong, but offering herself as a decoy for the empress, risking almost certain death, was a magnitude of devotion and duty many could claim to possess, but only a rare few actually did.

"Don't worry," he said to Fairy. "We're not going to let the Dragon Prince capture or kill you, if we can help it. He's already taken Sora. We're not going down without a fight."

"Thank you." Fairy wrapped her arms around Daemon and leaned heavily against his chest.

It was his turn to hold *her* up.

That evening, Daemon paced the edge of the bluff, keeping watch as the wind made the sand ripple like an ocean. Prince Gin and his ryuu were coming. He could feel it, even though his gemina connection with Sora was silent, and even though the Imperial Guard lookouts hadn't seen movement on the desert floor below.

There was a small chance that the Dragon Prince would actually want to negotiate with Empress Aki. If that was the case, the taigas hoped that Fairy resembled the empress enough that the decade that had passed since the Blood Rift would be explanation for the changes in her appearance. Then the burden would be on Fairy's acting skills. Empress Aki had given her a crash course in her mannerisms and, more important, on terms that were acceptable for a temporary cease-fire.

But honestly, the chance of that happening was very, very slim, and Daemon and the others here were just buying a little more time for the Society to move the rest of its warriors into place to prepare for a showdown in the Imperial

City. Most likely, the Dragon Prince was going to kill his sister. Why leave her alive if he could take over the kingdom in one fell swoop?

Daemon stopped on the southern part of the plateau.

Fairy could die. And the rest of the taigas here—maybe me too—could be brainwashed puppets. Very soon.

The Society had sent only thirty taigas to Copper Bluff. The Council and most of the Imperial Guards remained in the capital to protect the real empress. They had sent just enough of a contingent to look believable that Fairy was Empress Aki, yet not too many that Prince Gin would find a windfall of taigas to bring to his side.

Daemon's stomach curled into a ball and cowered.

We are sacrificing ourselves for the sake of the kingdom.

Broomstick stepped up beside him, glanced over, and put his fists over his heart. No words were necessary.

Daemon nodded and mirrored the gesture.

They were sacrifices. But they would go down fighting.

CHAPTER FORTY-SEVEN

On the third day after the dragonfly message at the Striped Coves, a dozen Imperial Guards stood outside Empress Aki's tent in Dassu Desert. Another dozen patrolled a bit farther out, like an orbit around the empress, and a handful more kept watch still farther out along the edges of Copper Bluff, looking for the approach of the Dragon Prince's army.

Sora and Hana had made themselves invisible on the climb up to the plateau, commanding the ryuu particles to sweep away their footprints in the sand along the way. Now they were at the very edge. The Imperial Guards couldn't see them, and so they remained standing in their places, vigilant but relaxed. Hana would create a diversion and take care of the guards here and the others who would charge in from the outer parts of the plateau. Sora would take advantage of the distraction and execute the empress.

As soon as they summited the bluff, Sora made to sprint to the tent.

Hana grabbed her by the wrist. "Hold on, you're being

297

sloppy. You're—" She dropped Sora's wrist like it had scalded her. "You're burning up!"

Sora grinned as she nodded. Every cell inside of her seemed to be on fire. She could hardly think straight. Everything in her head was an accelerated, blurry swirl. It was a fever, but not the kind that would confine her to bed—this was a fever of anticipation.

"I'm going to garrote the empress with her own gold hair. But before that, I'm going to tell her all the things we're going to do once Prince Gin is emperor. All the ways he's going to dismantle her kingdom and rebuild it. All the glory we'll achieve. She tried to prevent us from making Kichona into an empire and paradise, but the joke's on her—she'll die and we'll still get the Evermore."

Hana's eyes were as big as Autumn Festival cakes. "Um . . . okay."

Sora blinked at her, confused. "You don't want me to make the empress suffer?"

"No, yes, I mean . . . just don't take too long doing it. More time means more opportunity to mess up. The most important thing is that Empress Aki dies."

Sora grinned again, the flame growing inside as she thought about carrying out the Dragon Prince's orders. "I can do that."

Hana watched her for another minute before nodding. "All right. Remember the objective. Don't lose your head. Let's go."

They sneaked closer to Empress Aki's tent, pausing as necessary to weave between the Imperial Guards on patrol. When they were fifty yards away, a servant walked out of the tent. She held the flap open for a moment as she talked to one of the nearby guards.

Sora glanced at Hana.

"Good luck," Hana whispered.

"I don't need luck." Sora winked.

The servant finished her conversation and was leaving to fetch something. Sora darted for the tent.

She slipped inside just as the flap swung shut.

CHAPTER FORTY-EIGHT

Fairy's tent—actually, the empress's—was expansive, as befitting royalty. Flickering candles in glass pyramids hung from the ceiling, lighting the main room with their soft glow. A plush sofa took up one of the far corners of the tent, its blue silk upholstery hemmed in gold, several fluffy pillows positioned at the armrests. There was a dining area, with a low table and comfortable cushions on the floor, and the entire tent was perfumed with the sweetness of sparkling rose-apple sidra. It was an expensive luxury from the north of Kichona, and if Fairy was going to die masquerading as the empress, she might as well enjoy these last moments as if she really were royalty.

In the back of the tent, in a portion partitioned off by a heavy velvet curtain, Fairy sipped on the sidra while sitting at the empress's vanity. Her gold hair was done in curls and braids, and her gown flowed elegantly to the carpeted ground. It was the prettiest she'd ever looked, but she didn't preen as she might've before. Instead, she wore the clothes with a mixture of dread and pride. Dread, because she was all dolled up for her funeral. Pride, because she'd volunteered for this.

Broomstick and Wolf lounged on a couple of armchairs. The Imperial Guards were outside, patrolling the bluff and protecting all sides of the tent.

"You don't have to stay here with me," Fairy said, as she painted eyeliner in dramatic wings like the empress wore. "In fact, you should really get as far away as possible from this tent. The closer you are, the more likely you'll die when the ryuu come for me." Her hands shook, and the eyeliner went a bit jagged.

"I'm not leaving your side," Broomstick said. He fiddled with a new kind of fuse he'd been working on. The taiga weapons masters were always looking to improve the Society's arsenal, and Broomstick had offered to help with developing a new smoke bomb. But his hands were shaking too. Their entire gemina bond was.

Wolf polished his sword furiously. It was already as shiny as a mirror. "You've been insisting that we leave since I got here—and probably before that—but stop. We're not going to let you die. Or if you do, we're going to die with you."

Fairy's eyes welled with tears, and she stopped trying to fix her crooked makeup. Maybe it was selfish, but if this was the end, she really did want her friends by her side. She nodded, unable to say anything.

"Do you think they're close?" Broomstick asked. None of them believed Prince Gin would follow instructions and send only two ryuu.

She dabbed away her tears—the eyeliner was a mess now, but who cared—and said, "The Imperial Guards will sound the alarm once they see the ryuu approach."

"We still need to be on alert," Wolf said, staring intently at the velvet curtain. "The ryuu aren't like ordinary soldiers. Once they arrive, we might not have much notice. They could just blow in here like a sandstorm. Or an actual sandstorm."

They didn't say anything for a moment. Fairy put the eyeliner away and pushed around the other makeup in the cherrywood box but didn't apply anything else. Broomstick pretended to concentrate on his fuse. Wolf kept polishing his sword with such ferocity, it was as if he were trying to grind it into a different, smaller blade.

Everything was quiet.

Too quiet.

Fairy started to hum an Autumn Festival song to fill the silence. It was about a poor farmer whose wheat had not grown, and his neighbors who brought him gifts of bread and new seeds to help.

The velvet curtain behind her lifted. A familiar voice interrupted her song.

"Hello, Your Majesty."

It was Spirit.

Fairy's heart leaped. In the same instant, though, horror suffocated her hope as she processed the sadistic bite in Spirit's tone. She must be under the Dragon Prince's spell.

"Stop! I'm not—" But before Fairy could finish, she was yanked out of her seat and put in a headlock. A knife pressed against her throat, although there was no visible arm to hold it. Fairy tried to cry out, but the pressure on her neck had disabled her voice box.

"Freeze, Sora!" Wolf shouted, as he and Broomstick jumped up from their chairs.

The arm around Fairy's neck materialized. If she'd been able to, she would have gasped. Spirit had been invisible.

"Daemon? Broomstick?" Spirit said, confused.

"What are you doing here?" Wolf asked.

"I'm here to kill the empress." Her voice was fire, not like the same kind of flame it usually was. This was hot in a zealous kind of way, like a forest fire on a rampage.

Fairy tried to jab her with her elbow, but Spirit just tightened her grip.

"Prince Gin hypnotized you," Wolf said. "You'll do whatever he says."

"Shut up," Spirit said, jerking Fairy against her body. "I'm my own person. I do what I want, and what I want is to help Prince Gin usher Kichona into an age of glory. And then, if we succeed, Kichona will become a paradise, and we will be immortal."

Broomstick took a cautious step closer, at the same time giving Fairy a warning look not to struggle, because their friend was unpredictable. "That's just a myth, Spirit," he said gently. "It's not real."

"It *is* real. We just haven't achieved it yet because there hasn't been a warrior worthy of turning Kichona into the vast empire Zomuri wanted. But now we have Prince Gin, and he'll do it. He's already pushed magic beyond what taigas have known for centuries. He'll push our kingdom beyond what we know too. He'll make the Evermore real."

"Sora . . ." Wolf said, taking a step closer.

"Shall I slit the empress's artery and kill her right away,

or slice her in a hundred different, shallow places and let her bleed slowly to death before your eyes?"

"Spirit," Fairy said. Or, she tried to say it, but her roommate's chokehold was tight, and she could barely get out a whisper.

"I don't want to hear from you," Spirit said. The tip of her knife pierced Fairy's skin.

"You're hurting her!" Broomstick said. "That's—"

But Wolf had unhooked his bo. He lunged at Spirit, trying to reach her around Fairy.

Spirit dodged. She threw Fairy into the air, and somehow, Fairy remained floating there, where no one could reach her. A strip of her dress tore itself off and gagged her.

Broomstick gawked.

"Try to get her down!" Wolf instructed him.

Meanwhile, Spirit drew her sword and advanced on Wolf with rapid slashes.

He spun his bo up, down, left, and right, to block the blows. "You're not yourself, Sora. Think hard. Remember Kaede City? Do you remember what happened to the taigas there?"

"I remember wanting to join Prince Gin." She faltered. "And . . . you prevented me!" In anger, she rushed at Wolf.

He thrust the end of his bo into Spirit's stomach. It forced the air out of her, and she doubled over.

Spirit recovered and swung her sword at the bo. Wolf shifted its angle at the last second and caught the blade in a nick in the wood. He twirled the bo, which wrenched the sword from Spirit's hand.

"I don't even know why I'm fighting you," she said, her voice full of frigid disdain. "It's the empress that matters."

She unsheathed a knife from her sleeve and aimed it up to the tent's ceiling. She pulled back her arm to throw.

Fairy saw her entire life in a split second. The faint memory of being a tenderfoot, waking up each morning in the nursery, where it always smelled of warm milk and tea biscuits. The night they became Level 1 apprentices, when Luna's moonbeams lit up the grassy amphitheater, and the triplicate whorls on Fairy's and Broomstick's backs glowed at the same moment, bonding them as geminas. The first day of chemistry class when she was thirteen, when she discovered her love for botanicals and potions. All the nights she stayed up late with Spirit, laughing over a prank they'd pulled or rehashing Fairy's latest boy-conquering escapades.

It had been a good life. And it would be a noble ending.

Fairy closed her eyes and waited for the knife.

CHAPTER FORTY-NINE

No!" Daemon jumped at Sora. The air around him crackled, as if charged with electricity. He tackled her, and as soon as they collided, a jolt blasted through Sora's body.

She lay flat on her back, the wind knocked out of her. The knife fell out of her hand. Daemon kept her pinned.

And all his fear gushed through their gemina bond, like a dam that had burst. It swept over Sora, and for a moment, she was completely submerged in the whirlpool of his terror that she would kill the empress, that he would hurt Sora, and that Sora was irretrievably lost.

Suddenly, Sora's vision turned blue with bright light. The sensation was vaguely familiar, as if it had happened before. It whipped at her skull like a lash of lightning. The brightness reached inside, targeting her love of Prince Gin, trying to rip away the roots of it in her mind.

She tried desperately to hold on. The instinct to fight was so strong.

Daemon's emotion didn't relent. When Sora grabbed

onto a tendril of her loyalty to the Dragon Prince, a lasso of blue sparks yanked it away. Her mind tried again, and again, holding on to each root, and yet each time, the light in their gemina bond wrenched the tendril out of her brain.

And then the dedication to Prince Gin was gone, all the porridgy mush and cloudy, unquestioning bliss, cleaned out completely.

But Sora didn't feel empty. Daemon was here.

On top of her.

"Hello," she whispered. It was all she could manage as she tried to sort out what it was she was feeling. She wanted to flip him off her, as if they were sparring. She also wanted to hug him, because all their time apart fell on her in an avalanche, and she missed him like she missed breathing. And then there was his closeness, both physically and through their gemina bond, that overwhelmed her and made her feel like she was drowning again.

He looked her intensely in the eyes. "Is it you? Did I really break the spell again?"

Sora nodded, still trying to breathe and recover from his tackle.

Then it began to sink in. She had been about to kill the empress. Holy heavens. Horror washed over Sora, and she just let herself go limp on the ground. "The Dragon Prince. I . . . He . . . I didn't know what I was doing."

"I know."

"I'm sorry. So incredibly sorry."

Daemon climbed off her. "It's okay. You're you again. Everything is all right now."

It wasn't, though. At that moment, the ryuu particles in the tent began to vibrate, as if trying to contain their excitement but unable to. And the magic closer to the tent's entrance was actually bouncing off itself, reacting like magnetic waves near a ryuu.

Hana was right outside. She must be nearly finished fighting the Imperial Guards. She'd be inside any minute.

Sora felt paralyzed. What was she supposed to do? If Hana saw Daemon and Broomstick, she'd think they were getting in Sora's way, and she would kill them. Prince Gin wasn't here; there was no one to charm taigas to join the ryuu. So Hana had been executing the taigas outside one by one.

But if Sora protected Daemon and Broomstick, then Hana would know that the spell had been broken. Sora would be the enemy again. And that would mean losing the inroads they'd made in their reconciliation.

And there was another thing. Sora had promised her mother that she'd be the best person she could, because Hana hadn't had the opportunity to. Well, now her sister *did* have the chance. She was one of the original ryuu, so she hadn't needed to be enchanted to follow Prince Gin. Which meant Sora could possibly get through to her and convince her that the goals Prince Gin and the ryuu aspired to were wrong. Hana had had her future stolen from her by the Dragon Prince. She deserved to get it back.

Sora made her decision. It was inelegant, but it was the only way to save everyone she loved.

"I'm sorry," she said to Broomstick. She grabbed Daemon's bo and whacked Broomstick in the back of the head. He slumped to the carpeted floor.

Daemon gaped, not understanding what had suddenly

changed—again—in Sora. But he had daggers in both hands, poised to fight.

"I don't have time to explain," Sora said. "But you have to trust me." She commanded the ryuu particles to knock him unconscious. He sprawled out across the floor.

Hana pushed through the tent flaps, just as Sora caught the empress's body in her arms. She held her in a headlock again, Empress Aki's back pressed against Sora's chest.

"Stay quiet," Sora whispered so quietly, her words almost got lost in the swirls of the empress's gold hair. "I have to pretend to kill you right now. If I don't, my sister will do it for real in about thirty seconds."

She reached for the tiny, hidden pocket sewn into the inside of her collar and retrieved the pink rira disk that was meant to be Sora's way out if things went awry. She broke off half of it and crammed it in Empress Aki's mouth.

"This much won't kill you, but it'll slow your vital systems to the point of seeming like you're dead. You'll wake up in about a week, maybe less. Understand?"

The empress nodded her head but didn't say anything. Thank the gods.

"Good, now swallow it."

Empress Aki did as she was told.

"Are you taking your time torturing her to death, or what?" Hana asked. Her voice grew nearer. From the sound of it, she was halfway across the tent, although she hesitated in the middle, as if debating whether she could actually watch the assassination she couldn't execute herself.

The rira would hit the empress's bloodstream soon, but Sora still needed an explanation for why there wouldn't be a visible garrote wound across her throat. She'd have to make a show of the empress's death for Hana to witness.

I'm sorry for what I'm about to do, she said silently to Empress Aki.

Sora wrapped her left hand around her throat. The feel of the empress's fragile neck sickened Sora.

But this was what she had to do to save the kingdom.

Sora tightened her fingers. Empress Aki let out a frantic, gurgling cry. Tears formed in Sora's eyes. She held the leader of Kichona's life in her hands.

The velvet curtain flew open, revealing Hana on the other side.

Empress Aki gave a final, weak writhe against Sora's grasp. Then she went limp as Sora pushed on a pressure point while pretending to snap her neck.

Sora swallowed the nausea cresting inside her and dropped Empress Aki down to the ground. She slumped like a sack of rice.

"What took you so long?" Hana asked. "I dispatched thirty taigas out there, while you took care of . . . two?" She kicked Daemon's side. Luckily, he and Broomstick were both facedown. Not that Hana would have recognized them after the decade that had passed since she saw them last, but still. Sora exhaled a little in relief.

"I was savoring the moment," Sora said. She narrowed her eyes and smiled, as if wickedly gleeful at her victory, as a ryuu would be. "I told her all the things Prince Gin is going to do for Kichona. All the things that will change once she's dead."

That made Hana smile too.

And it made Sora angry. Angry that her sister had been

raised to believe in Prince Gin's greedy goals. Angry that she had been molded from a sweet little girl into a bloodthirsty one. Angry that they were on opposite sides of this war.

But I will fix this, Sora swore. She would go back with Hana to the ryuu and work on swaying her away from the Dragon Prince while they marched toward the Imperial City. And then when they were close, she and Hana would break away and rejoin the taigas at the Citadel. They knew a lot about the ryuu; Hana probably knew of weaknesses the Society could exploit.

They would be the Teira sister team, but on the side of good. As it was supposed to be.

"Well, there's nothing left to do here," Hana said. "I guess we have to get the empress's body back to Prince Gin now."

She hesitated, though.

She's still having trouble with the idea of the empress being murdered, Sora thought. Which boded well for Sora's hopes of persuading Hana away from the Dragon Prince's side.

"I'll take care of the body," Sora said.

Hana smiled bravely. "Thank you. I'll, um, wait for you outside."

As she left the tent, Sora stooped to pick up Empress Aki. It was the first time she looked at her face-to-face.

Oh gods. It wasn't the empress. It was Fairy in disguise.

If it hadn't been for Daemon's strange ability to shock Sora out of Prince Gin's spell, she would have killed Fairy, thinking she was the empress. Actually, she would have killed Daemon and Broomstick too, when they tried to defend Fairy.

"Stars," Sora whispered, falling to her hands and knees.

Prince Gin's ability to brainwash everyone he came across was terrifying. *He told us to stop at nothing. He told us bloodshed was good. I . . . I would have murdered my best friends.*

She saw clearly now what he could do when he had control of every magical warrior in Kichona and took them across the sea to ravage the mainland. They would be a tsunami of death, ruination with no mercy.

Sora doubled over and vomited onto the floor.

CHAPTER FIFTY

Daemon came to shortly after Sora was gone. He shook Broomstick lightly to wake him. There were a hundred thoughts racing through Daemon's head, but the first—and most important—one was:

"Fairy."

He jumped to his feet, but she was nowhere to be found.

"She was right here," he said.

Broomstick shoved through the velvet curtain and began overturning everything in the tent. "Fairy! Where are you?"

"They took her," Daemon said, running past Broomstick. He stopped short as he burst out of the tent.

Imperial Guards. Some on the ground. Some suspended upright, as if held up by invisible string. Pools of blood, coagulating and sticky and already attracting flies with their iron tang.

And every single warrior was missing body parts—arms,

313

legs, entire midsections of their torsos. The absent parts were nowhere to be seen.

"Good gods," Daemon said. Why hadn't Prince Gin hypnotized them, like he had at the other cities? Why kill these taigas?

Broomstick emerged from the tent and froze in horror when he saw the grisly murders.

"Is she . . . ?" he whispered.

Daemon shook his head. "Fairy isn't among them."

Broomstick exhaled in relief. But then his eyes grew wide again. "Just because she isn't here doesn't mean she's alive. The ryuu meant to kill Empress Aki."

Oh no, Daemon thought. Prince Gin must not have come. That's why Sora and the other ryuu killed the Imperial Guards, instead of adding them to their army.

"I think Fairy is gone because the ryuu had to take her body back to the Dragon Prince as proof," Daemon said.

"No." Broomstick crumpled to the ground, not caring that he collapsed among dismembered corpses.

It still didn't add up, though. *I got through to Sora, I'm sure of it*, Daemon thought. If she had her mind back, she wouldn't have killed Fairy. She would have thought of some way to trick the other ryuu into thinking Fairy—the empress—was dead.

To test his theory, he reached out through their gemina bond. It was the kind of gentle nudge he and Sora would always send each other in the mornings, to check if the other was awake.

A moment later, a reassuring nudge came back to him, like the foamy touch of low tide on bare feet.

Daemon nodded. She was all right.

He pulled Broomstick up and out of the graveyard of mutilated bodies. "Sora's with Fairy. She'll keep her safe."

"Are you mad? Did you not see what I saw? Spirit is a ryuu. We have to go after Fairy." He started to run toward the dirt road that led down the side of the bluff.

Daemon caught up and grabbed him. "Sora is still one of us."

"You're not thinking clearly," Broomstick said, every single one of his knives in his hands. "She's your gemina. It's affecting your judgment."

"And the fact that Fairy is your gemina is affecting *your* judgment," Daemon said. "But . . . okay. Test your gemina bond. Can you still feel her on the other end?"

Broomstick pursed his lips as he tried to connect to Fairy. "No. It's like a cemetery in my head," he said, choking back his despair.

"Sora must have done something to knock her out. If they have to present a body to Prince Gin, Fairy has to look like a dead empress."

Broomstick shook his head skeptically.

Daemon took him by the shoulders. "I know this is hard. Trust me. I just went through thinking my gemina was taken by the ryuu or dead. And I care about Fairy too! But I have a gut feeling that she's all right, that this is all part of Sora's plan. Whether or not you believe in Sora right now, the reality is that we can't go after Fairy. You see what ryuu can do." He waved behind them, but he didn't look. The image of the carnage was burned into his memory forever. "If we chase after Fairy, we will walk straight into the entire ryuu army and they'll kill us in half a second. Then we'll be no good to anybody."

Broomstick sagged. The five knives he had in each hand fell to the dusty ground.

Daemon picked them up. "Let's go home. We have to tell Empress Aki and the Council everything that's happened. They'll know what to do."

"Do you actually believe that?"

Daemon sighed. "I have to."

CHAPTER FIFTY-ONE

The president of the Striped Coves' most famous jeweler—Tiger Pearl Trading Company—had supposedly offered his home to Prince Gin, and this was where Sora and Hana found him when they returned from Copper Bluff. They were still covered in Dassu Desert's fine brown sand, but Hana had insisted they report on their success immediately. Hana levitated Fairy's body behind them. Her eagerness to please Prince Gin had overridden her squeamishness over the empress's assassination.

One of the jeweler's servants led Sora and Hana to the fourth floor of the mansion, out through a sunroom, and onto a cliff-side patio that overlooked the Kichona Sea. Prince Gin sat at a table, watching the waves while drinking a bottle of fine whiskey and nibbling on chili-dusted peanuts.

It was Sora's first look at him since regaining command of her mind. She clenched her fists to keep herself in check, fighting the urge to fling herself across the table, smash the whiskey bottle, and use it to cut the prince's throat.

"Your Highness, the empress is dead," Hana said, dumping Fairy's gold-haired body to the floor.

Sora winced at the impact. Fairy might seem dead, but she could still be hurt.

Hana frowned at Sora's reaction. Sora slapped a smug smile on her face, as if she too were pleased with the empress's death.

Was her sister suspicious that Sora was no longer under Prince Gin's spell? But she couldn't be. There was no precedent for anyone breaking out of his hypnosis. *I'm just jumpy*, Sora thought. But it was a good reminder to be more vigilant in how she acted, just in case.

Hana eyed her for another second before she turned back to Prince Gin. "We should have the kingdom light fireworks in your honor," she said.

Prince Gin set his cup down on the table. He turned slowly from the ocean to Sora and Hana.

"We won't throw a party at the death of the empress. Despite her shortcomings, she was still my sister. The kingdom will mourn her for thirty days, as custom dictates when a member of the royal family dies."

"My apologies, Your Highness." Hana bowed again.

Prince Gin frowned as he looked down at Fairy. "Aki is prettier than I remember. She was never the kind of beauty that would turn heads if she wasn't royalty, but now . . ."

Sora froze. Did he know it wasn't his sister?

She cleared her throat. "Ten years can change a person," Sora said. "I imagine being empress and revered by the entire kingdom could make anyone glow and become more beautiful."

Prince Gin picked up his whiskey and sipped it.

Sora held her breath. How stupid could she be? Hana had just caught her wincing at dropping Fairy's body on the floor, and now Sora had put herself out there again for scrutiny. And yet, it had to be done. She couldn't let them doubt that this was Empress Aki.

He contemplated the body before him some more. Finally, he said, "I suppose time does change people."

Prince Gin set his whiskey down and turned to Hana. "We're in mourning, but that doesn't mean we can't move forward with our plans. We'll march to the capital, where I will take the throne. The Society is sworn to the crown. They'll follow my orders out of duty or, if necessary, through magic. We'll hold my coronation as soon as the mourning period is over. And then you'll have your fireworks." He winked at Hana, as one does when giving a child what she's coveted for so long.

Hana blushed.

"Virtuoso, prepare the ryuu to head to the capital. We'll leave in the morning."

"With pleasure, Your Majesty," she said, addressing him by the title reserved for the emperor or empress. But, Sora supposed, if Aki was dead, the Dragon Prince *would* be His Majesty. She again had to keep herself from leaping across the table and slitting his throat.

Oblivious—or perhaps because he was so powerful—he turned his back on them and went back to gazing at the ocean.

I guess we're dismissed.

Hana levitated Fairy's body, and she and Sora left the patio.

"Do you want to help me plan Emperor Gin's coronation

319

parade and celebrations?" Hana asked.

Emperor Gin. A foul taste formed in Sora's mouth, and she hadn't even said the words aloud.

But she had to go along. She had to stay undercover within the ryuu until they were close enough to the Citadel that she could abscond with Fairy's body. And if possible, with Hana too.

"I'd love to," Sora lied. "The emperor's homecoming will be one Kichona will remember forever."

While Sora and Hana had been gone, the ryuu had found where the citizens and remaining taigas of the Striped Coves were hiding, and Prince Gin had enchanted them all to return home. Now word of Empress Aki's demise spread quickly through the city. Prince Gin gathered everyone into the main square and tailored the story to be one of a flaw in his sister's heart like the one that had killed their father, a secret she'd kept from the people of Kichona.

"But there's no reason to worry," he'd said. "The gods could see our kingdom's future, and they summoned me home just in time. I am blessed to be able to continue the Ora family line as your humble servant, and I'll honor my sister's life by ushering Kichona into a new era of greatness and prosperity."

Every word he said was magicked as if dipped in rich caramel and chocolate. The people ate it up. "Long live the Emperor!"

But Sora was immune to his brainwashing because her gemina bond was open again, and this time, she knew to cling to her connection to Daemon. Back on the ship, she'd been so surprised to see her sister alive that she'd stopped paying attention to her bond with Daemon as he escaped. That had weakened his ability to help her fight off Prince Gin's charm. Now, though, Sora held firmly to her connection, constantly sending and receiving emotion from Daemon. She still didn't understand how he could resist the Dragon Prince's spells, but whatever it was, she wasn't going to let go of it.

With her sense of self intact, Sora watched the prince, horrified by how easily he could charm everyone.

He couldn't be allowed to take over the Citadel. He couldn't be allowed to conduct the Ceremony of Two Hundred Hearts. He couldn't be allowed to wage war on the mainland, to pursue the Evermore. A glacial chill shivered through Sora's spine.

By the time the ryuu mobilized for their journey to the capital the next morning, small shrines to Empress Aki lined the cobblestone streets, her painting surrounded by white chrysanthemums and mourning ribbons. But gracing every window were new banners—yellow and green, not the traditional Ora colors, but Prince Gin's adopted ones for his ryuu army.

As they departed the Striped Coves and began to head inland, Sora's thoughts turned to Fairy, Broomstick, and Daemon. As a survival mechanism, she hadn't let herself think about them much since Copper Bluff. It was as if she could temporarily deny it had happened if she cordoned off that part of her brain.

Now, however, on horseback for a journey that would take several days, Sora had nowhere to hide from the guilt of leaving her friends. If something happened to them, she wouldn't be able to forgive herself.

Did she give Fairy the right amount of the rira disk? Did Daemon and Broomstick get back to the Citadel safely? Would she ever be able to make it up to them, the fact that she'd tried to murder them in her hypnotic haze?

If only Sora could be in two places at once—here with her sister, and there with her friends and the Society, where she belonged.

That is, if the Society would have her back. Her gut twisted as she thought about how this looked. She'd started this by breaking the rules and sneaking off on a self-appointed mission. Then she'd gotten herself captured, ostensibly joined the ryuu, learned their magic, and used it in an assassination attempt against the empress. And Sora hadn't gotten a chance to tell Daemon and Broomstick that Virtuoso was actually Hana, and that's why she was staying behind.

Put that way, the facts looked bad. Very bad.

Sora's horse stopped. The gelding ahead of her had lifted his tail. He let out an avalanche of dung.

Yeah, she thought. *That's how I feel.*

The ryuu on the horse next to her laughed as he rode past. "I'd find a handkerchief to wrap around my nose and mouth if I were you. Shitstorm there lives up to his name. That is only the first of his many 'gifts' he'll leave on the road in front of you."

Nines.

She steered her horse around the steaming pile.

The army rode onward into the countryside, making good time. The rice paddies were green and flooded with water, and the terraces on the hills behind it were lined with what were probably sweet potato plants. The tiger

322

pearls from the Striped Coves were one facet of Kichona, and these quiet farm communities were another— different, yet equally important. Sora tried to envision what would happen to them if Prince Gin won this fight against Empress Aki.

He would begin wars against other kingdoms, and their soldiers would come to Kichona's shores in retaliation. In her mind, Sora saw foreign warriors lighting the sweet potato terraces aflame, burning a sickly, syrupy smoke. She watched the rice paddies dry up, their plants uprooted, farmers' bodies impaled by hoes. She heard the screams of scared children, and of even more frightened mothers who tried to protect their babies' innocence while enemies pushed up the women's skirts against the farmhouse walls.

She also saw that the ryuu could do the same in other countries. Right now, they restrained themselves from too much destruction, because Prince Gin needed to preserve the kingdom he meant to rule. But she remembered how easily Prince Gin had beheaded the harbormaster at Tiger's Belly, how he'd designated Hearts throughout Kichona— including babies!—without a thought to sacrificing their lives, and how he'd told the Black Widows they could have their way with their prisoners once the war began. If this was what restraint looked like, the Dragon Prince and his ryuu would be disastrous abroad.

How was Sora going to stop them?

Prince Gin's army could control the ocean's waves. They could summon hordes of stinging wasps. They could unleash fire as if from a dragon's mouth, suck the air out of lungs, and boil the water inside a man until he burst from within. And that was just a sampling of the ryuu's abilities.

The taigas don't stand a chance. The answer set in like rot, rank and damp.

But then Sora adjusted her posture on her saddle and sat taller. The taigas might not stand a chance fighting the ryuu as they were. *But what if I could find a way to undermine the ryuu's magic?* It would level the playing field, at least a bit.

In front of her, Shitstorm lifted his tail again. Sora pulled her horse's reins to the left and trotted around the gelding.

There was always more than one path to get where you needed to go. And if anyone could find it, Sora could.

CHAPTER FIFTY-TWO

Daemon and Broomstick rode up to the behemoth gates at the Citadel. A dozen guards perched in watch stations above, arrows aimed at those who dared approach. Others were poised to drop down and attack, should they be needed.

"Who goes there?" the lead warrior asked.

Daemon and Broomstick dismounted. They fell to their knees, splayed their hands wide before them, and pressed their foreheads to the ground.

"Welcome back, apprentices," the warrior said upon recognizing them. There was a pause. Then he asked, "Broomstick, where's the rest of the team that went to Dassu Desert?"

Broomstick remained on the ground for a moment before he had the strength to rise and answer. "They're dead."

The guard froze as he processed this.

"All of them?"

Daemon nodded. It was too complicated to explain what

had happened to Sora and Fairy. Besides, that report should be directed at the Council.

In grim silence, the guards opened the fortress gates. Daemon and Broomstick entered.

As they returned their horses to the stables, Broomstick said, "Do you really believe she's still alive?"

They hadn't talked about it the entire journey back from Copper Bluff, but it had loomed over them. Fairy had been so incredibly brave to pose as the empress. She'd known that death might be the price. But Daemon refused to acknowledge it. He could remember the smell of her hair, like plums and sweet cream. He could hear her voice, lilting and teasing, always something scandalous to say just to get a smile out of him. He stopped working to unsaddle his horse. "I . . . I have to believe Fairy's alive."

"But what if . . ." Broomstick cast his eyes downward and fiddled with the reins still in his hands. "What about the possibility that Sora is one of them?"

"No." Daemon left the saddle and turned to Broomstick. He met his gaze and didn't let go. "I can resist the Dragon Prince's charm somehow, and Sora seems to benefit from my immunity. I feel her constantly through our gemina bond now, not like before, when she was hypnotized. If she's still with the ryuu, she has a very good reason for it."

Broomstick said nothing.

Conviction swelled in Daemon's chest. He put his hands on Broomstick's shoulders. "If we don't believe in each other," Daemon said, "what have we got left? Prince Gin wants to tear the Society apart. But we have control over this. We get to decide whether we stand with one of our best friends. It's been the four of us since we were kids. We can't abandon each other now when we need our friendship the most."

Silence.

"Fairy will be okay," Daemon said. "So will Sora. They are the strongest, most tenacious people we know."

Broomstick kicked at the dirt on the stable floor. But he nodded.

A Level 8 apprentice ran into the stable. Daemon and Broomstick spun to face him.

"Wolf and Broomstick, the Council requests your presence immediately."

Daemon leaned on his horse. This was going to be a very difficult report to give.

"Do we have time to change into our formal robes?" Broomstick asked.

"No. They want you now."

"All right," Daemon said. "Tell them we're on our way."

CHAPTER FIFTY-THREE

Aki's rooms at the Citadel were more spartan than she was accustomed to, but she didn't complain. She didn't need much, and besides, the Society was equipped to house warriors, not empresses pretending to be in Dassu Desert. The taigas had done as much as they could to make this feel like home while she was in hiding. They had knocked down a wall between two suites to form a single enormous one, with a receiving room, an office, a parlor, a meditation room, and of course, her bedchamber. The floors were done simply in reed mats as with the rest of the quarters in the building, and the furniture was utilitarian, but the walls of her temporary rooms had been repainted navy, and they'd found gold fabric to pin up as drapery.

The windows, however, remained papered in black, which took some getting used to after spending a lifetime in the bright, crystalline light of Rose Palace. Nevertheless, these were trifling details. After all, Aki's kingdom was on the brink of war.

One of her Imperial Guards stepped into the receiving room, where Aki sat on a simple bamboo chair, reading the latest reports from the taigas around the island. All major outposts had been evacuated. Many of the squadrons were coming here, to the Citadel, on Aki's orders. Whether or not a temporary cease-fire was reached in Dassu Desert, she suspected Gin would eventually march to Rose Palace to try to take the throne.

"Your Majesty, the Council is here."

They might have an update on whether her brother had agreed to a cease-fire and further discussions, or if he'd killed her decoy. Aki's stomach swan dived in the most unregal way.

"Thank you," she said, barely keeping her voice steady. "Send them in."

Glass Lady, Strategist, Bullfrog, Renegade, and Scythe filed in. They had two apprentices with them. Broomstick had been one of the rogues she'd appointed for the mission. For a moment, Aki dared to hope that it had gone well.

Except Fairy and the Imperial Guards who'd gone to the desert weren't here.

Aki's hope plummeted.

The councilmembers and apprentices lay on the ground in deep bows. "Your Majesty."

Aki pulled herself together as best she could and nodded as they rose. "You have word on my brother?"

"Yes," Glass Lady said. "As you predicted, Prince Gin wanted you dead. However, there is a bit of a twist we did not foresee. Broomstick and Wolf will report to you, since they were there."

Wolf shuffled his feet.

Poor boy, Aki thought. He was only seven years younger than she was, but he'd spent his life in school thus far, not exposed to the harsh realities that she'd dealt with—not only the Blood Rift that began her reign, but also the daily problems of the kingdom that had to be solved, from poor weather affecting the harvests to tiger pearl shipments lost at sea to pirates. The happenings at Copper Bluff—and of Prince Gin's return, in general—were an awful lot for an apprentice to have to handle.

Wolf composed himself quickly and began to recite everything that had happened, not just at Copper Bluff, but from the moment he and Spirit went back to Takish Gorge to investigate the mysterious camp again. As he recapped the events, Aki stopped feeling sorry for him. Instead, she marveled at his strength. He'd watched in horror as Gin charmed taigas to his side and chose innocents as sacrifices for the Ceremony of Two Hundred Hearts, and yet Wolf had pushed on, at personal risk, to infiltrate their ship. He'd snuck into Gin's cabin, stolen the ryuu's list of targets, escaped capture, and swam to Tiger's Belly to transmit his reconnaissance to the Citadel. He'd lost his gemina, both physically and emotionally.

And somehow, Wolf was still standing. *I'm sorry*, Aki thought. *I completely underestimated you.*

When he finished his report, Glass Lady spoke. "There will be consequences to your leaving the Citadel without permission. It was a flagrant violation of the rules, as well as reckless. As apprentices, you and Spirit do not yet understand the complexities of the politics Empress Aki must handle, nor the intricacies of military strategy. You could have triggered something the Society would not be able to handle."

Wolf's face flushed, but he nodded while continuing to stand at attention.

"Nevertheless," Aki interjected, "I do appreciate your efforts." She understood that the apprentices had to follow certain rules to maintain order in the school, but she also thought the commander was being too rigid in light of what Wolf and his friends had accomplished.

"There is one thing I don't understand, though," Aki said. "If Spirit can use ryuu magic now, why didn't she turn on them at Copper Bluff, and why didn't she return with you?"

Wolf and Broomstick shifted uncomfortably in place.

"We've been asking ourselves the same question the entire journey back," Wolf finally said.

Bullfrog cleared his throat. "If I may suggest an explanation, Your Majesty."

Aki dipped her head.

"It seems possible that Spirit succumbed to the Dragon Prince's charm," Bullfrog said. "She may have spared Wolf and Broomstick because they used to be her friends. But otherwise, she's a ryuu."

Wolf shook his head. "I won't believe that Spirit actually joined the ryuu. She's acting as our spy or she has some other plan. I got through to her. I can feel her in our gemina bond again."

"Perhaps she is lying to you through your connection," Glass Lady said.

"No," Wolf said. "Sora—Spirit—wouldn't do that."

Aki sighed. "It's hard to swallow the possibility that someone you love and know well would turn on you. Even now, a decade later, I sometimes can't believe that the Blood Rift really happened, that my own brother would be willing to kill me to get what he wants."

"But—" Wolf said.

"I'm not saying that Bullfrog is right," Aki said. "Yet we must consider it a possibility. We will proceed with the plan to pretend I'm dead and hope that Gin lets his guard down. But we will also be prepared for battle, as best as we can against their magic."

Wolf nodded but his posture was resigned.

"In the meantime," Aki said, turning to Glass Lady and the rest of the Council, "I want round-the-clock surveillance tripled around the fortress walls. Set traps throughout the Citadel should the ryuu breach our perimeter or use their invisibility to get inside. Get the tenderfoots out of here—I don't want a repeat of the fire during the Blood Rift. And I want to address all the taigas, to strengthen their loyalty and attempt to deflect my brother's charm."

"Yes, Your Majesty," Glass Lady said. "Anything else?"

Aki rose from her chair. "Just be ready to fight."

CHAPTER FIFTY-FOUR

Jade Forest was a lush gem of gnarled tree trunks covered in fuzzy moss and logs bridging over bubbling creeks, everything bright green and pure, a peaceful barrier that separated the Imperial City from the ryuu and Prince Gin's mindless, violent vision of Kichona's future. Sora and the others set up camp for the night, pitching their tents to the melody of a symphony of crickets and unrolling their sleeping mats next to a pond full of water lilies the size of dinner platters. It was a deceptive interlude before what Sora knew would be more bloodshed, and panic exploded like a geyser inside her chest.

She had to leave tonight, while everyone was asleep, to return to the Citadel. She would steal Fairy's body and take her too. But Sora didn't have a specific plan for before or after that. She'd stayed with the ryuu to convince Hana to return to the Society with her, but she hadn't found the right opportunity yet, and time was running out. And Sora had no idea what she was going to do when she made it back to the Citadel. What, exactly, was she going to tell the Council? How in the world would they put an end to this before Prince Gin claimed the crown and followed through on the Ceremony of Two Hundred Hearts? Before the wars really began?

Sora started breathing too quickly. She tried putting her head between her knees.

"Are you all right?" Beetle walked up to her.

She looked up at him and blinked.

"You look like you just ate a durian," he said.

"Huh?" Sora hastily composed herself. "Oh, it was nothing. I was light-headed, is all. I'm so hungry. Ever since I've become a ryuu, it seems I can't keep up with my appetite."

"Join the club." Beetle opened two pouches on his belt to reveal rice crackers and jerky and nuts. He tossed a package of bite-sized molasses cookies to Sora. "You'll get used to the hunger. Your body is adjusting right now. Your brain has to expend a lot of energy to be able to grasp and keep hold of its understanding of ryuu magic. It's a huge change from seeing the world as you knew it before. And with that extra burnt energy comes hunger." He winked and walked off toward the mess area of camp, presumably to pilfer more snacks.

Sora exhaled and her head drooped between her knees again. But then she tore the corner off the paper pouch of cookies. Maybe getting something into her stomach *would* help calm her down.

She took small bites and chewed deliberately, forcing herself into a sugar-and-flour-centered meditation. After two cookies, her breathing began to slow.

Maybe instead of contemplating the overwhelming task of stopping the momentum of the Dragon Prince's world war, it would help if Sora focused on a smaller scale. She began to think methodically about the advantages the ryuu had over the taigas. If there was a weakness that could be exposed, the Society might have a chance.

All right, she thought. *Let's start at the beginning.*

Ryuu power was based on the same magic as the taigas'.

Taigas needed mudras and chants to cast spells, whereas the ryuu didn't. Therefore, ryuu could fight physically and magically at the same time, whereas taigas could only do one or the other.

Taiga spells were impressive, but the taigas didn't know how to do more than enhance their own existing physical skills. Ryuu used the same magic, but they understood it on a more fundamental level, and so they could control things outside of their bodies—weather, elements, insects, inanimate objects.

Sora drummed her fingers on her knee. If it were a battle between taiga magic and ryuu magic, the ryuu would win every time. So what she needed to do was find a way to stop the ryuu from being able to use their magic at all. But how? It's not like the taigas could just bind all the ryuu's hands in iron shackles. Ryuu didn't need to form mudras to cast their spells. All they needed was a thought, and the magic did their bidding.

She grumbled at the emerald particles floating in the air in front of her. They sparkled, oblivious to her frustration.

Sora blinked at them and sat up straight. A smile touched the corner of her lips.

The ryuu might not rely on mudras and chants like taigas did, but they still relied on something else—they needed to be able to *see* the magic they were calling in order to use it. Hence, Prince Gin gifting them with Sight.

If we can blind them, we'll have a chance.

The taigas wouldn't be able to count on throwing stars and shooting arrows at the ryuu's eyes, though. Too many ryuu would be able to defend themselves from that kind of attack. Sora needed to come up with a way to surprise them and to blind them all at once.

Enchant handkerchiefs to tie around their eyes?

No, same problem as relying on weapons. It would be too difficult to control so many at once and get all the ryuu.

An enormous blanket?

Or a giant mirror. Sora thought of Fairy primping whenever they were going on leave, doing her hair and makeup so she could seduce as many boys as possible when they went into town. Sometimes, her compact would catch the sunlight and throw a blinding flash onto Sora's side of the room.

But where could she find a mirror big enough?

She remembered what Hana had said a while ago, at the beginning of training—*Follow the magic, and it will take you exactly where you need to go.* Hana had meant it physically, but what if it could be something more? What if it could guide Sora to what she wanted or needed?

"All right," she said quietly to herself. "Let's see how well this magic can understand my thoughts." She focused in front of her until the emerald particles appeared, swirling in the air.

"Take me where I need to go."

The green particles danced into a line, and a path shimmered before her.

She followed it through the trees, climbing over slippery mossed boulders and snagging her ankles in the dense foliage. She crossed a creek and trailed the magic up an incline, pushing her way through branches all the way.

Fifteen minutes outside of camp, she came to a clearing at the top of a hill. Sora commanded the magic to sharpen her vision.

Everything came into focus. Straight through the trees, the Imperial City stood proudly—the Citadel's dark, forbidding walls guarding the bottom, and Rose Palace presiding above, its crystal walls gleaming brightly under the moon.

So brightly, it was as if it were a sign from Luna herself.

Sora gasped and stared with her mouth open. Adrenaline cartwheeled through her veins, the same wondrous, satisfied feeling she got whenever she came up with a new scheme. A grin spread across her face. She knew what she needed to do.

"Thank you, little magic particles. You really did show me the way."

There was a very slight noise behind her, imperceptible to anyone but those with the most sensitive of taiga ears. Sora whipped around, throwing stars already between her fingers.

Hana emerged from the trees, hands up. "It's just me," she said. "I saw you leave camp, and I was curious. I'm sorry if I'm interrupting."

Sora shook her head and put her throwing stars back in the band across her chest. "You're not. I wanted to see the stars." It was the first excuse that came into her head. So many countless nights she'd spent with Daemon on the rooftops at the Citadel, just contemplating the sky.

She suddenly wondered what he was doing now. Was he above the dormitory, stretching his arm up as he often did, reaching for the stars that always seemed to have a pull on him?

"Ah," Hana said. "You had to get out from under the trees to see."

Sora nodded.

Her sister walked up to the crest of the hill and stood beside her.

"Do you remember the myth you used to tell me when I was little?" Hana pointed at a rabbit constellation.

"The one about the god of night's children?"

"Yeah."

"That was your favorite."

Hana continued looking at the stars. Next to the rabbit, there was a giraffe, and at the top of the giraffe's head sat a monkey. There was a whole menagerie of animals. "Do you think . . ." she hesitated. Then she fiddled with her hair and said, "Do you think you could tell the story to me now?"

The smile that spread across Sora's face was so bright, it outshone the moon. "I'd love to."

They found a patch of moss, as thick and soft as a blanket, and lay beside each other. As their breaths slowed and their chests rose and fell in sync, Sora called to the ryuu particles around them, asking them to illustrate the story she was about to tell. They swirled around her eagerly, then floated above Hana's head, mimicking the nightscape of stars.

Sora started the fable as their mother had written it, still pristine in her memory as if she had recited it to her little sister only yesterday.

Millions of miles in the sky, the gods look upon us from the heavens. To mortals, Celestae is perfect, a paradise no soul would ever want to leave.

But gods, like humans, sometimes grow tired of what they already have. The god of night, in particular, loved descending from the sky. He was very handsome. His face was composed of sharp angles, like the lines of constellations. His eyes smoldered like nebulas, mysterious and multicolored. And light followed wherever he went, like a comet trailing its king. One look from him sent mortal women tumbling head over heels, irretrievably in love.

Over the millennia, he fathered many children. But being a god, he was not accustomed to sharing. Instead, he took all his offspring from his mortal lovers so that his children could live with him in Celestae.

One day, a woman named Tomi refused the god of the night his child. She held their son close to her breast and would not relinquish him to live in the sky.

"Why do you do this?" the god of night had asked. "Our son is a demigod. He belongs in Celestae, where he can drink of sweet nectar and frolic in fields made of dreams. He will live a good life. He will live forever. This is the way it has always been for my children."

Tears ran down Tomi's face as she stroked her baby's fat cheek. "I love you, my lord. But I love my baby even more. Half of him comes from you, but the other half comes from me. If you take him and I never see him again, I shall die."

The god of the night frowned. He had never thought of it from his lovers' point of view. Yet their boy belonged in Celestae, with others like him. He would be unhappy, relegated to earth.

"My beautiful Tomi," the god said, kissing away the stream of her tears. Each touch of his lips left glimmers of starlight on her skin. "Tell me. What is your favorite animal?"

She looked up at the god, confused, her eyes rimmed in red. "A lion. But I don't understand."

"I must take our son with me. You know this to be true. But you will see him again." The god of night held out his arms for the baby.

Tomi hugged their son tightly. "How? When?"

"Every night. You need only look up to Celestae, and you will see him, a lion in the sky."

"What if he does not like Celestae?"

"He will," the god of night promised. "But if he ever wishes to leave, I will not stop him. That, I can promise you."

With that, the god gently took their boy from his mother. As they faded away, returning to the realm of the divine, Tomi felt a heavy sadness in her heart. And yet she did not cry.

When the sun set that evening, she did as she was told. She walked out into the chilly air and looked up toward Celestae.

Where there had been nothing before, now there was a constellation, a lion, bright against the night. The stars glimmered, as if her son were winking at her, and a small smile graced Tomi's face.

And from then on, all of the god of night's children appeared in the night sky, a parade of constellations bidding "good eve" to their mothers and assuring the mortal world that all was well in the universe.

At the end of the story, Sora's ryuu particles faded away, like a constellation at dawn.

Hana clapped softly. "It's just like I remember it. After

we'd left Kichona, I used to tell the story to myself when I couldn't sleep, but I never got it right. It's because the fable was missing you."

Sora's eyes prickled with tears, thinking of little Hana, shivering and scared after the Blood Rift, clinging to the one story that had been theirs.

"I'm here now," Sora said.

Hana nodded. "I know."

Impulsively, she leaned over and kissed Hana on the tip of her nose like she used to do when they were little.

Hana drew away, face contorted in horror. She quickly looked around, as if worried someone had seen.

"I'm sorry," Sora said. "I'm not sure what came over me. I just . . . I'm happy to have you back in my life."

Hana still looked horrified. But then her expression mellowed into a conflicted mixture of pleasure and disdain, as if her two halves—the little sister half and Virtuoso half—couldn't decide who was in charge. "I'm . . . happy to have you back too," she said. "But don't kiss me like that again. At least, um, when others can see."

"Okay, stinkbug."

Hana laughed despite herself. "Stinkbug. I haven't heard that nickname in a very long time."

They lay quietly in the moss for a little while. But the ryuu were going to march to the Imperial City at sunrise, and Sora had to leave tonight to beat them back to the Citadel. If she was going to take Hana with her, she'd have to test the waters now.

The temperature seemed to drop several degrees. Sora shivered. But it was time. "That story made me think about the gods," she said slowly. "They're all-powerful.

They can make women fall in love with them, give up their children. What's to stop them from making humans their playthings?"

Hana frowned. "You mean, they'd toy with us like dolls?"

"Something like that."

"That's a horrible thought."

"Why?" Sora asked.

"Because what if I didn't want to do what the god wanted? If we were toys, he could make us do anything. Kiss someone you find revolting. Smack yourself in the face. Jump off a cliff."

"You're right," Sora said.

"I'd fight back if they did that," Hana said.

"And if you couldn't? What if you couldn't fight back against the gods?"

"Then . . ." Hana thought about it. "Then I'd rather not live. What would be the point of having a life, if I didn't have free will? At least a doll doesn't actually have a mind of its own."

Sora let it sink in for a moment.

Hana turned to her, the moss pressed like a pillow against her face. "Is something wrong?"

Sora sighed. "What's wrong is Prince Gin and what he's doing."

Her sister sat up suddenly. "What are you talking about?"

This was it. Sora was about to reveal that she'd broken free of the Dragon Prince's spell. Instinctively, she sat up too and began to reach for her weapons, anticipating a fight.

But then she looked at Hana. The sweet little tenderfoot

had been there only minutes ago, asking for their bedtime story. She wasn't a ryuu, not entirely. And she had accepted Sora back into her life. Hana was capable of seeing the world in more than black and white. Sora had to do this—for Hana, for herself, and for her parents, who, if they knew their baby was still alive, would do everything in their power to shake her from her misguided faith in the Dragon Prince.

Sora moved her hand away from her knife. "I know Prince Gin is using ryuu magic to take over people's minds. I'm not sure how I broke free from the hypnosis, and I understand that you may want to bring me to him for the execution I was originally sentenced to, but if I'm to die . . . please give me a minute to explain. It's all I ask."

Hana's shock painted itself in circles across her face—round eyes, open mouth.

The freckles across her nose jerked as she wrinkled it and pulled herself together. She rose to one knee and drew her sword, the short one she wore at her hip. "You'd better talk quickly."

Sora swallowed and nodded. "Prince Gin is playing god. He's stealing people's free will and making them his toys. He wants to start wars, using not only us, but also ordinary Kichonans, as his soldiers. And for what? To pursue the legend of Zomuri and his immortal paradise? Stories are fun to tell, but they're just that. Stories."

"No," Hana said, shaking her head like she was trying to wake from a bad dream. "You don't know what you're talking about."

"Hana, lives are at stake, for a mythological reward that either doesn't exist or is impossible to attain. I know Prince Gin raised you, and you helped to build this army, but it's not too late to change your mind, to leave the sky like some constellations do."

That was how ancient Kichonans had explained stars that inexplicably disappeared. They were the god of night's children, making the choice to leave their father to return to their mothers on earth.

Her sister pointed her sword at Sora's chest. "No. Prince Gin wants what's best for Kichona." A sob caught in her throat. "That's what he told us. That's what he told *me*."

Her blade wavered. Sora inched closer and slowly reached over to Hana's hand. Her fingers closed over Hana's.

"I'm going back to the Citadel," Sora said gently. "Come with me. We'll defend our right to possess our own minds, and the peaceful way of life that Kichonans have had for centuries."

"But Prince Gin promised us more," Hana said, dropping her arm by her side.

Sora could see the wanting in her sister's eyes. Hana had grown up in an impoverished camp for exiles, in the rough mountains of Shinowana. To her, life was an injustice that needed to be corrected. And what the Dragon Prince promised must really seem like heaven on earth.

"Hana, you're home," Sora said. "This is a blessed kingdom, with plentiful harvests, joyful traditions, and friends and family. It may not be Zomuri's Evermore, but it's real. Come with me."

Her sister looked at the outline of the Citadel and Rose Palace on the hilly horizon beyond that.

"Sora . . . I love you."

"I love you too." Her heart soared like a nightingale taking flight.

Hana raised her sword again.

Sora tumbled backward on the moss. She scrambled for her own blade, but Hana had her sword point at Sora's throat.

"I love you," Hana began again, focused intensely on Sora's eyes, "and that's why, if you want to leave, I won't stop you. But I won't come with you, because my place is here. And if you go . . . it will be the end of us. For good this time."

Sora's nightingale heart plummeted from its height, wings broken.

"But—"

"My decision is made," Hana said. "Now it's up to you." She held Sora's gaze.

It was an impossible choice.

At the same time, there was no choice. Sora couldn't stay with the ryuu and fight for Prince Gin. She had to put the kingdom first. She had to defend the possession of their own wills, their lives.

Even if it meant losing Hana. Again.

Sora's lungs constricted. Her breaths came in short, tight gasps. Then she couldn't breathe at all.

But Hana seemed to understand what the conclusion was. She nodded sadly at Sora, sheathed her sword, and walked away.

And Sora cried.

CHAPTER FIFTY-FIVE

The tenderfoots were evacuated from the Citadel the same evening, and the Council called a meeting of all the remaining taigas. There were more than usual, for many taigas had been summoned from their posts around Kichona to the Imperial City.

The sound of wine-barrel drums filled the amphitheater as taigas filed in, finding places to sit on the arced benches carved into the grassy knoll. The commander and the rest of the councilmembers stood in the center of the black stage. Daemon and Broomstick settled into the back row with the rest of the Level 12s.

When everyone had sat down, Glass Lady stepped forward and said, "Thank you all for coming. As you know, the Dragon Prince is approaching with his army. They wield formidable magic different from ours and intend to finish what they started with the Blood Rift ten years ago. Not only that, but the Dragon Prince is also actively recruiting taigas to his side, using a powerful form of hypnosis. We must be prepared to use everything we have to fight them."

A taiga warrior in the front row rose and bowed to indicate that he had a question.

Glass Lady nodded at him.

"Commander, can you tell us more about their magic?" he shouted so the entire amphitheater could hear.

"I think the one best suited to answer your question would be a taiga who has actually witnessed what the ryuu can do." She found Daemon in the audience. "Wolf or Broomstick, would you brief everyone?"

This was so unexpected, Daemon's nerves hardly had time to twitch. But Broomstick was actually twitching, so Daemon would have to be the one to address the audience. He stood from the bench and hurried to the stage, taking the steps in a single bound. He bowed deeply to each councilmember before turning to the crowd.

Stars, there are a lot of people, he thought, his nerves finally catching up. He clasped his hands together behind his back to still the jittering, hoping the gesture came across as confident military poise rather than what it really was—an apprentice not used to being the center of attention. That was usually Sora's job.

This is for her as much as it is for Kichona. Daemon took a deep breath, enough to calm himself so he could speak, and began.

His voice carried through the cold night air. He told the taigas about the green particles of magic and how the ryuu could control them without mudras or chanted spells. He told them about the initiation ceremony, with Prince Gin giving new recruits Sight and the ryuu shoving them off the roof. He told them about the fearsome powers that the ryuu displayed, each one with a different talent far beyond what taigas could do.

When Daemon finished, the amphitheater remained completely silent. But it was not the serene type of quiet associated with the middle of the night. It was the silence of warriors who had never met an enemy they couldn't vanquish, not in the thousand-year history of the kingdom, suddenly faced with a foe more powerful than they could comprehend. Daemon quivered in the echo of his words too. He didn't know where Sora and Fairy were and how to get them back. He didn't know how the taigas could fight the ryuu. He didn't want to think what would happen if Prince Gin prevailed.

Someone walked up beside Daemon.

"Thank you, Wolf," Empress Aki said. "That was very informative."

The silence of the audience broke as they registered the empress's surprise appearance. They fell like dominoes to bow before her. Daemon too dropped to his knees and laid himself before her. "Your Majesty," he said.

She waited a minute for the taigas to finish paying their respects. When all had risen again, she smiled kindly at Daemon. "You may return to your seat," she said quietly.

He gave another quick, shallower bow and left the stage.

"Thanks for getting me off the hook," Broomstick whispered when Daemon slid back onto the bench beside him. "I can't say you didn't scare everyone shitless, but you did well."

"Everyone should be scared," Daemon said.

Broomstick merely nodded.

In front of them, Empress Aki stood regally in a black silk gown, embroidered with tiny gold suns that matched her hair.

"My noble taigas," she said, walking along the edge of the stage and looking purposefully at every section of the amphitheater. "Kichona is a respected kingdom. We are proud of the people and things we produce here—from rose apples to tiger pearls, daily catches of fish to famed pagoda temples for the gods. We treat our trade partners with respect, and in turn, they reciprocate, and we are known as fair, upstanding citizens of the world.

"It is my honor to rule over this illustrious kingdom. And it is Kichona's blessing to have the Society of Taigas at its defense. For centuries, your legacy has been the basis of legends, stories carried from our shores and spread across the globe.

"Now, we are about to engage in battle against an army that seems on the outside more impressive than our own. They will dazzle and frighten with their magic. They will maim and bloody and not hesitate to kill. They will attempt to initiate the quest for the Evermore with the Ceremony of Two Hundred Hearts."

Empress Aki paused at the center of the stage, letting the gravity of what she was saying sink in. Taigas slaughtered. Two hundred men, women, and children with their hearts cut out of their chests. The commencement of an unprecedented era of bloodshed and war.

Daemon held his breath, as did, it seemed, all the other

apprentices and warriors around him.

"But do not forget this," the empress said, again turning to look at each section of the crowd, so that every single taiga felt the golden warmth of her attention. "You are part of something greater than just this army assembled here, in the amphitheater, at this present time. You are part of a vast, proud history, a thousand years of taigas who have fought daunting foes and prevailed. You are part of not only the Society but the kingdom itself.

"You *are* Kichona."

The Council fanned out behind her, arms crossed over their chests, backs straight, black scabbards gleaming under the moonlight. It was an impressive picture, and Daemon's chest swelled with pride.

We may be about to face the ryuu, but the taigas are not something to trifle with either.

Then Empress Aki did something no one had ever seen before, in the long history of the kingdom: she dropped to her knees and bowed, stretching her body along the floor, lying prostrate before the taigas.

"Your Honors," she said, paying her respects.

The entire amphitheater gasped.

The ability to inspire others to follow was not Prince Gin's alone. It was in the Ora blood, and Empress Aki hadn't needed magic to charm the taigas. She had simply opened her heart and brought them into it, made them feel as one with her and the kingdom.

At that moment, Daemon understood that while he may not be special, he was still a part of the Society, an important part of Kichona with his own role to play.

The Council pressed their fists over their chests.

Every single apprentice and warrior rose from their seats and followed.

"Cloak of night. Heart of light," they shouted in unison.

It was a pledge of love and of loyalty.

And it was a battle cry.

CHAPTER FIFTY-SIX

Sora's eyes were puffy from crying, and her nose was red from where the thread of the green triplicate whorls on her sleeve had rubbed her skin raw. Only fifteen minutes away, the ryuu camp would have settled in for the night, Hana among them. Sora already felt her absence keenly.

In the distance, though, Rose Palace continued to shine like a beacon beneath the moon. Sora may have wrecked her chances with her sister, but she still had a shot at saving Kichona. She knew the ryuu's strengths and weaknesses. She had a plan.

The Society needed her.

Sora smothered the last of her sniffles and rose to her feet, standing tall in the clearing. There was work to do, and not much time for it. First, she had to rescue Fairy, and then they had to make their way back to the Citadel. There, Sora would have to convince the Council and Empress Aki to let her destroy Rose Palace as a weapon against the ryuu.

Easy.

Sora laughed humorlessly to herself.

And yet, the challenge energized her. This was what it meant to aspire for more, to become the best person she could be. She would give herself completely to Kichona, or she would die trying.

Sora made herself invisible and snuck back to the ryuu camp. Amazingly, their size had doubled in the time that Sora had been gone. It was no longer just ryuu now, but also an adjacent camp of pilgrims, the Hearts that Prince Gin had chosen in Paro Village, Sand Mine, Kaede City, Tiger's Belly, and the Striped Coves. Two hundred boys and girls, men and women, from one to a hundred years old. Sora stopped short and looked at them.

A boy just a couple years younger than her, arms and legs still lanky because he hadn't had the chance to grow into them. A woman with wrinkles as thick and heavy as a shar-pei dog's. A little boy cradled in her arms, on the cusp of toddlerhood, squirming as he sucked on his thumb. And 197 more, all people who'd had their own minds not that long ago, but who now milled around with the distant, contented glimmer in their eyes that Sora was all too familiar with.

She started in their direction.

"Great-grandmother," Sora said, as she approached the old woman holding the baby. "You shouldn't be here. Bad things are about to happen. You have to flee."

But the woman smiled, the corners of her mouth lifting the heavy curtains of the wrinkles around it. "My dear child, this is exactly where I need to be. I am honored to be chosen by the Dragon Prince. You are a taiga. You should understand the joy of giving yourself in service to your kingdom."

Sora shook her head. "No. He's controlling you. This . . . This isn't what you want."

The woman continued beaming as she cuddled the wriggling child. "Yes, Your Honor, it is. I was nothing but a seamstress before, but now I get to be something more."

"But . . ."

The little boy began to cry. The old woman cooed at him, then drifted away, forgetting her conversation.

Sora almost went after her.

And then she saw a girl with an abalone comb in her hair. Sora stopped moving.

It was the girl from the marketplace at Kaede City who had tried to get Daemon to go out with her on a date. But the flirtatious glimmer was gone from her eyes. She moved as if in a trance, humming a chirpy melody, like a soundtrack to her own dream.

Seeing a Heart whom Sora had known before, now completely dispossessed of her boldness, was like a bucket of ice water in Sora's face, a reminder that it was useless to try to talk the Hearts out of what they were doing. Sora had had too much experience with Prince Gin's magic, from the taro-pastry-loving woman in Paro Village who was overjoyed at being chosen as a Heart, to the indomitable taiga warriors who'd fallen prey to hypnosis. Even Sora herself. Talking would do no good. Sora had to push forward with her plan. The only hope was fighting against Prince Gin with the rest of the Society and putting a stop to him before he asked these two hundred souls to cut out their own beating hearts.

She tiptoed toward the northern edge of the ryuu camp, where most of the warriors had turned in for the night. Fairy's body was in a covered wagon, a small distance away from the rest of the ryuu, because the cart had been enchanted to a chilly temperature to prevent the empress from decomposing. Sora hoped it wasn't too cold for an actual, living body.

When she got closer to the wagon, though, she made herself invisible and stopped to survey the situation. There were a dozen ryuu ringing the cart.

Did Hana suspect anything? Was she herself here? If so, that would be trickier, because she'd be able to see Sora, even in invisible form.

Minutes ticked by. The ryuu guarding the wagon may have been numerous, but they were also tired from marching all day, and most were sitting or reclined on the ground, keeping sleepy watch in equidistant posts around the wagon. Only a couple of them bothered to actively patrol the area, but even they kept a wide berth from the cart itself to avoid its cold.

And there was no Hana in sight—ordinary or invisible.

Satisfied with this, Sora began her approach. She waited for one of the patrolling ryuu to pass, then slipped past him silently, taking care to move cautiously and not stir the air, a blade of grass, or a speck of dirt. She slinked between two of the reclined guards, one actually asleep and snoring, and crawled up into the covered wagon bed.

Sora shivered as she inched herself inside. The beams of wood were icy to the touch, and perhaps it was her imagination, but the air seemed tinged blue from the chill. She leaned over Fairy's body and nearly let out a cry.

Frost tipped her roommate's dark lashes. That heart-shaped face, usually so lively, was deathly pale and unmoving, like a statue carved of marble. Her hair had taken on a sheen not caused by the gold of her disguise but from the slick layer of ice that coated each strand. Sora touched a trembling hand to Fairy's cheek, afraid it would confirm there was nothing there but a corpse.

But despite the cold, Fairy's skin was still soft. There was no blush to it, no warmth, but it wasn't stiff like it would have been were she dead. Sora collapsed in relief on Fairy's chest.

"I'm sorry I did this to you," she whispered. "But you are so brave, and I'm proud of you. I'm proud of us. Just hang in there a little while longer. We're going home tonight."

She tucked a loose gold curl behind Fairy's ear and brushed the frost away from her lashes.

Then Sora took a long, deep breath and focused on the emerald dust currently making snowflakes in the cart.

Stop, she commanded. *Make her invisible instead.*

The snow stopped falling. It began to lift Fairy lightly off the makeshift bed of uniforms. Then it began to absorb her. Sora watched as Fairy's body turned sparkling green, invisible to the ordinary eye.

She directed the magic to carry Fairy out of the cart. It should have been an easy task, but Sora wasn't just steering a barrel of oranges. Fairy was a live person, and if she bumped into anything, she would get hurt. Sora asked more magic to bundle itself around Fairy, like a protective blanket.

She waited for the pacing ryuu to pass. Then Sora slid out of the wagon, and Fairy's levitating body followed.

A mere minute later, though, a ryuu behind her cried out, "The empress's corpse is missing!"

Dammit.

The ryuu's voice had been muffled—he must have been inside the cart itself—but in just a few seconds, the alarm would be raised.

Sora commanded the magic to tie itself like gags around the patrolling ryuu.

"Mmr rmph rroh!" The closest one tried to shout as he tore at his mouth.

Sora kicked him and slammed the heel of her hand into the back of his neck. He passed out immediately. She slid into the guard next to him, taking out his legs, and similarly knocked him unconscious.

The ten other ryuu on patrol came running, even though they couldn't see her. They knew that the empress was being kidnapped, and they'd seen their fellow guards fall. That's all they needed to dive into the fight headlong.

Sora drew her sword. She didn't want to kill them if she could help it, because some of these were new recruits and could hopefully be uncharmed in the future, restored as taigas. But she also didn't have the time to gently spare everyone. She needed to end this, quickly, before the rest of the camp woke up.

She had the benefit of invisibility, though. The ryuu had rushed to the spot where the other guards had fallen, but they didn't know where to attack next.

Sora smashed the butt of her sword into the heads of four ryuu, one right after the other in rapid succession. They tumbled to the ground.

The remaining six ryuu pinpointed her location. They

didn't bother with fighting the invisible gags around their mouths anymore. Instead, they focused their efforts and surrounded Sora, drawing their blades. They began to rush forward, some swords held high, some low.

Another second, and Sora would be skewered half a dozen ways.

She called on the magic to buoy her, and she leaped into the air as the swords impaled the space she'd just occupied.

The warriors ran the blades straight through each other. For a horrified moment, they stood there, eyes wide as blood spilled from their bodies, soaking their uniforms. Then, with muffled cries, they toppled over.

Five of them had been new recruits from Paro Village, Kaede City, and Tiger's Belly. Now they were just dead ryuu.

What have I done? Sora thought, landing on the ground beside them.

But this, as Prince Gin had pointed out, was the cost of war. No matter which side of right she was on, there would be inevitable wrongs.

Still, she staggered backward at the magnitude of what she'd done. She bumped into something and fell into the mud.

It was Fairy, her body still levitating but visible, pale and cold, defenseless and vulnerable. Her roommate's face wrenched Sora from her shock. She had to pull herself together. Her friend's life depended on it.

As did the lives of all the Hearts. And the entirety of Kichona's future, actually.

Sora gritted her teeth and pulled herself up from the mud. She kept her eyes on Fairy—refusing to look at the dead ryuu anymore—and refocused herself.

Make her invisible again.

Emerald dust rushed into Fairy's body and made her disappear.

Sora guided Fairy's floating form through camp. She had to hurry, in case anyone decided to check on the guards by the empress's cart. But she also had to be extra careful and quiet at the same time. Sora jumped whenever a ryuu turned in his sleep.

We're invisible. They can't see us. Keep going.

The horses were in the woods just outside camp. They were nearly there. They only had to get past Prince Gin's tent.

But Sora hovered for a moment outside where her sister slept. If only she'd had longer with Hana. If only the fate of the kingdom weren't hanging in the balance, with Sora being the sole taiga who could give Empress Aki and the Society a chance against the ryuu.

If Sora wanted enough time to report to the Council and put her plan into motion before the ryuu arrived at the Citadel, she had to leave now.

She looked at Hana's tent once more, then pressed onward out of the camp, into the woods with Fairy's body floating behind her.

Now, back to her friends, back to the Society. Back to the original point of her mission—bringing her knowledge about Prince Gin to the taigas, then stopping him before the Ceremony of Two Hundred Hearts set everything in blood-curdling motion.

Sora chose a horse, secured Fairy on the saddle, and climbed on behind her. Sora willed the ryuu particles to show her the path between trees, and she rode hard, letting herself go, surrendering herself and trusting the magic to guide her. Sora's horse bounded over logs and darted in and out between the gnarled, lichen-covered trunks. They moved so swiftly, the horse's feet hardly touched the ground before they propelled onward and over the next creek, the next cluster of boulders, the next copse of trees.

After a while, the damp moss and thick foliage of Jade Forest gave way to the Field of Illusions. The black-and-white sands were a dizzying obstacle, their ever-changing patterns too disorienting for all but taigas who were trained to look beyond them.

Unfortunately, almost all the ryuu were former taigas. They would have no trouble getting across, especially since they could also rely on their magic to show them the clear green path forward.

Sora pushed her horse even faster. Every minute was going to be essential for the Society to prepare for this fight. She had to get back.

They charged through the Field of Illusions, the horse's hooves spraying sand like fistfuls of scatter shot, the tiny metal pellets Daemon carried as throwing weapons. "Sorry for the bumps," she said to Fairy, whose body bounced violently in front of Sora. "Almost there."

The sand bit into their skin as they barreled forward. The patterns grew more frenzied. Staircases that looked like they descended straight down to the hells. Hills that crested then dropped off precipitously. Swirls that spun forward and backward at gut-churning speed.

Sora lost track of the emerald path, its particles blending in with the flurrying sand.

But they were almost there. She had to hold on to her focus.

Ignore the illusions. Keep an eye on the outline of the Citadel up ahead.

Concentrate on the ryuu path.

The emerald particles reappeared then, glittering brighter than before. Sora homed in on them, refusing to let go. Out of the corner of her eye, the towering, oil-slick fortress walls of the Citadel grew clearer, larger, as they sprinted closer.

The last illusion asserted itself. It became an ever-shifting set of tiny black-and-white rectangles, flashing so rapidly, it could induce seizures.

"Jump!" Sora shouted at the horse.

They leaped over the final stretch of sand.

Then it was over. Home loomed before them, ten stories of black fortifications and heavy, impenetrable gates. Sora exhaled and hugged Fairy. They'd made it. They had escaped Prince Gin and his ryuu.

And yet, the ache of killing those guards and of abandoning Hana didn't lessen with distance. In fact, it pulled on Sora, as if part of her had been left behind and had stretched too tautly now. The pain might be a constant—a punishment and a reminder—that she would have to live with.

Choices, unfortunately, had consequences.

CHAPTER FIFTY-SEVEN

Daemon paced near the bridge of a little lake. The Council had divided the Citadel into hundreds of sections, each one manned by large teams of taigas cycling through patrol and sleeping shifts. Bramble, one of the warriors in this lake section, jogged up to Daemon. She was in her thirties and an expert at nunchucks; she'd been one of the apprentices' sparring teachers. "Good evening, Wolf. Your shift is over. I can take your position."

"Thank you, Your Honor. Did you sleep well?"

"Well enough."

Daemon nodded. The floor in the boathouse wasn't the most accommodating of surfaces, but it was better than sleeping out on the dirt, which was what the taigas in a lot of the other sections had to do. It was fine either way, though. Taigas were accustomed to sleeping outdoors while on missions. This was no different; only slightly strange because their actual beds were in the dormitories not too far away.

"Anything notable during your shift?" Bramble asked.

"No. It was a boring day."

"Well, I doubt that will last for long. The ryuu must be coming."

Daemon's stomach pitched.

"Go get some sleep," Bramble said. "I think the rest of your team are already at the boathouse."

He nodded stiffly. The taigas were preparing, in the best way they knew how, for Prince Gin. But no matter how much detail Daemon and Broomstick told them about the ryuu and Copper Bluff, there was only so much they could comprehend without seeing the ryuu for themselves. The councilmembers were the only ones who'd gotten a taste of the threat at Isle of the Moon. The rest of the taigas were just, well, bracing themselves.

And then there was the matter of Sora returning. Gods, Daemon hoped he was right that she was on their side. He felt her presence through their gemina bond; she periodically sent him the feeling of steady reassurance, like a lily pad bobbing evenly on a calm pond. There were others, like Bullfrog, who doubted her, but they were wrong. Sora wanted to be the very best taiga she could be, and if anyone understood the desire to prove themselves, it was Daemon.

Besides, she was with Fairy, right? The ryuu had taken the body of who they thought was the empress, as proof that Prince Gin should wear the crown. Sora probably went back to the ryuu to ensure that Fairy was safe.

Daemon closed his eyes. He thought about the day he arrived in Dassu Desert, so exhausted, he wanted to tumble from his horse. He could still feel what it was like when Fairy hugged him, her swan-like chest against his chest, her laughter in the face of death. She had held him up first, and then he'd held her. There was so much life in her. Even when she'd needed support, it had still been like holding a fire-cracker in his hands.

She was safe, wasn't she?

Daemon was unraveling like a rope that had been exposed to the elements for too long.

But his shift was over for now, so he held himself together as best he could and bowed to Bramble, then jogged off the bridge to the boathouse, where Broomstick and two Level 7 apprentices had started a pot of oat porridge over a fire outside. The warriors on their shift were reporting to the Council.

"I could eat twigs right now, I'm so hungry," Daemon said, as he sat down in the dirt.

"Luckily, we don't have to." Stingray, one of the younger apprentices, handed him a bowl of sliced apples.

Stingray glared at Wirecutter, another Level 7. "You're stirring the pot the wrong way. It's supposed to go clock-wise, not counterclockwise."

"It's oat porridge," Wirecutter snapped back. "Right or left won't make a difference."

Stingray grumbled.

Everyone was on edge.

The porridge bubbled over. Instead of waiting for the bickering kids to handle it, Daemon grabbed a pair of pot-holders and took it off the fire.

Despite the bubbling and being stirred the "wrong" way, the porridge had cooked just fine. Daemon ladled steaming portions into bowls and topped them with dried, salted fish and scallions. They ate in silence except for the clacking of utensils and the slurping of porridge.

When they were done, Stingray yawned, and Wirecutter yawned a second after him. They sometimes snapped at each other like brothers, but they were also geminas, and it was as if the fatigue were contagious through their connection.

"It's been a long watch," Daemon said, finding some comfort in being the older-brother figure, "and the Dragon Prince is going to arrive any day now. We should all turn in and get some rest while we can."

"Agreed," Broomstick said.

Stingray and Wirecutter yawned again and trudged into the boathouse without protest.

"Should we clean up?" Daemon asked.

"Nah," Broomstick said. "The warriors will be back soon. Just put a lid on the porridge."

Daemon left the bowls of dried fish and scallions out for the warriors and covered the pot. Then he and Broomstick headed into the boathouse.

He thought it would be hard to get any rest, knowing that Prince Gin and Sora were coming. But the weight of fatigue pressed in on him, and after being on his feet for twelve hours, the sleeping mat felt like a plush down mattress. Daemon crawled under his blanket, and sleep hit him over the head.

CHAPTER FIFTY-EIGHT

Sora and Fairy emerged from the Field of Illusions and faced the grand fortress walls of the Citadel. Sora made herself visible. The particles lowered Fairy onto the ground before her, and her body also reappeared.

They were home. They were safe. Sora finally let herself breathe.

"Who goes there?" the guards shouted as soon as the moon cast its light upon them.

She bowed to the ground and splayed her fingers flat before her. "It is Spirit. I've returned with urgent news for the Council on the Dragon Prince's imminent return. And I've brought Fairy, who's in a rira-induced coma."

There was no response for a few moments. All Sora could hear was her pulse pounding in her ears.

A long minute later, the iron gates began to open on their silent hinges. Bullfrog, one of the councilmembers, strode out.

"Your Honor," Sora said, hurrying forward, "I'm so glad to see you. I came to tell you—"

"Save your breath," Bullfrog said, drawing his sword.

Sora's heart leaped into her throat. "I don't understand."

Except she could. Everything she'd done with the ryuu could be explained, but the truth was less believable than what it looked like from the outside—that she'd been brainwashed by Prince Gin and sent to deceive the taigas.

Bullfrog advanced.

Sora took several steps backward. But she couldn't pull a weapon on a councilmember. What was she supposed to do?

"Spirit," Bullfrog said, "you are under arrest."

She continued to back away. "No, please. Let me explain. I know how to defeat Prince Gin and his army. I came to report to you."

"Your allegiance cannot be trusted," Bullfrog said. "You made an attempt on Empress Aki's life. You murdered Imperial Guards. You are possibly still under the Dragon Prince's charm, sent here on his orders to mislead us."

"It's not true!" Sora turned, looking for another way out.

But several other taigas had descended from the fortress walls. They came at her from all sides, even behind her. She was surrounded.

"I'm sorry to do this," Bullfrog said as he stepped so close to her, she could smell the remnants of rice and pickled plum on his breath. "But until we defeat Prince Gin and find a way to undo his spell on our taigas, you must be considered a threat. And neutralized."

Before Sora could protest more, Bullfrog sheathed his

sword, choked off her windpipe, and jabbed a needle into her throat.

For an instant, Sora saw stars. And then the stars burst in a blinding explosion, and her knees gave way, dropping her to the ground and flinging her into unconsciousness.

CHAPTER FIFTY-NINE

At first, Daemon dreamed of clouds and clear blue sky.

Soon, though, the clouds began to melt and come back together again, swirling and sliding and changing from white to silver to green. One morphed from a blotch into a green cat. It was like being in the middle of a hallucination. The sky shifted suddenly to green—in fact, everything looked as if he were dreaming through an emerald-tinted lens—and the clouds billowed and started to funnel into Daemon's head, tickling his temple as the wisps drifted in through his ear and wafted inside his skull.

What is this? Daemon thought.

Somewhere in the back of his head, a girl giggled. It sounded almost like Sora, if Sora giggled. Which she did not. She laughed, but she didn't giggle.

Daemon, you're here! the girl said.

What in all hells—? Daemon blinked and shook himself awake.

Even with his eyes open, though, he didn't see reality.

The green-tinged dream pushed on.

Aren't the stars pretty? the girl said.

Who are you? What's happening?

The girl really did sound like Sora, if she were drunk. But again, impossible. Sora didn't ever drink enough to lose control. Two small cups of sake, and she would cut herself off.

The girl sighed. *I don't know who I am. Am I a taiga or a ryuu? Or both? A taigryuu?* She giggled. But then she grew pensive again. *What kind of soldier am I, though, if I have no weapons? Or maybe I do, I don't know. They were on me when I came to the gate. . . . I think Bullfrog injected me with genka after he knocked me unconscious?*

Oh gods, it *was* Sora. Or at least a version of Sora. She'd come back to the Citadel, only to be confronted by the councilmember most vehement in his belief that she'd succumbed to Prince Gin's charm. So Bullfrog had subdued her by shooting her with genka, a botanical drug used to pacify violent prisoners.

This is a dream, right? Sora asked. *I'm dreaming that you're in my head, Daemon. . . . Ooh, look, a green serpent! Isn't it pretty?*

Daemon smiled drowsily, at Sora missing him and her being back, and at the green stars shaped like a serpent. But the constellation's tongue—a green comet of some sort—flicked as it floated by, licking Daemon's cheek with a stinging twitch. The sharpness roused him.

He batted the serpent constellation away. How was this happening? Sora was hallucinating because of the genka, but she'd somehow pulled Daemon into her dream.

Maybe this was another facet of ryuu power. The Society had thought they understood magic, but they hadn't even scraped the surface. And here was something even more, an extra dimension to gemina bonds. Maybe, in her drugged state, Sora's new powers had expanded the connection she and Daemon shared.

Sora, I know you're, uh, slightly giddy, but I need you to listen to me closely. Where are you?

In the stars?

Daemon looked up. It seemed they were indeed flying among the stars. He wondered if they were seeing the same thing.

I mean, where is your actual body? he asked. A shooting star whooshed by him, so close it nicked his arm. He massaged the burn, but it vanished quickly, as dream burns do.

In a room . . .

Sora, I need you to focus. This is important.

He could feel her try to pull herself together.

Lemme try . . . to see . . . the wakeful world, she said.

Her thoughts struggled to make progress, like she was slogging through a swamp. But eventually, she said, *I see it. It's a fancy room. A big one.* Sora's voice cartwheeled groggily, and he could see the physical manifestation of it, jeweled green spirals spinning in slow motion in the air.

He had to find her in real life, outside of this dream.

Big, fancy room. Hmm.

The councilmembers had large suites, lavishly furnished. Perhaps she was being kept prisoner in Bullfrog's quarters?

Daemon needed to alert the other taigas. And he needed to get to Sora before the rest of the ryuu arrived. He tried to shake himself out of the dream. But the stars reached out with tendrils of light that held him fast, like vines wrapped around his arms.

Sora, let go of the connection. You have to let me out of your delirium.

Huh? Her dizziness spun through him. *But I don't want to be separated from you again.*

Daemon's breath caught in his throat. Sora had always been self-sufficient, an island in a sea of taigas. But now she needed him.

You won't lose me, Sora. You found me. And I'm coming for you right now. But you need to stop projecting. You need to let me out of the hallucination.

Silence.

Sora . . .

All right.

He felt her hold on for another moment, and then the starlight released him and he fell through the darkness,

down

down

down

until he hit the earth with a jolt. His eyes sprang open to reality, and he bolted up from where he lay on the boathouse ground. Early morning traces of light greeted him.

It was real, Daemon told himself, even though a part of him still wasn't sure whether it had just been a realistic dream.

No. It was real. I know Sora; it felt *like her.* Despite the fact that his gemina was drugged, being reconnected in that hallucination was the most whole Daemon had felt since they'd been separated on Prince Gin's ship. He actually felt more than whole.

He strapped his bo onto his back and shook Broomstick awake.

Broomstick was up in less than a second, knives in hand. "Ryuu?" he asked.

"Sort of," Daemon said. "Sora."

"Here?" He looked around the boathouse.

"It's hard to explain. She came back to help us, but Bullfrog didn't believe her and drugged her with genka. Somehow, though, in her delirious state, she connected with me through a dream."

Broomstick tensed. "Wait. Where's Fairy?"

Stars. Daemon hadn't thought to ask about her. *I'm a terrible friend.*

But he'd been asleep, under the dream influence of Sora's hallucination. It wasn't an excuse, but it was an explanation.

"I don't know," Daemon said. "We have to find Sora and wake her up. She'll tell us where Fairy is."

They ran toward the councilmembers' residence.

When they arrived, Daemon slowed his pace. Broomstick tilted his chin up toward a window on the back of the building's second floor.

Daemon nodded and curled his fingers in a series of simple mudras. "I am a spider, I am a spider, I am a spider," he chanted under his breath. The spell took, and he leaped onto the wall and scurried up to the second floor. He paused outside the window to listen through the rice paper screen . . . nothing.

And then, a giggle, like a little girl telling herself a joke. Only that girl was Sora. It was the same delirious giggle from his dream.

He peeled the paper off the window frame without a sound. From the corner of the window, he peeked inside.

She was there, toppled over on the reed mats, her hands

and feet bound. Relief and anger flooded through Daemon like a river through a broken dam. Anger at himself for letting this happen, and anger at Bullfrog for not trusting her.

Daemon shot a quick nod to Broomstick below. He began to scale the wall too. Daemon abandoned peeling away the rice paper and just burst through the window. He swung himself into the room.

Sora didn't register his arrival. He rushed to her side and tried to shake her awake.

"Hmm?" she said. Her eyes remained stubbornly shut.

"It's me, Daemon," he said. "You have to wake up."

"All right . . . after one more ride on this shooting star." She giggled.

Broomstick slipped in through the window.

"Sora." Daemon shook her again.

"We need to counteract the genka," Broomstick said as he began opening and shutting drawers. "Look for an antidote."

Daemon searched through the closet and lifted the reed mats to check beneath them. "There's nothing here," he said.

Broomstick sighed. "Now what?"

"I have an idea." Daemon crouched next to Sora.

"Sora, do you remember when you spoke to me through the connection and we saw the serpent constellation? And we flew through the stars?"

She opened her eyes and smiled drowsily. "When everything was ryuu emeralds?"

"Um, yeah. That." Daemon had no idea what she was talking about, but he pressed on. "You and I were seeing the same thing. We didn't just share feelings; other senses are potentially involved. So I was wondering . . . can you transfer the genka to me through the bond? I mean, not the actual genka, but its effects—the fogginess, the hallucinations, the intoxication?"

"I don't . . . I don't understand."

"It's all right. Just, uh, close your eyes again and try to reach out to me through our bond." He hoped allowing her to shut her eyes wouldn't send her careening back into the dream world and away from the real world.

The room around Daemon began to distort and swirl. He could almost feel the genka dribbling into his veins, if not in actuality, then in essence. Before he slipped away into the hallucination completely, he grabbed onto Broomstick's arm. Daemon needed something to tether himself to reality so he could communicate coherently with Sora before the drug submerged him.

Daemon?

Hi, Sora.

It worked. He exhaled, both relieved and a bit disbelieving. They could literally communicate through their gemina bond.

You really did come for me, Sora said.

I said I would, and I did. Listen, I'm going to try to draw the delirium from you, all right? And then you need to help Broomstick. You need to promise you'll leave me and go stop the ryuu.

What will happen to you?

Don't worry about me. But the Society—and Kichona—needs you. Do you promise?

I promise.

All right.

Broomstick put his hand on Daemon's. It grounded him.

The room around Daemon had already vanished, replaced instead by Sora's feverish green hallucination, which involved throwing stars flinging themselves every which way at moving targets. They always hit the bull's-eye.

Daemon smiled.

Then he concentrated on the muddy edges of his vision and on the feeling of being adrift. He collected the random clouds that floated among the throwing stars. He pulled away the giggles that floated in the air.

Give them to me, Sora.

His burden grew heavier, yet it was strangely light, like an ever-growing bundle of cotton on his shoulders and inside his head. Soon his skull cavity would be stuffed full with clouds and nonsensical laughter.

He couldn't feel Broomstick's hand anymore, even though it was probably still there. The throwing stars disappeared, replaced instead by a wolf cub, a bunny, and a kangaroo, all made of blue stars. They frolicked among lightning bolts, running to dodge them. Daemon giggled. What a foreign but glorious feeling; it was like being six years old again.

Thank you, Daemon, a girl's voice said from somewhere that seemed very far away. *I won't let you down. I promise.*

Daemon shrugged. He didn't even know what the girl was promising. Was it something they'd discussed?

The constellation wolf cub bounded toward him. Daemon tossed a meteor out into the dark sky, and the little wolf chased it, leaving a streak of bright blue behind him.

He's a good pet, Daemon thought as he giggled again. *Even if he is a myth.*

CHAPTER SIXTY

With ryuu magic, Sora broke the cuffs around her wrists as easily as if they were made of paper. She didn't want to think about what had just happened with Daemon. In fact, she didn't remember most of what had happened after Bullfrog injected her with genka, but she had a lingering feeling that something unexpectedly intimate had just taken place. She also knew that Daemon lay on the floor with a childlike grin on his face, and that Broomstick was standing several feet away. Too far for a friend, too close for an enemy.

"Broomstick—"

"Wolf risked everything for you just now," he said cautiously. "Not only by taking the delirium from you—though I still don't understand how—but also by rescuing you. You're under arrest by a councilmember. Freeing you could be grounds for treason."

Sora stumbled as she closed the distance between them. It seemed that everyone wanted to try her for treason. But that was all the more reason to make sure at least her friends were on her side.

"I know." Sora steadied herself. She put her hand on Broomstick's shoulder. "I also know that you're liable to be tried for treason too by accompanying Wolf. Thank you."

Broomstick jerked backward. He still had a crazed look in his eyes. "Please tell me we were right to do it, Spirit. Tell me Fairy's alive. I want to trust you, but my gemina bond feels like a gods-damn cemetery, and if you didn't keep her safe, I swear I will break you in half."

Sora nodded carefully. She was a good fighter and she had ryuu magic, but Broomstick was two hundred pounds of muscle, and she didn't doubt the lengths he'd go to to avenge his gemina, especially if Sora proved to be the enemy. "You can trust me," she said softly. "I gave Fairy rira to fake her death. I brought her back with me. . . . I don't know where Bullfrog took her. To the infirmary, I'm guessing."

He stared intensely at her for another moment as he processed this.

"Broomstick, I promise I'm telling the truth. I love Fairy. I love you and Daemon too. And . . . if we don't believe in each other, what do we have left?"

He flinched. "That's what Wolf said to me too." His fists began to unclench.

But then he let out a barrage of new questions. "What happened at Copper Bluff? Why did you spare us? Why did you go back to Prince Gin, and then turn around and leave them again? I don't get it." He looked pointedly at her uniform.

Sora was suddenly very aware of her green belt and the green triplicate whorls on the cuffs of her tunic. She looked like a ryuu, and she'd actually been one for some time—she'd nearly killed her friends. She tried to shake off the guilt, because she hadn't been herself, but it clung to her like a parasite.

"I know I did a lot of bad things . . . but I will make it up to you. I swear." To avoid Broomstick's scrutiny of her and her uniform, Sora looked down at Daemon. "Let me try to explain while we hide him. I think the closet would be a good place."

She called on the ryuu particles to make Daemon quiet for as long as the genka had hold of him. Broomstick stepped forward and began to pick up Daemon's feet, as if they were going to hoist him up. But Sora commanded the emerald dust to lift his slumbering body.

Broomstick took in a sharp breath. "Stars. How did you—? Oh, right," he said, as if he'd suddenly remembered Sora levitating Fairy's body inside the tent at Copper Bluff. "Ryuu magic."

Sora nodded apologetically.

"S-sorry. I just . . ." He composed himself, still wary of her, but listening. "Go on."

"My sister is alive," Sora said. "Hana didn't die during the Blood Rift. Prince Gin's warriors actually kidnapped some of the tenderfoots to train as the next generation of their army, for when he would return to Kichona. Hana was one of them. She goes by Virtuoso."

"What?" Broomstick cocked his head, as if he'd heard Sora wrong. In the meantime, the emerald particles floated Daemon into the closet and lowered him onto some spare bedding. The doors slid gently shut.

Without something else to do, Sora faced Broomstick

now. "She's been raised by a power-hungry, vengeful prince, and she doesn't remember anything else. Her whole world is shaped by the Dragon Prince's story. She's a ryuu through and through. But she's my baby sister, Broomstick. I couldn't abandon her. I was making progress reconnecting with her. So I had to go back with her after Copper Bluff. I wanted to get through to her and show her how wrong Prince Gin is. I wanted to bring her back to our side."

Broomstick sank down into one of Bullfrog's chairs, an elegant piece of black wood and soft black leather. "Stars, Spirit. Here I was whining about putting myself out there one time, while you've been working undercover with the gods-damn Dragon Prince, risking your life every second you're there, and simultaneously wrestling with the discovery that your little sister is still alive and beguiled by the enemy. I am a sorry excuse for a taiga for ever doubting you."

Sora kneeled beside him. "It's perfectly understandable. I know that what I've done doesn't look good on its face."

"But still. I *know* you. My loyalty shouldn't have wavered. I should've been more like Wolf."

She thought of how Daemon looked whenever he climbed to the top of a tree, smiling as if the heavens replenished him. How he'd become wild again in Takish Gorge, speaking with the alpha wolf. And how he'd somehow jolted her from the Dragon Prince's hold, through sheer determination in their gemina bond.

In a sky littered with asteroids, he was the North Star.

Sora's stomach fluttered, as if it were full of dragonflies. It was a new feeling that she didn't quite understand, but what she did know was this: "No one is like Wolf."

Broomstick nodded solemnly.

"You two made a bold move by saving me," Sora said. "Now let me make it worth it. I have a plan, but I need you to convince the Council and spread the word to the other taigas. They won't believe it, coming from me."

"Tell me what I need to do."

Sora pulled up another chair. "I assume Wolf explained how ryuu magic works?"

"Yes."

"Good. Now, there's no way the taigas are going to be able to match the ryuu in a fight. Prince Gin and his army are on the edge of Jade Forest; they'll be here within hours, and even if I could teach everyone how to command ryuu magic, there simply isn't enough time for them to learn and master it."

Broomstick's knuckles whitened as he squeezed the armrest on his chair. "This doesn't sound too promising."

"Exactly," Sora said. "That's why we can't actually fight. We have to stop the battle before it ever begins, before they can overwhelm us and conduct the Ceremony of Two Hundred Hearts. We have to undermine the ryuu's Sight."

"What do you mean?"

Sora held her hand in front of her. "Right now, there is emerald-colored dust swirling in the air. The ryuu have to be able to see it in order to command it to do things. But if we blind them, they won't have magic. However, we will. Or, worst case, we fight hand to hand, and the odds are even. Better for us, actually, because we outnumber them."

Broomstick relaxed his hold on the armrest and leaned forward. "So how do we blind all of them? We can't just poke out the ryuu's eyes individually when they march on the main gates. I have a feeling the Dragon Prince won't take well to that kind of welcome."

She stood from her chair and walked over to the window, which had a view of Rose Palace on the top of the hill. It glimmered as if it were the crown of all of Kichona. "I do have something in mind, if I can get it to work. It involves breaking off a huge chunk of crystal, floating it to the gates of the Citadel, and raising it at just the right angle in the sun when the ryuu arrive."

"You're going to tear apart Empress Aki's castle to use it as a giant magnifying glass?" His eyes were wide.

"If I can control the magic," Sora said. "I have no idea if I'm strong enough. But yes, that's the plan."

Broomstick chuckled despite himself. "If anyone can pull this off, it's you, Spirit."

She didn't laugh, though. She kept her gaze on Rose Palace. "Yes, well . . . Let's hope that's true."

CHAPTER SIXTY-ONE

Fairy startled awake and sat straight up. Her mouth tasted like sand. And everything was too bright.

She squinted at all the white around her. *Where am I?*

Everything that had happened at Copper Bluff came rushing back to her. The invisible ryuu putting her in a headlock. Wolf breaking Prince Gin's spell. Spirit, giving her rira and promising she would be all right.

That must mean she was somewhere safe, right? Because Spirit had been bad but then she was good. She must have been, if Fairy was still alive.

She frowned. She was so confused.

Am I back at the Citadel? But no, it was white here, and everything at the Citadel was black.

Except the infirmary. The inside of the Society infirmary was white. But how would she have gotten back here?

Fairy shoved aside the thin blanket that covered her. She threw her legs over the cot and stood up.

Rather, she *tried* to stand up. But her muscles were as wobbly as yuzu jelly. She grabbed for the rails on the side of the cot, missed, and fell to the ground with a crash.

No one ran to her aid. No doctors. No nurses.

But also, no ryuu.

She didn't know whether to be relieved or upset that she'd been left all alone.

And where was Broomstick? Or Wolf? Had they made it out of Copper Bluff?

Fairy began to cry.

She hated it. But she couldn't stop the tears.

Five minutes later, though, Broomstick burst through the infirmary doors. "Fairy?" he shouted as he tore down the corridor.

"Broomstick!" she shouted. She sobbed at the sound of his voice.

Stop crying, she reprimanded herself. *You're a taiga, for gods' sake.*

The confusion began to clear in her head, and she could feel their gemina bond light up. Broomstick's relief and happiness flooded in.

She reached up for the cot's rails again, and this time, she managed to pull herself up. Her arms and legs prickled with pins and needles, but it was a vast improvement from being composed of jelly. The rira had worn off her brain first, and now it was wearing off the rest of her body.

Broomstick careened around the corner, into the room. He helped her sit on the cot, then threw his arms around her and held her tight. "You're alive. You're alive and you're all right."

"I'll only be alive if you don't squeeze me to death," Fairy said, gasping.

"Oh, sorry." He released her but kept grinning and shaking his head, as if the fact that she was awake hadn't quite sunk in.

She was still working on believing it too. As all the feeling returned to her limbs, though, she was able to smile. No more stupid tears.

"How long was I out?" Fairy asked. "And where is everyone? I fell and made a racket, but no one came."

Broomstick let out a long exhale. "Do you remember what happened in the desert?"

"Yes."

"Well . . ." He quickly caught her up, from how her body had been taken as evidence of the empress's death to this very moment, when Spirit was on her way to demolish Rose Palace, Wolf was delirious from gemina-transferred genka, and Broomstick was supposed to alert the Council of the plan to blind the ryuu when they arrived. Which was a matter of hours.

Fairy blinked at him. "You're saying I didn't miss much while I was unconscious."

Broomstick shook his head and laughed. "Something like that."

"Well, I guess since it's been incredibly boring in the past few days, we'd better go out there and make something interesting happen, huh?" Fairy scooted off the cot. She wasn't feeling disoriented or sleepy anymore; the shock of all that had happened dispelled it.

And she'd been out of action for too long. Time to get

back into it. "Go do what you need to do to spread word of Spirit's plan. I'm going to grab my potions from my room. I might be able to mix together an antidote to genka for Wolf."

"It might not work, since he didn't actually get shot with genka," Broomstick said. "Spirit is the one with the genka in her system. Wolf only has the effects."

Fairy frowned. "It's still worth trying. If we're going to battle the ryuu, we're going to need all the taigas we can get, and Wolf is one of our best fighters."

Broomstick put his fist over his heart. "Cloak of night."

She shook her head. "Wrong salute."

"You're right." He pounded his fists to his chest again. "Work hard."

"Mischief harder."

Fairy let herself look at her gemina for a few more seconds, while at the same time basking in the fierce, brotherly love Broomstick sent through their connection. Heavens, it felt good to be back.

CHAPTER SIXTY-TWO

Your Majesty," one of the Imperial Guards said, "I'm sorry to bother you in these early hours, but there is an apprentice here to see you. She's not on your schedule, but she insisted it was urgent. She has news of Prince Gin."

Aki rose from the meditation cushion. "Who is this apprentice?" she asked.

"She says her name is Spirit."

"The one the Council arrested? Interesting." Aki nodded. Spirit was the chief rogue, the one who'd plotted the fireworks at the palace. Some of the councilmembers thought she might be a traitor, but Aki thought they were shortsighted, limited by how they understood the world. Spirit saw and did things differently than tradition dictated. It was precisely what Aki needed, and she'd judge for herself whether Spirit was loyal or not. "Please send her in."

Spirit entered the room and laid herself on the ground in the requisite bow. When she rose, she said, "Your Majesty, thank you for meeting with me. I don't have much time. I came to ask permission to break off part of your palace. It's the only way to defeat the ryuu."

Both of Aki's brows shot straight up. "I knew that you were creative, but this was more than I imagined."

"I know I'm asking a lot. More than a lot. You don't even know who I am, and—"

"You are asking for a great deal, but you're wrong about one thing: I do know who you are."

"Oh." Spirit looked around nervously, as if anticipating guards jumping at her.

"Some of the Council believe you're working for my brother," Aki said. "But I don't. If you were, I'd already be dead, wouldn't I?"

Spirit nodded carefully. It must be strange—scary, even—for the empress to talk about assassination. "Yes, Your Majesty. If I were a ryuu sent to kill you, you wouldn't have even known I was here."

"All right," Aki said, settling back onto her meditation cushion and surprised even at herself for feeling so calm and sure about Spirit. But now was the time for action, not over-thinking. "Explain to me why I should let you demolish part of my palace. The Council has a battle plan. How is yours better?"

She didn't say anything. Instead, Spirit held her arms out in front of her. Almost immediately, they disappeared from view, as if they'd been sliced off at the elbow.

Aki gasped. "How . . . ? What did you do?"

"I can make myself invisible," she said, her arms reappearing. "I'm not the only ryuu who can. There are others who can make blood boil. They can form hurricanes. Cloud the sky with an army of locusts. Bend steel to their will.

The Council doesn't comprehend the full power of the ryuu. But I've trained with them. I know what they can do, and we don't stand a chance fighting them the old way."

The old way, Aki thought. That was, indeed, how Glass Lady and the others at the Citadel had been operating. In the busy lead-up to confronting Gin, she'd forgotten her frustration with the Council. But it was because of their inability to adapt, their sticking to traditional methods of warfare, that Aki had taken matters into her own hands and asked Fairy and Broomstick to go to Copper Bluff.

If it was true what Spirit said about the ryuu, then following the Council's strategy of simply fighting Gin's warriors head-on was a prescription for death. Not only for the soldiers themselves, but also for Kichona. Once the Ceremony of Two Hundred Hearts was completed, Gin would turn their peaceful kingdom into a war machine. Tiger pearls and whispering maple leaves would be replaced with blood and destruction. And the people would no longer be themselves at all once he hypnotized them. They'd just be extensions of Gin's will.

"This isn't simply the Rift all over again, is it?" Aki said.

"No, Your Majesty. You won't win against Prince Gin this time, unless—"

"We think and fight differently."

Spirit nodded. Her jaw set with a determination that reminded Aki of herself when she was young and fighting for the kingdom.

"My brother is almost here?" Aki asked.

"Yes."

Aki touched the locket at her throat. He was coming. The man who used to be just a boy, her other half. The brother who used to play pirates versus taigas with her. Her partner in crime, sneaking into the palace kitchen together to steal peach pies.

The man who'd also torched the Imperial City, who was obsessed with the Evermore, and who would bring blood and destruction to Kichona again.

She inhaled deeply and waved her hand toward the hill outside her window. "You have my permission to do whatever you need to Rose Palace."

"Really?" Spirit's eyes widened, like a child who wasn't sure if she'd truly been given free reign to do the one thing she'd never been allowed to do.

"Yes. You have my permission on one condition . . ." Aki stood. "You let me come with you. If we are to do things differently, then I want to be an active part of this. I will not sit in a gilded room while the taigas fight for me."

Spirit's eyes grew wider, if that was possible. "It would be an honor, Your Majesty."

"Let me change into something more practical," Aki said, gesturing at the gown sweeping at her feet and heading toward her bedroom. "But let's be clear about this mission to dismantle my palace—it is also an honor for *me* to be able to join *you*."

CHAPTER SIXTY-THREE

The gray of night still had a tenuous hold on the sky when Sora and Empress Aki slipped out the rear gates of the Citadel. It may have been Prince Gin who was the sibling blessed with magic, but now the empress was in a taiga uniform, and with her hair pulled back in a simple bun, a knife on her belt, and her commanding stride, she really could have passed as a young warrior.

Empress Aki had also found Sora a taiga uniform to wear. Sora stretched an arm out in front of her. It felt good to see a sleeve without the ryuu's green whorls embroidered there.

I can wield their magic, but I am still a taiga, and I always will be.

Instead of heading up the winding road to Rose Palace, though, Empress Aki turned toward the Field of Illusions guarding the Citadel's western fortress walls.

Sora hesitated. "Where are we going?"

"A secret that only the Imperial Guard and I know. And now you." The empress winked.

She sprinted onto the sand, which immediately began to shift beneath her, in front of her, all around her.

In a matter of seconds, the empress was already fifty yards into the illusions. How was she so fast?

"Wait!" Sora ran after her. "Your Highness, you need a taiga guide or else—"

"Or else this will happen?" Empress Aki stopped abruptly in the middle of a black-and-white spiral of sand that swirled and made the ground look like a three-dimensional vortex that would swallow them whole.

And then it did swallow her.

"No!" Sora shouted.

But the empress's laugh came from deep beneath the sand. "Spirit, stand in the middle. Follow me."

Sora rushed into the spiral to the spot where Empress Aki had just been. She jerked herself backward at the last second when she realized there was a hole there. Her toe almost slipped down.

"It's all right, Spirit," Empress Aki said from below. "There's a soft landing down here."

Sora looked around to see if anyone was watching. She took a breath and stepped into the hole.

She let out a small cry as she plummeted. But as the empress had promised, she landed on her feet on a thick mat. Not unlike the ones the Society used for training.

"Is that—?" Sora began to ask.

"A sparring mat?" Empress Aki said. "Yes. I have many. Are you surprised?"

"I . . . I shouldn't be." It made sense now why the empress could run so fast. How could Sora have thought that the ruler of their kingdom would just sit around in her throne room? Especially since she'd grown up with a twin brother who trained as a taiga; she couldn't command magic, but there was no reason she wouldn't have learned the other drills for physical conditioning and fighting. And Empress Aki had fought the Blood Rift—and won—when she was only fifteen.

"Good. Because sparring mats are the least of my surprises."

It was only then that Sora really took in where they were. It was an underground room. The floor was striped in black and white, as if the Field of Illusions had been beaten into submission and the sand packed tight as stone. Cypress beams held up the ceiling. And the walls were covered in ceramic tiles, some blue, some gold, and some with the Ora tiger crest painted on them.

"Is this some kind of safe room?" Sora asked, still gaping.

"You'll see," Empress Aki said.

"Does the commander know about it?"

"Like I said, only me, the Imperial Guards, and you."

Despite the fact that they were on the brink of war with Prince Gin, Sora grinned. She had stepped up to her potential. And now someone was taking her seriously, letting her in on a part of history almost nobody else knew.

Empress Aki produced a necklace with a locket on it and pressed the locket into one of the tiger tiles.

A dusty corner of the floor began to sink down into the ground, revealing a stairway.

"What in all h—" Sora stopped before she cursed in front of the empress.

"Do you think you could use some of my brother's fancy magic to light the way in an underground tunnel?" Empress

Aki asked. "There are lanterns around here, but it would be faster if you were able to—"

Sora shook herself out of her shock and conjured an orb of light in her hands, and then several more. They floated in the air around her.

"Well, then," the empress said, "that takes care of that."

They descended into the cool earth, into a tunnel that ran through the mountain. It went under the Citadel, up beneath the winding road, under the crystal waters of the moat, to the palace. Every thousand yards, a solid iron door sealed and separated the next section of the tunnel from the previous one, and each door was secured by a tiger tile that required the locket medallion to be pressed into it— sometimes it was the tile on the upper right of the left wall, sometimes in the middle of the right wall, sometimes on a spot halfway from the center to the bottom left corner, et cetera. Sora watched in awe as Empress Aki unlocked each door without a moment's hesitation, the solution to each one memorized.

On the way to the palace, Sora had explained to the empress what she wanted to do with the crystal. Now they emerged from the tunnels through a panel in the floor of the courtyard where Sora and the other Level 12s had performed their exhibition match.

"I thought you could use that slab of crystal," Empress Aki said, pointing to where her chair had been that night. It was the part of the courtyard wall etched with the imperial family's crowned tiger and the motto "Dignity. Benevolence. Loyalty."

"It's a good size," Sora said. "But are you sure? I could break down a piece of less significance."

Empress Aki looked right at the crest. "No. This one sends the right message."

Yes, it does, Sora thought. She'd already known that these principles were the underpinnings of the kingdom. But now Sora also understood that they were the foundation on which she herself had been made. Dignity, benevolence, and loyalty had molded her and her friends, and if they adhered to them, these same principles would guide them into who they were going to be—people as noble and selfless and good as Empress Aki. Hopefully.

Sora nodded at the crystal wall. "The facets of the etching will also make the light sparkle more, be more unpredictable to the ryuu."

Four Imperial Guards arrived. They seemed unsurprised to find that the empress had returned to the palace, as if she'd told them it was a possibility all along.

"You should take cover, Your Majesty," Sora said. "This could get messy."

"I'll wait in the tunnel." She pressed her locket medallion into the secret panel and descended into the courtyard floor. Her Imperial Guards went with her.

Sora stood alone before the wall. She hadn't mentioned to the empress that she wasn't sure how or even *if* she could break off a piece of the palace.

What is the best way to do this?

The fire ryuu had told a story about melting the edges of an iceberg before, but that was no help. Sora wasn't a master at fire magic, and crystal wouldn't melt at the kind of temperatures she could manage.

She could try to command the magic to form giant hands and wrench the wall away, but that might cause irreparable damage to the rest of the palace. Sora shuddered thinking of all the cracks she'd create, and how they'd spread, shattering the rest of Rose Palace because of the fractures.

Okay. No wrenching the wall.

What she needed was a clean break.

"A saw."

Actually, several saws. The kind used to cut diamonds. *Gods, please let my imagination be enough to guide the magic to do what I need it to do.*

Sora looked for the emerald particles. She called for as many of them as possible, and they rushed in from all over, sparkling streaks through the sky and into the courtyard. She willed the magic into long, sharp, steady blades. She directed them to the top of the wall, one enormous green saw poised over the right side, the other on the left.

Cut, she thought.

They began to slide back and forth, slowly, as if sawing through wood, and spewing splinters as if they were sawing through wood as well. Except these splinters were made of crystal. Sharp crystal.

Sora leaped as far as she could and covered her head under the shower of needles. *Stop!* she commanded the saws.

They ceased their motion. But some of the particles started to dissipate as she lost control over them, because she was looking at the blood seeping into her uniform from the many places her skin had been pierced.

Deal with the wounds later, she told herself. *They're just splinters.*

A hundred or so of them, but still. *Just splinters.*

Sora turned back to the saws and yelped as she saw them disintegrating back into the air, the particles wandering off because she wasn't paying attention to them.

No! Back into formation.

The magic hesitated, as if momentarily confused. Then most of the particles began to drift back into the shape of their saws.

She exhaled.

All right. Cutting back and forth on crystal was dangerous. Perhaps she had to approach this more like chopping vegetables.

Slice straight down, she willed the magic.

At first, she couldn't see anything happening. But then she noticed a thin line appear on either side of the wall where it was separating from the rest of the palace. Her green knives worked slowly but steadily.

The floor panel on the far side of the courtyard opened. Empress Aki stuck out her head. "Everything all right?"

"It is now," Sora said. "You can come out from the tunnel, although you should probably stay on that side of the courtyard, just in case."

Empress Aki and her Imperial Guards emerged. One of them noticed Sora was injured. "I'll get her some bandages," he said.

He returned a few minutes later and dressed her wounds. Sora breathed into his touch. It was actually helpful to have someone else with her, grounding her as she focused intensely on the saws.

She began again. The wall trembled, and the Ora crest glinted in the faint light of the impending sunrise.

The saws neared the bottom. Sora's eyes began to cross; the concentration was taxing.

And then, the last, final slice.

She exhaled deeply and closed her eyes for a moment. Then she turned to Empress Aki. "Your Majesty, we have our magnifying glass."

"Excellent. Can you get it down to the Citadel?"

Sora was tired, but she nodded. There would be time for rest later. "I'll use magic to levitate it down the hill."

Empress Aki looked up at the purpling sky to gauge the time. "You go on ahead. I just need to do one thing here at the palace. I want to go to Sola's temple to pray."

"But—"

"Don't worry. I have some Imperial Guards with me, and I'll leave by way of the secret tunnels again. You need to get to the Citadel, though. It's imperative that you arrive before my brother's army does, if you are to have them all in one place at the fortress gates to blind them."

Sora didn't like the idea of leaving the empress behind. But she was the sovereign, which meant Sora didn't really have a choice. Besides, Empress Aki's reasoning made sense, and she did have a contingent of Imperial Guards, the best warriors in the kingdom.

"All right, Your Majesty. Be safe. I'll see you back at the Citadel soon."

CHAPTER SIXTY-FOUR

Fairy slipped into Bullfrog's room the same way Broomstick had—through the window. She'd stopped by the dormitory to grab vials of wood-ear mushroom powder and swallow's saliva, which could be combined to form an antidote to genka. Unfortunately, she didn't have much wood ear; her old stash was in the satchel she'd given to Spirit, and Fairy hadn't had time since to forage for more.

I hope what I have is enough to wake Daemon.

As soon as she was inside Bullfrog's quarters, she found her way to the bedroom and slid open the closet door.

"Oh, Wolfie," she said, as she saw him slumped in a heap on top of the spare bedding. It was a little sad to see him like this, a ferocious, wild animal from the woods reduced to a grinning fool with spit dribbling down his chin.

It was almost the same as what had happened to her. Fairy may not be an orphan raised by wolves, but she was pretty formidable too. And she'd also been completely disarmed, a trophy for the Dragon Prince to carry victoriously in his arms.

"I understand sacrifices must be made for the greater good, but let's not do it like this," she said, partly to herself, partly to Wolf. "Idle drooling really doesn't suit the League of Rogues."

Quickly, she poured the wood-ear powder into an empty vial, then used a dropper to add half an ounce of swallow's saliva. The concoction let off a noxious brown cloud that stunk of steaming-hot cow dung.

Fairy wrinkled her nose as she carried it over to the closet. "I'm sorry, but you're going to have to drink this."

He kept snoring quietly.

She turned him onto his back and tried to pry open his lips with her free hand. "Wolf. Open your mouth."

"Mm mm mmmm." He kept his lips firmly pursed.

Fairy swirled the vial of wood ear and swallow's spit. Its odor had shifted from fresh dung to fertilizer now. Slightly mellower, but still awful.

"I don't have the patience for this. Sorry. Again." She kicked Wolf hard in the side, and he opened his mouth as if yelping, although no sound came out. She poured the contents of the vial onto his tongue. Then she smacked her hand over his mouth so he couldn't spit it out.

He struggled but finally swallowed. She removed her hand from his mouth.

Wolf's voice came back to him, a bit muddled, and he started singing nonsense. "Ba dij do, Ba dij pa-kow . . ."

"Come on, come on, come on," Fairy said. "Please work." She looked at her completely empty vial of wood ear, but even if it was enough to counteract the genka, there was still a chance it wouldn't work. After all, Spirit had been the one who was actually injected with genka.

Suddenly, Wolf gasped. He blinked. Then he looked up and smiled groggily.

"It's really unfair that you're so damnably handsome, even when you're drugged," Fairy said. "You're lucky I have a great deal of restraint."

He laughed, but it came out a bit sluggishly. "You made me a genka antidote."

"You're very observant."

"And you're awake. The rira wore off."

"Again, very observant. It would've been hard for me to make you an antidote if I was in a coma."

He sighed. "Glad you're okay. You were so brave . . . at the bluff." His eyelids fluttered shut. "Still sleepy. Miss the sparkly green dragons."

"No." Fairy shook him. "If you fall back asleep, I swear to the gods, I will kiss you against your wishes."

"I should definitely fall asleep then."

Fairy's heart skittered, like a hound's at the start of a foxhunt. Was he actually flirting back? Wolf never did that. He always shrugged aside her comments as if they were jokes.

She looked at his lips. They were very kissable. And then she remembered the day this past summer, when she'd seen him stepping out of one of the deep soaking tubs in the bathhouse (yes, she'd been in the towel closet with a conquest, but that didn't mean she wasn't allowed to look at other boys too). The water had beaded on Wolf's broad shoulders and dripped off the planes of his chest down to where the towel was wrapped around his waist . . .

Stop it. He's your roommate's gemina, she told herself.

"Come on," Fairy said, pulling Wolf to his feet. She retrieved another small glass vial from her belt, took his hand, and poured a small handful of what looked like little brown rocks into his palm. "Here, eat these."

He wobbled while trying to stand. "What are they?"

"Cocoa nibs. Highly caffeinated."

"Ah." Wolf popped them into his mouth. The nibs would hopefully counteract the last of the genka's effects.

He shook his head at the bitterness and blinked a few times, eyes bright and clear. Then he tilted his head as he looked down at Fairy.

She wrinkled her nose. "What are you staring at?"

"You're alive. You're awake."

Fairy waved him off. "We already went over this."

But he kept staring. "I worried . . . *we* worried that you might not have survived. I wanted to believe that you were safe, but we just didn't know. And over the past few days, I couldn't stop thinking about the feel of you in my arms in the desert, the life in you like a flame, and I . . ."

A silent hum began to build in the air between them, the kind of subtle vibration that only the two people involved can perceive. The thrill of the start of a foxhunt flitted through Fairy's chest again.

"You what?" she prompted.

"I . . ." Wolf shook his head as if dissuading himself from speaking. But then he looked at her again and said, "Your hair is still gold." He reached a tentative hand out, as if he wanted to touch it.

She held her breath.

"You were ready to give your life for the empress," he

said, hand still hovering just a fraction of an inch away from her hair. "You could have died. You almost did. I've always known you were bold, but that . . . Fairy, I'm in awe of you."

His fingers found a stray lock of hair. They grazed her cheek as he pinned it back into place.

Fairy's entire body vibrated at his touch. She looked at his mouth again. He was definitely awake now. She could kiss him, feel his tongue on hers, press herself against that glorious chest she'd seen in the bathhouse.

She met his gaze and raised her eyebrows, just a little, as if asking permission.

He nodded, dipped his head, and parted his lips.

His mouth was warm and soft at first. Gentle, as if he didn't want to hurt her.

But Fairy was no fragile thing. She pressed her lips against Wolf's, showing him what they could do. Her tongue found its way to his—hot and fluid.

And then Wolf let himself go, threading his hands through her hair and pulling her to him, smashing their mouths and bodies together. It was like he'd been released from a cage, his wanting fueled even more by his relief that she was alive.

Fairy smiled as she pressed herself harder into him and wondered why she'd never thought to do this with him. It's not like Spirit cared. She and Wolf were like Fairy and Broomstick—together since childhood, like siblings.

Wolf's hands began to trail down Fairy's neck, along the collar of her tunic. He was just about to slip them beneath the fabric when she gasped and pulled away. "No."

He startled and backed away. "I'm sorry. I didn't mean to—"

"It's all right. I mean, I wanted it. But we can't right now." Fairy hastily pulled her disheveled hair back into the semblance of neatness. "The ryuu are coming. We have to help."

Wolf cursed at himself under his breath. "How could I forget? I'm so selfish."

"No, you're not. You're just human."

He sighed.

"We'll finish this later. I promise," Fairy said. "Come on, we're meeting everyone at the main gates. I'll fill you in on the way there."

She held out her hand.

Wolf took it.

CHAPTER SIXTY-FIVE

Broomstick found Glass Lady in the armory. She was pacing through the weapons racks, taking inventory of what they had at their disposal.

"Commander," he said, jogging to keep up with her long stride. "Can I speak with you?"

"Unless you are reporting a breach of our perimeter by the ryuu, I don't have time," she said, marching on to the racks of swords.

"No, they haven't been sighted yet, but—"

"Then go back to your post, Broomstick. You are derelict in your duties."

"No." He planted himself in front of her and crossed his arms.

Glass Lady looked at him, aghast. "I beg your pardon?"

"Commander, you have to listen to me. We know how to defeat the ryuu."

"You're at risk of heaping more punishment upon yourself and your friends."

"I know." Broomstick took a step closer to her. "And that's why you should know this is important. The ryuu's one weakness is sight. They have to be able to see the magic before they can call it to do their bidding. We believe they'll be here shortly. We have a plan to blind them, but then we'll only have a short window of opportunity to take them out while they're vulnerable."

Glass Lady frowned, but it wasn't the disappointed one she usually wore when it came to Sora and her friends' shenanigans. She was thinking over what Broomstick said.

He was afraid to breathe while she considered it, as if even a slight puff of air could nudge her back into dismissing him as an overeager apprentice.

"I thought Sight was what gave them power," she said.

He exhaled. She was actually listening. "Yes, it is. But ironically, vision is also their weakness. Like taigas have to use their hands to form mudras, ryuu have to use their eyes to control their power."

She nodded slowly. "And what, exactly, is your plan?"

Broomstick explained how Sora was going to use a crystal wall as a magnifying glass to blind the ryuu when they approached the Imperial City. If they didn't have Sight, they wouldn't be able to access their magic. The taigas would have to be ready to pounce on the ryuu before they regained their ability to see. "It might only be a matter of seconds," he said.

Glass Lady fingered the throwing stars on her belt. "Yes, but before the ryuu showed up, taigas were the most formidable warriors in the world. If the ryuu don't have their magic, we only need a few seconds to neutralize them."

"Exactly," Broomstick said. "And we outnumber them."

Thanks to Wolf, he thought. It was because of his reconnaissance that Empress Aki could interrupt her brother's strategy to secretly amass an army. Prince Gin had managed to put together only a couple hundred ryuu on his way here. In comparison, there were now over five thousand taigas at the Citadel.

"They won't all come to the front gates," Glass Lady said.

"Most probably will," Broomstick said. "Even though Spirit brought Fairy back here, the ryuu still don't know that she wasn't the empress. Prince Gin will likely march here as planned, believing he is the new emperor."

"I think that's right," Glass Lady said, beginning to walk toward the armory's exit and gesturing for Broomstick to follow her. "We'll assemble most of our troops at the main gates, but we'll leave in place some forces on the perimeters. Spirit's crystal will have to do the brunt of the work. But I'll order mirrors stripped from bedrooms for the patrols on the other edges of the fortress walls, in case they also need to blind ryuu incursions."

Broomstick couldn't help the stupid grin that plastered itself across his face. She'd really listened to him. His crew was back and safe. They had a plan. And Glass Lady had actually heard what he had to say. "Thank you, Commander."

She glanced over at him as they left the armory and veered toward Warrior Meeting Hall. "For what?"

"For believing in me. For believing in *us*."

Glass Lady shrugged as if it meant nothing. But then she

gave Broomstick a small wink, so quick, he almost thought he imagined it.

"I always knew you and your friends had the potential to be great taigas," she said. "I was just waiting for you to believe in it yourselves."

CHAPTER SIXTY-SIX

Hana woke to the sky purpling with the dawn. She should have been excited about the march to the Imperial City. This was going to be a watershed moment in the dream Prince Gin had plotted for years.

Instead, there was a heaviness in her chest, like a ball of iron right beneath her sternum. Today was also supposed to be the day when she and Sora fought against the taigas, a sister ryuu team.

But that day would never be.

Hana lay on her sleeping mat for a few more minutes, the first morning in a long time that she hadn't jumped out of bed. Had she made a mistake in letting Sora go?

Why do I care? I gave her a choice, and she chose the taigas over me.

The iron ball in Hana's chest grew heavier, though. Love was an unwelcome guest in her heart.

And then she thought of something that made a dreadful morning even worse—if Sora had chosen the taigas over the ryuu, it also meant she'd chosen Empress Aki over Prince Gin.

"The body!"

Hana tore out of the tent and sprinted toward the cart at the edge of camp that held Empress Aki's corpse.

Please let everything be where it's supposed to be.

The ryuu who were supposed to be guarding the body were dead or unconscious.

"Gods dammit!" she screamed. "You fools! How could you let her past you? How could you allow her to steal the empress from right under your nose?"

The ryuu lay on the ground, unmoving.

But Hana's questions were really directed at herself anyway. She had trusted too easily. She should have known. Sora's priority had always been the Society and her friends.

Hana's anger ripped the cart apart. The wooden frame that held the canvas cover broke into pieces and flew into the air, then rocketed straight down, spearing themselves just inches from each of the ryuu.

She stormed back into the main part of camp.

"Pack up now!" she yelled at the ryuu.

"B-but we haven't had breakfast yet," one of them dared to say.

Hana glared at him. Her fury could burn a hole straight through his head.

"I don't care. Pack up camp and be ready to move out in thirty minutes. Today, we destroy my sister and her precious Society, and we put Emperor Gin on the throne."

CHAPTER SIXTY-SEVEN

Inside the Citadel, Sora commanded the ryuu particles to set her massive magnifying glass against the inside of the fortress wall. Sweat poured down her temples from the effort of floating and steering the crystal from Rose Palace. It had taken longer than she wanted, not only from being careful, but also because she'd decided it would be safest if she and the magnifying glass were invisible. Doing so drained nearly everything Sora had in her.

But the commotion of gathering troops at the main gates roused Sora. She hurried over, pushing past squadrons who were still assembling, ignoring the surprised calls of apprentices who hadn't known that she was back home. She stopped only when she found Broomstick.

A moment later, Daemon and Fairy appeared, framed by the rising sun. An avalanche of relief roared through Sora when she saw her roommate. "You're all right!"

Then she noticed that Fairy and Daemon were holding

hands, and a different kind of avalanche crashed down on her, one that made her sick to her stomach, even though she had no right to feel that way.

Gods. Sora blinked as comprehension set in. It was jealousy.

She looked at Daemon's and Fairy's fingers intertwined, and Sora realized that, in the back of her mind, she'd always assumed he was hers. She had taken their togetherness for granted. She'd mistaken her attachment to him as mere partnership.

But now, seeing him with someone else, she understood. She'd loved him since the day he arrived at the Citadel like a wolf cub, with his unkempt tufts of hair and feral eyes, the way he crouched on all fours and snarled at the other tenderfoots. She had imagined him as a boy out of one of her mother's Kichonan fables. Everyone else had wanted to tame him. Sora had been the only one who wanted him to keep his wildness.

Fairy cocked her head at Sora, as if to ask if everything was okay.

Sora took a deep breath and forced herself to smile. What else could she do? Sora hadn't tried to make a move on Daemon. Besides, the Society wouldn't have allowed it. Geminas couldn't get involved with each other like that.

So she nodded. Yes, it was fine. Everything was fine.

Besides, she couldn't afford to waste time on her feelings right now. Glass Lady always said curiosity killed the cat, but sentimentality killed the taiga. Maybe this was what she meant.

"I heard about your sister," Daemon said. For once, he didn't pick up on Sora's emotion through their gemina bond. Or, more accurately, the fact that she wanted to shut off the spigot of her emotions. Maybe he was too wrapped up in Fairy to feel the subtle change in his and Sora's connection. "I thought the reason you left Copper Bluff was to keep Fairy safe," he continued. "But now I also know it was because of Hana."

Sora sighed and closed her eyes. It took a second before she opened them again and answered.

"Yes. She's alive. She's on the wrong side, but she's alive."

Daemon looked at his feet and shook his head. "I'm sorry I wasn't there for you when you found Hana. You must have a hundred different feelings about it."

"I shouldn't. I don't want to feel anything right now except the drive to stop Prince Gin."

"Taigas aren't superhuman. We have emotions, just like regular people. But no matter what happens, I'm here for you. *We're* here for you." He looked to his right and left, at Fairy and Broomstick.

Sora nodded, feeling at the same time his comforting reassurance through their bond. "I know."

Glass Lady ran up to them. "The ryuu are approaching. Please tell me everything is in place."

Sora blinked, confused for a second that the commander was talking to them, mere apprentices.

"Spirit," Glass Lady snapped. "Broomstick said you were preparing a magnifying glass of some sort. Where is it?"

Sora shook herself out of her surprise. After all, she had come up with the plan, and it was a good one. Good enough, she hoped. "Yes, Commander. It's right over there." She pointed at the slab of Rose Palace propped a short distance away, against the inside of the Citadel's walls.

Glass Lady actually took a step back at its size. "That's the weapon? The Ora imperial crest?"

"Yes, Commander," Sora said. "Do you like it?"

A small smile actually crept onto Glass Lady's face. "I do, Spirit. Very much."

Sora grinned at Daemon. See? She'd been right. The road to becoming legendary didn't have to be without irreverence.

Glass Lady grew serious again. "Everyone in your places. Let's get to the top of the fortress walls."

From there, they looked down on the main gates. The ryuu were indeed nearly upon them. As they marched, their fire, bone, insect, and other magic was on full display. Glass Lady inhaled sharply as wasps swarmed above the ryuu in a noisy storm cloud, flames licked toward gates, and stones rolled up to the walls and began piling themselves to form steps.

Sora frowned. Something was wrong. The realization shot through her gemina bond like an arrow.

"What is it?" Daemon asked.

"This isn't all of the ryuu," Sora said.

"Maybe they're going to attack other parts of the fortress," Fairy said.

Broomstick peered through a spyglass and shook his head. "No signs of approach from the other sides of the Citadel. And we haven't heard alarms from the perimeter."

Where's the other half of the army? Sora wondered. Were they so arrogant that they thought they could defeat an entire fortress full of taigas and decided to use only a fraction of their forces?

"It's better for us," Daemon said. "After you blind them,

there will be fewer for us to fight."

Sora kept shaking her head, though. "I worry what the other half is doing. If—"

Hana rode forward. Sora froze. She couldn't remember what she was going to say. All she could focus on was her sister and the seething hatred in her eyes, so intense, it felt as if they burned a hole straight through Sora's heart.

She had to look away.

"Commander," Hana said, raising her voice and sounding ever Virtuoso. "We have come home to mourn Empress Aki's death, and to usher in the reign of Emperor Gin. We bring with us the gift of new magic to the Society. Open the gates, and let your returned warriors in."

Glass Lady nodded subtly at Sora to set her plan in motion.

"What is your name, child?" Glass Lady said to Hana.

Hana scoffed. "I am no child. I am Virtuoso, and I am second in command of this army."

"Well, *child*," Glass Lady said, her voice oozing the same venomous disdain as Hana's, "I may be old-fashioned, but I think current etiquette still dictates that it is rude to try to force one's way into another's home." She gestured at the stone staircase the ryuu were building with their magic, and the flames that had begun to heat the iron of the gates orange. "You claim to come here respectfully," Glass Lady continued, "and yet you begin from a position of utter *dis*respect. Therefore, we must treat you in kind."

She waved her hand, and taigas appeared from their hiding places just below the top of the fortress walls. Others waited on the foot- and handholds below them, ready to pounce on the ryuu once Sora blinded them.

She focused the emerald particles around her. *Make the crystal invisible. Bring it to me.*

With Sora keeping the wall invisible, the ryuu wouldn't know what was blinding them. They wouldn't be able to shoot it down. The only one who could understand—who could see invisible things—was Hana.

Sora's entire body trembled with the effort of moving the crystal. She'd forgotten how much energy she'd already used to cut the wall from the palace and transport it here. There wasn't much in her reserves.

Daemon noticed. He placed his hands on Sora's shoulders, the heat of his touch steadying her. It was like when the Imperial Guard had bandaged her wounds while she was working on cutting the crystal from the palace walls, except tenfold, because this was Daemon.

Sora's hold on the magic strengthened, and the slab of crystal rose faster from the ground where she'd left it, soaring through the air toward them.

Hana sneered at Glass Lady, her attention, at least for now, on the commander. "Your old-fashioned view of the world is exactly why I'll replace you as leader of the Society once Emperor Gin wears the crown," Hana said. "Now I'm going to ask you one more time to let us in."

The commander glanced at Sora.

The slab of Rose Palace hovered just below the top of the fortress walls, where Hana couldn't see it.

Now! Sora ordered.

The crystal shot up into the sky, directly in front of the sun. Sora rotated it from side to side.

The light blasted down upon the ryuu, not in a beam of pink, but rather in a brilliant, intense spectrum, everything from red to violet, as the light filtered through the prism of the Ora tiger crest. It was beautiful and painfully glaring, all at once.

The ryuu shrieked as they were blinded. Some shielded their eyes. Others clawed at them, as if they could rip away the brightness of the light.

"Attack!" Glass Lady shouted.

Taigas swarmed over the fortress walls, climbing up and over like an army of fire ants. They rained down on the ryuu below, throwing stars and darts tipped in genka. The goal was not to kill them—most of the ryuu were taigas who had recently been hypnotized by Prince Gin—but to blind them, knock them out, and then imprison them until the Society could figure out how to undo the Dragon Prince's spell. Sora kept turning the magnifying glass in the sky, varying the rays of sunlight unpredictably, so that any direction a ryuu looked for their emerald dust, they'd immediately be confronted with more of the blinding light. But her trick with the magnifying glass would handicap the ryuu for only a minute, maybe less, before they figured out a way to avoid looking at it. The taigas needed to incapacitate the ryuu quickly.

Hana roared, her anger audible even through the chaos of the fight.

The stone stairs her ryuu had been building were only six stories high, still four stories from the top of the fortress walls. But four floors wasn't impossible for a ryuu to jump.

"Watch out for Virtuoso!" Sora said.

Hana shielded her eyes from the flashing light above and sprinted up the stones. She pushed off the last one and leaped up.

Others began to follow her lead. Beetle—Sora's friend—kept his gaze to the earth, where cicadas, centipedes, and thousands of other antennaed things crawled out of the dirt. They climbed on top of each other and created a moving platform to carry him and a few others up. At the same time, the fire ryuu doubled her efforts on the gates, their lower bars red-hot, while another ryuu who could work with metal coaxed it to bend. Another minute or two, and they would have a hole large enough to let themselves through.

Hana landed on the top of the fortress wall. Sora glanced over, and her stomach curdled at the way her sister's face twisted, her eyes narrowed, and that cute button nose now scrunched, nostrils flared in anger. Sora's spell on the magnifying glass almost slipped.

Taiga officers began to shout new commands to the different squadrons.

"Stay up on the wall and continue shooting any ryuu you can with genka darts!"

"Drop down to the ground and draw your weapons!"

"Remember—if they can't see, they can only fight like we can, and we outnumber them. Go!"

Grasshopper spells were cast. Taigas jumped down from the ten-story fortress walls, into the melee below. They drew swords and sickles and chains, also dipped with genka.

Some taigas and ryuu would die. The Society would try to spare as many as they could, but stopping Prince Gin's army was the priority.

In the meantime, Beetle, Firebrand, and other ryuu were making progress on the wall.

Sora trembled under the concentration required to keep the piece of Rose Palace in the air. Sweat soaked her entire uniform. Her eyes were beginning to cross.

But she held on.

Fairy and Broomstick ran past her to fight the ryuu who were landing at the top of the wall.

"Be careful!" Sora yelled after them.

"'Careful' isn't part of the League of Rogues' motto," Fairy shouted back.

League of Rogues. Sora liked the sound of that.

But she didn't have time to respond. Beetle and his insects lunged at Fairy and Broomstick. Hana smirked at Sora.

"You won't be needing that anymore," Hana said, as she commanded green particles to wrench the magnifying glass from Sora's magic's grip.

It wasn't even a fight. Sora was already exhausted, and her hold slipped as soon as Hana's stronger one snatched at the crystal.

The beautiful piece of Rose Palace smashed on the ground inside the Citadel, flattening six taiga apprentices who had been running toward the gates to provide reinforcements. The remnants of the etched Ora crest shattered.

Sora stared at it in horror.

But Bullfrog and the other councilmembers leaped into action.

"Shoot for their eyes!"

"Kill if you have to!"

Stars, no. The new ryuu were just taigas beneath their enchantment. And the original ryuu . . . they were misguided in their beliefs, but they were still Luna's soldiers. Kichonans.

Sisters.

Hana stalked toward Glass Lady.

"I'm relieving you of command, old lady," she said.

"Over my dead body," the commander said.

That only made Hana smile. "Watch me."

She faded from view and laughed.

Glass Lady gaped, paralyzed for a moment. She didn't know how to fight something she couldn't see.

Behind them, Beetle's insect horde dove down for attack.

"Fairy!" Broomstick shouted. "Now!"

She flung a vial of something into the air. Broomstick hurled a small, liquid-filled sphere at it.

The two collided. The glass of both the vial and sphere shattered, and whatever was inside reacted to the other and hissed before it exploded.

Beetle's buzzing army dropped dead instantaneously.

He screamed, then drew his sword and charged at Fairy.

Meanwhile, Hana was running at Glass Lady.

"She's on your left!" Sora yelled at the commander. Sora was the only one who could see where her sister was.

But it was too late. Hana reappeared, whipped out a stiletto blade from her sleeve, and said to Glass Lady, "I told you I'd take command over your dead body." She slashed it across the commander's neck and pushed her over the edge of the fortress wall.

At the same moment, Beetle ran right into Broomstick's sword.

"No!" Sora shouted.

Everything seemed to happen in slow motion. Glass Lady's jaw dropped as her throat split open, spilling her life in crimson rivulets. Beetle held Broomstick's blade in his hands, looking down at his impaled stomach in disbelief.

Then Glass Lady and Beetle both fell, ten stories to the ground. Their bodies smashed into the dirt, bouncing at the impact.

Sora screamed.

The ryuu below were fighting back with the full force of their magic. Balls of fire, burning taigas like meat on a spit. Storms of icicles, shot straight through like spears.

The Society was not relenting either. They had numbers on their side. They regrouped in squadrons, each one targeting a single ryuu, and charged. Blades flashed. Darts and throwing stars gleamed as they flew.

Bodies fell.

Hana looked down at them without emotion, her face now a cruelly placid mask. When she turned to Sora, she was equally collected. The eyes that had lit up at seeing Sora perform ryuu magic were now flat, as if she felt nothing for her sister.

"Hana—"

"I don't have anything to say to you." She stalked toward Sora, spinning her sword in her palm.

Daemon dispatched the ryuu beside him and came to Sora's side. He growled, sounding more like a wolf than she'd ever heard before. "If you lay a finger on her," he said, "you'll pay for it." Fairy and Broomstick came up behind him.

"No," Sora said. "Back away, Daemon. All of you. You won't see her coming if she turns herself invisible again."

"We're not going to—"

"Back away!" Sora shouted. "If I die, the League of

Rogues has to continue the fight. Kichona needs you."

Daemon, Fairy, and Broomstick stood still. Hana watched them, amused.

"Aren't you going to listen to her?" she taunted. "You're like a litter of puppies, still following my sister around like when we were kids. Nothing about you taigas has changed."

"Maybe you're right," Sora said. "But I'd rather not change than become a tool for Prince Gin to use."

"He's not using me."

"He is, Hana."

"Stop calling me that! And the emperor isn't using me. He trusts me and respects me! Which is more than I can say about you. It was a shame I even gave you a second chance."

No, Sora thought. *I refuse for this to be the end of me and Hana.*

It was only a postponement. It had to be. Sora needed to save Kichona first, but then she'd make a third chance for her and Hana. Somehow.

No matter what happened next, as long as Sora was alive, she'd come back for her sister. Hells, even if Sora died, her ghost would devote itself to Hana. It would be a fitting afterlife for a taiga named Spirit.

"Now that Prince Gin is the emperor—" Hana was saying.

Fairy stepped forward. "I hate to break it to you, but he's not. His sister is still very much alive."

Hana smirked. Which was much more dangerous than a glare.

Sora froze.

"Did you think that would surprise me?" Hana said. "When Spirit revealed that she wasn't under Prince Gin's spell anymore and the 'empress's' body disappeared from camp, I put two and two together. My sister has always been a schemer. I figured she must have been up to something, and you weren't a corpse; otherwise, you wouldn't be worth stealing. So yes, I already know the empress is still alive. Why do you think only half the ryuu are here? The rest are already inside Rose Palace. And they've got the Hearts with them."

Holy heavens . . . Sora's chest clenched. She'd thought the ryuu would have to get past the Citadel first. But Prince Gin had been raised in the imperial family, too. He would know about the trapdoor in the Field of Illusions and the secret network of tunnels underground . . .

Empress Aki wouldn't know he was coming.

Emerald dust eddied around Hana, then dove into her, saturating her with magic. She vanished.

Sora summoned her own whirlwind of ryuu particles. She absorbed them and went invisible too.

No one else would be able to see them fight. Or die.

Hana called on more magic, which rushed to her and formed itself into a hundred tiny daggers and flew at Sora.

She conjured a shield of her own emerald dust and deflected the knives, each one pinging against her shield.

"Not bad," Hana said. "But basic." She formed a sack with the magic and brought it down over Sora's head, tightening the bottom like a noose around her neck.

Sora panicked and sucked in too much air, and suddenly there wasn't enough oxygen. She clawed at the balloon surrounding her. The noose around her throat kept tightening.

Can't breathe. Can't fight. Can't . . .

As her brain fogged, the one thing she could think was

how, when Hana was a tenderfoot, she always wanted to do whatever Sora was doing. If Sora was juggling apples, Hana wanted to juggle apples. If Sora was sparring against three others at the same time, Hana wanted to spar against three others.

If Sora was being suffocated by an invisible balloon . . .

On the brink of passing out, Sora issued one last desperate command to the ryuu magic.

Throw a bag over Hana's head too.

A mirror-image balloon appeared and tightened itself around Hana's neck. Her eyes bugged.

But Hana had a stronger killer instinct than Sora did. Instead of standing there and losing consciousness, she ran for Sora and butted her head straight into Sora's stomach.

They both lost control of ryuu magic, the emerald particles bursting out of their bodies like a shower of glitter.

They both became visible, and the suffocating balloons around their heads exploded away.

They both flew off the top of the fortress wall.

CHAPTER SIXTY-EIGHT

S ora!" Daemon yelled. He dove off the fortress wall after them.

Everything around him went blue and bright, like lightning. Everything rumbled like thunder. Daemon felt sparks on his skin, electrical charges in his bones. It was terrifying and thrilling. Adrenaline vibrated through his veins.

For a moment, time slowed, as if the universe were stretching. Daemon flew off the wall like an arrow shot through water, straight and true but not as fast as reality ought to be.

He aimed himself at Sora to intercept her fall. Hana held on to her. But as Daemon reached Sora, he drew power from the buzzing light around him. He snatched Sora out of her sister's weakening grip.

As soon as he touched her, the sparks on his skin enveloped Sora too. She gasped as the world went blue.

Daemon hugged her close to his chest, and they flew forward together, defying gravity.

He landed in a cypress tree, as softly as if his feet were made of air. He set Sora down on a branch.

Then all of a sudden, time sped up again.

Daemon looked back at the fortress walls. Ryuu and taiga bodies alike littered the dirt, the ground a deep red, as if paint had spilled down from the heavens. But the taigas had overwhelmed them. They began securing the ryuu who were still alive, blindfolding them to prevent them from using Sight when they woke from the genka, and shackling their hands behind them with iron gloves and cuffs so they couldn't form mudras for taiga spells. And the remaining ryuu were fleeing, running back into Jade Forest.

Hana wasn't there.

"Where is she?" Sora whispered.

"I don't know." He'd seen her fall toward the ground when he took Sora from her grip.

"But she isn't . . . dead, right?"

Daemon searched for her again. "Maybe she's invisible."

Sora shook her head. "I'd be able to see her." She collapsed against Daemon and exhaled. "She's not there. She's not dead on the ground."

But an instant later, Sora snapped away from Daemon. "What in all hells!" Her eyes were wide, and she stepped backward on the branch, putting distance between them. "What are you?"

Daemon shook his head. "I don't know what you're talking about. I'm me."

Sora stared at him, mouth agape.

Their gemina bond was electric, like the times when he'd zapped Sora out of Prince Gin's spell. But the energy now was even louder, so unruly it hurt his ears, and he didn't know what was happening.

"Why are you staring at me like that?" He began to panic. Had Hana done something to him?

Sora reached out tentatively, almost as if scared. But then she touched his face. And stroked his hair.

A couple weeks ago, he would have wanted this. But he had just kissed Fairy, and everything was confusing, made worse by the crackling electricity in his bond.

And there was something about the way Sora's fingers felt in his hair that wasn't right.

He stiffened.

The caution in her touch, however, began to fade.

"It really is you," she whispered incredulously.

"I . . . of course it's me. Please, Sora, what are you talking about?"

She took his hand in hers and lifted it for him to see.

It wasn't a hand. It was a paw, engulfed in brilliant blue light.

He gasped. "What did they do to me?"

She touched his face again. Stroked his hair. "The ryuu didn't do this. I think you did."

Daemon whimpered. He didn't know what she meant.

A tear trickled down Sora's cheek, but she was smiling. "You just flew across the sky," she said, shaking her head in awe. "You've spent your life not knowing where you came from and worried that you weren't good at magic. But that's because you don't need to *use* magic, like the rest of us do."

"I don't understand." He couldn't tear his eyes away from his paw. His *paw*.

"You don't need magic because you *are* magic." She waved her hand up and down the length of his body.

Daemon looked. He was a wolf. An actual wolf with paws and midnight-blue fur that lit up with a buzzing, bright light, as if he were surrounded by stars. But inside, he was still himself. He felt the same. He had the same memories. Even his voice was still his own. "What . . . ? How?"

"There's so much more magic in this world than we knew," Sora said, and he knew she wasn't only talking about the ryuu. "Remember the Kichonan myths? The god of night brings all his children to Celestae with him, but they're allowed to shine like constellations at night so their mothers on earth can still see them. Sometimes, though, the god of night's children decide they belong down here, among people like their mothers, rather than in the heavens. And when they descend, they take human form and their constellations disappear from the sky."

Suddenly, a brief scene—a memory?—flashed before him. Daemon was running in the dark, surrounded by stars. The sky rumbled, and the planets shook. His fur stood on end.

Sora's mouth dropped open again, as if she'd just realized something. "It's your birthday today, Daemon."

He'd forgotten. There had been too much going on. "What does my birthday have to do with anything?"

"I don't know if it does," Sora said. "But there used to be a wolf constellation in the sky, and it disappeared eighteen years ago. I think you're one of the god of night's sons. You're a demigod."

Daemon frowned and shook his head. "That's crazy."

"Sometimes crazy is true."

It would explain why he'd been immune to Prince Gin's spell. Daemon wasn't an ordinary taiga.

He shook out his fur. There was power in these lupine muscles, the kind he'd envied in his cub brothers and sisters when he was young. But now that he was an actual wolf, all he wanted was to be human again.

But maybe that was the point. Maybe he'd craved being human, and that's why he came back to earth. But it also made sense why he loved being up in the trees and on rooftops, close to the sky. If it was true that he was one of the god of night's children, there'd always be a part of him that missed his first home.

And yet none of that mattered right now. Daemon was a taiga—even if he wasn't a typical one—and that meant putting the kingdom before himself. Whether he was a demigod or something else, figuring it out would have to wait.

To be honest, it was a little overwhelming, and Daemon was relieved to have an excuse to deal with it later.

"Come on," he said to Sora. "We need to go after Virtuoso and Prince Gin."

"We might be too late," she said.

"Maybe. But remember? I can fly now." He grinned and felt electric, both inside and out. "Get on."

CHAPTER SIXTY-NINE

The light shining through the crystal in Sola's temple was even deeper crimson than the last time Aki was here. She kneeled at the shrine, her torn handkerchief before her with a new bloodstain on it now, knees aching from waiting for the goddess's attention.

But Sola hadn't come. Was she irritated at being summoned again so soon? Perhaps she would not heed Aki's call.

Outside, the temple fountain bubbled as it always did. There were several Imperial Guards posted on the spiraling gold stairs. Aki should have been perfectly alone.

Nevertheless, she knew the instant he was there. The air stilled and, at the same time, grew colder, like the icy chill before a winter storm.

"Hello, sister," Gin said, as he entered.

She turned around slowly. "You were supposed to think I was dead."

Gin shrugged. "And you were supposed to think that of

me. Funny how even after a decade apart, we're still twins in our thoughts."

He was taunting her. Reminding her of how differently they'd felt ten years ago. How those differences had split not only them but the entire kingdom, for a bloody night.

"I wouldn't let you bring war to Kichona's shores a decade ago, and I won't let you do it now."

He stalked closer to her. "Ah, but you don't have to give me permission. I'm stronger now than I was then."

Aki took a step backward. "You're distorting the magic Luna gave you as a taiga. You're brainwashing our own people. You must know that isn't right!"

Her brother pursed his lips, and for a moment, he looked remorseful. But then he shook his head. "It's for the greater good. Sometimes, sacrifices must be made. In the long run, Kichona will be better for it."

Gin was still obsessed with the Evermore. He'd been that way since they were younger, and Aki wouldn't be able to dissuade him now.

But *he* could persuade *her* of anything, if he wanted to. If she gave him more time, he could hypnotize her too. He could command her to abdicate, and the throne would be his.

She couldn't let that happen.

Aki dove for his knees. Gin yelped as she took him down. He was the fighter, not her, and she'd caught him by surprise.

She took advantage of it and scrambled onto his back, locking her arms and legs around him. She jerked him into a headlock and tightened her grip, choking him to cut off both the air and blood to his brain.

Just a few seconds, and he would be unconscious. After

that, she wasn't sure what she'd do. Killing him would be the surest way to stop him.

But she couldn't kill her own brother, even if he'd sent his ryuu to make an attempt on her life. Aki would have to hope the taigas arrived soon.

She squeezed tighter. Gin grappled at her arms, trying to loosen her hold. He gasped for air. His legs kicked.

Suddenly, someone appeared out of thin air. It wasn't Sola.

It was a girl. A ryuu.

"Enough," she said.

Aki went flying across the temple. She slammed into the crystal wall and crashed down into the incense as she landed on Sola's shrine. Ash and rice poured out of the pot, onto her bloody handkerchief, snuffing out the smoke and smothering her entreaties to Sola to intervene and save the kingdom.

She gasped, the wind knocked out of her. What just happened? Where had that girl come from?

Gin glowered as he rose to his feet. He rubbed his throat. "That wasn't very nice of you to attack me, Aki. I came here and tried to have a polite conversation with you, and this is what I get?"

She crawled backward through the ash and rice, but there was nowhere else she could go. She was trapped. She found her voice, though, because gods dammit, she was an empress, and she would not be bullied.

"It wasn't exactly a polite conversation, Gin."

"Only because you're so stubborn. But I did try while you still possessed your own mind."

Aki paled. She crossed her arms in front of her face, as if that would stop him from hypnotizing her. "No. Gin, don't.

We can talk. We can think of a solution. We can—"

"It's too late." He looked at her intently, and her mouth smacked shut.

She tore at her lips with her fingers, but they wouldn't budge.

Gin kneeled before her, an ivory-handled dagger in his hands. "I was going to kill you, but I've changed my mind. I have a better idea."

"Mrrr!" Her pulse pounded in her ears as panic grew.

He spun the knife's handle. "All of Kichona already thinks you're dead. You made sure of that, thank you very much. I simply have to ask you to abdicate the throne, and then make you disappear. You should suffer in exile, like I had to all those years."

Aki's heart didn't slow at learning that she wasn't going to die. What really mattered was not letting Gin become emperor.

But he smiled like a dragon, and she knew she was lost.

A moment later, warmth like a summer breeze enveloped her. It reminded her of birthday parties as a little girl, playing hide-and-seek in the palace with Gin, and their father scooping them both up and twirling them until they all fell dizzy to the floor with laughter.

"Everything is wonderful, isn't it?" Gin said.

Aki nodded. The red light in the temple, which had seemed ominous before, now took on a dark beauty, like sitting inside a hummingbird feeder full of the sweetest nectar.

"And you agree that abdicating in my favor is what is best for Kichona?" Gin asked.

"I do," Aki said. She didn't know why she hadn't seen his perspective before. But then again, he always had been a visionary. She was the twin who saw what was before them. He was the twin who saw what was possible.

"Then make it official," Gin said, reaching out and holding her hand. "Give me the throne."

She smiled at his touch. It was just like when they were children, holding hands as they splashed through fountains and searched the gardens for dandelions to make wishes on. "I don't want to be empress anymore," she said. "I abdicate. I give you the throne."

Gin's grip on her hand tightened. His eyes glistened, but Aki didn't understand why. Were they happy tears? And yet, he frowned.

"I'm sorry," he whispered.

Aki just grinned at him.

He squeezed her hand once more, then released it and turned away without looking at her.

"Virtuoso," he said to the ryuu who'd been standing behind him at attention. "You know what to do."

The girl nodded. She looked at Aki and narrowed her eyes.

It happened in an instant. Aki had no clue what had happened, but she gasped. Everything around her seemed tinted, as if a green haze had descended upon the world.

"What did you do?" she asked, gaping at the temple around her. A second ago, the walls had seemed like rubies. Now they were unpolished emeralds.

"You're camouflaged to the rest of the world," Virtuoso said. "You still exist, but . . . you don't."

Gin, still looking in the other direction, let out a long sigh. The warmth and contentment Aki had felt vanished, replaced by deep chill.

He'd released her from his spell.

"Oh gods, what have you done?" Aki asked.

"I didn't want it to be this way," Gin said. "But I have to put the kingdom first." He glanced over his shoulder at Virtuoso. "Take my sister away and stash her somewhere no one will ever find her."

"With pleasure, Your Majesty." Virtuoso produced a length of rope and a gag.

"No," Aki said, backing up against the temple wall, everything still green. "Gin, don't."

"I'll take care of our kingdom, Aki. I promise. I'll make our family and all the gods proud."

"Gin!" Aki screamed.

Virtuoso grabbed her, sinking her fingernails into the skin on her neck, and tied the gag roughly around her neck.

"See you later, *princess*," she said. Then she slammed the heel of her hand into the back of Aki's head, and all the green in the world went black.

CHAPTER SEVENTY

Sora and Daemon flew through the air in a bright blue blur. The electricity around him tingled on Sora's skin, and while ryuu power had felt like sparklers inside her, now she and Daemon literally cast off sparks, and the energy he generated blazed through their gemina bond, powering them with more adrenaline than she'd ever felt in her life.

But the thrill was extinguished as they arrived at the base of the quartzite hill that led up to Rose Palace. The dusty-pink crystal wasn't there to greet them.

The palace was gone. Mounds of shattered crystal lay in its place.

"Holy heavens," Daemon growled, as he stopped in midair. He landed on the ground, and they gaped at the destruction in front of them.

Rose Palace had been a part of Kichona's Imperial City for a millennium. And now it was just a pile of debris.

Sora gasped. "The empress is inside. We have to get up there!"

The ground began to vibrate. The crystal remnants of the palace clinked against each other as the earth shook. Daemon froze, and Sora held on to his fur more tightly.

"What's happening?" he asked.

Suddenly, spires of bloodstone pierced through the top of the hill, sending rose crystal flying like daggers everywhere.

Sora threw out some ryuu particles. They arced around them like a shimmering, emerald shield, forming a barrier in the air.

The shards of crystal struck with vicious speed.

She inhaled sharply and held on to her magic.

The shield remained steady and caught the crystal spears. They quivered, their momentum cut short.

Daemon let out a long breath.

The hill whimpered. Then there was a deafening crack, as more bloodstone shot out of the ground, like dark fangs puncturing the rocky hill. The moat around it, once clear as ice, now bubbled, thick and murky and green. And the black stone streaked with red kept rising from the bowels of the earth.

A new castle.

Sora's and Daemon's jaws dropped. Behind them, the taiga army arrived.

"Gods help us," Renegade, one of the councilmembers, said of the growing castle. He wasn't even fazed by the fact that Sora was sitting on a giant, electric blue wolf. After the displays of ryuu magic at the Citadel, the appearance of a magical wolf and a new, black palace were just two more unfathomable additions to the morning.

As they watched, flags unfurled at the top of the

bloodstone towers. Most were long banners, yellow and green like Sora had first seen at the Takish Gorge camp. They flicked their forked tongues in the wind. But on the highest towers, a new flag was raised. Instead of the Ora tiger wearing a crown—the symbol that had flown over Kichona for hundreds of years—an emerald dragon held the crown in its claws.

Sora's stomach pitted.

At the top of the castle walls, the ryuu army emerged. Their numbers had been reduced, but they still peered down the hill at the taigas as if they were the ones with the advantage.

They were.

"Long live Emperor Gin, ruler of all Kichona!" they chanted.

Sora snapped out of her horrified stupor. She whirled to Renegade and the three other councilmembers who'd come to the front line. "The empress! She was in Rose Palace when it collapsed. We have to save her."

"If she was in the palace, she's probably dead," Renegade said.

Sora shook her head, aghast. "But there's a chance she's alive."

Scythe stepped forward. "If Prince Gin wanted her dead, then she's already dead. If he wanted to keep her alive, then he will for some time. He won't have spared her life just to kill her right away. Either way, it would do the kingdom harm if we tried to attack them now. The ryuu have their powers back, and we can't lead the taigas straight to Prince Gin. He'll use his magicked charm to convert most of us, even if we try to resist."

"So we just retreat?" Sora looked from the councilmembers to the castle and back again. She couldn't believe what they were saying. Beneath her, Daemon's muscles tensed, and he sparked brighter blue.

Bullfrog, the councilmember who had arrested and drugged her earlier, approached them. "Spirit, I didn't listen to you before, and I was wrong. I'm sorry. But now we're operating on the advice you gave us—the taigas cannot win against the ryuu when they have the full force of their magic. Therefore, we have to retreat, temporarily, to regroup."

"And do what?" she asked.

"Learn to see the world in a new way," he said, looking directly at Daemon's wolf form. "There is magic we never thought possible. We need to understand it and harness it. Only then will we have a chance."

"But we're not giving up," Sora said, beginning to understand.

"We are not giving up," Renegade confirmed.

Sora looked forlornly at the castle. She had left the empress up there, unprotected, and now the empress might be dead. Prince Gin had claimed the throne, and soon he would declare war on their neighboring kingdoms. And whatever she had managed to mend with Hana during their time together was now ruined, shattered like rose crystal.

"You did the best you could, Spirit," Bullfrog said softly, the usual croak in his voice barely audible. "You did better than the rest of us. It's time for us to catch up. Don't worry. The Society has protected Kichona for a millennium. You don't get that far without adapting and learning new tricks."

"I was naive to think we could beat the Dragon Prince that easily," Sora said.

"No," Daemon said. "You weren't naive. You were optimistic and daring, and that's exactly what the Society needed. Without you, we'd all be conscripted to Prince Gin's army already."

"But instead, you're a magic wolf," she said glumly.

Daemon laughed, though, and it shook his shoulders and almost knocked Sora off his back. She had to grab a handful of fur so she didn't slide off. "Don't get me wrong," he said, "I'd like to figure out sooner rather than later how to change back into human form, but I'm not all that upset."

"You're not?"

"No. I've finally got magic now."

That made Sora smile. A little.

Meanwhile, Renegade turned to the taigas behind them and shouted, "Retreat!"

The army turned and began marching. They would have to leave the Imperial City. Until they came up with a stronger plan, it wouldn't be safe to stay so close to Prince Gin and his ryuu.

Not all the taigas retreated, though. From the far end of the army, Fairy and Broomstick pushed their way up the road to Sora and Daemon.

"Spirit, are you okay?" Fairy asked, shoving aside the last of the taigas, despite their appalled scowls that she would blatantly ignore the councilmembers' orders to retreat. "We thought you were going to die when you and Virtuoso fell off the Citadel's wall. And, Wolf, you're . . . a wolf."

Daemon laughed so deeply, it vibrated through his body and through Sora's. She held more tightly to his fur.

"What, exactly, happened?" Broomstick asked.

"I think he's the missing wolf from the sky," Sora said.

Fairy ran her fingers through the fur behind Daemon's ears. "A demigod, huh? Sexy."

He leaned into her touch and growled in a content, low rumble.

Sora flinched. But then she reminded herself that she didn't have a claim on Daemon, not like that. And she never would. They were geminas.

Because of that, she tried to act like everything between them was the same as it had always been, though it felt like wading upriver in a storm. "Wow," Sora said, rolling her eyes affectionately at Fairy. "You're still a flirt, even in the middle of a war."

"It's evidence of good character that I'm consistent," she said.

Daemon nudged Fairy playfully with his nose.

Sora looked away. She had to think about something else. "Come on, we should probably catch up with the rest of the taigas."

But then a voice boomed from the top of the hill. "Did you think it would be that easy to walk away from me?"

"Prince Gin." Sora paled.

Suddenly, the road beneath them roiled and broke open. It roared as more spears of bloodstone shot out of the ground, like thousands of dragon talons. One of the claws knocked Daemon into the air. Sora screamed and clung to his back.

He righted himself before they hit the ground, and they darted into the sky.

Beneath them, the path that had once led to Rose Palace continued to rip itself asunder. More talons pierced through the earth. Some speared straight through unfortunate taigas. Others closed around them and lifted them ten stories off the ground, trapping the soldiers in prisons of stone dragon claws. Those who were trapped tried fruitlessly to smash the claws or pry them apart as the talons curled together, the spaces between narrowing to close the prisoners in.

"Wolf! Help!" Fairy teetered at the top of one of the talons. She held Broomstick by the back of his tunic, but the fabric was slipping. If she lost her grip, he would fall into the stone claws' clutches.

"Hang on," Daemon shouted.

Sora pressed herself flat onto his neck and clamped her legs to his sides. They dove straight down. Blue light streaked behind them. The wind shrieked in Sora's ears.

As they descended, new claws shot out of the ground and tried to snatch them from the air. Daemon swerved.

"Crow's eye!" Sora clung to his fur as they dodged in and out.

"I can't hold Broomstick much longer!" Fairy shouted. The talon she perched on began to close toward the others, threatening to impale her on another claw.

"Go now!" Sora yelled into Daemon's ear.

He darted out of reach of another stone claw and streaked toward Fairy and Broomstick again.

Sora held out her hand.

Broomstick reached.

Their fingers met and locked. "Let go!" Sora said to Fairy.

She released Broomstick, and Sora swung him up onto Daemon's back. They flew up and away from the claws.

"Are you all right?" Sora asked.

Broomstick nodded, securing himself into Daemon's blue fur. "We have to go back for Fairy."

"Already on it." Daemon looped around and dove down again.

"My dear taigas," Prince Gin's voice projected from his bloodstone castle to the soldiers captured below. "Your empress is dead. I am the ruler of Kichona now, which means the Society answers to me."

"Hurry!" Sora said. "He's going to hypnotize everyone!"

Daemon growled and flew faster. Sparks flew in Sora's face, briefly burning as they bounced off her skin.

They neared the dragon's claw. Sora stretched her arm out again, and Broomstick held her waist to help keep her on Daemon's back.

"Fairy! Give me your hand!"

Fairy climbed up onto the talon, trying to keep her balance as it shook her, attempting to jostle her into the cage of taiga prisoners in its palm below.

Daemon swooped down. Sora reached. Fairy jumped.

Another stone claw shot up out of nowhere. "Stars!" Daemon jerked out of the way at the last second, changing their trajectory.

Fairy was left with no one to catch her.

"Wolf!" she screamed. She began to fall toward the ground.

The blue light around him exploded, sparking and buzzing so brightly, Sora and Broomstick had to shield their eyes.

He flew at the speed of lightning, sound falling behind them, and snatched Fairy out of the air with his teeth.

It wasn't until they were high up in the sky, out of the reach of the stone claws, that Sora realized they were all safe.

"Oh gods," Fairy said, her breaths fast and shallow.

"Literally," Sora said of Daemon. She reached down for her roommate, and together, she and Broomstick pulled Fairy onto Daemon's back.

Below them, Prince Gin's voice rumbled as he continued to address the taigas. "Bow to your new emperor."

"Don't listen to him," Daemon growled. The blue around him flashed like an electric storm.

In the stone claws, though, a hush rolled through the taiga ranks, like a tumbleweed blowing through a deserted town. One by one, the soldiers inside the talon prisons fell to their knees, stretched their arms forward, and lay prostrate on the stone floor. "Long live Emperor Gin, ruler of all of Kichona!"

Sora braced herself for the warm, campfire comfort of Prince Gin's hypnosis. She watched Fairy and Broomstick too for that familiar, contented glaze in their eyes that infected everyone under the Dragon Prince's spell.

But it didn't get to them. Daemon's electricity sparked ferociously blue around them like a shield. It was similar to the orbs some of the ryuu had used, but even better—this was the magic of a demigod.

Still, it didn't help the others. "The Society is gone," Broomstick said sadly. "There's only the four of us left."

They all stared helplessly at the taigas below, whose minds had been stolen from them. From Bullfrog, the most opinionated councilmember, to the young Level 8s who had joined in the fight. Their free will had been brainwashed away. And now the Dragon Prince controlled an entire magical army.

As if on cue, Prince Gin emerged from inside the bloodstone castle, onto the large balcony of the tallest

444

spire. "My loyal ryuu, the day I've dreamed of my entire life has finally come. Today, we begin our quest to make Kichona the greatest empire in history. Zomuri will give our island a paradise and immortality that, until now, has only existed in mythology. My dear ryuu, I promise that if we fight together, we will be rewarded. We will achieve the Evermore."

Cheers broke out from the dragon claws, and from the existing ryuu lined up around the castle.

"Long live Emperor Gin!"

"Long live Kichona!"

"To the Evermore!"

Then two hundred men, women, boys, and girls filed out onto the balcony where Prince Gin stood.

Daemon snarled. "The Ceremony of Two Hundred Hearts."

Sora's own heart plummeted as if off the highest spire of the bloodstone castle.

"If we don't stop him," Fairy said, "he'll declare war on the world?"

"Yes," Sora said. "And the *world* will declare war on *us*. Kichona as we know it will be gone."

"What do we do?" Daemon asked.

Bullfrog and the other councilmembers had been wrong. The taigas couldn't retreat. They had to try to stop this now.

Sora looked down at the two hundred people below. "We have to take out Prince Gin."

Daemon flew an arc in the sky to line himself up with the tower.

Hana stepped onto the balcony.

At first, relief lifted the tension off Sora's shoulders. Her sister was alive.

But the relief was quickly followed by a dizzying dread, as Hana turned her eyes up toward Sora and her friends. She raised her hand, as if commanding them to stop.

The fur on Daemon's back bristled, a ridge of midnight blue. He prepared to dive at Prince Gin.

"No," Sora said. "We can't."

"What? I thought we were going after him?"

But Sora could see something none of the others could. "My sister . . . She has Empress Aki."

"How? Prince Gin announced that she was dead."

Sora shook her head. Hana had infused the empress with ryuu particles and made her invisible. Empress Aki was bound and unconscious, and Hana held her by the back of her taiga uniform collar.

Satisfied that Sora had seen her, Hana unsheathed a sword and pressed it to the empress's throat.

"Hana, please!" Sora shouted. "Don't do it!"

"Come any closer, and her death is on you," Hana said.

"We have to stop," Sora told Daemon.

He growled, but they hovered in the sky, neither approaching nor retreating. Sora squeezed her eyes shut and pressed herself against Daemon's neck. How had it come to this?

When she looked up again, Prince Gin was nodding his approval at Hana. Then he began to pace in front of his assembled Hearts.

"I've chosen each of you to make history for our kingdom. You give your lives today, but great honor will be bestowed upon your families, and your names will live on for eternity."

A murmur of happiness rippled through the Hearts.

"My lord Zomuri," Prince Gin shouted, his voice echoing like a funeral gong, "I sacrifice these two hundred Hearts for you, as a symbol of my dedication to your glory."

He waved his arm at the people assembled before him. In unison, they pulled out short, stout daggers and positioned them over the center of their chests.

"No." Sora gasped.

"I can't watch," Broomstick said. He and Fairy buried their faces in Daemon's fur.

But Sora couldn't tear her eyes away from the horror, and Daemon, ever her gemina, forced himself to look too. He sent waves of calm to her through their bond, like the sensation of lying in a meadow under the summer sun, even as he tremored beneath Sora, trying to stay strong.

She loved him a little more for it.

The Hearts began to shout.

"Long live Emperor Gin!"

"Long live Kichona!"

"To the Evermore!"

All at once, the two hundred sacrifices stabbed themselves with their knives. And then, possessed by Gin's magic, they resisted going into shock, and they sawed through their own flesh, plunged their hands in, and wrenched out their own, still-beating hearts, holding them up to the sky.

The hardest to watch were the small children, their chests a mangled mess because they were too uncoordinated to slice out their hearts cleanly. And the worst part was, they didn't cry. Possessed, they just kept stabbing at themselves as blood and chunks of flesh smacked onto their tiny feet, until finally, they'd gashed themselves open entirely, and their little hearts spilled out onto the tower floor.

Then suddenly, the sacrifices dropped their knives and toppled over, one on top of another. Finally dead.

Tears streamed down Sora's cheeks, and matching ones matted the fur on Daemon's face. A violent sob racked Sora's body. Horror and grief weighed down their gemina bond, as if it had been filled with sand.

"Is it over?" Fairy whispered from where her face was still buried.

"Yes," Sora choked. "But don't look. Whatever you do, don't look."

For a long moment, everything was eerily quiet.

Then a deep, low rumble began to emanate from the ground, distant at first, as if it came from the center of the earth. It grew louder as it came closer, like thunder surfacing. Suddenly, a giant burst out of the ground. His otherworldly laugh shook the entire Imperial City.

Sora could only stare, jaw open.

Zomuri swooped down and began tossing hearts in a sack, as if they were potatoes.

"How can he do that?" Fairy whispered. She'd abandoned not looking and, like Sora, now couldn't stop.

"I think he eats them," Sora said weakly. Like potatoes.

"Emperor Gin Ora," Zomuri boomed. "You have proven your dedication through the Ceremony of Two Hundred Hearts."

On the bloodstone tower, Prince Gin fell prostrate on the ground, right in the midst of the corpses. He bowed to

Zomuri, his body sticky with blood.

The god finished collecting his hearts and licked all twenty of his fingers. "I hereby anoint you Savior of Kichona, Warrior of Glory, Seeker of the Evermore. Go forth and make an empire in my name. And when I am satisfied, I shall grant you and your kingdom the paradise you deserve."

Everything shook—the ground, the air, Sora's resolve.

And like all gods, who do not stay among humans for long, Zomuri disappeared.

Prince Gin rose slowly to his feet. He turned to the ryuu and the captured taigas in the stone claws. "Tonight, we celebrate. And tomorrow, we set forth on our quest for the Evermore."

His soldiers whooped and shouted.

The prince turned to the sky. "I see you up there, Spirit. You and your flying pet may be out of my reach for now, but you've seen a glimpse of Kichona's future. This is the end for you. The next time we cross paths, I'll see to it that your sister kills you."

No. Sora leaned over, searching for her sister, and nearly toppled off Daemon. Fairy latched onto her.

"Don't die on us," Fairy said. "We need you. Kichona needs you."

"It's over," Sora said. "Hana's taken Empress Aki. The entire Society has been hypnotized. And the quest for the Evermore has officially begun."

She slouched. "Kichona is lost. We're the only ones with our wits about us, because we're protected by Daemon's shield."

"The kingdom's not lost," Daemon said. "We didn't

449

fight this hard just to give up now. But first, we need to get out of here."

If it weren't for his decisiveness, Sora wouldn't have been able to do it.

He soared past the clouds. He flew so high, the sky changed color, darker here where the sun had not yet reached. He turned westward, but kept flying up, up, and up still.

"You'll fix this," he said.

Sora shook her head and buried it into his neck. "I can't."

Fairy scooted up and hugged her. "Then *we'll* fix this. Together."

"The League of Rogues." Broomstick's hand rested on Sora's shoulders.

She sat up slowly and remembered her mother's entreaty—*Be more. Do more.*

No one said Sora had to do it alone.

Her friends were right. They couldn't lie down and give up. Their kingdom was at stake—not just the island, but the people. People like her mother and father up on Samara Mountain. People like Empress Aki. People like the taigas who'd been taken.

But there were no more taigas left to fight.

Except for us.

"We're going to need something bigger than ourselves," Sora said.

"Tell us what to do, and we're in," Daemon said.

"Even if it's something crazy?"

Fairy shrugged. "I've already impersonated the empress and died once. I'm not sure there's anything crazier than that."

"I might be a demigod wolf," Daemon offered. "That's possibly crazier."

"What they mean is 'yes,'" Broomstick said. "Let's save Kichona."

What had happened with Prince Gin today was terrifying. But what could happen if he was allowed to keep going . . .

A magical army that would drown the mainland in blood. A war that would come to Kichona's shores.

And an empire of millions of mindless puppets, all under Prince Gin's control.

Sora shuddered. They had to stop him. It was their duty. Their calling.

Daemon flew farther and farther away. Stars sprinkled Sora's vision. They had flown away from day, into the night.

The darkness gave her hope.

"All right, then," Sora said. "Let's do this."

"Really?" Fairy said.

Sora nodded. "Work hard."

"Mischief harder," they said.

They held on tightly to his fur, shadows on a constellation, and they shot higher, into midnight sky. And then Sora glared back at the earth in defiant challenge.

"You're wrong, Dragon Prince," she whispered. "This is definitely not the end."

ACKNOWLEDGMENTS

Having written another series before this one, I thought *Circle of Shadows* would be easy to write. It turned out, though, that I had to wrangle with this book a bit, and I'm very grateful to my editor, Kristin Rens, for understanding what I wanted this story to be and patiently guiding me to get it there.

Thank you to Kelsey Murphy, Jon Howard, Audrey Diestelkamp, Michelle Taormina, Alison Donalty, Epic Reads, and everyone else at HarperCollins who has worked on *Circle of Shadows*. And thank you to Ronan Le Fur for the gorgeous cover art. I'm blessed to have such an exceptional team bringing my books to life. Your love for what you do is truly dazzling.

As always, I'd like to thank my agent, Brianne Johnson, as well as the rest of the Writers House crew, including Alexandra Levick, Cecilia de la Campa, and James Munro. You are the unsung heroes behind the scenes, and I see you and all that you do.

This journey wouldn't be as fun without my readers, and a special shout-out to the ever-enthusiastic Skye Guard! Thank you to every single one of you loyal soldiers for spreading the love of my stories. I adore you forever and ever.

I'd be remiss not to mention Sara Raasch, Jennifer Nielsen, Amie Kaufman, Kerri Maniscalco, and Karen Grunberg, my critique partners and early readers; Brittany Press, the Major General of the Skye Guard; Julia Jin, who did the beautiful art of Sora, Daemon, Fairy, and Broomstick for the trading cards; Hafsah Faisal, my design wizard; Angela Mann and all the booksellers at Kepler's Books; YA Lunch Break, my beloved book club; and all my incredible author friends, whose names would fill an entire book if I listed everyone, because the author community is really *that* awesome and generous and wonderful.

And last, but never least, thank you to my family, who are always my biggest fans. Thank you to my parents, Andrew and Margaret Hsu, for being so proud of me that your hearts might burst. Thank you to Tom, for throwing my life wide open in the very best of ways; I could not write a better love story than the one I'm living with you. And thank you to Reese, for your curiosity and joy and endless little kisses and hugs. I love all of you with my entire soul.

Turn the page for a sneak peek
at CLOAK OF NIGHT, the sequel
to CIRCLE OF SHADOWS.

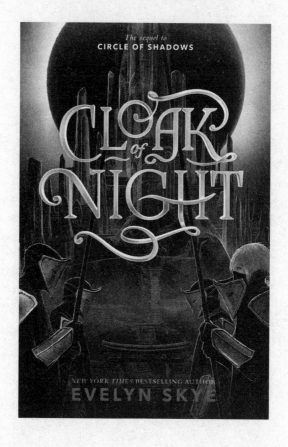

CHAPTER ONE

Empress Aki woke up completely disoriented and with a skull-hammering headache.

She opened her eyes slowly, because even that movement hurt her head. There was dirt beneath her, and the air here was sharp and sour, as if a crate of cleaning solution had been left open and undiluted. Her throat ached from breathing it.

What is this place? Aki certainly wasn't in the Imperial City anymore.

The last thing she remembered was her brother, Gin, taking control of her mind and forcing her to abdicate the throne in his favor and then one of his ryuu turning everything in the world green and knocking her unconscious.

Carefully, the former empress rose, bracing herself against a wall. She was still in the taiga uniform she'd donned before the battle with Gin, and now her sleeves caught on the jagged rock walls.

Aki was in a grotto of some sort. A waterfall crashed

twenty yards away from her, and a pool of churning water spanned the short distance between the grotto floor and the base of the falls.

She crept along the narrow ledge of rock around the edge of the pool. Surely this was more than a mere grotto. Gin wouldn't leave her alone if she could simply swim her way out.

She approached the underside of the waterfall and stretched her hand toward it.

The droplets burned her fingers, and Aki jerked her arm away. "Nines!" she cursed, falling backward onto the ground. Wisps of smoke rose from her fingertips.

Acid.

Instinctively, she began to plunge her hand into the pool to cool it down, but she caught herself at the last moment. The pool might be filled with the same thing.

Aki cradled her hand and gaped at the torrent of acid raining down in front of her. Was this a fabricated prison that the ryuu had created? Or was this a real waterfall, and they'd somehow transformed the water into something deadly? In either case, it was terrifying.

A girl laughed from the other side of the grotto. Aki startled but didn't see anyone there. She scurried back to the opposite part of the cave.

Out of thin air, the girl materialized.

Virtuoso. Aki grit her teeth from both the pain of the acid burn and seeing the ryuu who had knocked her out during the battle at Rose Palace.

The girl didn't even bother with a greeting before she stalked over, kneed Aki in the stomach, and shoved her onto the slick ground.

Tears stung Aki's eyes. "Please. You have to let me go," she said.

"No," Virtuoso said curtly.

"I demand it."

Virtuoso shrugged.

Aki had nothing. She was a prisoner. She couldn't cast spells like her brother and the ryuu and taigas could. No one knew where she was, or even that she was still alive. She might as well be dead.

She slouched against the wall, no longer bothering to hide the fingers burned by the acid.

Virtuoso laughed at Aki's blistering skin. "I see you've discovered that these are no ordinary waterfalls."

"You did this?"

"It was my idea. Another ryuu executed it for me. Want to go for a swim?" she sneered.

"I thought my brother wanted me alive. You know, so I could suffer in exile as he had to. Isn't that what he said before he had me thrown in here?"

Virtuoso glared daggers at her.

Aki set her jaw. She refused to give away the fear chewing at her bones.

The acid in front of Virtuoso began to boil. What in Sola's name was this? Aki pressed herself even harder against the wall to get as far away from it as possible.

An enormous emerald bubble—seven or eight feet in diameter—rose from the depths of the acid. The orb bobbed to shore and opened as if it were yawning. It was empty, except for a large armchair.

Virtuoso glowered at Aki. "There's a small cell behind this rock wall, sheltered from the acid. Squeeze through the crevice over there"—she pointed to a person-sized crack in the grotto wall, obscured by the falls' shadows—"and you'll find a mattress, water, and food. Enough to survive. Barely."

Then she stepped into her green bubble, sat in it like the captain of a small ship, and sank into the water, leaving Aki behind.

Alone.

Possibly for the rest of her life, because Gin wanted her to rot here as punishment.

She hugged her knees to her chest and looked at the curtain of acid locking her into this prison.

But there was still one hope, even if it was a small one.

"League of Rogues," Aki whispered. "If you're out there, please don't give up on me."

CHAPTER TWO

Hana clenched her fists as she rode away in her bubble. As Virtuoso, Emperor Gin's second-in-command, she was supposed to want to snap the former empress's neck in the grotto. But there was a part of Hana that was relieved she wasn't allowed to kill Princess Aki. Prisoner or not, she was still royalty.

Unfortunately, it was that kind of wishy-washy commitment that had made Hana weak before. She'd fallen for her sister's attempt to reconcile, letting Sora go instead of turning her in. *If I had revealed Sora as a mole in our ranks, the Society of Taigas wouldn't have been warned of the impending attack, and the ryuu could have taken the Imperial City without as much ryuu bloodshed.* They also could have avoided killing some taigas who would have been valuable once they were brainwashed and turned into ryuu.

That had all been because Hana had wavered in her allegiance.

I won't make that mistake again, she thought. From now on, whatever Emperor Gin wanted, she would be single-mind-edly dedicated to him and his pursuit of the Evermore.

"Nothing will sway me," Hana said aloud, as if doing so would further bind her to the pledge. "Nothing."

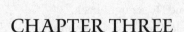

CHAPTER THREE

It's a strange thing, Sora thought, *when a boy you've known your entire life is suddenly an enormous electric wolf.* It was stranger still to ride on his back as he flew through the night, sparks flickering off his blue fur. She, Fairy, and Broomstick clung to Daemon, bracing themselves against the biting chill.

They'd fled Kichona, beaten and terrified, after Prince Gin—the Dragon Prince—seized the throne. But now, just hours later, the decision nipped at the edges of Sora's mind.

They were supposed to be the protectors of the kingdom. Was it irresponsible to abandon their people?

But the rest of the Society of Taigas had been beaten, and if Sora and her friends had stayed, Prince Gin might have captured and hypnotized them, too. And then Kichona would have no one left to save them.

Still, it felt wrong to run away.

"Turn around," she said to Daemon.

"What?"

"Turn around. We need to go back."

"Are you out of your mind?" Daemon said, his voice half growl. "Prince Gin just took over the minds of every warrior we know, and we only barely escaped."

"Which means that the prince won't expect us yet," Sora said. "He probably thinks we'll disappear for a while to lick our wounds. No one would guess we'd turn around after losing a battle and fly straight back."

With a reluctant sigh, Daemon changed directions and headed back to Kichona.

Eventually, a crescent-shaped island came into view. Isle of the Moon had been the retreat of the Society of Taigas' council, before the ryuu destroyed it. Even from this height, Sora could see the red bridges smashed into ponds and the toppled Constellation Temple.

But its devastation also made Isle of the Moon the perfect place to regroup before they returned across the channel to Kichona's main island. No one would expect them to choose this as a hideout.

"Try touching down on that strip," Sora said, pointing to a narrow clearing.

"I hardly know how to fly, let alone land," Daemon said. "I might dash us all to pieces."

"You can do it," she said, even though they'd only discovered his magic hours ago. She tapped into the mental bond she shared with Daemon and sent him a ribbon of reassurance. It coursed through their connection like the scent of salt water and sunshine on a summer day, and she could immediately feel the muscles in his shoulders release some of their tension.

She looked down again at the island. The destruction was even more stark as they got closer. Gardens were flooded.

Beams from broken buildings littered the ground. Rainbow koi swam in puddles on top of broken rooftops instead of in the carefully tended ponds they'd once called home.

"I'm going to aim for that meadow at the edge of the woods," Daemon said. "There's slightly more space there. Everyone, hold on."

Sora leaned into the fur on the back of his neck and hugged him, feeling his lupine strength beneath her, and for just a moment, she let the wonder of Daemon's transformation sweep over her. Even though he was a wolf, he smelled like cypress trees and sky, like a boy born of the forest and the stars. Every nerve in her body tingled, awake in a way she'd never before experienced.

Fairy tightened her grip around Sora's waist, bringing Sora out of her thoughts. Broomstick stretched from behind Fairy and wrapped his arms around both of them, his reach long enough to secure them all together. Daemon began his descent.

The wind stung Sora's face, and her ears felt tight from the pressure of flying downward at such speed. A flock of birds squawked and broke formation to allow Daemon through. The open air quickly gave way to treetops, and then—

"Jump!" Daemon shouted as he careened, out of control, toward the grass below.

Sora leaped off his back, tucked her body into a ball, and somersaulted as she hit the ground. She rolled once, then sprang to her feet, as agile as if she'd intended such a landing all along. Beside her, Fairy also landed lightly, as did Broomstick, his massive body graceful from years of taiga training. It didn't matter that he was the size of a small rhinoceros;

he moved like an acrobat—strong and fluid and effortless.

Daemon was not as lucky. He crashed into the meadow, bouncing several times, and stopped only when he'd skidded several hundred feet into the wet, sandy remnants of a meditation garden. His groan rumbled like an unhappy thunderbolt.

They rushed to him.

"Wolf!" Fairy cried. Sora was the only one who called Daemon by his birth name. Likewise, he was the only one who called her Sora.

He rose on wobbly legs, his paws crossing awkwardly as he stumbled.

Broomstick reached him first and braced Daemon against his own frame. "Steady, there."

Daemon grinned sheepishly, which was quite an accomplishment for a wolf. "I told you I might crash."

"But you're all right?" Sora asked.

"Ego bruised, but that's the worst of it."

She nodded. "Let's find a place to settle down. It's been quite a day."

That was, of course, a massive understatement, but so much had happened since the sun rose that morning, Sora could only process parts of it at a time. Prince Gin had hypnotized the entire Society of Taigas except Sora, Daemon, Fairy, and Broomstick. He had also destroyed Rose Palace, sacrificed two hundred innocent people in a bloody ceremony, and possibly murdered his sister, the empress. It was almost too much to bear.

"Hey-o," Daemon said, "that house over there looks intact."

Sora and Fairy followed him and Broomstick. Upon closer

inspection, the building wasn't a house but a large hall, possibly a meeting space for when the Councilmembers had their annual retreat. Also, it wasn't so much "intact" as not falling down. The front door barely hung on its hinges, the rice paper on the windows was torn open, and the glass ceiling was completely shattered. But it was the best they had.

"Let's see if there's any food," Sora said, "and figure out a plan."

"Can we sleep a little before we have to think again?" Daemon asked. His shoulders slouched from the effort of flying for hours with three people on his back.

Sora paused. Time was of the essence. If Empress Aki was still alive, they'd have to find her quickly before Prince Gin had a chance to move her out of the Imperial City.

But when Sora looked at Daemon, she knew what the answer had to be. His muscles trembled beneath his fur, and the gales outside had almost blown them out of the sky several times as he tired.

"Yes, of course," Sora said. "We should definitely sleep. I'm sorry I didn't think of it before."

They walked through the creaky front door. It was indeed a meeting space, which apparently doubled as a dining hall, too. Smashed plates and teacups and the moldy remnants of a meal lay in the mess of broken tables and chairs.

Broomstick eyed the room warily, as if the ryuu who had done this might still be lurking, just waiting for them to let down their guard before they sprang again. "We can take turns on watch."

Sora waved him away. "I'm having trouble shutting off my brain. You guys go ahead and get some sleep."

Fairy hesitated.

"I swear I'll wake you if I need someone to take over," Sora said.

Daemon stumbled into the far corner of the hall and collapsed on a pile of tablecloths. Within seconds, he was snoring wolfishly.

Broomstick and Fairy went off to find their own nooks to sleep in.

Or at least Broomstick went to find his own space. Fairy went straight to Daemon's corner of the room and settled against his blue fur.

Sora's chest knotted; she'd almost forgotten about the two of them holding hands before the Citadel battle. It had been difficult to see, since Sora had only just realized her feelings for Daemon then, too.

But the Society of Taigas forbade romantic relationships between geminas. So if Daemon was going to be with anyone other than Sora, she was glad it was Fairy. There was something lovely about your favorite people in the world coming together.

Right?

Annoyed at herself, Sora distracted her mind by clearing the debris on the floor to make some space—none of the chairs were sturdy enough to sit in—and cast a simple spell to light a fire next to her. They were indoors, but with the shattered glass ceiling, they might as well be outside.

Then Sora finally had time to think about everything that had happened.

Empress Aki was missing—possibly dead. Prince Gin had sworn loyalty to Zomuri, god of glory, and dedicated the kingdom to the pursuit of the Evermore, a mythological paradise obtained through war and bloodshed. And every single one of the Society's leaders—no, *all* the taigas—were either dead or brainwashed and under the prince's control.

Sora curled up next to her fire. What was she going to do? There really was no one left except her, Daemon, Fairy, and Broomstick. Her earlier confidence faded.

Eventually, though, Sora's fatigue caught up to her, and she dozed off.

A while later, she startled awake. The fire next to her had burned out. She scrambled to her feet.

"Don't worry," Broomstick said from nearby. "I was awake about the time you fell asleep. It's been quiet."

"That makes me nervous," Sora said as she stretched.

"Makes me nervous, too." Broomstick rubbed his hands over his head. It was normally shaved, but now platinum fuzz was beginning to show.

Sora's own hair had seen better days as well. It was limp and greasy against her face, and the white-blond roots had started to grow out while the black dye faded on the rest. Her tunic and trousers were in similar shape, mud-spattered and wrinkled, no longer the formidable black uniform taigas were used to wearing. She was pretty sure she smelled a bit like old cheese, too. Ugh.

At least the nap had done her some good. She still didn't know how the four of them could save a kingdom, but she wasn't drowning in utter despair anymore. The wheels in her brain creaked, eager to turn and come up with a plan.

But there was also something else. Sora finally understood Empress Aki's imperial crest, the one with the crowned tiger and the words "Dignity. Benevolence. Loyalty."

It was about giving yourself to something bigger.

Sora took a deep breath. What lay ahead of them was going to be the most difficult task they had ever faced. She had to be prepared.

"We should start brainstorming our next steps," Sora said.

"I'll wake Fairy and Wolf." Broomstick rose and headed to the back of the hall.

A few seconds later, he yelped.

Fear rose like an alarm in Sora's chest as she sprinted to help him. Were they being attacked?

When she reached Broomstick, though, it was apparent he didn't need help. At least, not in the way Sora had imagined.

Fairy was still next to Daemon, but he wasn't a furry, electric-blue wolf anymore. He was six feet two inches of stark-naked, tautly muscled boy on a bed of tablecloths. The only hint of his wolfishness was his hair, which had lost its black taiga dye in his transformation and was now its natural midnight blue.

Sora's jaw dropped, her pulse beating traitorously at double time.

"Good gods, you two!" Broomstick said. "I don't normally care what you do on your own time, but here? When Spirit and I were twenty yards away?"

Both Fairy and Daemon seemed just as shocked as Broomstick and Sora, though. Daemon curled up into a ball and desperately heaped tablecloths on himself to cover up. Fairy had sprung to her feet and leaped away from him, her eyes wide.

"It's n-not . . . ," she said. "We didn't . . ."

"When did I turn back into a human?" Daemon asked,

curling more tightly into himself.

The four of them stood frozen for another moment, brains trying to catch up with the scene before them.

Suddenly, Broomstick snorted. "You had no idea he was naked, did you?" he said to Fairy.

"None." She shook her head to emphasize the point.

The real evidence, though, was the hot rush of Daemon's embarrassment through his and Sora's gemina bond. He was absolutely mortified.

"Oh, Daemon." Sora summoned her cloak from the other side of the room. It flew swiftly to him, and he yanked it to his body. Her poor gemina. He was possibly a demigod, but he was also still the boy she knew, self-conscious and uncertain in his magic. They didn't know the extent of his powers or how to control them, and this surprise was an unfortunate result.

"We'll find an extra set of clothes for you in the council-members' rooms," Sora said. "You can join us when you're, uh, ready."

"Thanks," Daemon said, his embarrassment still burning through their bond.

Sora began to walk away, with Fairy and Broomstick right behind her. She almost expected a joke from one of them, Broomstick especially, about how teasing Fairy and Daemon was part of his sacred duty as a best friend.

But there wasn't a single word. Their usual lighthearted banter was gone, as if the weight of Prince Gin's fledgling reign was already taking its toll.

Everything had changed.